NIGHTWOOD

Books by Djuna Barnes

The Book of Repulsive Women (1915)
A Book (1923)
Ladies Almanack (1928)
Ryder (1928)
A Night among the Horses (1929)
Nightwood (1936)
The Antiphon (1958)
Spillway (1962)
Creatures in an Alphabet (1982)

posthumous publications

Smoke and Other Early Stories (1982)
Interviews (1985)
New York (1989)
Poe's Mother: Selected Drawings (1995)
At the Roots of the Stars: The Short Plays (1995)

DJUNA BARNES

NIGHTWOOD

The Original Version and Related Drafts

Edited and with an Introduction by
Cheryl J. Plumb

Dalkey Archive Press

The Publisher wishes to thank New Directions Publishing Corp. for permission to incorporate its authorized edition of *Nightwood* into this critical edition.
The related drafts are reproduced by permission of the Archives and Manuscripts Department, McKeldin Library, University of Maryland, College Park,
MD.

Library of Congress Cataloging-in-Publication Data
Barnes, Djuna.
    Nightwood : the original version and related drafts / edited and with an in-
troduction by Cheryl J. Plumb. — 1st ed.
    p.   cm.
    Includes bibliographical references.
    1. Barnes, Djuna. Nightwood—Criticism, Textual. 2. Lesbians in literature.
3. Lesbians—Fiction. I. Plumb, Cheryl J., date. II. Title.
PS3503.A614N5   1995   813'.52—dc20   94-36949
ISBN 1-56478-080-5

Partially funded by grants from the National Endowment for the Arts and the
Illinois Arts Council.

Dalkey Archive Press
Illinois State University
Campus Box 4241
Normal, IL 61790-4241

NATIONAL
ENDOWMENT
FOR THE
A R T S

*Printed on permanent/durable acid-free paper and bound in the United States of
America.*

CONTENTS

INTRODUCTION

DJUNA BARNES REFERRED to *Nightwood* as "my life with Thelma."[1] A silverpoint artist from St. Louis, Thelma Wood was the model for the character Robin Vote. Wood's relationship with Barnes, lasting approximately nine years, was both idyllic and destructive. That life ended, or changed character, by December 1927, though a reconciliation of sorts appears to have taken place in 1928. The source of significant information regarding Djuna Barnes, Emily Coleman's diary indicates in 1933 that Barnes had not lived with Thelma for five years. They saw each other, however, through the years of *Nightwood*'s composition. These years were very difficult for Barnes, both emotionally and financially. The breakup with Thelma was followed by an interlude with Charles Henri Ford, by a frustrating and futile relationship with Peter Neagoe, and constant tension with her family.

The hope of financial success with *Ryder*, on the best-seller list in September 1928, faded quickly, and by the end of 1929 the royalty had dwindled to $8.77, just as the October 1929 crash took its toll on the American economy. Barnes's *Theatre Guild* work from late 1929 to September 1931 was her last steady journalistic income. In April 1934 she wrote Coleman that she had earned $200 in the last seven months. During these years she was supported at various times by grudging family members, by wealthy patrons like Eustace Seligman and Peggy Guggenheim, and by a brief stint as a writer with the W.P.A. On 10 January

[1]Djuna Barnes, letter to Emily Coleman, 14 December 1935, Emily Holmes Coleman Papers, Special Collections, University of Delaware, Newark, Delaware (abbreviated CP). Letters from Emily Coleman to Djuna Barnes are in the Djuna Barnes Papers, Special Collections, University of Maryland at College Park Libraries, College Park, Maryland. In some instances where carbons of Barnes's letters are at the University of Maryland, an abbreviation (BP) indicates the archive. The letters are printed as written without correction of spelling or punctuation.

1936 Barnes wrote Coleman that it was "unendurable" to have charity, but she also acknowledged that "only through charity, god damn, damn, shall I ever be able to have my life to myself to do my work in, but on the other hand it makes you feel so bloody, when gift money is not given (and when is it?) not only with the whole wish but the whole heart." Despite the uncertainties of these years, Barnes had an asset, in addition to her own talent, in Emily Coleman's friendship—a friendship that was not always easy, but that was indispensable at this time of her life.

When Coleman met Barnes in Paris in 1929, she prompted suspicion and dismissal on Barnes's part, and on Coleman's side less than whole-hearted interest. But gradually as they both gathered around Peggy Guggenheim and her entourage, Coleman's intensity and passion for life and literature won grudging respect from Barnes; for Coleman, her side of the friendship was sealed when she read *Nightwood*, even the first version: it spoke to her. She expressed "intense excitement" at the part about jealousy and watching the loved one wake up, yet she judged that "most of the book is sentimental shit of the worst kind (Thelma and Fitzie), then these wonderful truths" (diary, 15 December 1932).

Coleman—college-educated, author of the published novel *Shutter of Snow*, and writing a second—encouraged Barnes, offered her support and suggestions, finally taking on the role of collaborative reader. Asserting that she had had the "greatest reverence" for the text, she wrote that Barnes wouldn't change anything if "she didnt believe it. . . . But the trouble was (as John [Holms] said about her) first she wouldnt believe a word I said and then she would believe everything." Coleman expressed her realization that she had to be "careful" (diary, 21 October 1937).

Under these circumstances *Nightwood* was written, its title changing at various times from "Bow Down" to "Anatomy of the Night," to "Through the Night" and "Night without Sleep," and finally to *Nightwood*. Andrew Field credits Eliot with coming up with the title.[2] In fact, Barnes announced the title to Coleman on 23 June 1935: " 'Nightwood,' like that, one word, it makes it sound like night-shade, poison and night and forest, and tough, in the meaty sense, and simple yet singular, . . . Do you like it?" Coleman didn't. But Eliot did concur in Barnes's choice, a choice evidenced by its appearance as the typescript title. Coleman, however, continued to object, preferring "Anatomy of the

[2]Andrew Field, *Djuna: The Formidable Miss Barnes* (Austin: University of Texas Press, 1985), 212.

Night," with Barnes resolving in May 1936 to let Eliot decide; he would know the English market. When Eliot wrote Coleman that he objected to "Anatomy of the Night" because Lionel Johnson had written a poem of that title, Coleman responded with her argument, but informed Eliot that Barnes would do as he suggested. Only later in October 1936 did Barnes write Coleman of her discovery that the title was Thelma's name: "Nigh T. Wood—low, thought of it the other day. Very odd."

Eliot himself mentioned the title, among other issues, while answering an inquiry by Barnes about Coleman's representation of her role regarding *Nightwood*, this during the period when Barnes quarreled with Coleman over her essay on the novel. Coleman's essay was to have been published in a magazine that Charles Henri Ford edited, but Barnes objected to the essay as inaccurate and "too sticky," and Coleman withdrew it, protesting the changes Barnes and Ford had made (29 November 1944). In his letter Eliot objected that Barnes was being unfair to Coleman, that Coleman had never given him "the impression that she had anything to do with writing the book," acknowledging that "she had practically forced the book down my throat," and admitting that he hadn't "appreciated it at first." He stated that "she was wrong about the title certainly: *Nightwood* is right" (23 July 1945).

When he turned to the issue of editing, he credited himself and Frank Morley, apparently forgetting that much of what he and Morley had taken out had been marked or suggested by Coleman. Or to be fair, he may simply have regarded his decision as independent. This letter, to be addressed more fully later, has caused scholars to question Eliot's role in editing *Nightwood*. Coleman's role with respect to *Nightwood* is less well known.

Exactly when the novel was begun is not certain, but perhaps as early as 1927, the first breakup with Thelma. Barnes's 20 September 1935 letter to Coleman establishes the circumstances and points to a date between 1927 and 1931: "God knows who could have written as much about their blood while it was still running. I wrote it you must remember . . . when I still did not know whether Thelma would come back to me or not (and knew that as I wr[o]te it I should have to read it so to her) whether I could live with her again or not; in that turmoil of Charles [Ford] and Morocco, sickness, Hayford Hall—everything, then the end here in New York. . . . when I realized that being here was death (and is) for me." Barnes's Guggenheim application of November 1930 gives some insight into her plans: she outlined two projects: one was "to research the relationship of the Jew and the court for a book in progress whose chief figure is an Austrian Jew." And the second "a creative religious history" (BP). Thus, the character Felix, whose role was much criticized by Coleman, was an early element of the book.

Though her application was not funded, Barnes wrote through the summer of 1932 at Hayford Hall, Peggy Guggenheim's summer residence in England. On 28 August, Coleman recorded that she and John Holms (Guggenheim's current lover) had talked to Barnes about her book. Coleman questioned why she wrote of Dan Mahoney (the model for Doctor O'Connor): "You should write of Thelma." Barnes claimed that she "had written about Thelma," and "could not face Thelma's reading it." Later in the evening Coleman recorded that Barnes had read a part about Ford to Holms.

In December 1932 Coleman reported that Thelma had come back to Barnes, "needing her protection," and had "tried to resuscitate their old relation, and it hasn't worked." On the 14th Barnes had left her book for them to read, and Coleman wrote that Holms had found a part that was quite wonderful, and she observed that it "gave you a sudden quick feeling of fear for Djuna." Dated five years later is a diary entry recording a far less positive response: "John sitting with the ms. of Nightwood on his knee at Hayford Hall and groaning: 'Its *awful*. Its impossible. I ought to do something to it. I cant. I *cant*.' He found 70 pages so awful that he didn't think he'd ever see Djuna again" (21 October 1937). Four days later, after Barnes had left her book with them, they met Thelma and Barnes for dinner at Café Flore; Barnes had received her first rejection letter from Liveright's T. R. Smith. Coleman commented that it was the "most intelligent letter I ever saw from an American publisher." He wanted her to write it over again. Barnes "had had her cry," Coleman observed, "and was feeling gay."

Soon Barnes began the second version of the novel, again writing through the summer of 1933 at Hayford Hall, returning to New York in September. In February 1934, she wrote that her book was at the publishers, but she had heard nothing. Less than two months later, 20 April 1934, she wrote Coleman: "I can't get the book accepted anywhere, it is now at the fifth publisher." She added that publishers were not interested in the book because "they all say it is not a novel; that there is no continuity of life in it, only high spots and poetry—that I do not give anyone an idea what the persons wore, ate or how they opened and closed doors, how they earned a living or how they took off their shoes and put on their hats. God knows I don't." The ironic tone of her comment demonstrates that even amidst rejection after rejection and criticism regarding the novel's apparent lack of form and realistic treatment she had no interest in compromise that would produce a realistic novel, or in what she labeled the "safety" of the realistic novelist. Her position was elaborated in a second letter, written after the book's publication. Barnes distinguished between two kinds of writers: the poet and the "plain home variety": "With the correct artist we contemplate life, with the poetic artist we make a new one. . . . . Realistic values sit before one, to interpret or not, as the eye is good or off focus; with the spiritual life the critic (or novelist) has to more than record, he has to understand with a sixth sense that is almost a kind of collusion, not an appraisal, the one is safe, the other is danger" (BP: 5 January 1939). Barnes numbered herself among the poetic artists.

While trying to place the novel, Barnes sought article assignments and sent around a short story, but conditions in the literary world were "dreadful"; "nothing goes down now," she noted, "but Erskine Caldwell sort of thing—very stark brutal literature wanted—swift moving and bloody" (20 April). In February she had written Coleman that she had completed an article on Arab marriage and that she had three to go, and so was "able to sit less heavily on brother's back." Her distress and isolation were complete, for she found Americans "empties," explaining the term as factory "lingo" for cardboard boxes.

On 29 August 1934, Barnes received another rejection letter from T. R. Smith, who explained that many of the criticisms he had made of the first version applied also to this. He found the early part "clear enough," but stated that it was difficult "to extricate the story from the mass of brilliant and somewhat mad writing." He suggested that something be done about O'Connor. Though he considered O'Connor a "brilliant commentator on life," it was true too that he "frequently became a bore." While Smith acknowledged "brilliant writing," "unusually broad observation of life and behavior," and "keen philosophy," he felt it a "pity that the book succeeds only in being a rambling, obscure complicated account of what the average reader will consider 'God only knows.'" He asked if it would be possible for her to rewrite. And once more, a year later, hearing that it had been rewritten, he requested to see what was then the third version of the novel, but again the outcome was the same. By 13 December 1934, Barnes reported more rejections and added: "am rewriting parts."

Frustrated by rejections, Barnes found revision difficult. But in this process Emily Coleman served her well. After Coleman's late April visit in 1935, Barnes wrote her in Hartford (5 May), responding to Coleman's desire to show the manuscript to publisher Ben Huebsch when she returned at the end of May: "If you imagine there was just a little work to do on it, you are mad my love, the whole damned floor is a mess of it, no table big enough to spread it all out on, so I crawl about on the floor. . . . I still do not think La Somnambule the perfect title—Night Beast would be better xcept for the debased meaning now put on that nice word beast." Returning to an issue Coleman had raised about who should share dialogue with the doctor in "Watchman, What of the Night?" Barnes answered, "No, how can my doctor have the Watchman Chapter with Nora or Catherine? He has about half the book with her now, he'd better talk a word or two to someone else." But in pencil she wrote, "I'll think it over" (2 May 1935). Catherine was a character based on Barnes's friend Eleanor Fitzgerald (Fitzie), but the character was later combined with Nora.

Barnes tried to work on "La Somnambule" but could not: "it seems so riddled and so fixed at the same time—I hurled a few of the condemned sentences out, and then took to my bed like a stricken tree." On 15 May the revision was not yet going well: "I can do the technical things, but the creative work, no, not now—I am so troubled with Chandler, and life known as love on the wing, and do I hate me for it, damned women anyway, all women, damned and should be buried with their hot hearts and lack of worldly sense."

On 17 May she observed: "It lies here on the floor, and I circle around it like the murderess about the body, but do nothing. I seem to have no will power, only an awful despair. And after all the trouble you took with my book, its really bastardly." But by 23 June, she had "rearranged" (her word) up to chapter 3: "And what a nice bit that's going to be. How to bring Nora in, her American home, what she is like, to whom talking and then her meeting with Robin, the Paris home, etc, etc."

Barnes's 28 June letter reported substantial progress: she had revised up to the middle of chapter 4, which was originally "Watchman, What of the Night?" not " 'The Squatter.' " The first chapter is "as was"; "the second, 'La Somnambule,'. . . leaves off pretty nearly as it does now, with Robin leaving Felix, and reappearing with Nora." Barnes changed chapter 3 from a working title of "Beast of the Waste Wood" to "Night Watch." The chapter began, as it does now, with "Nora's country home, herself, then how she goes to the circus in America and how there she finds Robin." Particularly interesting is what she has cut: "All of the people of her salon cut out with children, lovers, Altamonte etc." Characterized in these letters are a substantial shortening of the narrative, dropping of characters and combining of characters, and also a practice of shifting parts from one place to another: Altamonte, for example, is taken from Nora's salon in America and transferred to Germany where he is portrayed as a count at the party where O'Connor, Nora, and Felix meet before Robin enters the story.

The 28 June letter continues, Barnes describing "how Robin becomes restless and wants to go back to Paris, where Nora buys the house in the rue Barbe de Jouy, then the rest of it as you recall, the night, the departure into it of Robin, Noras anxiety, her dream, the scene of Robin and the statue and the final paragraph where Nora falls to her knees by the window." By this time she had accepted Coleman's suggestion that Doctor O'Connor talk to Nora in "Watchman": "Of course to bring that lovely part about Matthew in bed into this chapter, and take it out of 'Where the Tree Falls' and away from Felix is pretty bloody. . . ." Very interesting, in terms of what Barnes saw as the center of the book at this point, is her conclusion that all of these changes make it "still more the Doctors and Noras book."

Though initially revision had been difficult, when Barnes was finally able to work in June 1935, she declared the process "a kind of glee of despair":[3] "Now its rather fun to cut the book up and hurl chapter after chapter into the fireplace, like a puzzle, all of the rest of it all over the floor, and me crawling after lines like a fly after honey. Everyone thinks I'm crazy to change it, suddenly, when everyone before thought I was crazy to write it, and then crazy to send it out, and then crazy not to throw it away, and then madder still not to keep on mailing it out, etc etc, if you *know* what I mean!!"

This letter clarifies speculation about Eliot's role in cutting *Nightwood* that has troubled Barnes scholars, a problem raised by two of Eliot's letters, the first dated 23 July 1945, referred to earlier, and the second 13 August 1936. In the first Eliot credited Morley and himself with cutting "a lot": "It was one of those rare books in which cutting out a lot of stuff perfectly good in itself actually improved the

[3]The phrase itself comes from Barnes's recollection of the process in a letter to Coleman, 22 September 1936.

whole." In the second, to Barnes in Paris, he stated his preference for the shorter version because he found it more "satisfactory." His comments were directed to O'Connor's role. Eliot explained that the problem was not that his conversation "flags at all," but he believed "too much distorts the shape of the book." Pointing out there was much in the book besides the doctor, he wrote: "we don't want him to steal everything." He also wrote that he didn't think he had taken "any unfair advantage of the liberty" that she had allowed. These comments, together with Barnes's report of the original length of the book, have led scholars to speculate as to just how much Eliot took out of *Nightwood*—and when. A few of his blue pencil marks appear, along with a notation by Barnes identifying them as Eliot's, on some of the fragments of earlier versions of the novel; thus the question did Eliot influence Barnes's revision of the second version. Evidence indicates that he did not. Barnes's 28 June letter clarifies that "chapters" had been thrown away long before Eliot entered the picture. Certainly the version that Barnes revised in early 1935 was the one rejected by T. R. Smith in August 1934. Thus, the shorter version that Eliot preferred was the typescript version with the cuts noted on it by Coleman. Another letter of Eliot's, 18 June, adds support to this conclusion, for there he wrote that he and Morley are "now engaged in reading and collating the two copies of the text that you left with me," two copies implying that they are of the same text. Additionally, Coleman's diary (28 December 1936) confirms Barnes's statement about discarded chapters. In reading Eliot's introduction to *Nightwood*, Coleman worried about how Eliot saw her role with respect to the cutting that produced the third version: "When I see how Eliot loves the book, I become even more sick to think what he must wonder about what was cut out. If only Djuna had preserved what was cut out—nothing could vindicate me more. But she threw away the awful parts in New York." Coleman fretted: "If only he could have seen the book as it was when I first saw it." The phrase "when I first saw it" might be construed to mean the first version of December 1932; however, the context clearly identifies her reference as to the second version: "what she threw away in New York." Thus, it seems very unlikely that Eliot ever saw a complete second version, and he certainly did not see any part of it until after he had accepted the July 1935 typescript, for he was not in contact with Barnes or Coleman before October 1935, and no one else could have provided the second version.

By 11 July 1935, Barnes wrote Coleman that she had finished the book. She described its conclusion: "when they see each other Robin goes down with the dog, and thats the end. I do not go any further than this into the psychology of the 'animal' in Robin because it seems to me that the very act with the dog is pointed enough, and anything more than that would spoil the scene anyway; as for what the end promises (?) let the reader make up his own mind, if hes not an idiot he'll know." Despite what appears to be Barnes's sanguine appraisal of the reader's ability, she had evidence from the reading of her friend Marion Bouché that readers might find it both puzzling and disturbing: "How, tho, you could write such a thing about someone you once loved is a mystery." Barnes explained (to Coleman): "Oh God, I said, I didn't, it was someone else, but whom I also loved, in another way." She added: "The look of horror that will be seen on all public faces, if the book ever does get into print, was on hers, and that in spite of the fact that she is fond of me, so you see what I'll get" (17 May 1935). Her anticipation of difficulty was not sufficient, however, to move her to change the section, though later she altered a word or two to lessen the sexuality of the passage.

In the same letter she asked Coleman for "only survivor lines" that Coleman had sent to Edwin Muir. What she refers to here apparently are the extracts that Coleman had typed—extracts that are based on the second version of the novel—and returned to Barnes, who sent them to Marion. Because Barnes referred in her 17 May letter to Marion's comments, it is likely that Marion returned them to Barnes before Coleman revisited on her way back to Europe. Thus, when Coleman cited Barnes's book before the end of July when the third version arrived, she was probably referring to the extracts. These were also given to Muir, who sent them to Eliot in September.

After Barnes finished the novel in July, she arranged for Sylvia Satin, former secretary of Peter Neagoe, to type it. She informed Coleman that the manuscript was only "250 pages!!" She added, "You can see where my once one hundred and ninety thousand word book has gone." One hundred and ninety thousand words, at 280 words a page, a figure Barnes used, is equivalent to approximately 670 pages. The typescript is 212 pages. Coleman's 11 August response to the letter was "I can't believe your book can only be 65-66,000, then it never was 100,000. I'm quite certain we could not have taken out more than 15,000 words. What became of the rest?" It is likely the disparity resulted because Barnes approximated the total number of words of the first version, while Coleman's reference point was the difference between version two and version three.

By July, then, Barnes had a final typescript and two carbons: the ribbon typescript went to Clifton Fadiman of Simon and Schuster, who responded on 25 July that "no standard publishing house could take it." It is likely that this copy also went to T. R. Smith for his third rejection. The first carbon went to Emily Coleman, and one, of course, for herself: "I meant to keep the first, pig that I am, for myself, but decided that no one but myself could read the third" (24 July).

Coleman had helped Barnes rethink organization and characters in April and May of 1935, and again she performed valuable service to Barnes as editor between August and November, when she mailed the manuscript to T. S. Eliot. Coleman's letter of 27 August 1935 is indispensable for anyone tracing changes in the typescript. Her suggestions fall into three groups: the first is a general overview of the work with an eye to what Coleman regarded as compositional weaknesses that Barnes might address in terms of her future writing. The second group includes structural suggestions that could be integrated into version three, and the third group offers editing suggestions—three typed pages of them, single-spaced. Many of these Barnes accepted, noting them in her copy of the typescript. Most of the others she rejected. In the first category, in fact, Coleman's point had more to do with Barnes's character as it influenced her work. Coleman referred to her as having a "deadly introversion," which was "almost pathological." The problem, she claimed, was that Barnes didn't communicate to people the things she really felt. It was one reason why Barnes "had such trouble with conversation. Your people speak to themselves." She almost pleaded, "If you would get yourself aired out inside, what comes out of you would more sweetly see the light of day. As it is, when it comes out the light of day dazzles it." Coleman also asserted that Barnes did not have a consistent point of view, that she needed to believe something: "In this book you believe one thing half the time, and another—the opposite thing—the other half."

In terms of the second kind of comment, those with structural implications, Coleman declared it "artistically MUCH better than it was—readable in fact," but still a "failure artistically" because Barnes had not stayed with the tragedy of Robin and Nora, but had shifted the "center of emotion from Felix—to start with—to the Doctor—to Robin—to Nora—to Felix (Guido)—to the Doctor—to Nora." Coleman asserted that the story of Felix and Robin distracted from the tragedy of Robin and Nora. In fact, when she mailed the text to Eliot, she suggested that chapters 1 and 6 might be removed to give it unity, as she informed Barnes (5 November 1935). She argued that the doctor slowed the narrative and would inevitability bore the listener. She accused Barnes of forgetting Nora. She observed of "The Possessed": "the dog, much better, with Robin, and as the end," indicating that this scene was once not the last chapter. And as the excerpts reveal, in the previous version Jenny witnessed the scene with Robin and the dog: "And at this moment Robin began going down. Sliding down she went, as Jenny beat sobbing against the door" (CP).

Comments of the third category focus on careful reading of the text; for example, when Coleman questioned the phrase "Where? Where?" Barnes replied that it was there "when the dog and Nora were Fitzie"; thus the phrase was no longer applicable (20 September 1935).

While it is difficult to assess fully Coleman's role, the correspondence and excerpts indicate that Coleman precipitated major changes regarding character, action, and outcome, and careful editing with respect to phrasing of the July typescript. Upon rereading the text, preparatory to sending it to Eliot, Coleman exclaimed: "Thank God, thank God you agreed to combining Nora and Catherine, to removing the two sons of Nora—and to having the Doctor talk to Nora—at that important point—and not to Felix" (5 November), further revealing the character of her advice. Coleman's letter points to significant reorganization and condensation.

Barnes responded to the majority of the changes suggested in Coleman's August letter on 20 September and 8 November, beginning the first letter: "Your beautiful, painful, maddning letter recd." She had been unable to answer it until now, Barnes declared, because it had sent her "into a state of the most appaling [sic] misery. To have someone love my book so much is a terrible responsibility, and it frightens me to death about the next. Hithertofore I had nobody to live up to but myself, now I have you." She reported that she had made all the alterations that Coleman suggested except she had not cut any of the doctor's stories. If they had to be cut, it could be done later. She defended Felix's role, justifying it in terms of Robin's reality (as experienced by Barnes): "Robins marriage to Felix *is* necessary to the book for this reason (which you can not know, not having lived with a woman having loved her and yet circulated in public with that public aware of it) that people *always* say,

'Well of course those two women would never have been in love with each other if they had been *normal*, if any man had slept with them, if they had been well f—— and had born a child.' Which is ignorance and utterly false, I married Robin to prove this point, she had married, had had a child yet was still 'incurable'" (8 November 1935). Her justification reveals not only her susceptibility to public opinion but also a not-so-latent corrective aim. She denied she had been mean to Felix, noted that his remarks on French and Italian priests were correct, "my own as a matter of fact" (although elsewhere she denied this, attributing the remarks solely to the doctor). She said if "The Possessed" sounded sexual, she couldn't change it, though she suggested crossing out "Mistress." She exclaimed: "I'll never have a reader like you again. Of that I am more and more convinced" (8 November 1935).

However, Barnes did not always take Coleman's advice. Her defense of Felix's story and O'Connor's "loquacious raving" and her resistance to further structural changes suggest that while Coleman's sense of structure had helped her transform *Nightwood*, Barnes had also come to have a sense of its structure and unity that differed from the conventions of the traditional realistic novel—and from Coleman's expectations. Coleman's concept of unity focused on the "tragedy of Nora and Robin," primarily Nora, but Barnes chose to surround the story of Nora and Robin with a concept of "disqualification,"[4] as she referred to it. Stated less privately, she seems to refer to an awareness of a sense of shame, a suggestion that individuals who incurred public dismissal or scrutiny suffered because of what had happened to them or what they were, that is, Jewish, homosexual, or alienated from the values of a dominant culture.

Thus, Barnes's defense of Felix and O'Connor suggests that while she had considered the structural advice, it was not something she wished to change, though many of Coleman's comments regarding phrasing were accepted. With respect to Coleman's other objections,

[4]In a letter, Barnes defined the term in the context of a fight she had had with Eustace Seligman, who had brought her and twenty other luncheon guests to see "the expensive horse, then the middle class horse, and then that poor demented dog, who *knew* he was being looked at for what had happened to him, for his disqualification, you could see it in the way he would not turn his eyes aside, too damned to make his eyeballs turn from you, it reminded me of that look the Baroness [von Freytag-Loringhoven] gave me long ago, just before she said 'Shall I trust you?' " (20 September 1935).

Barnes acknowledged that "a great deal of my writing is intuition, remembrance of time and pain," but she exclaimed that thought had been part of the book. If Coleman meant "thought" in terms of not having plot and structure, Barnes admitted that Coleman was right: "Perhaps its all right for others, but for me it seems so queer to write a synopsis of chapter and plot and all that sort of thing, and then hang your feelings on it."

With respect to *Nightwood*, what Barnes and Coleman shared most clearly was a desire to probe human nature beneath the surface, though here too they differed, with Coleman asserting on occasion that Djuna did not know the significance of what she was writing and Barnes responding in teasing exasperation at Coleman's presumption that in certain places Emily knew more about what Barnes was writing than Barnes did. For example, in her diary entry for 23 June 1936, Coleman recorded Djuna's jesting: "You know that girl is wonderful. She'll show you your own writing and say, 'Read that—and try to appreciate.' She'll show you passages from your book and say, 'You don't know what it means!' She'll introduce you to your own mother and tell you you ought to get to know her." Part of the difference between them was that Coleman believed in an afterlife. For Coleman, afterlife meant Christian resurrection, but for Barnes, her afterlife was life after Thelma, life after that death. Thus, Coleman argued that Barnes's insights and the language expressing them implied belief in an afterlife, an assertion that Barnes denied.

Nevertheless, Coleman's role was a remarkable element of *Nightwood's* coming to print. What the record shows is that Coleman's intense excitement over the human truths of *Nightwood* helped keep Barnes focused on the work, willing to rewrite, able to hear Coleman's demand for a clearer structure to carry the reader, and yet able to execute her own version of that structure. And in terms of the gritty scrutiny of the stray phrase, Coleman's advice was taken more often than not. When Coleman worried about whether people would think she had "mutilated" the work, Barnes assured her "if anyone ever came out in print suggesting that mutilations had been done to that ms., she would answer it" (diary, 21 October 1937).

But Coleman's role with respect to *Nightwood* was not limited to seeing the manuscript revised for the third time; she was also instrumental in getting it to Eliot and perhaps indispensable in ensuring his careful reading. Coleman's campaign for the book's publication began in July

1935 with sending excerpts to Edwin Muir who sent them to Eliot (BP: 10 July 1935). On 1 August 1935, when Coleman received the revised typescript, she sent it to Ben Huebsch, a partner at Viking, apparently in London at this time, for his consideration, then to Muir for his advice. On 25 October 1935, Coleman, on Muir's advice, wrote Eliot of her wish to discuss the manuscript with him. Eliot, having seen the excerpts, had written her that he did not believe it would *do* as a novel. But after receiving Coleman's letter, he asked to see the book. Coleman informed Barnes that she had written of the book's faults, but "in just the right way." Later Coleman explained her strategy to Barnes as not wishing to appear as an "undiscriminating friend." Because Muir had indicated that Eliot would be interested in work that other publishers could not or would not consider, Coleman mentioned that the book had been turned down by every publisher in America, by some of them twice. Among the negative points she raised: she believed two earlier books by the author to be "worthless"; it would probably not have "a wide sale"; there seems to be no "organic" structure; that though the author has "unconscious" intelligence, she lacks a kind of intellect; that the author "cannot create character . . . has no sense of dramatic action, and can only describe people"; the theme is homosexuality. "It will thus be apparent," she wrote, "that the book is an artistic failure." She anticipated Eliot, "Perhaps you will conclude that the book is worthless—as a novel, or whatever it was intended to be." She concluded: "But I think you will agree with me that it contains as extraordinary writing as has been done in our time: that the human truths revealed in it (the light it sheds on the relation of good to evil, in this life) make it a document which absolutely must be published" (CP).

This improbable letter must have made a curious impression on Eliot. She built on it in a second letter, a combination of flattery and indignation. She quietly remonstrated with him for drawing from the excerpts an unfavorable comparison to Kay Boyle's work, suggesting if he saw this similarity, it "would seem futile" to send the manuscript. She conceded, however, that perhaps the excerpts do not "form enough of a connection to bring out what seems to me the extraordinary value of Miss Barnes's book." Indeed, the excerpts don't form a connection; they are sixteen single-spaced pages of passages that appealed to Coleman because of their "human truths" and descriptive power.

Essentially, she grabbed Eliot by the lapels and demanded that he appreciate what she valued in the book: "Does not the description of the circus woman . . . make you know something you did not know before?. . . . What about the passage, 'The woman who presents herself as a picture forever arranged'? What about the terrible ten pages of the jealous life?" Or, "Can you read that and not see that something new has been said about the very heart of sex?—going beyond sex, to that world where there is no marriage or giving in marriage—*where no modern writer ever goes?*; Did you read the passage about the 'Tupenny Upright'?" She seemed resigned: "I almost despair in sending you this manuscript. If I have not communicated to you what the book is, the excerpts themselves having failed to rouse you (who are among the few living beings who could be so aroused), the manuscript itself may not move you." She cited a few more electric passages and suggested quietly, "I do not think you will find that Miss Kay Boyle moves in such realms."

How close this version is to the letter actually sent is problematic; a second draft, undated but similar, is even more provocative, carrying what she described as a couple of phrases that might have made him mad: for example, "I cannot believe that you will not recognize the book (however tedious parts of it may be) as a product of genius; if you do not, I can only think that something very dreadful must have happened to you to have made you so blind." Presumably, this is one of the phrases that her close friend Peter Hoare suggested she delete. This draft is single-spaced and undated, and for those reasons and its tone, it appears to be the first draft of the letter dated 31 October, then re-dated 1 November. It seems likely that the letter that was sent was similar to the second draft. But her strategy worked, or perhaps her passion worked, or perhaps *Nightwood* itself worked. On 26 January 1936, Coleman reported that Eliot liked the book, that he and another director wanted to publish it, but they must convince the chairman, Faber, whom she described as a "hard-headed businessman." She included a typed copy of Eliot's letter: he was "very much impressed"; he wrote that the "excerpts when taken by themselves gave me a rather misleading impression," and that "the book is one to be taken seriously." To Coleman's delight he commented that "what you say in criticism is true." He pointed to a need for revision in the beginning and advised "*strongly* the omission of the last chapter, which is not only superfluous, but really an anti-climax. The Doctor is so central a character, and so vital, that I think the book ends superbly with his last remarks." Coleman agreed that this could work "because that is the way the book ended in the first place." As

Coleman concluded, it was now certain that the book would be published. It was, of course, but with "The Possessed" as the final chapter.
Barnes stuck to her position, and Eliot, as his preface shows, came
around.

Finally, on 27 April 1936, Coleman received a note from Eliot: "I
really believe that we are now getting to the point at which something
can be done about 'Nightwood.' I should like very much to see you and
have a talk with you about the book and about Miss Barnes." The problem he and Frank Morely presented was that "the book might be taken
up by the censor." Morley indicated they were prepared to make a definite offer, "it was just a question of how amenable she would be." When
Eliot suggested because of his conversation with Coleman, before
Morley joined them, that apparently Barnes was "a tiger who is eating
out of Mrs. Coleman's hand," Coleman became frightened, "because
Djuna cannot be said to eat out of my hand. But I guaranteed that she
would be amenable about small omissions" (diary, 28 April 1936). Coleman recorded that they planned to bring it out in an expensive edition in
order to attract the right audience and avoid prosecution. "E. says the
English are against Lesbianism particularly." And she observed, "E. and
M. like brothers, conspiring."

And so 3 June 1936, Barnes met T. S. Eliot. Coleman entered in her
diary Barnes's narration of this session with Eliot and Morley. Barnes
reported that with respect to Eliot's corrections, she had said, "I'll take
anything from you, Mr. Eliot." But later in considering the manuscript when they got on to "balls, testicles, and pubic hair . . . they were
embarrassed and Djuna vigilant." Djuna reported that Eliot had "that
wise but lenient look when he corrected her spelling." She questioned,
"Who can spell?" Then added, "Eliot, I can tell from your face that you
can spell." Later that evening of Eliot's changing "bugger" to "boys,"
Barnes exclaimed, "Imagine trying to wake Eliot up!" Yet she had liked
him.

What textual changes were made at this meeting or at two subsequent
meetings, occurring around 12 June and before 23 June, according to
Coleman's diary? Before Coleman sent the manuscript to Eliot in early
November, she had marked out certain passages, and pages which she
identified as stories of the doctor that slowed the narration; they will
"infuriate Eliot" she wrote Barnes. She stated, almost absently, that "the
Jenny chapter can go before 'Watchman, What of the Night?' (If you
don't agree, it can be changed later.)"

In her letter of 8 November 1935, Barnes had responded to Coleman's *fait accompli*: "the Jenny chapter can go before 'Watchman, What of the Night?' Only its such a let down (I think) from the 'Ah' in the last chapter, the 'Night Watch.' " She apparently did not notice or remember Coleman's other points, hence her irritation with Coleman when she returned from her meeting with Eliot. Barnes may have been upset with Coleman because of her note regarding the omission of Felix's story or the manner in which Coleman marked out some words. But Coleman was sensitive as to how Eliot regarded her and hurt to hear Barnes's comment: "That girl would take anything out with a meat-axe."

Coleman's judgment about chapter arrangement, accepted after the fact by Barnes, was apparently confirmed by Eliot, for in all subsequent editions, as in the Dalkey Archive edition, the Jenny chapter, " 'The Squatter,' " precedes "Watchman, What of the Night?" For it appears to be a change that Barnes came to prefer. All of the sections suggested for cutting by Coleman were confirmed by Eliot except for the section where the doctor and Felix discuss Jenny. Overall, approximately thirteen pages were deleted. Other than these pages, most of the phrases blue-penciled by Eliot (Frank Morley's comments are identified as in red by Barnes on the typescript, and there appears to be a sort of hierarchical consistency to this use) relate to sexuality or religion.

All in all, the editorial hand was light; certainly because he anticipated potential difficulty with censors, Eliot blurred sexual, particularly homosexual, references and a few points that put religion in an unsavory light. However, meaning was not changed substantially, though the character of the work was adjusted, the language softened. Beyond that, there is the standard tightening of a phrase or two, punctuation, and spelling. After the June meetings with Eliot, Barnes returned to Paris and Eliot sailed for the United States on 22 August. Any other editorial matters were to be taken up with Morley, who, according to Barnes's account of Kay Boyle's report, "is *positive* he'll go to jail for my book and said he was 'proud' to!!" (13 July 1936).

What remained for Eliot was "the blurb," or jacket copy, and the preface. At first Barnes was hesitant. To Coleman she wrote: "You must know that I am in a fever to see what Eliot wrote. What a beast he is, I would much have preferred no blurb at all, in fact I think all blurbs should be stopped by an act of state, – it may be different in England, but a few things like that would kill the book in America" (20 September

1936). In fact, when she saw the blurb, she was pleased: "I like it because I hate blurbs, and understatement delights me when it is so thoroughly well done, so British, so somber, so sober, . . . I could have done without the line to the effect that it had 'nothing to offer those of easy optomism' [sic]. That is the line that will kill it if any" (22 September 1936). It also seems likely that Eliot used the preface for the first American edition to set the work as a philosophical examination of universal human nature, leading attention away from its homosexual theme.[5] Barnes's approval of Eliot's comments and their use in the first American edition and in most later editions suggests that his preface voiced, in her view, an acceptable reading of the work.

It may not have been the text that she had hoped would be published, but she could live with the compromise, given her fears that it would not be published. Perhaps, however, one action speaks to Barnes's abiding interest in the original third version of this work: she saved *all* copies of the typescript, not just the first carbon with Eliot's emendations.

"Dropped into oblivion" is the phrase Emily Coleman used in her essay on *Nightwood* to describe the public's awareness of the novel in January 1944. Royalty statements, small in 1937 and 1938, and dwindling thereafter, seemed to bear out her appraisal. By 1945 the book was out of print in the States. Harcourt, Brace had destroyed their plates, and Barnes was having difficulty finding a publisher to re-issue the work. She tried Maxwell Perkins at Scribner's, Henry Simon of Simon and Schuster, and Bennet Cerf at Random House, before being approached by James Laughlin of New Directions in July 1945. Laughlin's decision to keep *Nightwood* in print and his efforts on her behalf contributed much to her reputation.

Back in 1935 Djuna Barnes had written to Emily Coleman that her friend Scudder Middleton had read *Nightwood*, loved it, and pronounced it "the most terrifying mad creation from the left lobe of the brain, damned and utterly sad" (19 August 1935). He doubted that "anyone will ever print it." And she added, "so do I, and that makes me crazy." Again on November 8 she confessed, "I am worried for my book, I feel it will never get published somehow." But her fears were less accurate than the prediction of Coleman in her letter of 27 August 1935: "There is no

---

[5]This point was made by Leigh Gilmore, "Obscenity Law and *Nightwood*: Legal, Literary, and Lesbian Identities," Djuna Barnes Centennial Conference, October 1992, University of Maryland, College Park, Maryland.

doubt that, if you live, you will become famous. Its not possible that you should not. . . . People you never heard of and could . . . never talk to, dreadful intellectuals, and Bloomsbury potentates, passionate lovers of literature, seers and prophets—will be among your audience! It is funny, considering that you have never talked to them. But you will get a chance to, in the future!"

The Dalkey Archive edition preserves and presents the original voice, unmuted by the fear of censorship. Barnes's readers are undoubtedly familiar with the foreword to *Ryder* where she damns the effects of censorship on literature, the "havoc of this nicety, and what its effects are on the work of imagination," a statement that Paul West in the afterword to Dalkey's edition of *Ryder* considers the "key to almost everything she wrote." That a similar foreword did not precede *Nightwood* may be because by June 1936 the book meant so much more to her and she knew what its chances had been—and T. S. Eliot was T. S. Eliot. She wrote Coleman after the American edition of *Nightwood* had come out with Eliot's introduction that she "loved Eliot because he has been angelic to me" (15 December 1938). And to Peter Hoare in May 1970 Barnes wrote after seeing Coleman much changed: "I would have liked to show her and the 'public' my 'thanks' to her for her part in my 'career.' " Barnes dedicated her last book *Creatures in an Alphabet* to Emily Coleman. As Coleman noted in her diary on 21 October 1937, "When all is known . . . the story of Coleman and Barnes over the ms. of Nightwood in NY in 1935 will become a saga, a unique thing in literature, as indeed it was."

*

The editor wishes to thank Timothy D. Murray and Rebecca Johnson Melvin, Special Collections, University of Delaware, and their staff for access to and assistance in using the Emily Holmes Coleman Papers; appreciation is also due Beth Alvarez, Curator of Literary Manuscripts, Special Collections, University of Maryland at College Park Libraries, for access to the Djuna Barnes Papers, and to other members of the Maryland staff—all of whom have been very helpful: Lauren Brown, Tim Pyatt, Anne Turkos, Warren Stephenson, and Janette Pardo; also special thanks to former Curator of Rare Books and Literary Manuscripts, Blanche Ebeling-Koning.

I am grateful to Herbert Mitgang of the Authors League Fund, Literary Executor of the Djuna Barnes Estate, and Joseph Geraci, Literary Executor of the Estate of Emily Holmes Coleman, for permission to quote from unpublished material.

The editor wishes also to acknowledge the following colleagues: Linda Itzoe for discriminating advice regarding fine points of acceptable usage; Mary Lynn Broe, Nancy Levine, and Jane Marcus, who in various ways aided and encouraged the project; Wesley Blessing, who has been a valued assistant in proofing text, researching annotations, and double-checking emendations; and Steven Moore, my editor at Dalkey Archive, who has been patient, and ingenious in finding some of the more obscure of Barnes's allusions. My appreciation also goes to patient and supportive friends who have listened, encouraged, and distracted (when necessary). Thanks are also due my son, Hylon Plumb, IV, the cartographer who made the map on pp. 216-17.

This project has been aided by research support from the Institute of Arts and Humanistic Studies, from the Research and Graduate Studies Office, both of Penn State University, and an Advisory Board Grant from Penn State York Campus.

The editor wishes to dedicate this book to the memory of two very special friends: Mary Frances Plumb Blade and Ellis Blade.

*

In the text that follows, three different marks are used to indicate material in the textual apparatus:

* – emendations to the copy-text (pp. 152-86)
† – textual notes (pp. 187-210)
° – explanatory annotations (pp. 211-31)

NIGHTWOOD

To Peggy Guggenheim
and John Ferrar Holms

o

1

Bow Down

EARLY IN 1880, in spite of a well-founded suspicion as to the advisability of perpetuating that race which has the sanction of the Lord and the disapproval of the people, Hedvig Volkbein, a Viennese woman of great strength and military beauty, lying upon a canopied bed, of a rich spectacular crimson, the valance stamped with the bifurcated wings of the House of Hapsburg, the feather coverlet an envelope of satin on which, in massive and tarnished gold threads, stood the Volkbein arms, – gave birth, at the age of forty-five, to an only child, a son, seven days after her physician predicted that she would be taken.

Turning upon this field, which shook to the clatter of morning horses in the street beyond, with the gross splendour of a general saluting the flag, she named him Felix, thrust him from her, and died. The child's father had gone six months previously, a victim of fever. Guido Volkbein, a Jew of Italian descent, had been both a gourmet and a dandy, never appearing in public without the ribbon of some quite unknown distinction tinging his buttonhole with a faint thread. He had been small, rotund, and haughtily timid, his stomach protruding slightly in an upward jutting slope that brought into prominence the buttons of his waistcoat and trousers, marking the exact centre of his body with the obstetric line seen on fruits, – the inevitable arc produced by heavy rounds of burgundy, schlagsahne, and beer.

The autumn, binding him about, as no other season, with racial memories, a season of longing and of horror, he had called his weather. Then walking in the Prater he had been seen

carrying in a conspicuously clenched fist the exquisite handkerchief of yellow and black linen that cried aloud of the ordinance
of 1468 issued by one Pietro Barbo, demanding that, with a   o
rope about its neck, Guido's race should run in the Corso for
the amusement of the Christian populace, while ladies of noble
birth, sitting upon spines too refined for rest, arose from their
seats, and, with the red-gowned cardinals and the *Monsignori*,   o
applauded with that cold yet hysterical abandon of a people that
is at once unjust and happy; the very Pope himself shaken down   *
from his hold on heaven with the laughter of a man who forgoes
his angels that he may recapture the beast. This memory and
the handkerchief that accompanied it had wrought in Guido (as
certain flowers brought to a pitch of florid ecstasy no sooner
attain their specific type than they fall into its decay) the sum
total of what is the Jew. He had walked, hot, incautious and
damned, his eyelids quivering over the thick eyeballs, black with
the pain of a participation that, four centuries later, made him a
victim, as he felt the echo in his own throat of that cry running   * †
the *Piazza Montanara* long ago, "Roba vecchia!", – the degrada-   o
tion by which his people had survived.   *

Childless at fifty-nine, Guido had prepared out of his own
heart for his coming child a heart, fashioned on his own preoc-   *
cupation, the remorseless homage to nobility, the genuflexion
the hunted body makes from muscular contraction, going down
before the impending and inaccessible, as before a great heat. It
had made Guido, as it was to make his son, heavy with imper-
missible blood.

And childless he had died, save for the promise that hung at
the Christian belt of Hedvig. Guido had lived as all Jews do
who, cut off from their people by accident or choice, find that
they must inhabit a world whose constituents, being alien, force
the mind to succumb to an imaginary populace. When a Jew
dies on a Christian bosom he dies impaled. Hedvig, in spite of
her agony, wept upon an outcast. Her body at that moment
became the barrier and Guido died against that wall, troubled
and alone. In life he had done everything possible to span the   †
impossible gap, the saddest and most futile gesture of all had

been his pretense to a Barony. He had adopted the sign of the cross; he had said that he was an Austrian of an old, almost extinct line, producing, to uphold his story, the most amazing and inaccurate proofs: a coat of arms that he had no right to and a list of progenitors (including their Christian names) who had never existed. When Hedvig came upon his black and yellow handkerchiefs he had said that they were to remind him that one branch of his family had bloomed in Rome.

He had tried to be one with her by adoring her, by imitating her goose-step of a stride, a step that by him adopted, became dislocated and comic. She would have done as much, but sensing something in him blasphemed and lonely, she had taken the blow as a Gentile must – by moving toward him in recoil. She had believed whatever he had told her, but often enough she had asked: "What is the matter?" – that continual reproach which was meant as a continual reminder of her love. It ran through his life like an accusing voice. He had been tormented into speaking highly of royalty, flinging out encomiums with the force of small water made great by the pressure of a thumb. He had laughed too heartily when in the presence of the lower order of title, as if, by his good nature, he could advance them to some distinction of which they dreamed. Confronted with nothing worse than a general in creaking leather and with the slight repercussion of movement common to military men, who seem to breathe from the inside out, smelling of gunpowder and horse flesh, lethargic yet prepared for participation in a war not yet scheduled (a type of which Hedvig had been very fond), Guido had shaken with an unseen trembling. He saw that Hedvig had the same bearing, the same though more condensed power of the hand, patterned on seizure in a smaller mould, as sinister in its reduction as a doll's house. The feather in her hat had been knife-clean and quivering as if in an heraldic wind; she had been a woman held up to nature, precise, deep-bosomed and gay. Looking at the two he had become confused as if he were about to receive a reprimand, not the officer's, but his wife's.

When she danced, a little heady with wine, the dance floor had become a tactical manoeuvre; her heels came down staccato and trained, her shoulders as conscious at the tips as those which carry the braid and tassels of promotion; the turn of her head held the cold vigilance of a sentry whose rounds are not without apprehension. Yet Hedvig had done what she could. If ever there was a massive *chic* she had personified it – yet somewhere there had been anxiety. The thing that she had stalked, though she herself had not been conscious of it, was Guido's assurance that he was a Baron. She had believed it as a soldier "believes" a command. Something in her sensitory predicament – upon which she herself would have placed no value – had told her much better. Hedvig had become a Baroness without question.

In the Vienna of Volkbein's day there were few trades that welcomed Jews, yet somehow he had managed, by various deals in household goods, by discreet buying of old masters and first editions and by money changing, to secure for Hedvig a house in the Inner City, to the north, overlooking the Prater, a house that, large, dark and imposing, became a fantastic museum of their encounter.

The long rococo halls, giddy with plush and whorled designs in gold, were peopled with Roman fragments, white and dissociated; a runner's leg, the chilly half-turned head of a matron stricken at the bosom, the blind bold sockets of the eyes given a pupil by every shifting shadow so that what they looked upon was an act of the sun. The great salon was of walnut. Over the fireplace hung impressive copies of the Medici shield and, beside them, the Austrian bird.

Three massive pianos (Hedvig had played the waltzes of her time with the masterly stroke of a man, in the tempo of her blood, rapid and rising – that quick mannerliness of touch associated with the playing of the Viennese, who, though pricked with the love of rhythm, execute its demands in the duelling manner) sprawled over the thick dragon's-blood pile of rugs from Madrid. The study harboured two rambling desks in rich and bloody wood. Hedvig had liked things in twos and threes. Into the middle arch of each desk silver-headed brads had been hammered to form a lion, a bear, a ram, a dove and in

their midst a flaming torch. The design was executed under the
supervision of Guido who, thinking on the instant, claimed it as
the Volkbein field, though it turned out to be a bit of heraldry
long since in decline beneath the papal frown. The full length
windows (a French touch that Guido thought handsome) overlooking the park were curtained in native velvets and stuffs from
Tunis and the Venetian blinds were of that peculiarly sombre
shade of red so loved by the Austrians. Against the panels of
oak that reared themselves above the long table and up to the
curving ceiling hung life-sized portraits of Guido's claim to
father and mother. The lady was a sumptuous Florentine with
bright sly eyes and overt mouth. Great puffed and pearled
sleeves rose to the pricked-eared pointings of the stiff lace
about the head, conical and braided. The deep accumulation of
dress fell about her in groined shadows, the train, rambling
through a vista of primitive trees, was carpet-thick. She seemed
to be expecting a bird. The gentleman was seated precariously
on a charger. He seemed not so much to have mounted the
animal, as to be about to descend upon him. The blue of an
Italian sky lay between the saddle and the buff of the tightened
rump of the rider. The charger had been caught by the painter
in the execution of a falling arc, the mane lifted away in a dying
swell; the tail forward and in, between thin bevelled legs. The
gentleman's dress was a baffling mixture of the Romantic and
the Religious, and in the cradling crook of his left arm he carried a plumed hat, crown out. The whole conception might
have been a Mardi Gras whim. The gentleman's head, stuck
on at a three-quarter angle, had a remarkable resemblance to
Guido Volkbein, the same sweeping Cabalistic line of nose, the
features seasoned and warm save where the virgin blue of the
eyeballs curved out the lids as if another medium than that
of sight had taken its stand beneath that flesh. There was no
interval in the speed of that stare, endless and objective. The
likeness was accidental. Had anyone cared to look into the
matter they would have discovered these canvases to be reproductions of two intrepid and ancient actors. Guido had found
them in some forgotten and dusty corner and had purchased

them when he had been sure that he would need an alibi for the   *
blood.

At this point exact history stopped for Felix who, thirty years
later, turned up in the world with these facts, the two portraits
and nothing more. His aunt, combing her long braids with an
amber comb, told him what she knew, and this had been her
only knowledge of his past. What had formed Felix from the
date of his birth to his coming to thirty was unknown to the
world, for the step of the wandering Jew is in every son. No   o
matter where and when you meet him you feel that he has come
from some place – no matter from what place he has come –
some country that he has devoured rather than resided in, some
secret land that he has been nourished on but cannot inherit, for   †
the Jew seems to be everywhere from nowhere. When Felix's
name was mentioned, three or more persons would swear to
having seen him the week before in three different countries
simultaneously. One would say that he had brushed against him   †
as he climbed the steps of St. Patrick's; another that Felix had   o
been observed punting up the Thames; and the third, that it
could not be as he himself had just left Florence where Felix had
been noted admiring the primitives in the Uffizi.   o

Felix called himself Baron Volkbein, as his father had done
before him. How Felix lived, how he came by his money – he
knew figures as a dog knows the covey and as indefatigably he
pointed and ran – how he mastered seven languages and served
that knowledge well, no one knew. Many people were familiar
with his figure and face. He was not popular, though the posthumous acclaim meted out to his father secured from his
acquaintances the peculiar semi-circular stare of those who,
unwilling to greet with earthly equality, nevertheless give to   *
the living branch (because of death and its sanction) the slight
bend of the head – a reminiscent pardon for future apprehension, – a bow very common to us when in the presence of this
people.

Felix was heavier than his father and taller. His hair began
too far back on his forehead. His face was a long stout oval,
suffering a laborious melancholy. One feature alone spoke of

* Hedvig, the mouth, which, though sensuous from lack of desire as hers had been from denial, pressed too intimately close to the bony structure of the teeth. The other features were a little
* heavy, the chin, the nose, and the lids; into one was set his monocle which shone, a round blind eye in the sun.

He was usually seen walking or driving alone, dressed as if expecting to participate in some great event, though there was no function in the world for which he could be said to be properly garbed; wishing to be correct at any moment, he was tailored in part for the evening and in part for the day.

From the mingled passions that made up his past, out of a diversity of bloods, from the crux of a thousand impossible
* situations, Felix had become the accumulated and single – the embarrassed.

His embarrassment took the form of an obsession for what he termed "Old Europe": aristocracy, nobility, royalty. He spoke any given title with a pause before and after the name. Knowing circumlocution to be his only contact, he made it interminable and exacting. With the fury of a fanatic he hunted down his own disqualification, re-articulating the bones of the Imperial Courts long forgotten (those long remembered can alone claim to be long forgotten), listening with an unbecoming
* loquacity to officials and guardians for fear that his inattention might lose him some fragment of his resuscitation. He felt that
* the great past might mend a little if he bowed low enough, if he succumbed and gave homage.

In nineteen hundred and twenty he was in Paris (his blind eye had kept him out of the army), still spatted, still wearing his
* cutaway, bowing, searching, with quick pendulous movements, for the correct thing to which to pay tribute: the right street, the right café, the right building, the right vista. In restaurants
* ° he bowed slightly to anyone who looked as if he might be "someone," making the bend so imperceptible that the surprised person might think he was merely adjusting his stomach. His rooms were taken because a Bourbon had been carried from them to death. He kept a valet and a cook, the one because he looked like Louis the Fourteenth, and the other because she

resembled Queen Victoria, Victoria in another cheaper material, cut to the poor man's purse.

In his search for the particular *Comédie humaine* Felix had   ° *
come upon the odd. Conversant with edicts and laws, folk story
and heresy, taster of rare wines, thumber of rarer books and old
wives' tales – tales of men who became holy and of beasts that
became damned – read in all plans for fortifications and bridges,
given pause by all graveyards on all roads, a pedant of many
churches and castles, his mind dimly and reverently reverber-
ated to Madame de Sevigné, Goethe, Loyola and Brantôme.   °
But Loyola sounded the deepest note, he was alone, apart and   *
single. A race that has fled its generations from city to city has
not found the necessary time for the accumulation of that   *
toughness which produces ribaldry, nor, after the crucifixion of
its ideas, enough forgetfulness in twenty centuries to create
legend. It takes a Christian, standing eternally in the Jew's
salvation, to blame himself and to bring up from that depth
charming and fantastic superstitions through which the slowly
and tirelessly milling Jew once more becomes the "collector"
of his own past. His undoing is never profitable until some *goy*
has put it back into such shape that it can again be offered
as a "sign." A Jew's undoing is never his own, it is God's; his
rehabilitation is never his own, it is a Christian's. The Christian
traffic in retribution has made the Jew's history a commodity;
it is the medium through which he receives, at the necessary
moment, the serum of his own past that he may offer it again
as his blood. In this manner the Jew participates in the two
conditions; and in like manner Felix took the breast of this wet
nurse whose milk was his being but which could never be his
birthright.

Early in life Felix had insinuated himself into the pageantry
of the circus and the theatre. In some way they linked his
emotions to the higher and unattainable pageantry of Kings
and Queens. The more amiable actresses of Prague, Vienna,
Hungary, Germany, France and Italy, the acrobats and sword-
swallowers, had at one time or another allowed him their
dressing rooms – sham salons in which he aped his heart. Here

*   he had neither to be capable nor alien. He became for a little while a part of their splendid and reeking falsification.

The people of this world, with desires utterly divergent from his own, had also seized on titles for a purpose. There was a °   Princess Nadja, a Baron von Tink, a Principessa Stasera y Stasero, a King Buffo and a Duchess of Broadback: gaudy, cheap cuts from the beast life, immensely capable of that great disquiet called entertainment. They took titles merely to dazzle boys about town, to make their public life (and it was all they had) mysterious and perplexing, knowing well that skill is never so amazing as when it seems inappropriate. Felix clung to his title to dazzle his own estrangement. It brought them together.

Going among these people, the men smelling weaker and the women stronger than their beasts, Felix had that sense of peace *   that formerly he had experienced only in museums. He moved with a humble hysteria among the decaying brocades and laces °   of the Carnavalet; he loved that old and documented splendour with something of the love of the lion for its tamer – that sweat-tarnished spangled enigma that, in bringing the beast to † *   heel, had somehow turned toward him a face like his own, but which, though curious and weak, had yet picked the precise fury from his brain.

Nadja had sat back to Felix, as certain of the justice of his eye * °   as she would have been of the linear justice of a Rops, knowing that Felix tabulated precisely the tense capability of her spine with its lashing curve swinging into the hard compact cleft of *   her rump, as angrily and as beautifully as the more obvious tail of her lion.

The emotional spiral of the circus, taking its flight from the *   immense disqualification of the public, rebounding from its *   illimitable hope, produced in Felix longing and disquiet. The circus was a loved thing that he could never touch, therefore never know. The people of the theatre and the ring were for him as dramatic and as monstrous as a consignment on which he could never bid. That he haunted them as persistently as he did, was evidence of something in his nature that was turning Christian.

He was, in like manner, amazed to find himself drawn to the church, though this tension he could handle with greater ease; its arena, he found, was circumscribed to the individual heart.

It was to the Duchess of Broadback (Frau Mann) that Felix owed his first audience with a "gentleman of quality." Frau Mann, then in Berlin, explained that this person had been "somewhat mixed up with her in the past." It was with the utmost difficulty that he could imagine her "mixed up" with anyone, her coquetries were muscular and localized. Her trade – the trapeze – seemed to have preserved her. It gave her, in a way, a certain charm. Her legs had the specialized tension common to aerial workers; something of the bar was in her wrists, the tan bark in her walk, as if the air, by its very lightness, by its very non-resistance, were an almost insurmountable problem, making her body, though slight and compact, seem much heavier than that of women who stay upon the ground. In her face was the tense expression of an organism surviving in an alien element. She seemed to have a skin that was the pattern of her costume: a bodice of lozenges, red and yellow, low in the back and ruffled over and under the arms, faded with the reek of her three-a-day control, red tights, laced boots—one somehow felt they ran through her as the design runs through hard holi- day candies, and the bulge in the groin where she took the bar, one foot caught in the flex of the calf, was as solid, specialized and as polished as oak. The stuff of the tights was no longer a covering, it was herself; the span of the tightly stitched crotch was so much her own flesh that she was as unsexed as a doll. The needle that had made one the property of the child made the other the property of no man.

"Tonight," Frau Mann said, turning to Felix, "we are going to be amused. Berlin is sometimes very nice at night, *nicht wahr?* And the Count is something that must be seen. The place is very handsome, red and blue, he's fond of blue, God knows why, and he is fond of impossible people, so we are invited – " The Baron moved his foot in. "He might even have the statues on."

"Statues?" said Felix.

º   "The living statues," she said, "he simply adores them." Felix dropped his hat; it rolled and stopped.

"Is he German?" he said.

"Oh no, Italian, but it does not matter, he speaks anything, I think he comes to Germany to change money – he comes, he goes away, and everything goes on the same, except that people have something to talk about."

"What did you say his name was?"

"I didn't, but he calls himself Count Onatorio Altamonte, I'm sure it's quite ridiculous, he says he is related to every nation – that should please you. We will have dinner, we will have champagne." The way she said "dinner" and the way she said "champagne" gave meat and liquid their exact difference, as if by having surmounted two mediums, earth and air, her talent, running forward, achieved all others.

†   "Does one enjoy oneself?" he asked.

"Oh absolutely."

She leaned forward, she began removing the paint with the hurried technical felicity of an artist cleaning a palette. She

º   looked at the Baron derisively. *"Wir setzen an dieser Stelle über den Fluss—"* she said.

Standing about a table at the end of the immense room, looking as if they were deciding the fate of a nation, were grouped ten men, all in parliamentary attitudes, and one young woman. They were listening, at the moment of the entrance of Felix

*   and the Duchess of Broadback, to a middle-aged "medical student" with shaggy eyebrows, a terrific widow's peak, over-large dark eyes, and a heavy way of standing that was also apologetic. The man was Dr. Matthew O'Connor, an Irishman

*   from the Barbary Coast (Pacific Street, San Francisco), whose interest in gynaecology had driven him half around the world. He was taking the part of host, the Count not yet having made

*   his appearance, and was telling of himself, for he considered himself the most amusing predicament.

"We may all be nature's noblemen," he was saying, and the

mention of a nobleman made Felix feel happier the instant he
caught the word, though what followed left him in some doubt,   *
"but think of the stories that do not amount to much! That
is, that are forgotten in spite of all man remembers (unless he
remembers himself) merely because they befell him without
distinction of office or title – that's what we call legend and it's
the best a poor man may do with his fate; the other," he waved
an arm, "we call history, the best the high and mighty can do
with theirs. Legend is unexpurgated, but history, because of its   *
actors, is deflowered – every nation with a sense of humour is a
lost nation, and every woman with a sense of humour is a lost
woman. The Jews are the only people who have enough sense to   †
keep humour in the family; a Christian scatters it all over the
world."

"*Ja! das ist ganz richtig –* " said the Duchess in a loud voice,   o
but the interruption was quite useless. Once the doctor had
his audience – and he got his audience by the simple device of
pronouncing at the top of his voice (at such moments as irri-
table and possessive as a maddened woman's) some of the more
boggish and biting of the shorter early Saxon verbs – nothing
could stop him. He merely turned his large eyes upon her and
having done so, noticed her and her attire for the first time,   † *
which, bringing suddenly to his mind something forgotten but
comparable, sent him into a burst of laughter, exclaiming:
"Well but God works in mysterious ways to bring things up
in my mind! Now I am thinking of Nikka the nigger who used
to fight the bear in the *Cirque de Paris*. There he was, crouching
all over the arena without a stitch on, except an ill-concealed
loin cloth all abulge as if with a deep sea catch, tattooed from
head to heel with all the *ameublement* of depravity! Garlanded   o
with rosebuds and hack-work of the devil, was he a sight to see!
Though he couldn't have done a thing (and I know what I am
talking about, in spite of all that has been said about the black   *
boys) if you had stood him in a gig-mill for a week, though (it's   o
said) at a stretch it spelled Desdemona. Well then, over his belly   o
was an angel from Chartres, on each buttock, half public half
private, a quotation from the book of magic, a confirmation of

* † ° the Jansenist theory, I'm sorry to say and here to say it. Across
* †   his knees, I give you my word, 'I' on one and on the other, 'can,'
     put those together! Across his chest, beneath a beautiful caravel
     in full sail, two clasped hands, the wrist bones fretted with point
     lace. On each bosom, an arrow-speared heart, each with dif-
     ferent initials but with equal drops of blood; and running into
°   the arm-pit, all down one side, the word said by Prince Arthur
     Tudor, son of King Henry the Seventh, when on his bridal
     night he called for a goblet of water (or was it water?). His
     Chamberlain, wondering at the cause of such drought, re-
     marked on it and was answered in one word so wholly epi-
     grammatic and in no way befitting the great and noble British
     Empire that he was brought up with a start, and that is all we
     will ever know of it, unless," said the doctor, striking his hand
°   on his hip, "you are as good at guessing as Tiny M'Caffery."
        "And the legs?" Felix asked uncomfortably.
        "The legs," said Dr. O'Connor, "were devoted entirely to
     vine work, topped by the swart rambler rose copied from the
°   coping of the Hamburg house of Rothschild. Over his *dos*,
     believe it or not and I shouldn't, a terse account in early
     monkish script – called by some people indecent, by others
°   Gothic – of the really deplorable condition of Paris before
     hygiene was introduced, and nature had its way up to the knees.
     And just above what you mustn't mention, a bird flew carrying a
°   streamer on which was incised, 'Garde tout!' I asked him why all
     this barbarity, he answered he loved beauty and would have it
     about him."
        "Are you acquainted with Vienna?" Felix inquired.
        "Vienna," said the doctor, "the bed into which the common
*   people climb, docile with toil, and out of which the nobility
* ° fling themselves, ferocious with dignity – I do, but not so well
     but that I remember some of it still. I remember young Austrian
     boys going to school, flocks of quail they were, sitting out their
     recess in different spots in the sun, rosy-cheeked, bright-eyed,
     with damp rosy mouths, smelling of the herd childhood, facts
     of history glimmering in their minds like sunlight, soon to be
     lost, soon to be forgotten, degraded into proof. Youth is cause,

effect is age; so with the thickening of the neck we get data."

"I was not thinking of its young boys, but of its military superiority, its great names," Felix said, feeling that the evening was already lost, seeing that as yet the host had not made his appearance and that no one seemed to know it or to care, and † * that the whole affair was to be given over to this volatile person who called himself a doctor.

"The army, the celibate's family!" nodded the doctor. "His † * one safety."

The young woman, who was in her late twenties, turned from the group, coming closer to Felix and the doctor. She rested her hands behind her against the table. She seemed embarrassed. "Are you both really saying what you mean, or are you just talk- * ing?" Having spoken, her face flushed, she added hurriedly, "I am doing advance publicity for the circus, I'm Nora Flood."

The doctor swung around, looking pleased. "Ah!" he said, * "Nora suspects the cold incautious melody of time crawling, but," he added, "I've only just started." Suddenly he struck his thigh with his open hand. "Flood, Nora, why sweet God, my girl, I helped to bring you into the world!"

Felix, as disquieted as if he were expected to "do something" to avert a catastrophe (as one is expected to do something about an overturned tumbler, the contents of which is about to drip over the edge of the table and into a lady's lap), on the phrase "time crawling" broke into uncontrollable laughter, and though * this occurrence troubled him the rest of his life he was never able to explain it to himself. The company, instead of being silenced, went on as if nothing had happened, two or three of the younger men were talking about something scandalous, and the "Duchess" in her loud empty voice was telling a very stout man something about the living statues. This only added to the Baron's torment. He began waving his hands, saying, "Oh, please! please!" and suddenly he had a notion that he was doing something that wasn't laughing at all, but something much worse, though he kept saying to himself, "I am laughing, really laughing, nothing else whatsoever!" He kept waving his arms in distress and saying, "Please, please!" staring at the floor, deeply embarrassed to find himself doing so.

As abruptly, he sat straight up, his hands on the arms of the chair, staring fixedly at the doctor who was leaning forward as he drew a chair up exactly facing him. "Yes," said the doctor, and he was smiling, "you will be disappointed! *In questa tomba oscura* – oh unfaithful one! I am no herbalist, I am no Rutebeuf, I have no panacea, I am not a mountebank – that is, I cannot or will not stand on my head. I'm no tumbler, neither a friar, nor yet a thirteenth-century Salome dancing arse up on a pair of Toledo blades – try to get any love-sick girl, male or female, to do that to-day! If you don't believe such things happened in the long back of yesterday look up the manuscripts in the British Museum or go to the Cathedral of Clermont-Ferrand, it's all one to me; become as the wives of the rich Mussulmans of Tunis who hire silly women to reduce the hour to its minimum of sense, still it will not be a cure, for there is none that takes place all at once in any man. You know what man really desires?" inquired the doctor, grinning into the immobile face of the Baron. "One of two things: to find someone who is so stupid that he can lie to her, or to love someone so much that she can lie to him."

"I was not thinking of women at all," the Baron said, and he tried to stand up.

"Neither was I," said the doctor, "sit down." He refilled his glass. "The *fine* is very good," he said.

Felix answered, "No thank you, I never drink."

"You will," the doctor said. "Let us put it the other way, the Lutheran or Protestant church versus the Catholic. The Catholic is the girl that you love so much that she can lie to you, and the Protestant is the girl that loves you so much that you can lie to her, and pretend a lot that you do not feel. Luther, and I hope you don't mind my saying so, was as bawdy an old ram as ever trampled his own straw, because the custody of the people's 'remissions' of sins and indulgences had been snatched out of his hands, which was in that day in the shape of half of all they had and which the old monk of Wittenberg had intended to get off with in his own way. So of course after that, he went

wild and chattered like a monkey in a tree and started something he never thought to start (or so the writing on his side of
the breakfast table would seem to confirm), an obscene mega-
lomania – and wild and wanton stranger that *that* is, it must
come clear and cool and long or not at all. What do you listen to
in the Protestant church? To the words of a man who has been
chosen for his eloquence – and not too eloquent either, mark
you!, or he gets the bum's rush from the pulpit, for fear that in
the end he will use his golden tongue for political ends. For a
golden tongue is never satisfied until it has wagged itself over
the destiny of a nation, and this the church is wise enough to
know.

"But turn to the Catholic church, go into mass at any
moment – what do you walk in upon? Something that's already
in your blood. You know the story that the priest is telling as he
moves from one side of the altar to the other, be he a cardinal,
Leo X, or just some poor bastard from Sicily who has discovered that *pecca fortiter* among his goats no longer masses his
soul, and has, God knows, been God's child from the start, – it
makes no difference. Why? Because you are sitting there with
your own meditations *and* a legend, (which is nipping the fruit
as the wren bites), and mingling them both with the Holy
Spoon, which is that story; or you can get yourself into the
confessional, where, in sonorous prose, lacking contrition (if
you must) you can speak of the condition of the knotty, tangled
soul and be answered in Gothic echoes, mutual and instanta-
neous, – one saying hail to your farewell. Mischief unravels and
the fine high hand of heaven proffers the skein again, combed
and forgiven!

"The one House," he went on, "is hard, as hard as the gift of
gab, and the other is as soft as a goat's hip, and you can blame no
man for anything, and you can't like them at all."

"Wait!" said Felix.

"Yes?" said the doctor.

Felix bending forward, deprecatory and annoyed, went on: "I
like the gesture of the prince who was reading a book, when the
executioner touched him on the shoulder telling him that it was

time, and he, arising, laid a paper-cutter between the pages to
keep his place and closed the book."

    "Ah, said the doctor, "that is not man living in his moment, it
is man living in his miracle." He refilled his glass. "*Gesundheit*,"
he said, "*Freude sei Euch von Gott beschieden, wie heut' so immerdar!*"

    "You argue about sorrow and confusion too easily," Nora
said.

    "Wait!" the doctor answered. "A man's sorrow runs uphill;
true, it is difficult for him to bear, but it is also difficult for him
to keep. I, as a medical man, know in what pocket a man keeps
his heart and soul, and in what jostle of the liver, kidneys and
genitalia these pockets are pilfered. There is no pure sorrow.
Why? It is bedfellow to lungs, lights, bones, guts and gall!
There are only confusions, about that you are quite right, Nora
my child, confusions and defeated anxieties – there you have
us, one and all. If you are a gymnosophist you *can* do without
clothes, and if you are gimp-legged you will know more wind
between the knees than another, still it is confusion; God's
chosen walk close to the wall.

    "I was in a war once myself," the doctor went on, "in a little
town where the bombs began tearing the heart out of you, so
that you began to think of all the majesty in the world that
you would not be able to think of in a minute if the noise came
down and struck in the right place; I was scrambling for the
cellar – and in it was an old Breton woman and a cow she had
dragged with her, and behind that someone from Dublin,
saying, 'Glory be to God!' in a whisper at the far end of the
animal, (thanks be to my maker I had her head on); the hole
was no bigger than a tea-tray, and the poor beast trembling on
her four legs so I knew all at once the tragedy of the beast can
be two legs more awful than a man's. She was softly dropping
her dung at the far end where the thin Celtic voice kept coming
up saying, 'Glory be to Jesus!' and I said to myself, 'Can't the
morning come now, so I can see what my face is mixed up with?'
At that a flash of lightning went by and I saw the cow turning
her head straight back so her horns made two moons against

her shoulders, the tears soused all over her great black eyes.

"I began talking to her, cursing myself and the mick, and
the old woman, looking as if she were looking down her life,   *
sighting it, the way a man looks down the barrel of a gun for an   *
aim. I put my hand on the poor bitch of a cow and her hide was
running water under my hand, like water tumbling down from
Lahore, jerking against my hand as if she wanted to go, standing   *
still in one spot; and I thought, there are directions and speeds   *
that no one has calculated, for believe it or not that cow had
gone somewhere very fast that we didn't know of, and yet was   *
still standing there."

The doctor lifted the bottle. "Thank you," said Felix, "I
never drink spirits."   † *

"You will," said the doctor.

"There's one thing that has always troubled me," the doctor   *
continued, "this matter of the guillotine. They say that the
headsman has to supply his own knife, as a husband is supposed to supply his own razor. That's enough to rot his heart   *
out before he has whittled one head. Wandering about the
Boul 'Mich' one night, flittering my eyes, I saw one with a red   o
carnation in his buttonhole. I asked him what he was wearing
it for, just to start up a friendly conversation; he said, 'It's   † *
the headsman's prerogative,' – and I went as limp as a blotter   † *
snatched from the Senate. 'At one time,' he said, 'the executioner gripped it between his teeth.' At that my bowels turned   *
turtle, seeing him in my mind's eye stropping the cleaver with
a bloom in his mouth like Carmen, and he the one man who   o
is supposed to keep his gloves on in church! They often end
by slicing themselves up, it's a rhythm that finally meets their
own neck. He leaned forward and drew a finger across mine and
said, 'As much hair as thick as that makes it a little difficult,'
and at that moment I got heart failure for the rest of my life. I   † *
put down a franc and flew like the wind, the hair on my back
standing as high as Queen Anne's ruff! And I didn't stop until I
found myself spang in the middle of the Musée de Cluny,   o
clutching the rack."

A sudden silence went over the room. The Count was

standing in the doorway, rocking on his heels, either hand on the sides of the door, a torrent of Italian, which was merely the culmination of some theme he had begun in the entrance hall, was abruptly halved as he slapped his leg, standing tall and bent and peering. He moved forward into the room, holding with thumb and forefinger the center of a round magnifying glass which hung from a broad black ribbon. With the other hand he moved from chair to table, from guest to guest. Behind him, in a riding habit, was a young girl. Having reached the sideboard he swung around with gruesome nimbleness.

"Get out!" he said softly, laying his hand on the girl's shoulder. "Get out, get out!" It was obvious he meant it; he bowed slightly.

As they reached the street the "Duchess" caught a swirling hem of lace about her chilling ankles. "Well, my poor devil?" she said, turning to Felix.

"Well!" said Felix. "What was that about, and why?"

The doctor hailed a cab with the waving end of a bulldog cane. "That can be repaired at any bar," he said.

"The name of that," said the Duchess, pulling on her gloves, "is a brief audience with the great, brief, but an audience!"

As they went up the darkened street Felix felt himself turning scarlet. "Is he really a Count?" he asked.

°   "*Herr Gott!*" said the Duchess. "Am I what I say? Are you? Is the doctor?" She put her hand on his knee. "Yes or no?"

The doctor was lighting a cigarette and in its flare the Baron
* †   saw that he was laughing silently. "He put us out for one of those hopes that is about to be defeated." He waved his gloves from the window to other guests who were standing along the curb, hailing vehicles.

"What do you mean?" the Baron said in a whisper.

"Count Onatorio Altamonte, – may the name eventually roll
°   over the Ponte Vecchio and into the Arno, – suspected that he had come upon his last erection."

°   The doctor began to sing, "*Nur eine Nacht.*"

Frau Mann, with her face pressed against the cab window said, "It's snowing." At her words Felix turned his coat collar up.

"Where are we going?" he asked Frau Mann. She was quite gay again.

"Let us go to Heinrich's, I always do when it's snowing. He mixes the drinks stronger then, and he's a good customer, he always takes in the show."

"Very well," said the doctor, preparing to rap on the window.

"Where is thy Heinrich?"

"Go down *Unter den Linden*," Frau Mann said. "I'll tell you when." ○

Felix said, "If you don't mind, I'll get down here." He got down, walking against the snow.

Seated in the warmth of the favored café, the doctor, unwinding his scarf said: "There's something missing and whole about the Baron Felix—damned from the waist up, which reminds me of Mademoiselle Basquette who was damned from the waist down, a girl without legs, built like a medieval abuse. She used to wheel herself through the Pyrenees on a board. What there was of her was beautiful in a cheap traditional sort of way, the face that one sees on people who come to a racial, not a personal, amazement. I wanted to give her a present for what of her was missing, and she said, 'Pearls—they go so well with everything!' Imagine, and the other half of her still in God's bag of tricks! Don't tell me that what was missing had not taught her the value of what was present. Well, in any case," the doctor went on, rolling down his gloves, "a sailor saw her one day and fell in love with her. She was going up hill and the sun was shining all over her back, it made a saddle across her bent neck and flickered along the curls of her head, gorgeous and bereft as the figurehead of a Norse vessel that the ship has abandoned. So he snatched her up, board and all, and took her away and had his will; when he got good and tired of her, just for gallantry, he put her down on her board about five miles out of town, so she had to roll herself back again, weeping something fearful to see, because one is accustomed to see tears falling down to the feet. Ah truly, a pine board may come up to the chin of a woman and still she will find reason to weep. I tell you, Madame, if one gave birth to a heart on a plate, it would ✳

say 'Love,' and twitch like the lopped leg of a frog."

"*Wunderbar!*" exclaimed Frau Mann. "*Wunderbar*, my God!"

"I'm not through," said the doctor, laying his gloves across his knees, "someday I am going to see the Baron again, and when I do I shall tell him about the mad Wittelsbach. He'll look as distressed as an owl tied up in a muffler."

"Ah," exclaimed Frau Mann, "he will enjoy it. He is so fond of titles."

"Quite right too, in a way," said Doctor O'Connor. "Thinking of something great, even if it *is* all whichways, is better than thinking of nothing, all packed down tidy. And Ludwig knew death, among other things. Death is like taking your thumb out of a bowl of soup; it *has* to leave a hole, but it doesn't. So what of Ludwig? Called infirm because he'd had everything but a woman and a lace collar—and I wouldn't be too sure about the lace collar—though it is true that he had come near to taking Sophia, until he heard a Bürgermeister had got there ahead of him (they still have the shape of his head in a hatter's in München) so at that, the Wittelsbach threw Sophie's bust (marble) right out of the *Residenz Schloss* window and into the court, precariously near to the *Odeonsplatz* – and what a pretty bedroom window it was to be sure! The ceiling was of wrenched yellow silk with a knob in the center which rayed it like the rays of the sun – and that was supposed to be as much as to say, 'Welcome, my little pigeon!' Well, it smashed all to pieces (the bust) down there in the court, and a great humming it made, as much as to say, 'In a moment I'll be something nobody ever intended!' – and then being all different in the green grass. So I often think, what kind of a nature was it this man had, sitting there in his Winter Garden where he – all by himself – listened to music, riding about on his lake dressed up like Lohengrin in a boat like a swan. What's so crazy in that? If wanting a theatre all to yourself is madness, I'm madder than most; and if screaming would empty the world out I'd scream until I broke. After his death didn't they tear it down? Why? The blue water of the fountain was dripping into the ballroom – speaking of water," he added turning his head – "Where, for God's sake, are our drinks? So then I flew away through his chambers," he went on, "as dead as the past, and the pigeons out there in the *Platz* whitening the church and the pavement and the Fräuleins' Sunday bonnets, with their yesterday's oat. The rooms were all of a blue plush and a glitter of scrolling that it would have taken a blindman a lifetime to think up. I came to his bedchamber with its royal china to wash in – his ink-stand was nailed down and as large and rambling as the hand of a whore. There on an estrade, was the bed, which, because it hadn't been slept in since death, was an object *d'art*. Its wooden railing ran all before it to keep the people off, (the people love to leave egg-shells all over history). I could have vaulted the railing myself at a leap, if there had been any reason. So I stood there thinking what must have been in his heart when he sent for Wagner – can't you see Wagner creeping up the stairs, with his blood pounding, the script of an opera under his arm? Then what do I do but clap my eyes on a cross sunk in the parquetry, which was put there to remind the Mad King that one day he forgot himself, and put a hand on his nature, whereupon his rosary fell and lay there weeping. He had it inlaid, and whenever he felt that he was about to lay hands on himself, he put his best foot forward and over that sign and prayed like a good Wittelsbach that his hand might be withheld. My God, was that madness? I asked München's good women why they thought him mad – they said he 'wept a long while and then he got that way.' They loved him very much, they said, 'He whipped his servants.' Why not? They said, 'He used to call out his sledges at midnight and go roaring into the hills.' They said, 'A king has all privileges, but mustn't use them.' 'Sounds like love,' I said, 'all the love in the world and none of it used.' He, possibly, came to the same conclusion. He got to ordering his dinner up through a trap-door, all by himself eating his noodles and *schnitzel*. And is that crazy now? I've called it loneliness all my life." The doctor sighed, his elbows on the table – his hands lying one over the other. "Well, he ended it all," he continued, "by drawing the waters of Starnberg over him, after that he could do as he pleased. Turn belly up or back up and nobody to say him nay, until they snatched him out by the hair and laid him correctly face against the wall, which is called the grave. And it's strange and awful how many people there are who can do what they want only off a roof, or through a rope, or under water, or after the shot is silent. Up there in the palace there's an attendant wandering the great empty rooms with their plush chairs and

†   pillars, throne-room and ballroom (that seems like a terrific terminal and no trains coming in), who remembers him still, and for a mark will tell you how he was his valet – and you look out of the corner of your eye to see if he knows what that might mean – and if he knew, if he remembers. He said the king was so tall that he himself, six foot three, had to stand on the tips of his shoes to get at his tie. So suddenly I myself rose up on

*   tip-toes, right in the middle of that great fine room, and whispered, 'Was he large?' and it went echoing and bellowing through all those rooms like a great bull getting madder and madder the harder he ran; there had been no grandeur in that place for so long that echo couldn't be stopped. I stood there all dumbfounded, my eyes getting frightened, and he said, 'Oh very!' but did he know what I meant or was he thinking of character? To draw his mind off I said in a little whisper, 'Now my good man, where are the toilets? For dear's sake, I don't see

*   so much as a toureen or a tea caddy, much less a pot.'

* ○   " '*Lesen Sie österreichische Geschichte*,' he says, giving me a look of utter contempt. A bit of imperial and secret commode work I'll never know anything about, I thought to myself; 'but the crockery stoves are all in tiling,' I says, 'now why are they fed from the outside in, that is, from the hall?' All those Düsseldorf wenches doing scuttling and secret ash work where it would not meet the imperial eye – "

"That's an item to tell Felix in case he's forgotten," the "duchess" put in, "or doesn't know – "

"Which is all the same," grinned the doctor.

Frau Mann said: "It will give the poor fellow a feeling of power."

*   "Listen," the doctor said, ordering a round, "I don't want to talk of the Wittelsbach. Oh God, when I think back to my past,

everyone in my family a beauty, my mother, with hair on her   *
head as red as a fire kicked over in spring, (and that was early
in the eighties when a girl was the toast of the town, and going
the limit meant lobster à la Newburg). She had a hat on her as
big as the top of a table, and everything on it but running water;
her bosom clinched into a corset of buckram, and my father
sitting up beside her (snapped while they were riding on a
roller-coaster). He had on one of those silly little yellow jackets
and a tan bowler just up over his ears, and he must have been
crazy, for he was sort of cross-eyed – maybe it was the wind
in his face or thoughts of my mother where he couldn't do
anything about it." Frau Mann took up her glass, looking at
it with one eye closed – "I've an album of my own," she said
in a warm voice, "and everyone in it looks like a soldier – even
though they are dead."

"Halt!" said the doctor, "I remember rummaging through   †
the garret of our palatial mansion (called Spanish in those days),
and seeing rows of old dresses in silks that could stand up by
themselves – they could have gone to war just as they were.
There was enough spirit in those old materials to get shot, and
they were my only idea of metempsychosis, you could tell by the
way the bum bird-cages of bustles stood that they had been
good Catholics all the days of their lives, way back to begorrah,
and not afraid of love no matter what was going on. And speaking of love," he said, "I love nature as well as anyone, things all
growing quietly, getting used up and dying and saying nothing,
that's why I eat salad – which brings me to the night I popped
Tiny out to relieve him of his drinking, when something with
dark hands closed over him as if to strangle the life's breath out
of him and suddenly the other, less pleasing hand, the hand of
the law, was on my shoulder and I was hurled into jail, into
Marie Antoinette's very cell; and I thought, 'Well, if this latrine   °
was good enough for her, I'll stop my weeping,' and I thought,
'The dish of the eucharist, the last she took from, if shown me
now as it's shown in the Notre Dame, I'd simply die!' We, the
two blasphemed queens, she blasphemed twice, for wasn't it the
rule in her day that an expecting queen should have to deliver

herself amid all the rabble that they call the royal suite? There
they were, scrambling to get a sight of her luck, stepping on the
umbilical as if she were a prizefight and not a lady; and 'That,' I
said to myself as I was being dragged along, 'has been spared
me,' and then as I began to think of that I began to weep and
hurl my robin, with the dark all about me and the bats flying.

"Then the sergeant, who was going to take me to the
procureur after that black terrible ride in the Maria, came and
put his hand out and it was to put the manacles on me, but I
did not understand, so I just took his hand, and at that he sighed
and gave up the ghost and said, taking my hand in his, 'Oh for
God's sake!' and me walking beside him, feeling a little as if I
had a mother, a mother winnowed down, but still a mother – I
had always wanted one all to myself! They tossed bread into
my cell and it was made of wood and they said, 'If you want
water you can get it where you make it!' and with that they
left me until the court scene the next morning, and me all
bewildered, looking about for a place to lay my head that
wouldn't stop the traffic. Well, the next morning I was being
hurried along – holding on to my pants, because they had cut
the suspenders for fear of suicide. So there I was, covered with
snow and shame, shuffling along holding on to my pants, my
heart breaking, shuffling along in one loose shoe and the other
loose shoe – they'd snatched out the laces too for fear of hanging – and me looking right and left under my eyebrows – crying
and shamed, (crying and needing a friend and afraid I'd see
one). My God, to get into this for a thing that was less than
love! A mere accident, I'd had nothing whatsoever to do with,
and then an accusation. I don't believe that there is a thing that
lasts in this world, love least of all, and here was something that
I was never going to forget! Oh God! I was in a twitter, my heart
bleeding and my long golden curls catching in my French heels!
Me, with a face like a squirrel's, only fit to keep nuts in! When
I think how ugly He made me (me wanting to be a soprano
and sing a cadenza in an early Gaulish garden) I could weep for
injustice! Well, then I looked up and there standing above the
judge was *Notre Dame de la Bonne Garde* looking down at me.

I began praying right then and there, holding on to my pants, saying softly: 'If you get me out of this, darling, I'll say my beads smack down under you for thirty days!' And it's a crazy kind of prayer I'll be saying to her because I'm the little man who believes you should talk to these people. If they aren't your friends up there in the sky, then what are they? So why shouldn't I talk to her in that way?"

Frau Mann nodded, she wanted to say something, but she knew there was no hope.

"So I said, 'Why did you have me if you didn't want me,' " the doctor went on, " 'and weren't going to help me in our hour of trouble!' And there I was, draped over the railing, all of a swoop of misery, as heavy in my heart as Adam's off ox. And at that *Notre Dame de la Bonne Garde* seemed to sort of give me the high wink, and the judge let me off after all! So, as I went by him I whispered: 'I thank you, and I love you very much, *de tout mon coeur!*' He answered, soft and low, stabbing the blotter with a pencil: '*C'est le coeur d'une femme!*' 'Oui!' I said gentle, so perhaps I've got me a friend."

The doctor grinned, biting his teeth. Frau Mann tried to light a cigarette, the match wavered from side to side in her unsteady hand.

"You have very particular ideas, haven't you?" she said.

"I have," said the doctor, "I think it's a terrible world – this extremity, this badly executed leap in the dark called life. So I was thinking, where are all the birds and flowers? Anyway, there we were, sitting up like a row of Byzantine latrines, my hands to my lip, saying, 'Tragedy,' saying 'Horror,' saying 'Violence!' Silence, may it stand beside my mouth – note the Greek in that posture, the gesture histrionic! At that moment I was, for misery, as slain of detail as a marble from Carthage.

"If they must punish you for forgetting yourself – as if that were not awful punishment enough," he said reflectively, "Why don't they come to your house in the dark, when no one is looking, and let your drawers down and beat you up? It would be better for the pride of the race." Frau Mann was slightly tipsy, and the insistent hum of the doctor's words was making her

†   sleepy. "Listen to the music," she said.

     "Why should I," answered the doctor, "I've heard the music
* °   of musics, Albeniz' *Córdoba* under the fingers of my friend playing softly. Humming on the twilight it went, on the
moonlight it went, with his head thrown back so that his ears
were horizontal, he said to me, looking over his shoulder, 'Can't
you see all those grand Franciscans and the other monks of
†   Córdoba sitting in the Piazza with the great Spanish combs in
their hair!' And I said, 'Surely, but at this moment there are two
*   king snakes at the sill, making love as near as I can figure, by the
way they are swallowing each other.' He sort of screamed and
put his hands over his eyes, and I said, 'Now play something.'"

     Seeing that Frau Mann dozed, the doctor got up lightly and
tip-toed noiselessly to the entrance. He said to the waiter in
bad German: "The lady will pay," opened the door, and went
quietly into the night.

2

LA SOMNAMBULE

_o

CLOSE TO THE CHURCH OF *St. Sulpice*, around the corner in the *rue Servandoni*, lived the doctor. His small slouching figure was a feature of the *Place*. To the proprietor of the *Café de la Mairie du VIe* he was almost a son. This relatively small square, through which tram lines ran in several directions, bounded on the one side by the church and on the other by the court, was the doctor's "city." What he could not find here to answer to his needs, could be found in the narrow streets that ran into it. Here he had been seen ordering details for funerals in the *parlour* with its black broadcloth curtains and mounted pictures of hearses; buying holy pictures and *petits Jésus* in the *boutique* displaying vestments and flowering candles. He had shouted down at least one judge in the *Mairie du Luxembourg* after a dozen cigars had failed to bring about his ends.

He walked, pathetic and alone, among the pasteboard booths of the *Foire St. Germain* when for a time its imitation castles squatted in the square. He was seen coming at a smart pace down the left side of the church to go into Mass; bathing in the holy water stoup as if he were its single and beholden bird, pushing aside weary French maids and local tradespeople with the impatience of a soul in physical stress.

Sometimes, late at night, before turning into the *Café de la Mairie du VIe*, he would be observed staring up at the huge towers of the church which rose into the sky, unlovely but reassuring, running a thick warm finger around his throat, where, in spite of its custom, his hair surprised him, lifting along his back † * and creeping up over his collar. Standing small and insubordi-

nate, he would watch the basins of the fountain loosing their
skirts of water in a ragged and flowing hem, sometimes crying
to a man's departing shadow: "Aren't you the beauty!"

To the *Café de la Mairie du VI* he brought Felix, who turned
up in Paris some weeks after the encounter in Berlin. Felix
thought to himself that undoubtedly the doctor was a great liar,
but a valuable liar. His fabrications seemed to be the framework
of a forgotten, but imposing plan; some condition of life of
which he was the sole surviving retainer. His manner was that of
a servant of a defunct noble family, whose movements recall,
though in a degraded form, those of a late master. Even the
doctor's favorite gesture—plucking hairs out of his nostrils—
seemed the "vulgarization" of what was once a thoughtful
plucking of the beard.

As the altar of a church would present but a barren stylization
but for the uncalculated offerings of the confused and humble;
as the *corsage* of a woman is made suddenly martial and sorrow-
ful by the rose thrust among the more decorous blooms by the
hand of a lover suffering the violence of the overlapping of the
permission to bestow a last embrace, and its withdrawal, making
a vanishing and infinitesimal bull's-eye, of that which had a
moment before been a buoyant and showy bosom, by dragging
time out of his bowels—(for a lover knows two times, that
which he is given, and that which he must make)—so Felix was
astonished to find that the most touching flowers laid on the
altar he had raised to his imagination were placed there by the
people of the underworld, and that the reddest was to be the
rose of the doctor.

After a long silence in which the doctor had ordered and con-
sumed a *Chambéry fraise* and the Baron a coffee, the doctor remarked that the Jew and the Irish, the one moving upward, and
the other down, often meet, spade to spade in the same acre.

"The Irish may be as common as whale-shit—excuse me—
on the bottom of the ocean—forgive me—but they do have
imagination and," he added, "creative misery, which comes
from being smacked down by the devil, and lifted up again by
the angels. *Misericordioso!* Save me, Mother Mary, and never

mind the other fellow! But the Jew, what is he at his best? Never
anything higher than a meddler—pardon my wet glove—a   *
supreme and marvellous meddler often, but a meddler nevertheless." He bowed slightly from the hips. "All right, Jews
meddle and we lie, that's the difference, the fine difference. We
say someone is pretty for instance, whereas, if the truth were   *
known, they are probably as ugly as Smith going backward, but   *
by our lie we have made that very party powerful, such is the
power of the charlatan, the great strong! They drop on anything at any moment, and that sort of thing makes the mystic in
the end, and," he added, "it makes the great doctor. The only
people who really *know* anything about medical science are the
nurses, and they never tell, they'd get slapped if they did. But
the great doctor, he's a divine idiot and a wise man. He closes
one eye, the eye that he studied with, and putting his fingers on
the arteries of the body says, 'God, whose roadway this is, has
given me permission to travel on it also,' which, heaven help the
patient, is true; in this manner he comes on great cures, and   *
sometimes upon that road is disconcerted by that Little Man."
The doctor ordered another *Chambéry*, and asked the Baron   † *
what he would have; being told that he wished nothing for the   *
moment, the doctor added: "No man needs curing of his indi-   *
vidual sickness, his universal malady is what he should look to."
The Baron remarked that this sounded like dogma.
The doctor looked at him. "Does it? Well, when you see that   *
Little Man you know you will be shouldered from the path."
"I also know this," he went on: "One cup poured into another   *
makes different water, tears shed by one eye would blind if wept
into another's eye. The breast we strike in joy is not the breast
we strike in pain; any man's smile would be consternation on   *
another's mouth. Rear up, eternal river, here comes grief! Man   *
has no foothold that is not also a bargain. So be it! Laughing I
came into Pacific Street, and laughing I'm going out of it;
laughter is the pauper's money. I like paupers and bums," he
added, "because they are impersonal with misery, but me—me,   *
I'm taken most and chiefly for a vexatious bastard and gum on
the bow, the wax that clots the gall or middle blood of man

* † known as the heart or Bundle of Hiss. May my dilator burst and my speculum rust, may panic seize my index finger before I point out my man!"

* His hands (which he always carried like a dog who is walking on his hind legs) seemed to be holding his attention, then he
* said, raising his large melancholy eyes with the bright twinkle that often came into them: "Why is it that whenever I hear music I think I'm a bride?"

* "Neurasthenia," said Felix.

He shook his head. "No, I'm not neurasthenic, I haven't that
† much respect for people—the basis, by the by, of all neurasthenia."

"Impatience."

The doctor nodded. "The Irish are impatient for eternity, they lie to hurry it up, and they maintain their balance by the dexterity of God, God and the father."

* ° "In 1685," the Baron said, with dry humour, "the Turks brought coffee into Vienna, and from that day Vienna, like a woman, had one impatience, something she liked. You know of
° course, that Pitt the younger was refused alliance because he was foolish enough to proffer tea; Austria and tea could never go together. All cities have a particular and special beverage suited to them. As for God and the Father—in Austria they
° were the Emperor." The doctor looked up. The *chasseur* of the
* *Hôtel Récamier* (whom he knew far too well) was approaching them at a run.

* "Eh!" said the doctor, who always expected anything at any hour, "Now what?" The boy, standing before him in a red and
† ° black striped vest and flapping soiled apron, explained in Midi
* French that a lady in twenty-nine had fainted and could not be brought out of it.

* The doctor got up slowly, sighing. "Pay," he said to Felix,
* "and follow me." None of the doctor's methods being orthodox, Felix was not surprised at the invitation, but did as he was told.

On the second landing of the hotel (it was one of those
* middle-class hostelries which can be found in almost any corner

of Paris, neither good nor bad, but so typical that it might have been moved every night and not have been out of place) a door was standing open, exposing a red-carpeted floor, and at the further end, two narrow windows overlooking the square.

On a bed, surrounded by a confusion of potted plants, exotic palms and cut flowers, faintly oversung by the notes of unseen birds, which seemed to have been forgotten, left without the usual silencing cover (which, like cloaks on funeral urns, are cast over their cages at night by good housewives), half flung off the support of the cushions from which, in a moment of threatened consciousness she had turned her head, lay the young woman, heavy and dishevelled. Her legs, in white flannel trousers, were spread as in a dance, the thick lacquered pumps looking too lively for the arrested step. Her hands, long and beautiful, lay on either side of her face.

The perfume that her body exhaled was of the quality of that earth-flesh, fungi, which smells of captured dampness and yet is so dry, overcast with the odour of oil of amber, which is an inner malady of the sea, making her seem as if she had invaded a sleep incautious and entire. Her flesh was the texture of plant life, and beneath it one sensed a frame, broad, porous and sleep-worn, as if sleep were a decay fishing her beneath the visible surface. About her head there was an effulgence as of phosphorus glowing about the circumference of a body of water—as if her life lay through her in ungainly luminous deteriorations—the troubling structure of the born somnambule, who lives in two worlds—meet of child and desperado.

Like a painting by the *douanier* Rousseau, she seemed to lie in a jungle trapped in a drawing room (in the apprehension of which the walls have made their escape), thrown in among the carnivorous flowers as their ration; the set, the property of an unseen *dompteur*, half lord, half promoter, over which one expects to hear the strains of an orchestra of wood-winds render a serenade which will popularize the wilderness.

Felix, out of delicacy, stepped behind the palms. The doctor with professional roughness, brought to a pitch by his eternal fear of meeting with the law (he was not a licensed practitioner)

* said: "Slap her wrists, for Christ's sake. Where in hell is the water pitcher!"

He found it, and with amiable heartiness flung a handful against her face.

A series of almost invisible shudders wrinkled her skin as the
* water dripped from her lashes, over her mouth and on to the bed. A spasm of waking moved upward from some deep shocked realm, and she opened her eyes. Instantly she tried to get to her
† feet. She said: "I was all right," and fell back into the pose of her annihilation.

Experiencing a double confusion, Felix now saw the doctor, partially hidden by the screen beside the bed, make the movements common to the "dumbfounder," or man of magic; the
* gestures of one who, in preparing the audience for a miracle, must pretend that there is nothing to hide; the whole purpose that of making the back and elbows move in a series of "honesties," while in reality the most flagrant part of the hoax is being prepared.

Felix saw that this was for the purpose of snatching a few drops from a perfume bottle picked up from the night table; of dusting his darkly bristled chin with a puff, and drawing a line of rouge across his lips, his upper lip compressed on his lower, in order to have it seem that their sudden embellishment was
* a visitation of nature; still thinking himself unobserved, as if
* the whole fabric of magic had begun to decompose, as if the mechanics of machination were indeed out of control, and were
† * simplifying themselves back to their origin, the doctor reached out and covered a loose hundred franc note lying on the table.

With a tension in his stomach, such as one suffers when watching an acrobat leaving the virtuosity of his safety in a mad unravelling whirl into probable death, Felix watched the hand
- descend, take up the note, and disappear into the limbo of the doctor's pocket. He knew that he would continue to like the doctor, though he was aware that it would be in spite of a long series of convulsions of the spirit, analogous to the displacement in the fluids of the oyster, that must cover its itch with a pearl; so he would have to cover the doctor. He knew at the

same time that this stricture of acceptance, (by which what we must love is made into what we can love) would eventually be a part of himself, though originally brought on by no will of his own.

Engrossed in the coils of this new disquiet, Felix turned about. The girl was sitting up. She recognized the doctor. She had seen him somewhere. But, as one may trade ten years at a certain shop and be unable to place the shopkeeper if he is met in the street or in the *promenoir* of a theatre, the shop being a † * portion of his identity, she struggled to place him now that he * had moved out of his frame.

"*Café de la Mairie du VI*," said the doctor, taking a chance in order to have a hand in her awakening.

She did not smile, though the moment he spoke, she placed him. She closed her eyes, and Felix, who had been looking into * them intently because of their mysterious and shocking blue, found himself seeing them still faintly clear and timeless behind the lids—the long unqualified range in the iris of wild beasts * who have not tamed the focus down to meet the human eye.

The woman who presents herself to the spectator as a "picture" forever arranged, is for the contemplative mind the chiefest danger. Sometimes one meets a woman who is beast turning human. Such a person's every movement will reduce to an image of a forgotten experience; a mirage of an eternal wedding cast on the racial memory; as insupportable a joy as would be the vision of an eland coming down an aisle of trees, chapleted with orange blossoms and bridal veil, a hoof raised in the economy of fear, stepping in the trepidation of flesh that will become myth; as the unicorn is neither man nor beast * deprived, but human hunger pressing its breast to its prey.

Such a woman is the infected, carrier of the past—before her † * the structure of our head and jaws ache—we feel that we could eat her, she who is eaten death returning, for only then do we put our face close to the blood on the lips of our forefathers.

Something of this emotion came over Felix, but being racially incapable of abandon, he felt that he was looking upon a figurehead in a museum, which though static, no longer

roosting on its cutwater, seemed yet to be going against the
° wind; as if this girl were the converging halves of a broken
* fate, setting face, in sleep, toward itself in time, as an image
and its reflection in a lake seem parted only by the hesitation
* in the hour. In the tones of this girl's voice was the pitch of
* one enchanted with the gift of postponed abandon: the low,
drawling "aside" voice of the actor who, in the soft usury of his
* speech, withholds a vocabulary until the profitable moment
* † when he shall be facing his audience, – in her case a guarded
extempore to the body of what would be said at some later
period when she would be able to "see" them. What she now
said was merely the longest way to a quick dismissal. She asked
them to come to see her when she would be "able to feel better."

Pinching the *chasseur*, the doctor inquired the girl's name,
"Mademoiselle Robin Vote," the *chasseur* answered.

Descending into the street, the doctor desiring "one last
before bed" directed his steps back to the café. After a short
silence he asked the Baron if he had ever thought about women
and marriage. He kept his eyes fixed on the marble of the table
before him, knowing that Felix had experienced something
unusual.

The Baron admitted that he had, he wished a son who would
feel as he felt about the "great past." The doctor then inquired,
with feigned indifference, of what nation he would choose the
boy's mother.

* "The American," the Baron answered instantly. "With an
American anything can be done."

The doctor laughed. He brought his soft fist down on the
table—now he was sure. "Fate and entanglement," he said,
* "have begun again—the dung beetle rolling his burden up
hill—oh the hard climb! Nobility, very well, but what is it?"
The Baron started to answer him, the doctor held up his hand.
"Wait a minute! I know—the few that the many have lied about
well and long enough to make them deathless. So you must have
° a son," he paused. "A king is the peasant's actor, who becomes
so scandalous that he has to be bowed down to—scandalous in
the higher sense naturally. And why must he be bowed down to?

Because he has been set apart as the one dog who need not regard the rules of the house; they are so high that they can de-
fame God and foul their rafters! But the people—that's different—they are church-broken, nation-broken—they drink and
pray and piss in the one place. Every man has a housebroken
heart except the great man. The people love their church and
know it, as a dog knows where he was made to conform, and
there he returns by his instinct. But to the graver permission,
the king, the tsar, the emperor, who may relieve themselves on
high heaven—to them they bow down—only." The Baron, who
was always troubled by obscenity, could never, in the case of the
doctor, resent it; he felt the seriousness, the melancholy hidden
beneath every jest and malediction that the doctor uttered,
therefore he answered him seriously. "To pay homage to our
past is the only gesture that also includes the future."

"And so a son?"

"For that reason. The modern child has nothing left to hold
to, or to put it better, he has nothing to hold with. We are
adhering to life now with our last muscle—the heart."

"The last muscle of aristocracy is madness—remember
that—" the doctor leaned forward, "the last child born to
aristocracy is sometimes an idiot, out of respect—we go up—
but we come down."

The Baron dropped his monocle, the unarmed eye looked
straight ahead. "It's not necessary," he said, then he added, "But
you are American, so you don't believe."

"Ho!" hooted the doctor, "because I'm American I believe
anything, so I say beware! In the king's bed is always found, just
before it becomes a museum piece, the droppings of the black
sheep," – he raised his glass, "To Robin Vote," he said. "She
can't be more than twenty."

With a roar the steel blind came down over the window of
the *Café de la Mairie du VI*.

° Felix, carrying two volumes on the life of the Bourbons, called the next day at the *Hôtel Récamier*. Miss Vote was not in. Four afternoons in succession he called, only to be told that she had just left. On the fifth, turning the corner of the *rue Bonaparte* he ran into her.

* Removed from her setting, – the plants that had surrounded her, the melancholy red velvet of the chairs and the curtains, the
* sound, weak and nocturnal, of the birds, – she yet carried the quality of the "way back" as animals do. She suggested that they
* should walk together in the gardens of the Luxembourg toward which her steps had been directed when he addressed her. They walked in the bare chilly gardens and Felix was happy. He felt that he could talk to her, tell her anything, though she herself was so silent. He told her he had a post in the *Crédit Lyonnais*, earning two thousand five hundred francs a week; a master of
* seven tongues, he was useful to the bank, and, he added, he had a trifle saved up, gained in speculations.

He walked a little short of her. Her movements were slightly headlong and sideways; slow, clumsy and yet graceful, the ample gait of the night watch. She wore no hat, and her pale
* head, with its short hair growing flat on the forehead made still narrower by the hanging curls almost on a level with the finely arched eyebrows, gave her the look of cherubs in renaissance
† theatres, the eye-balls showing slightly rounded in profile, the
* temples low and square. She was gracious and yet fading, like an
* old statue in a garden, that symbolizes the weather through which it has endured, and is not so much the work of man as the work of wind and rain and the herd of the seasons, and though formed in man's image, is a figure of doom. Because of this,
* † Felix found her presence painful, and yet a happiness. Thinking of her, visualizing her, was an extreme act of the will; to recall her after she had gone, however, was as easy as the recollection of a sensation of beauty without its details. When she smiled,
† the smile was only in the mouth, and a little bitter, the face of an
* † incurable, yet to be stricken with its malady.

As the days passed they spent many hours in museums, and
* while this pleased Felix immeasurably, he was surprised that

often her taste, turning from an appreciation of the excellent,   † *
would also include the cheaper and debased, with an emotion as   *
real. When she touched a thing, her hands seemed to take the
place of the eye. He thought, "She has the touch of the blind
who, because they see more with their fingers, forget more in
their minds." Her fingers would go forward, hesitate, tremble,
as if they had found a face in the dark. When her hand finally
came to rest, the palm closed, it was as if she had stopped a cry-   *
ing mouth. Her hand lay still, and she would turn away. At such
moments Felix experienced an unaccountable apprehension.
The sensuality in her hands frightened him.   † *

Her clothes were of a period that he could not quite place.
She wore feathers of the kind his mother had worn, flattened
sharply to the face. Her skirts were moulded to her hips and
fell downward and out, wider and longer than those of other
women, heavy silks that made her seem newly ancient. One day
he learned the secret. Pricing a small tapestry in an antique shop
facing the Seine, he saw Robin reflected in a door mirror of a
back room, dressed in a heavy brocaded gown which time had
stained in places, in others split, yet which was so voluminous
that there were yards enough to refashion.

He found that his love for Robin was not in truth a selection;   *
it was as if the weight of his life had amassed one precipitation.
He had thought of making a destiny for himself, through laborious and untiring travail. Then with Robin it seemed to stand
before him, without effort. When he asked her to marry him it   *
was with such an unplanned eagerness that he was taken aback
to find himself accepted, as if Robin's life held no volition for   † *
refusal.

He took her first to Vienna. To reassure himself he showed
her all the historic buildings. He kept saying to himself that
sooner or later, in this garden or that palace she would suddenly
be moved as he was moved. Yet it seemed to him that he too was
a sightseer. He tried to explain to her what Vienna had been
before the war; what it must have been before he was born;
yet his memory was confused and hazy, and he found himself
repeating what he had read, for it was what he knew best. With

* methodical anxiety he took her over the city. He said, "You are
a *Baronin* now." He spoke to her in German as she ate the heavy
schnitzel and dumplings, clasping her hand about the thick
° handle of the beer mug. He said: "*Das Leben ist ewig, darin liegt*
* *seine Schönheit."*

They walked before the Imperial Palace in a fine hot sun that
fell about the clipped hedges and the statues warm and clear. He
* went into the *Kammergarten* with her and talked, and on into
† the *Gloriette*, and sat on first one bench, and then another,
though she asked why. Brought up short, he realized that he had
been hurrying from one to the other as if they were orchestra
† chairs, as if he himself were trying not to miss anything, though
now, at the extremity of the garden, he was aware that he had
* been anxious to see every tree, every statue at a different angle.

In their hotel, she went to the window and pulled aside the
* heavy velvet hangings, threw down the bolster that Vienna uses
against the wind at the ledge, and opened the window, though
° the night air was cold. He began speaking of Emperor Francis
° Joseph and of the whereabouts of Charles the First. And as he
spoke, Felix labored under the weight of his own remorseless
* re-creation of the great, generals and statesmen and emperors.
His chest was as heavy as if it were supporting the combined
weight of their apparel and their destiny. Looking up after an
interminable flow of fact and fancy, he saw Robin sitting with
* † her legs thrust out, her head thrown back against the embossed
cushion of the chair, sleeping, one arm fallen over the chair's
side, the hand somehow older and wiser than her body; and
looking at her he knew that he was not sufficient to make her
what he had hoped; it would require more than his own argument. It would require contact with persons exonerated of
their earthly condition by some strong spiritual bias, someone
of that old régime, some old lady of the past courts, who only
remembered others when trying to think of herself.

* On the tenth day, therefore, Felix turned about and re-
entered Paris. In the following months he put his faith in the
fact that Robin had Christian proclivities, and his hope in the
discovery that she was an enigma. He said to himself that pos-

sibly she had greatness hidden in the non-committal. He felt
that her attention, somehow in spite of him, had already been
taken, by something not yet in history. Always she seemed to be
listening to the echo of some foray in the blood, that had no
known setting; and when he came to know her this was all he
could base his intimacy upon. There was something pathetic in
the spectacle: Felix reiterating the tragedy of his father. Attired
like some haphazard in the mind of a tailor, again in the ambit
of his father's futile attempt to encompass the rhythm of his
wife's stride, Felix, with tightly held monocle, walked beside
Robin, talking to her, drawing her attention to this and that,
wrecking himself and his peace of mind in an effort to acquaint
her with the destiny for which he had chosen her: that she
might bear sons who would recognize and honour the past. For
without such love, the past as he understood it, would die away
from the world. She was not listening, and he said in an angry
mood, though he said it calmly, "I am deceiving you!" And he
wondered what he meant, and why she did not hear.

"A child," he pondered, "Yes, a child!" and then he said to
himself, "Why has it not come about?" The thought took him
abruptly in the middle of his accounting. He hurried home in a
flurry of anxiety, like a boy who has heard a regiment on parade,   *
toward which he cannot run, because he has no one from whom † *
to seek permission, yet runs haltingly nevertheless; coming face   *
to face with her, all that he could stammer out was, "Why is
there no child? *Wo ist das Kind? Warum? Warum?*"   o *

Robin prepared herself for her child with her only power, a
stubborn cataleptic calm, conceiving herself pregnant before
she was; and strangely aware of some lost land in herself, she
took to going out; wandering the countryside; to train travel,
to other cities, alone and engrossed. Once, not having returned
for three days, and Felix nearly beside himself with terror, she
walked in late at night and said that she had been halfway to
Berlin.

Suddenly she took the Catholic vow. She came into the
church silently. The prayers of the suppliants had not ceased
nor had anyone been broken of their meditation. Then, as if

some inscrutable wish for salvation, something monstrously
unfulfilled had thrown a shadow, they regarded her, to see her
going softly forward and down, a tall girl with the body of a boy.
Many churches saw her, St. *Julien le Pauvre*, the church of
St. *Germain des Prés*, Ste. *Clotilde*; even on the cold tiles of the
Russian church, in which there is no pew, she knelt alone, lost
and conspicuous, her broad shoulders above her neighbours,
her feet large and as earthly as the feet of a monk.

She strayed into the *rue Picpus*, into the gardens of the convent of *L'Adoration Perpétuelle*. She talked to the nuns and they,
feeling that they were looking at someone who would never be
able to ask for, or receive mercy, blessed her in their hearts
and gave her a sprig of rose from the bush. They showed her
where Jean Valjean had kept his rakes, and where the bright
little ladies of the *pension* came to quilt their covers; and Robin
smiled, taking the spray, and looked down at the tomb of
Lafayette and thought her unpeopled thoughts. Kneeling in the
chapel, which was never without a nun going over her beads,
Robin, trying to bring her mind to this abrupt necessity, found
herself worrying about her height. Was she still growing?

She tried to think of the consequence to which her son was
to be born and dedicated. She thought of the Emperor Francis
Joseph. There was something commensurate in the heavy body
with the weight in her mind where reason was inexact with lack
of necessity. She wandered to thoughts of women, women that
she had come to connect with women. Strangely enough these
were women in history, Louise de la Vallière, Catherine of
Russia, Madame de Maintenon, Catherine de Medici, and two
women out of literature, Anna Karenina and Catherine Heathcliff; and now there was this woman Austria. She prayed, and
her prayer was monstrous, because in it there was no margin left
for damnation or forgiveness, for praise or for blame – those
who cannot conceive a bargain cannot be saved or damned. She
could not offer herself up, she only told of herself, in a preoccupation that was its own predicament.

Leaning her childish face and full chin on the shelf of the
prie-Dieu, her eyes fixed, she laughed, out of some hidden

capacity, some lost subterranean humour; as it ceased, she   *
leaned still further forward in a swoon, waking and yet heavy,
like one in sleep.

When Felix returned that evening, Robin was dozing in a
chair, one hand under her cheek, and one arm fallen. A book   *
was lying on the floor beneath her hand. The book was the
memoirs of the Marquis de Sade; a line was underscored: *Et lui*   o
*rendant sa captivité les milles services qu'un amour dévoué est seul
capable de rendre*, and suddenly into his mind came the question:
"What is wrong?"

She awoke but did not move. He came and took her by the
arm and lifted her toward him. She put her hand against his
chest and pushed him, she looked frightened, she opened her
mouth but no words came. He stepped back, he tried to speak
but they moved aside from each other saying nothing.

That night she was taken with pains. She began to curse
loudly, a thing that Felix was totally unprepared for; with the   *
most foolish gestures he tried to make her comfortable.

"Go to hell!" she cried. She moved slowly, bent away from   *
him, chair by chair; she was drunk – her hair was swinging in
her eyes.

Amid loud and frantic cries of affirmation and despair, Robin
was delivered. Shuddering in the double pains of birth and fury,
cursing like a sailor, she rose up on her elbow in her bloody
gown, looking about her in the bed as if she had lost something.
"Oh for Christ's sake, for Christ's sake!" she kept crying like a
child who has walked into the commencement of a horror.

A week out of bed she was lost, as if she had done something
irreparable, as if this act had caught her attention for the first
time.

One night, Felix, having come in unheard, found her stand-   † *
ing in the center of the floor, holding the child high in her
hand as if she were about to dash it down, but she brought it
down gently.

The child was small, a boy, and sad. It slept too much in a

* quivering palsy of nerves, it made few voluntary movements; it whimpered.

Robin took to wandering again, to intermittent travel, from which she came back hours, days later, disinterested. People
* were uneasy when she spoke to them, confronted with a catastrophe that had yet no beginning.

Felix had each day the sorrow born with him; for the rest, he pretended that he noticed nothing. Robin was almost never home; he did not know how to inquire for her. Sometimes coming into a café, he would creep out again, because she stood
* before the bar—sometimes laughing, but more often silent,
* her head bent over her glass, her hair swinging; and about her people of every sort.

* One night, coming home about three, he found her in the darkness, standing back against the window, in the pod of the curtain, her chin so thrust forward that the muscles in her neck stood out. As he came toward her, she said in a fury, "I didn't want him!" Raising her hand she struck him across the face.

He stepped away, he dropped his monocle and caught at it swinging, he took his breath backward. He waited a whole second, trying to appear casual. "You didn't want him," he said.
* He bent down pretending to disentangle his ribbon, "It seems
* † I could not accomplish that."
* "Why not be secret about him?" she said. "Why talk?"

Felix turned his body without moving his feet. "What shall
* we do?"

She grinned, but it was not a smile. "I'll get out," she said. She took up her cloak, she always carried it dragging. She looked about her, about the room, as if she were seeing it for the
* † first time.

For three or four months the people of the quarter asked for her in vain. Where she had gone no one knew. When she was seen again in the quarter, it was with Nora Flood. She did not explain where she had been, she was unable or unwilling to give an account of herself. The doctor said: "In America, that's where Nora lives, I brought her into the world and I should know."

3

NIGHT WATCH   †

THE STRANGEST "SALON" in America was Nora's. Her house
was couched in the center of a mass of tangled grass and weeds.
Before it fell into Nora's hands the property had been in the   *
same family two hundred years. It had its own burial ground,
and a decaying chapel in which stood in tens and tens   *
mouldering psalm books, laid down some fifty years gone in
a flurry of forgiveness and absolution.

It was the "paupers" salon, for poets, radicals, beggars, artists, and people in love; for Catholics, Protestants, Brahmins,
dabblers in black magic and medicine; all these could be seen
sitting about her oak table before the huge fire, Nora listening,
her hand on her hound, the firelight throwing her shadow and
his high against the wall. Of all that ranting roaring crew, she
alone stood out. The equilibrium of her nature, savage and
refined, gave her bridled skull a look of compassion. She was   *
broad and tall, and though her skin was the skin of a child, there
could be seen coming, early in her life, the design that was to be
the weather-beaten grain of her face, that wood in the work; the   †
tree coming forward in her, an undocumented record of time.   *
                                                                     *
She was known instantly as a Westerner. Looking at her, for-   *
eigners remembered stories they had heard of covered wagons;
animals going down to drink; children's heads just as far as the
eyes, looking in fright, out of small windows, where in the dark
another race crouched in ambush; with heavy hems the women
becoming large, flattening the fields where they walked, God so
ponderous in their minds that they could stamp out the world
with him in seven days.

At these incredible meetings one felt that early American
history was being re-enacted. The Drummer Boy, Fort Sumter,
Lincoln, Booth, all somehow came to mind; Whigs and Tories
were in the air; bunting and its stripes and stars, the swarm
increasing slowly and accurately on the hive of blue; Boston
tea tragedies, carbines, and the sound of a boy's wild calling;
Puritan feet, long upright in the grave, striking the earth again,
walking up and out of their custom; the calk of prayers thrust
in the heart. And in the midst of this, Nora.

By temperament Nora was an early Christian; she believed
the word. There is a gap in "world pain" through which the
singular falls continually and forever; a body falling in observable space, deprived of the privacy of disappearance; as if
privacy, moving relentlessly away, by the very sustaining power
of its withdrawal kept the body eternally moving downward;
but in one place, and perpetually before the eye. Such a singular
was Nora. There was some derangement in her equilibrium
that kept her immune to her own descent.

Nora had the face of all people who love the people—a face
that would be evil when she found out that to love without
criticism is to be betrayed. Nora robbed herself for everyone;
incapable of giving herself warning, she was continually turning about to find herself diminished. Wandering people the
world over found her profitable in that she could be sold for
a price forever, for she carried her betrayal money in her own
pocket.

Those who love everything are despised by everything, as
those who love a city, in its profoundest sense, become the
shame of that city, the *détraqués*, the paupers; their good is
incommunicable, outwitted, being the rudiment of a life that
has developed, as in man's body are found evidences of lost
needs. This condition had struck even into Nora's house; it
spoke in her guests, in her ruined gardens where she had been
wax in every work of nature.

Wherever she was met, at the opera, at a play, sitting alone
and apart, the programme face down on her knee, – one would
discover in her eyes, large, protruding and clear, that mirrorless

look of polished metals which report not so much the object as
the movement of the object. As the surface of a gun's barrel,
reflecting a scene, will add to the image the portent of its construction, so her eyes contracted and fortified the play before
her in her own unconscious terms. One sensed in the way she
held her head that her ears were recording Wagner or Scarlatti,   °
Chopin, Palestrina, or the lighter songs of the Viennese school,
in a smaller but more intense orchestration.

And she was the only woman of the last century who could
go up a hill with the Seventh Day Adventists and confound the   °
seventh day, – with a muscle in her heart so passionate that
she made the seventh day immediate. Her fellow worshippers
believed in that day and the end of the world out of a bewildered
entanglement with the six days preceding it; Nora believed for   *
the beauty of that day alone. She was by fate one of those people
who are born unprovided for except in the provision of herself.   † *

One missed in her a sense of humour. Her smile was quick
and definite, but disengaged. She chuckled now and again at a
joke, but it was the amused grim chuckle of a person who looks
up to discover that they have coincided with the needs of nature
in a bird.

Cynicism, laughter, the second husk into which the shucked
man crawls, she seemed to know little or nothing about. She
was one of those deviations by which man thinks to reconstruct
himself.

To "confess" to her was an act even more secret than the
communication provided by a priest. There was no ignominy in   † *
her; she recorded without reproach or accusation, being shorn   † *
of self-reproach or self-accusation. This drew people to her and
frightened them; they could neither insult nor hold anything
against her, though it embittered them to have to take back
injustice that in her found no foothold. In court she would have
been impossible; no one would have been hanged, reproached
or forgiven, because no one would have been "accused." The
world and its history were to Nora like a ship in a bottle; she   *
herself was outside and unidentified, endlessly embroiled in a
preoccupation without a problem.

* °   Then she met Robin. The Denckman circus, which she kept
in touch with even when she was not working with it (some of
*   its people were visitors to her house), came into New York in
† *   the fall of 1923. Nora went alone. She came into the circle of
the ring, taking her place in the front row.

Clowns in red, white and yellow, with the traditional smears
on their faces, were rolling over the sawdust, as if they were in
the belly of a great mother where there was yet room to play.
A black horse, standing on trembling hind legs that shook in
*   apprehension of the raised front hooves, his beautiful ribboned
head pointed down and toward the trainer's whip, pranced
*   slowly, the fore-shanks flickering to the whip. Tiny dogs ran
about trying to look like horses, then in came the elephants.

A girl sitting beside Nora took out a cigarette and lit it; her
hands shook and Nora turned to look at her; she looked at her
suddenly because the animals, going around and around the
ring, all but climbed over at that point. They did not seem to
see the girl, but as their dusty eyes moved past, the orbit of their
*   light seemed to turn on her. At that moment Nora turned.

The great cage for the lions had been set up, and the lions
were walking up and out of their small strong boxes into the
arena. Ponderous and furred they came, their tails laid down
across the the floor, dragging and heavy, making the air seem
full of withheld strength. Then as one powerful lioness came to
the turn of the bars, exactly opposite the girl, she turned her
furious great head with its yellow eyes afire and went down, her
paws thrust through the bars and, as she regarded the girl, as
if a river were falling behind impassable heat, her eyes flowed
in tears that never reached the surface. At that the girl rose
*   straight up. Nora took her hand. "Let's get out of here!" the
girl said, and still holding her hand Nora took her out.

In the lobby Nora said, "My name is Nora Flood," and she
waited. After a pause the girl said, "I'm Robin Vote." She
*   looked about her distractedly. "I don't want to be here." But it
*   was all she said; she did not explain where she wished to be.
* †   She stayed with Nora until the mid-winter. Two spirits were
*   working in her, love and anonymity. Yet they were so

"haunted" of each other that separation was impossible.

Nora closed her house. They travelled from Munich, Vienna and Budapest into Paris. Robin told only a little of her life, but she kept repeating in one way or another her wish for a home, as if she were afraid she would be lost again, as if she were aware, without conscious knowledge, that she belonged to Nora, and that if Nora did not make it permanent by her own strength, she would forget.   †

Nora bought an apartment in the *rue du Cherche-Midi*, Robin   o
had chosen it. Looking from the long windows one saw a fountain figure, a tall granite woman bending forward with lifted head, one hand was held over the pelvic round as if to warn a child who goes incautiously.

In the passage of their lives together every object in the garden, every item in the house, every word they spoke, attested to their mutual love, the combining of their humours. There were circus chairs, wooden horses bought from a ring of an old merry-go-round, Venetian chandeliers from the Flea Fair,   *
stage drops from Munich, cherubim from Vienna, ecclesiastical hangings from Rome, a spinet from England, and a miscellaneous collection of music boxes from many countries; such was the museum of their encounter, as Felix's hearsay house had been testimony of the age when his father had lived with his   *
mother.

When the time came that Nora was alone most of the night and part of the day, she suffered from the personality of the house, the punishment of those who collect their lives together. Unconsciously at first, she went about disturbing nothing; then she became aware that her soft and careful movements were the outcome of an unreasoning fear—if she disarranged anything Robin might become confused—might lose the scent of home.

Love becomes the deposit of the heart, analogous in all   *
degrees to the "findings" in a tomb. As in one will be charted the taken place of the body, the raiment, the utensils necessary to its other life, so in the heart of the lover will be traced, as an indelible shadow, that which he loves. In Nora's heart lay the fossil of Robin, intaglio of her identity, and about it for its

maintenance ran Nora's blood. Thus the body of Robin could never be unloved, corrupt or put away. Robin was now beyond timely changes, except in the blood that animated her. That she could be spilled of this, fixed the walking image of Robin in an appalling apprehension on Nora's mind, – Robin alone, crossing streets, in danger. Her mind became so transfixed that, by the agency of her fear, Robin seemed enormous and polarized; all catastrophes ran toward her, the magnetized predicament; and crying out, Nora would wake from sleep, going back through the tide of dreams into which her anxiety had thrown her, taking the body of Robin down with her into it, as the ground things take the corpse, with minute persistence, down into the earth, leaving a pattern of it on the grass, as if they stitched as they descended.

Yet now, when they were alone and happy, apart from the world in their appreciation of the world, there entered with Robin a company unaware. Sometimes it rang clear in the songs she sang, sometimes Italian, sometimes French or German, songs of the people, debased and haunting, songs that Nora had never heard before, or that she had never heard in company with Robin. When the cadence changed, when it was repeated on a lower key, she knew that Robin was singing of a life that she herself had no part in; snatches of harmony as tell-tale as the possessions of a traveller from a foreign land; songs like a practised whore who turns away from no one but the one who loves her. Sometimes Nora would sing them after Robin, with the trepidation of a foreigner repeating words in an unknown tongue, uncertain of what they may mean. Sometimes unable to endure the melody that told so much and so little, she would interrupt Robin with a question. Yet more distressing would be the moment, when, after a pause, the song would be taken up again, from an inner room where Robin, unseen, gave back an echo of her unknown life more nearly tuned to its origin. Often the song would stop altogether, until unthinking, just as she was leaving the house, Robin would break out again in anticipation, changing the sound from a reminiscence to an expectation.

Yet sometimes, going about the house, in passing each other, they would fall into an agonized embrace, looking into each other's face, their two heads in their four hands, so strained together that the space that divided them seemed to be thrusting them apart. Sometimes in these moments of insurmountable grief, Robin would make some movement, use a peculiar turn of phrase not habitual to her, innocent of the betrayal, by which Nora was informed that Robin had come from a world to which she would return. To keep her (in Robin there was this tragic longing to be kept, knowing herself astray) Nora knew now that there was no way but death. In death Robin would belong to her. Death went with them, together and alone; and with the torment and catastrophe, thoughts of resurrection, the second duel.

Looking out into the fading sun of the winter sky, against which a little tower rose just outside the bedroom window, Nora would tabulate by the sounds of Robin dressing the exact progress of her toilet; chimes of cosmetic bottles and cream jars; the faint perfume of hair heated under the curling irons; seeing in her mind the changing direction taken by the curls that hung on Robin's forehead, turning back from the low crown to fall in upward curves to the nape of the neck, the flat uncurved back head that spoke of some awful silence. Half narcoticized by the sounds and the knowledge that this was in preparation for departure, Nora spoke to herself: "In the resurrection, when we come up looking backward at each other, I shall know you only of all that company. My ear shall turn in the socket of my head; my eyeballs loosened where I am the whirlwind about that cashed expense, my foot stubborn on the cast of your grave." In the doorway Robin stood. "Don't wait for me," she said.

In the years that they lived together, the departures of Robin became a slowly increasing rhythm. At first Nora went with Robin; but as time passed, realizing that a growing tension was in Robin, unable to endure the knowledge that she was in the way or forgotten; seeing Robin go from table to table, from drink to drink, from person to person, realizing that if she herself were not there Robin might return to her as the one who,

* ° out of all the turbulent night, had not been lived through, – Nora stayed at home, lying awake or sleeping. Robin's absence, as the night drew on, became a physical removal, insupportable and irreparable. As an amputated hand cannot be disowned, because it is experiencing a futurity, of which the victim is its forebear, so Robin was an amputation that Nora could not renounce. As the wrist longs, so her heart longed, and dressing she would go out into the night that she might be "beside herself," skirting the café in which she would catch a glimpse of Robin.

Once out in the open Robin walked in a formless meditation, her hands thrust into the sleeves of her coat, directing her steps toward that night life that was a known measure between Nora and the cafés. Her meditations, during this walk, were a part of the pleasure she expected to find when the walk came to an end. It was this exact distance that kept the two ends of her life—Nora and the cafés—from forming a monster with two heads.

Her thoughts were in themselves a form of locomotion. She walked with raised head, seeming to look at every passer-by, yet her gaze was anchored in anticipation and regret. A look of anger, intense and hurried, shadowed her face and drew her mouth down as she neared her company; yet as her eyes moved over the façades of the buildings, searching for the sculptured
* † head that both she and Nora loved (a Greek head with shocked
*   protruding eyeballs, for which the tragic mouth seemed to
*   pour forth tears), a quiet joy radiated from her own eyes; for this head was remembrance of Nora and her love, making the anticipation of the people she was to meet set and melancholy. So, without knowing she would do so, she took the turn that brought her into this particular street. If she was diverted, as was sometimes the case, by the interposition of a company of
*   soldiers, a wedding or a funeral, then by her agitation she seemed a part of the function to the persons she stumbled
*   against; as a moth by his very entanglement with the heat that
†   shall be his extinction is associated with flame as a component
* † part of its activity. It was this characteristic that saved her from

being asked too sharply "where" she was going; pedestrians who had it on the point of their tongues, seeing her rapt and confused, turned instead to look at each other. *

The doctor, seeing Nora, out walking alone, said to himself, * as the tall black-caped figure passed ahead of him under the * lamps, "There goes the dismantled—Love has fallen off her wall. A religious woman," he thought to himself, "without the joy and safety of the Catholic faith, which at a pinch covers up the spots on the wall when the family portraits take a slide; take * that safety from a woman," he said to himself, quickening his step to follow her, "and love gets loose and into the rafters. She * sees her everywhere," he added, glancing at Nora as she passed * into the dark. "Out looking for what she's afraid to find— Robin. There goes mother of mischief, running about, trying to get the world home."

Looking at every couple as they passed, into every carriage and car, up to the lighted windows of the houses, trying to discover not Robin any longer, but traces of Robin, influences in her life, (and those which were yet to be betrayed), Nora watched every moving figure for some gesture that might turn up in the movements made by Robin; avoiding the quarter where she knew her to be, where by her own movements the waiters, the people on the terraces might know that she had a part in Robin's life.

Returning home, the interminable night would begin. Listening to the faint sounds from the street, every murmur from the garden, an unevolved and tiny hum that spoke of the progressive growth of noise that would be Robin coming home, Nora lay and beat her pillow without force, unable to cry, her legs drawn up. At times she would get up and walk, to make something in her life outside more quickly over; to bring Robin back by the very velocity of the beating of her heart. And walking in vain, suddenly she would sit down on one of the circus chairs that stood by the long window overlooking the garden, bend forward, putting her hands between her legs, and begin to cry, "Oh God! Oh God! Oh God!" repeated so often that it had the effect of all words spoken in vain. She nodded and awoke

again and began to cry before she opened her eyes, and went
back to the bed and fell into a dream which she recognized;
though in the finality of this version she knew that the dream
had not been "well dreamt" before. Where the dream had been
incalculable, it was now completed with the entry of Robin.

Nora dreamed that she was standing at the top of a house,
that is, the last floor but one—this was her Grandmother's
room—an expansive, decaying splendour; yet somehow, though
set with all the belongings of her grandmother, was as bereft as
the nest of a bird which will not return. Portraits of her great-
uncle, Llewellyn, who died in the Civil War, faded pale carpets,
curtains that resembled columns from their time in stillness—a
plume and an ink well—the ink faded into the quill; standing,
Nora looked down into the body of the house, as if from a
scaffold, where now Robin had entered the dream, lying among
a company below. Nora said to herself, "The dream will not be
dreamed again." A disc of light, that seemed to come from
someone or thing standing behind her and which was yet a
shadow, shed a faintly luminous glow upon the upturned, still
face of Robin who had the smile of an "only survivor," a smile
which fear had married to the bone.

From round about her in anguish Nora heard her own voice
saying, "Come up, this is Grandmother's room," yet knowing it
was impossible, because the room was taboo. The louder she
cried out the further away went the floor below, as if Robin and
she, in their extremity, were a pair of opera glasses turned to the
wrong end, diminishing in their painful love; a speed that ran
away with the two ends of the building, stretching her apart.

This dream that now had all its parts, had still the former
quality of never really having been her grandmother's room.
She herself did not seem to be there in person, nor able to give
an invitation. She had wanted to put her hands on something
in this room to prove it; the dream had never permitted her to
do so. This chamber that had never been her grandmother's,
which was, on the contrary, the absolute opposite of any known
room her grandmother had ever moved or lived in, was nevertheless saturated with the lost presence of her grandmother,

who seemed in the continual process of leaving it. The architecture of dream had rebuilt her everlasting and continuous, flowing away in a long gown of soft folds and chin laces, the pinched gatherings that composed the train taking an upward line over the back and hips, in a curve that not only bent age but fear of bent age demands.

With this figure of her grandmother, who was not entirely her recalled grandmother, went one of her childhood, when she had run into her at the corner of the house—the grandmother who, for some unknown reason, was dressed as a man, wearing a billycock and a corked moustache, ridiculous and plump in tight trousers and a red waistcoat, her arms spread saying with a leer of love, "My little sweetheart!"—her grandmother "drawn upon" as a prehistoric ruin is drawn upon, symbolizing her life out of her life, and which now appeared to Nora as something being done to Robin, Robin disfigured and eternalized by the hieroglyphics of sleep and pain.

Waking she began to walk again, and looking out into the garden in the faint light of dawn, she saw a double shadow falling from the statue, as if it were multiplying; and thinking perhaps this was Robin, she called and was not answered. Standing motionless, straining her eyes, she saw emerge from the darkness the light of Robin's eyes, the fear in them developing their luminosity until, by the intensity of their double regard, Robin's eyes and hers met. So they gazed at each other. As if that light had power to bring what was dreaded into the zone of their catastrophe, Nora saw the body of another woman swim up into the statue's obscurity, with head hung down, that the added eyes might not augment the illumination; her arms about Robin's neck, her body pressed to Robin's, her legs slackened in the hang of the embrace.

Unable to turn her eyes away, incapable of speech, experiencing a sensation of evil, complete and dismembering, Nora fell to her knees, so that her eyes were not withdrawn by her volition, but dropped from their orbit by the falling of her body. Her chin on the sill she knelt thinking, "Now they will not hold together," feeling that if she turned away from what Robin was doing, the design would break and melt back into Robin alone. She closed her eyes, and at that moment she knew an awful happiness. Robin, like something dormant, was protected, moved out of death's way by the successive arms of women; but as she closed her eyes, Nora said "Ah!" with the intolerable automatism of the last "Ah!" in a body struck at the moment of its final breath.

4

"THE SQUATTER" *

JENNY PETHERBRIDGE WAS a widow, a middle-aged woman who ° * had been married four times. Each husband had wasted away and died; she had been like a squirrel racing a wheel day and night in an endeavour to make them historical; they could not * survive it.

She had a beaked head and the body, small, feeble, and ferocious, that somehow made one associate her with Judy; they ° did not go together. Only severed could any part of her have * been called "right." There was a trembling ardor in her wrists and fingers as if she were suffering from some elaborate denial. She looked old, yet expectant of age; she seemed to be steaming in the vapours of someone else about to die, still she gave off an * odour to the mind (for there are purely mental smells that have * no reality) of a woman about to be *accouchée*. Her body suffered ° † * from its fare, laughter and crumbs, abuse and indulgence. But put out a hand to touch her, and her head moved perceptibly with the broken arc of two instincts, recoil and advance, so that the head rocked timidly and aggressively at the same moment, giving her a slightly shuddering and expectant rhythm.

She writhed under the necessity of being unable to wear anything becoming, being one of those panicky little women who, no matter what they put on, look like a child under penance.

She had a fancy for tiny ivory or jade elephants, she said they were luck; she left a trail of tiny elephants wherever she went; * and she went hurriedly and gasping.

Her walls, her cupboards, her bureaux, were teeming with

second-hand dealings with life. It takes a bold and authentic
robber to get first-hand plunder. Someone else's marriage ring
was on her finger; the photograph taken of Robin for Nora sat
upon her table. The books in her library were other people's
selections. She lived among her own things like a visitor to a
room kept "exactly as it was when – ." She tiptoed, even when
she went to draw a bath, nervous and *andante*. She stopped,
fluttering and febrile, before every object in her house. She had
no sense of humour or peace or rest, and her own quivering
uncertainty made even the objects which she pointed out to
the company, as, "My Virgin from Palma," or, "The left-hand
glove of La Duse," recede into a distance of uncertainty, so that
it was almost impossible for the onlooker to see them at all.
When anyone was witty about a contemporary event, she would
look perplexed and a little dismayed, as if someone had done
something that really should not have been done; therefore
her attention had been narrowed down to listening for *faux pas*.
She frequently talked about something being the "death of
her," and certainly anything could have been had she been the
first to suffer it. The words that fell from her mouth seemed
to have been lent to her; had she been forced to invent a vocabulary for herself, it would have been a vocabulary of "ah" and
"oh." Hovering, trembling, tip-toeing, she would unwind
anecdote after anecdote in a light rapid lisping voice which one
always expected to change, to drop and to become the "every
day" voice; but it never did. The stories were humorous, well
told. She would smile, toss her hands up, widen her eyes;
immediately everyone in the room had a certain feeling of
something lost, sensing that there was one person who was
missing the importance of the moment, who had not heard the
story – the teller herself.

She had endless cuttings and scraps from journals and old
theatre programmes, haunted the *Comédie-Française*, spoke of
Molière, Racine and *La Dame aux Camélias*. She was generous
with money. She made gifts lavishly and spontaneously. She was
the worst recipient of presents in the world. She sent bushel
baskets of camellias to actresses because she had a passion for

the characters they portrayed. The flowers were tied with yards of satin ribbon, and a note accompanied them, effusive and gentle. To men she sent books by the dozen; the general feeling was that she was a well-read woman though she had read   *
perhaps ten books in her life.   †

She had a continual rapacity for other people's facts; absorbing time, she held herself responsible for historic characters. She was avid and disorderly in her heart. She defiled the very meaning of personality in her passion to be a person; somewhere about her was the tension of the accident that made the beast the human endeavour.

She was nervous about the future, it made her indelicate.   *
She was one of the most unimportantly wicked women of her time – because she could not let her time alone, and yet could never be a part of it. She wanted to be the reason for everything and so was the cause of nothing. She had the fluency of tongue   *
and action meted out by divine providence to those who cannot think for themselves. She was master of the over-sweet phrase, the over-tight embrace.

One inevitably thought of her in the act of love emitting florid *commedia dell' arte* ejaculations; one should not have   o
thought of her in the act of love at all. She thought of little else, and though always submitting to the act, spoke of and desired the spirit of love; yet was unable to attain it.   *

No one could intrude upon her, because there was no place for intrusion. This inadequacy made her insubordinate – she could not participate in a great love, she could only report it. Since her emotional reactions were without distinction, she had to fall back on the emotions of the past, great loves already lived and related, and over these she seemed to suffer and grow   †
glad.

When she fell in love it was with a perfect fury of accumu-   †
lated dishonesty; she became instantly a dealer in second-hand and therefore incalculable emotions. As, from the solid archives of usage, she had stolen or appropriated the dignity of speech, so she appropriated the most passionate love that she knew, Nora's for Robin. She was a "squatter" by instinct.   *

Jenny knew about Nora immediately; to know Robin ten minutes was to know about Nora. Robin spoke of her in long rambling, impassioned sentences. It had caught Jenny by the ear – she listened, and both loves seemed to be one and her own. From that moment the catastrophe was inevitable. This was in

* † nineteen hundred and twenty-seven.

At their subsequent engagements, Jenny was always early and

* Robin late. Perhaps at the *Ambassadeurs*, (Jenny feared meeting Nora). Perhaps dinner in the *Bois* – (Jenny had the collective

* income four dead husbands could afford) – Robin would walk in, with the aggressive slide to the foot common to tall people,

* † slurred in its accent by the hipless smoothness of her gait – her hands in her pockets, the trench coat with the belt hanging, scowling and reluctant. Jenny leaning far over the table, Robin far back, her legs thrust under her, to balance the whole backward incline of the body, and Jenny so far forward that she had to catch her small legs in the back rung of the chair, ankle out and toe in, not to pitch forward on the table, – thus they presented the two halves of a movement that had, as in sculpture, the beauty and the absurdity of a desire that is in flower

* but that can have no burgeoning, unable to execute its destiny;

* a movement that can divulge neither caution nor daring, for the fundamental condition for completion was in neither of them; they were like Greek runners, with lifted feet but without the relief of the final command that would bring the foot

* † down, – eternally angry, eternally separated, in a cataleptic frozen gesture of abandon.

† The meeting at the opera had not been the first, but Jenny,

* seeing the doctor in the *promenoir*, aware of his passion for

* gossip, knew she had better make it seem so; as a matter of fact she had met Robin a year previously.

Though Jenny knew her safety lay in secrecy, she could not bear her safety; she wanted to be powerful enough to dare the world – and knowing she was not, the knowledge added to that already great burden of trembling timidity and fury.

* On arriving at her house with the doctor and Robin, Jenny

* found several actresses awaiting her, two gentlemen, and the

Marchesa de Spada, a very old rheumatic woman (with an antique spaniel, which suffered from asthma), who believed in the stars. There was talk about fate, and every hand in the room was searched and every destiny turned over and discussed. A little girl (Jenny called her niece, though she was no relation) sat at the far end of the room. She had been playing, but the moment Robin entered she ceased and sat, staring under her long-lashed eyelids at no one else, as if she had become prematurely aware. This was the child Jenny spoke of later, when she called on Felix.

The Marchesa remarked that everyone in the room had been going on from interminable sources since the world began, and would continue to reappear, but that there was one person who had come to the end of her existence and would return no more. As she spoke, she looked slyly at Robin, who was standing by the piano speaking to the child in an undertone; and at the Marchesa's words Jenny began to tremble slightly, so that every point of her upstanding hair – it stood about her head in a bush, virile and unlovely – quivered. She began to pull herself along the enormous sofa toward the Marchesa, her legs under her, and suddenly she stood up.

"Order the carriages!" she cried. "Immediately! We will go driving, we need a little air!" She turned her back and spoke in agitation. "Yes, yes," she said, "The carriages! It is so close in here!"

"What carriages?" said the doctor, and he looked from one to the other. "What carriages?" He could hear the maid unlocking the front door, calling out to the coachmen. He could hear the clear ringing sound of wheels drawn close to the curb and the muttered cries of a foreign voice. Robin turned around and said, a malign gentle smile on her mouth, "Now she is in a panic, and we will have to do something." She put her glass down and stood, her back to the room, her broad shoulders drawn up, and though she was drunk, there was a withdrawal in her movement, and a wish to be gone.

"She will dress up now," she said. She leaned back against the piano, pointing with the hand that held her glass. "Dress up, wait, you will see." Then she added, thrusting her chin forward so that the cords in her neck stood out: "Dress up in something old."

The doctor, who was more uncomfortable perhaps than anyone in the room and yet who could not forbear scandal, in order to gossip about the "manifestations of our time" at a later date, made a slight gesture and said, "Hush!" And sure enough, at that moment, Jenny appeared in the doorway to the bedroom, got up in a hoop, a bonnet and a shawl, and stood looking at Robin who was paying no attention to her, deep in conversation with the child. Jenny with the burning interest of a person who is led to believe herself a part of the harmony of a concert to which she is listening, appropriating in some measure its identity, emitted short, exclamatory ejaculations.

There were, it turned out, three carriages in all, those open hacks that may still be had in Paris if they are hunted up in time. Jenny had a standing order with them and when they were not called upon still they circled about her address, like flies about a bowl of cream. The three cabbies were hunched up on their boxes, their coats about their ears, for though it was an early autumn night, it had become very chilly by twelve o'clock. They had been ordered for eleven and had been sitting on their boxes for the past hour.

Jenny, cold with dread, lest Robin should get into one of the other carriages with a tall slightly surprised English girl, seated herself in the farthest corner of the foremost *fiacre* and called, "Here, here," leaving the rest of the guests to dispose of themselves. The child, Sylvia, sat across from her, the ragged gray rug held in two clenched hands. There was a great deal of chattering and laughter, when to her horror Jenny saw that Robin was moving toward the second carriage in which the English girl had already seated herself. "Ah no, no!" Jenny cried, and began beating the upholstery, sending up a cloud of dust. "Come here," she said in an anguished voice, as if it were the end of her life. "Come here with me, both of you," she added in a lowered and choking tone; and assisted by the doctor, Robin got in, the young Englishwoman, to Jenny's consternation, taking the seat by her side.

Doctor O'Connor now turned to the driver and called out: "*Écoute, mon gosse, va comme si trente-six diables étaient accrochés à tes fesses!*" Then waving his hand in a gesture of abandon, he added: "Christ's sweet foot, where to but the woods, the sweet woods of Paris! *Fais le tour du Bois!*" he shouted, and slowly the three carriages, horse behind horse, moved out into the *Champs Elysées*.

Jenny, with nothing to protect her against the night but her long Spanish shawl, which looked ridiculous over her flimsy hoop and bodice, a rug over her knees, had sunk back with collapsed shoulders. With darting, incredible swiftness, her eyes went from one girl to the other, while the doctor, wondering how he had managed to get himself into the carriage which held three women and a child, listened to the faint laughter from the carriages behind, feeling as he listened, a twinge of occult mystery. "Ah!" he said under his breath. "Just the girl that God forgot." Saying which, he seemed to be precipitated into the halls of justice, where he had suffered twenty-four hours. "Oh God help us," he said, speaking aloud, at which the child turned slightly on her seat, her head, with large intelligent eyes directed toward him, which had he noticed, would have silenced him instantly (for the doctor had a mother's reverence for childhood). "What manner of man is it that has to adopt his brother's children to make a mother of himself, and in his sleep lies with his brother's wife to get him a future – it's enough to bring down the black curse of Kerry."

"What?" said Jenny in a loud voice, hoping to effect a break in the whispered conversation between Robin and the English girl. The doctor turned up his coat collar.

"I was saying, madame, that by his own peculiar perversity God has made me a liar –"

"What, what is that you say?" demanded Jenny, her eyes still fixed on Robin so that her question seemed to be directed rather to that corner of the carriage than to the doctor.

"You see before you, madame," he said, "one who, in common parlance is called a 'faggot,' a 'fairy,' a 'queen.' I was created in anxiety. My father, Lord rest his soul, had no happiness of me from the beginning. When I joined the army he relented a little because he had a suspicion that possibly in that fracas which occasionally puts a son on the list of 'not much left since,' I might be damaged. After all, he had no desire to see my ways corrected with a round of buckshot. He came in to me early in the dawn as I lay in my bed, to say that he forgave me, and that indeed he hoped to be forgiven; that he had never understood, but that he had, by much thought, by heavy reading, come back with love in his hand, that he was sorry, that he came to say so; that he hoped I could conduct myself like a soldier. For a moment he seemed to realize my terrible predicament: to be shot for man's meat, but to go down like a girl, crying in the night for her mother. So I got up in bed on my knees and crawled to the foot where he stood, and cast my arms about him and said, 'No matter what you have done or thought, you were right, and there's nothing in my heart but love for you and respect.'"

Jenny had shrunk into her rug and was not listening. Her eyes followed every movement of Robin's hand, which was laid now on the child's hand, now stroking her hair, the child smiling up into the trees.

"Oh," said the doctor, "for the love of God!"

Jenny began to cry slowly, the tears wet, warm, and sudden in the odd misery of her face. It made the doctor sad, with that unhappy yet pleasantly regrettable discomfort on which he usually launched his better meditations.

He remarked, and why he did not know, that by weeping she appeared like a single personality, who, by multiplying her tears, brought herself into the position of one who is seen twenty times in twenty mirrors – still only one, but many times distressed. Jenny began to weep outright. As the initial soft weeping had not caught Robin's attention, now Jenny used the increase and the catching in her throat to attract her, with the same insistent fury one feels when trying to attract a person in a crowded room. The weeping became as accurate as the monotonous underplay in a score, in spite of the incapacity of her heart. The doctor, sitting now a little slumped forward, said, in an almost professional voice (they were now long past the pond and the park, and were circling back again, toward the lower parts of town), "Love of woman for woman, what insane passion for unmitigated anguish and motherhood brought that into the mind?"

"Oh, Oh," she said, "Look at her!" She abruptly made a gesture toward Robin and the girl, as if they were no longer present, as if they were a vista passing out of view with the movement of the horses. "Look, she brings love down to a level!" She hoped that Robin would hear. *

"Ah!" he said. "Love, that terrible thing!" † *

She began to beat the cushions with her doubled fist. "What † * could you know about it? Men never know anything about it, why should they? But a woman should know – they are finer, more sacred; my love is sacred and my love is great!"

"Shut up," Robin said, putting her hand on her knee. "Shut * up, you don't know what you are talking about. You talk all the time and you never know anything. It's such an awful weakness with you. Identifying yourself with God!" She was smiling, and * the English girl, breathing very quickly, lit a cigarette. The child remained speechless, as she had been for the duration of the drive, her head turned as if fixed, looking at Robin, and trying to hold her slight legs, that did not reach the floor, from shaking with the shaking of the carriage.

Then Jenny struck Robin, scratching and tearing in hysteria, * striking, clutching and crying. Slowly the blood began to run down Robin's cheeks, and as Jenny struck repeatedly Robin began to go forward as if brought to the movement by the very blows themselves, as if she had no will, sinking down in the small carriage, her knees on the floor, her head forward as her arm moved upward in a gesture of defense; and as she sank, Jenny also, as if compelled to conclude the movement of the first blow, almost as something seen in retarded action, leaned forward and over, so that when the whole of the gesture was completed, Robin's hands were covered by Jenny's slight and bending breast, caught in between the bosom and the knees.

And suddenly the child flung herself down on the seat, face outward, and said in a voice not suitable for a child, because it was controlled with terror: "Let me go! Let me go! Let me go!"

The carriage at this moment drew smartly up into the *rue du Cherche-Midi*. Robin jumped before the carriage stopped, but Jenny was close behind her, following her as far as the garden.

† *
*   It was not long after this that Nora and Robin separated; a little later Jenny and Robin sailed for America.

5

Watchman, What of the Night? °†

About three in the morning, Nora knocked at the little glass door of the concierge's *loge*, asking if the doctor was in. In the anger of broken sleep the concierge directed her to climb six flights, where at the top of the house, to the left, she would find him.

Nora took the stairs slowly. She had not known that the doctor was so poor. Groping her way she rapped, fumbling for the knob. Misery alone would have brought her, though she knew the late hours indulged in by her friend. Hearing his "come in" she opened the door and for one second hesitated, so incredible was the disorder that met her eyes. The room was so small that it was just possible to walk sideways up to the bed, it was as if being condemned to the grave, the doctor had decided to occupy it with the utmost abandon.

A pile of medical books, and volumes of a miscellaneous order, reached almost to the ceiling, water-stained and covered with dust. Just above them was a very small barred window, the only ventilation. On a maple dresser, certainly not of European make, lay a rusty pair of forceps, a broken scalpel, half a dozen odd instruments that she could not place, a catheter, some twenty perfume bottles, almost empty, pomades, creams, rouges, powder boxes and puffs. From the half open drawers of this chiffonier hung laces, ribands, stockings, ladies' underclothing and an abdominal brace, which gave the impression that the feminine finery had suffered venery. A swill-pail stood at the head of the bed, brimming with abominations. There was something appallingly degraded about the room, like the rooms

* in brothels, which give even the most innocent a sensation of
* having been accomplice; yet this room was also muscular, a
* ° cross between a *chambre à coucher* and a boxer's training
† * camp. There is a certain belligerence in a room in which a
* woman has never set foot; every object seems to be battling its
* own compression, and there is a metallic odour, as of beaten
iron in a smithy.

In the narrow iron bed, with its heavy and dirty linen sheets,
* † lay the doctor in a woman's flannel night gown.

* The doctor's head, with its over-large black eyes, its full gun-
metal cheeks and chin, was framed in the golden semi-circle of
a wig with long pendent curls that touched his shoulders, and
falling back against the pillow, turned up the shadowy interior
of their cylinders. He was heavily rouged and his lashes painted.
† It flashed into Nora's head, "God, children know something
* they can't tell, they like Red Riding Hood and the wolf in bed!"
* † But this thought, which was only the sensation of a thought, was
of but a second's duration, as she opened the door; in the next,
the doctor had snatched the wig from his head, and sinking
* down in the bed drew the sheets up over his breast. Nora said, as
quickly as she could recover herself: "Doctor, I have come to
* † ask you to tell me everything you know about the night. "As she
spoke, she wondered why she was so dismayed to have come
upon the doctor at the hour when he had evacuated custom and
gone back into his dress. The doctor said, "You see that you can
ask me anything," thus laying aside both their embarrassments.
She said to herself: "Is not the gown the natural raiment of
extremity? What nation, what religion, what ghost, what dream
* has not worn it—infants, angels, priests, the dead; why should
not the doctor, in the grave dilemma of his alchemy, wear his
* dress?" She thought: "He dresses to lie beside himself, who is so
* constructed that love, for him, can be only something special; in
* † a room that, giving back evidence of his occupancy, is as mauled
as the last agony."

"Have you ever thought of the night?" the doctor inquired
* with a little irony; he was extremely put out, having expected
someone else, though his favorite topic, and one which he

talked on whenever he had a chance, was the night. "Yes," said
Nora, and sat down on the only chair. "I've thought of it, but
thinking about something you know nothing about does not
help."

"Have you," said the doctor, "ever thought of the peculiar
polarity of times and times; and of sleep? Sleep, the slain white   *
bull? Well, I, Doctor Matthew-Mighty-grain-of-salt-Dante-   o *
O'Connor, will tell you how the day and the night are related
by their division. The very constitution of twilight is a fabulous
reconstruction of fear, fear bottom-out and wrong side up.
Every day is thought upon and calculated, but the night is not
premeditated. The Bible lies the one way, but the night gown
the other. The Night, 'Beware of that dark door!' "

"I used to think," Nora said, "that people just went to sleep,
or if they did not go to sleep, that they were themselves, but
now," she lit a cigarette and her hands trembled, "now I see that
the night does something to a person's identity, even when
asleep."

"Ah!" exclaimed the doctor. "Let a man lay himself down in
the Great Bed and his 'identity' is no longer his own, his 'trust'
is not with him, and his 'willingness' is turned over and is of
another permission. His distress is wild and anonymous. He
sleeps in a Town of Darkness, member of a secret brotherhood.
He neither knows himself nor his outriders, he berserks a fearful dimension and dismounts, miraculously, in bed!

"His heart is tumbling in his chest, a dark place! Though
some go into the night as a spoon breaks easy water, others go
head foremost against a new connivance; their horns make a dry
crying, like the wings of the locust, late come to their shedding.

"Have you thought of the night, now, in other times, in   *
foreign countries—in Paris? When the streets were gall high
with things you wouldn't have done for a dare's sake, and the
way it was then, with the pheasants' necks and the goslings'   *
beaks dangling against the hocks of the gallants, and not a
pavement in the place, and everything gutters for miles and
miles, and a stench to it that plucked you by the nostrils and
you were twenty leagues out! The criers telling the price of

* wine to such effect that the dawn saw good clerks full of piss
* and vinegar and blood-letting in side streets where some wild
princess in a night shift of velvet howled under a leech; not to
o mention the palaces of Nymphenburg echoing back to Vienna
with the night trip of late kings letting water into plush cans and
* fine woodwork. No," he said, looking at her sharply, "I can see
you have not! You should, for the night has been going on for a
long time."
* She said, "I've never known it before—I thought I did, but it
* was not knowing at all."
* "Exactly," said the doctor, "you thought you knew, and you
hadn't even shuffled the cards—now the nights of one period
are not the nights of another. Neither are the nights of one city
the nights of another. Let us take Paris for an instance, and
o France for a fact. *Ah, Mon Dieu! La nuit effroyable! La nuit, qui
est une immense plaine, et la coeur qui est une petite extrémité!* Ah,
* † good Mother mine, *Notre Dame de la Bonne Garde!* Intercede for
me now, while yet I explain what I'm coming to! French nights
are those which all nations seek the world over—and have you
* noticed that? Ask Doctor Mighty O'Connor, the reason the
* doctor knows everything is because he's been everywhere at the
wrong time and has now become anonymous."
"But," Nora said, "I never thought of the night as a life at
* all—I've never lived it—why did she?"
"I'm telling you of French nights at the moment," the doctor
went on, "and why we all go into them. The night and the day
are two travels, and the French—gut-greedy and fist-tight
though they often are—alone leave testimony of the two in the
dawn; we tear up the one for the sake of the other, not so the
French.
"And why is that, because they think of the two as one continually, and keep it before their mind as the monks who repeat,
'Lord Jesus Christ, Son of God, have mercy upon me!' some
twelve thousand or more times a twenty-four hours, so that it is
finally in the head, good or bad, without saying a word. Bowing
down from the waist, the world over they go, that they may
revolve about the Great Enigma—as a relative about a cradle—

and the Great Enigma can't be thought of unless you turn the head the other way, and come upon thinking with the eye that you fear, which is called the back of the head; it's the one we use when looking at the beloved in a dark place, and she is a long time coming from a great way. We swoon with the thickness of our own tongue when we say, 'I love you,' as in the eye of a child lost a long while will be found the contraction of that distance —a child going small in the claws of a beast, coming furiously up the furlongs of the iris. We are but skin about a wind, with muscles clenched against mortality. We sleep in a long reproachful dust against ourselves. We are full to the gorge with our own names for misery. Life, the pastures in which the night   *
feeds and prunes the cud that nourishes us to despair. Life, the permission to know death. We were created that the earth might be made sensible of her inhuman taste; and love that the body might be so dear that even the earth should roar with it.   *
Yes, we who are full to the gorge with misery, should look well around, doubting everything seen, done, spoken, precisely because we have a word for it, and not its alchemy.

"To think of the acorn it is necessary to become the tree. And   *
the tree of night is the hardest tree to mount, the dourest tree to scale, the most difficult of branch, the most febrile to the touch, and sweats a resin and drips a pitch against the palm that computation has not gambled. Gurus, who, I trust you know, are Indian teachers, expect you to contemplate the acorn ten years at a stretch, and if, in that time, you are no wiser about the nut, you are not very bright, and that may be the only certainty with which you will come away, which is a post-graduate melancholy—for no man can find a greater truth than his kidney will allow. So I, Doctor Matthew Mighty O'Connor, ask you to   *
think of the night the day long, and of the day the night through, or at some reprieve of the brain it will come upon you   †
heavily—an engine stalling itself upon your chest, halting its wheels against your heart, unless you have made a roadway for   *
it.

"The French have made a detour of filthiness—Oh, the good dirt! Whereas you are of a clean race, of a too eagerly washing

people, and this leaves no road for you. The brawl of the Beast
leaves a path for the Beast. You wash your brawl with every
thought, with every gesture, with every conceivable emollient
° * † and *savon*, and expect to find your way again. A Frenchman
° makes a navigable hour with a tuft of hair, a wrenched *bretelle*, a
rumpled bed. The tear of wine is still in his cup to catch back
° the quantity of its bereavement; his *cantiques* straddle two backs,
night and day."

† * "But, what am I to do?" she said.

* "Be as the Frenchman, who puts a *sou* in the poor-box at
night that he may have a penny to spend in the morning—he
can trace himself back by his sediment, vegetable and animal,
and so find himself in the odour of wine in its two travels, in
and out, packed down beneath an air that has not changed its
position during that strategy.

"The American, what then? He separates the two for fear of
indignities, so that the mystery is cut in every cord; the design
° wildcats down the *charter mortalis*, and you get crime. The
startled bell in the stomach begins to toll, the hair moves and
drags upward, and you go far away backward by the crown, your
conscience belly out and shaking.

"Our bones ache only while the flesh is on them. Stretch it as
thin as the temple flesh of an ailing woman and still it serves to
ache the bone and to move the bone about; and in like manner
the night is a skin pulled over the head of day that the day may
be in a torment. We will find no comfort until the night melts
away; until the fury of the night rots out its fire."

* "Then," Nora said, "it means I'll never understand her—I'll
always be miserable—just like this."

"Listen! Do things look in the ten and twelve of noon as they
look in the dark? Is the hand, the face, the foot, the same face
* and hand and foot seen by the sun? For now the hand lies in a
shadow, its beauties and its deformities are in a smoke—there is
a sickle of doubt across the cheek bone thrown by the hat's
* brim, so there is half a face to be peered back into speculation.
A leaf of darkness has fallen under the chin and lies deep upon
the arches of the eyes; the eyes themselves have changed their

colour. The very mother's head you swore by in the dock is a heavier head, crowned with ponderable hair.

"And what of the sleep of animals? The great sleep of the elephant, and the fine thin sleep of the bird?"

Nora said: "I can't stand it, I don't know how—I am frightened. What is it? What is it in her that is doing this?"

"Oh, for God's sake!" the doctor said, "give me the smelling salts." She got up, looking among the debris on the stand. Inhaling, he pushed his head back into the pillow, then he said:

"Take history at night, have you ever thought of that, now? Was it at night that Sodom became Gomorrah? It was at night, I swear! A city given over to the shades, and that's why it has never been countenanced or understood to this day. Wait, I'll be coming to that! All through the night Rome went burning. Put that in the noontide and it loses some of its age-old significance, does it not? Why? Because it has existed to the eye of the mind all these years against a black sky. Burn Rome in a dream, and you reach and claw down the true calamity. For dreams have only the pigmentation of fact. A man who has to deal in no colour cannot find his match, or, if he does, it is for a different rage. Rome was the egg, but colour was the tread."

"Yes," said Nora.

"The dead have committed some portion of the evil of the night, sleep and love, the other. For what is not the sleeper responsible? What converse does he hold, and with whom? He lies down with his Nelly and drops off into the arms of his Gretchen. Thousands unbidden come to his bed. Yet how can one tell truth when it's never in the company? Girls that the dreamer has not fashioned himself to want, scatter their legs about him to the blows of Morpheus. So used is he to sleep that the dream that eats away its boundaries finds even what is dreamed an easier custom with the years, and at that banquet the voices blend and battle without pitch. The sleeper is the proprietor of an unknown land. He goes about another business in the dark—and we, his partners, who go to the opera, who listen to gossip of café friends, who walk along the boulevards, or sew a quiet seam, cannot afford an inch of it; because, though

we would purchase it with blood, it has no counter and no
*† till. She who stands looking down upon her who lies sleeping
knows the horizontal fear, the fear unbearable. For man goes
*† only perpendicularly against his fate. He was neither formed
to know that other nor compiled of its conspiracy.

†   "You beat the liver out of a goose to get a *pâté*; you pound the
o muscles of a man's *cardia* to get a philosopher."

    "Is that what I am to learn?" she asked bitterly.

*   The doctor looked at her. "For the lover, it is the night into
* which his beloved goes," he said, "that destroys his heart; he
wakes her suddenly, only to look the hyena in the face that is her
† smile, as she leaves that company.

    "When she sleeps is she not moving her leg aside for an
unknown garrison? Or in a moment, that takes but a second,
* murdering us with an ax? Eating our ear in a pie, pushing us
aside with the back of her hand, sailing to some port with a ship
† full of sailors and medical men? Or is confessing bottom up
(though keeping the thread in the tatting), to a priest who has
the face of a butcher, and the finger of our own right hand
placed where it best pleases? And what of our own sleep? We
go to it no better—and betray her with the very virtue of our
days. We are continent a long time, but no sooner has our head
touched the pillow, and our eyes left the day, than a host of
merrymakers take and get. We wake from our doings in a deep
sweat for that they happened in a house without an address, in a
street in no town, citizened with people with no names with
which to deny them. Their very lack of identity makes them
ourselves. For by a street number, by a house, by a name, we
cease to accuse ourselves. Sleep demands of us a guilty immunity. There is not one of us who, given an eternal incognito, a
* thumbprint nowhere set against our souls, would not commit
* rape, murder and all abominations. For if pigeons flew out of
* his bum, or castles sprang out of his ears, man would be
* troubled to know which was his fate, a house, a bird or a man.
Possibly that one only who shall sleep three generations will
come up uninjured out of that unpeopled annihilation." The
doctor turned heavily in bed.

"For the thickness of the sleep that is on the sleeper we 'forgive,' as we 'forgive' the dead for the account of the earth that lies upon them. What we do not see, we are told, we do not mourn; yet night and sleep trouble us, suspicion being the strongest dream and dread the thong. The heart of the jealous knows the best and the most satisfying love, that of the other's bed, where the rival perfects the lover's imperfections. Fancy gallops to take part in that duel, unconstrained by any certain articulation of the laws of that unseen game.

"We look to the East for a wisdom that we shall not use—and to the sleeper for the secret that we shall not find. So, I say, what of the night, the terrible night? The darkness is the closet in which your lover roosts her heart, and that night-fowl that caws   *
against her spirit and yours, dropping between you and her the awful estrangement of his bowels. The drip of your tears is his implacable pulse. Night people do not bury their dead, but on the neck of you, their beloved and waking, sling the creature, husked of its gestures. And where you go, it goes, the two of you, your living and her dead, that will not die; to daylight, to life, to grief, until both are carrion.

"Wait! I'm coming to the night of nights—the night you want to know about the most of all—for even the greatest generality has a little particular; have you thought of that? A   † *
high price is demanded of any value, for a value is in itself a   *
detachment. We wash away our sense of sin, and what does that bath secure us? Sin, shining bright and hard. In what does a Latin bathe? True dust. We have made the literal error. We have used water, we are thus too sharply reminded. A European gets out of bed with a disorder that holds the balance. The layers of his deed can be traced back to the last leaf and the good slug be found creeping. *L'Echo de Paris* and his bed sheets were   °
run off the same press. One may read in both the travail life has had with him—he reeks with the essential wit necessary to the 'sale' of both editions, night edition and day.

"Each race to its wrestling! Some throw the beast on the other side, with the stench of excrement, blood and flowers, the three essential oils of their plight! Man makes his history with the one hand and 'holds it up' with the other.

"Oh God, I'm tired of this tirade. The French are dishev-elled, and wise, the American tries to approximate it with drink. It is his only clue to himself. He takes it when his soap has washed him too clean for identification. The Anglo-Saxon has made the literal error; using water, he has washed away
*   his page. Misery melts him down by day, and sleep at night. His preoccupation with his business day has made his sleep insoluble."

Nora stood up, but she sat down again. "How do you stand it then?" she demanded. "How do you live at all, if this wisdom of yours is not only the truth, but also the price?"

"Ho, nocturnal hag whimpering on the thorn, rot in the
*   grist, mildew in the corn," said the doctor. "If you'll pardon my song and singing voice, both of which were better until I gave my kidney on the left side to France in the war—and I've drunk myself half around the world cursing her for jerking it out—if I had it to do again, grand country though it is—I'd be the girl found lurking behind the army, or up with the hill folk, all of which is to rest me a little of my knowledge, until I can get back
* o   to it. I'm coming to something. *Misericordia*, am I not the girl to
*   know of what I speak? We go to our Houses by our nature—and
*   our nature, no matter how it is, we all have to stand—as for me, so God has made me, my house is the pissing port. Am I to blame if I've been summoned before and this my last and oddest call? In the old days I was possibly a girl in Marseilles thumping the dock with a sailor, and perhaps it's that memory that haunts
o   me. The wise men say that the remembrance of things past is all that we have for a future, and am I to blame if I've turned up this time as I shouldn't have been, when it was a high soprano I wanted, and deep corn curls to my bum, with a womb as big as the king's kettle, and a bosom as high as the bowsprit of a fish-ing schooner? And what do I get but a face on me like an old child's bottom—is that a happiness, do you think?
o   "Jehovah, Sabaoth, Elohim, Eloi, Helion, Jodhevah, Shaddai! May God give us to die in our own way! I haunt the
† o   *pissoirs* as naturally, in search of my man, as Highland Mary

her cows down by the Dee—and by the Hobs of Hell, I've seen
the same thing work in a girl looking for her woman, but I'll
bring that up later! I've given my destiny away by garrulity, like
ninety per cent of everybody else—, for, no matter what I may
be doing, in my heart is the wish for children and knitting. God,
I never asked better than to boil some good man's potatoes and
toss up a child for him every nine months by the calendar. Is it
my fault that my only fireside is the out-house? And that I can
never hang my muffler, mittens and Bannybrook umbrella on   ° *
anything better than a bit of tin boarding as high as my eyes,
having to be brave, no matter what, to keep the mascara from
running away? And do you think that those circular cottages   †
of delight have not brought me to great argument? Have you
ever glanced at one when the night was well down, and seen it
and what it looked like and resembled most, with its one coping
and a hundred legs? A centipede. And you look down and   † *
choose your feet, and, ten to one, you find that you have picked   †
a bird with a light wing, or an old duck with a wooden knee, or
something that has been mournful for years. What? I've held
argument with others at long tables all night through about
the particular merits of one district over another for such
things, of one cottage over another for such things. And do
you suppose I was agreed with, and had any one any other one's
ideas? There was as much disagreement as there might have
been, had we all been selecting a new order of government.
Jed would say North, and Jod would say South, and me sitting
between them going mad because I am a doctor and a collector
and a talker of Latin, and a sort of petropus of the twilight and   °
a physiognomist that can't be flustered by the wrong feature
on the right face, and I said that the best port was at the *Place*   ° *
de la Bastille. Whereupon I was torn into parts by a hundred
voices,—each of them pitched in a different *arrondissement*,   °
until I began clapping like the good woman in the shoe, and
screaming for silence; and for witchery I banged the table with a
formidable and yelled out loud: 'Do any of you know anything   °
about atmosphere and sea level? Well,' I says, 'sea level and
atmospheric pressure and topography make all the difference

in the world!' My voice cracked on the word 'difference,' soaring up divinely, and I said: 'If you think that certain things do not show from what district they come, yea, even to an *arrondissement*, then you are not out gunning for particular game, but simply any catch, and I'll have nothing to do with you! I do not discuss weighty matters with water wits!' And at that I ordered another and sat with my chin up. 'But,' said one fellow, 'it's the face that you tell by.' 'Faces is it!' I screamed, 'the face is for fools! If you fish by the face you fish out trouble, but there's always other fish when you deal with the sea. The face is what anglers catch in the daylight, but the sea is the night!' "

Nora turned away— "What am I to do?

"Ah, mighty uncertainty!" said the doctor. "Have you thought of all the doors that have shut at night and opened again? Of women who have looked about with lamps, like you, and who have scurried on fast feet? Like a thousand mice they go this way and that, now fast, now slow, some halting behind doors, some trying to find the stairs, all approaching or leaving their misplaced mouse-meat, that lies in some cranny, on some couch, down on some floor, behind some cupboard; and all the windows, great and small, from which love and fear have peered, shining and in tears? Put those windows end to end and it would be a casement that would reach around the world; and put those thousand eyes into one eye and you would have the night combed with the great blind searchlight of the heart."

Tears began to run down Nora's face.

"And do I know my Sodomites?" the doctor said unhappily, "and what the heart goes bang up against if it loves one of them, especially if it's a woman loving one of them. What do they find then, that this lover has committed the unpardonable error of not being able to exist—and they come down with a dummy in their arms. God's last round, shadow boxing, that the heart may be murdered and swept into that still, quiet place where it can sit and say: 'Once I was, now I can rest.'

"Well, that's only part of it," he said, trying to stop her crying, "and though your normal fellow will say all are alike in the

dark, negro or white, I say you can tell them, and where they *
came from, and what quarter they frequent, by the size and
excellence—and at the Bastille (and may I be believed) they
come as handsome as *mortadellas* slung on a table.   † ° *

"Your *gourmet* knows for instance from what water his fish
was snatched, he knows from what district and to what year
he blesses his wine, he knows one truffle from another and
whether it be Brittany root or if it came down from the North,
but you gentlemen, sit here and tell me that the district makes
no difference—is there no one who knows anything but myself?
And, must I, perchance like careful writers, guard myself against
the conclusions of my readers?

"Have I not shut my eyes with the added shutter of the night
and put my hand out? And it's the same with girls," he said,   *
"those who turn the day into night, the young, the drug addict,
the profligate, the drunken and that most miserable, the lover
who watches all night long in fear and anguish. These can never
again live the life of the day. When one meets them at high
noon they give off, as if it were a protective emanation, something dark and muted. The light does not become them any
longer. They begin to have an unrecorded look. It is as if they
were being tried by the continual blows of an unseen adversary.
They acquire an 'unwilling' set of features: they become old
without reward, the widower bird sitting sighing at the turnstile of heaven, 'Hallelujah! I am sticked! *Skoll! Skoll!* I am   *
dying!'

"Or walks the floor, holding her hands; or lies upon the floor,   †
face down, with that terrible longing of the body that would, in
misery, be flat with the floor; lost lower than burial, utterly   *
blotted out and erased so that no stain of her could ache upon
the wood, or snatched back to nothing without aim—going
backward through the target, taking with her the spot where she
made one—"   † *

"Yes!" Nora said.

"Look for the girls also in the toilets at night, and you will
find them kneeling in that great secret confessional crying
between tongues, the terrible excommunication:

" 'May you be damned to hell! May you die standing upright! May you be damned upward! May this be damned, terrible and damned spot! May it wither into the grin of the dead, may this draw back, low-riding mouth in an empty snarl of the groin! May this be your torment, may this be your damnation! God damned me before you, and after me you shall be damned, kneeling and standing away till we vanish! For what do you know of me, man's meat? I'm an angel on all fours, with a child's feet behind me, seeking my people that have never been made, going down face foremost, drinking the waters of night at the water hole of the damned, and I go into the waters, up to my heart, the terrible waters! What do you know of me? May you pass from me, damned girl! Damned and betraying!'

"There's a curse for you," he said, "and I have heard it."

"Oh!" Nora said, "Don't—don't!"

"But," he continued, "if you think that is all of the night, you're crazy! Groom, bring the shovel! Am I the golden-mouthed St. John Chrysostom, the Greek who said it with the other cheek? No, I'm a fart in a gale of wind, an humble violet, under a cow pad. But," he said with sorrow, "even the evil in us comes to an end, errors may make you immortal—one woman went down the ages for sitting through *Parsifal* up to the point where the swan got his death, whereupon she screamed out, 'Godamercy, they have shot the Holy Grail!'—but not everyone is as good as that; you lay up for yourself in your old age, Nora my child, feebleness enough to forget the passions of your youth, which you spent your years in strengthening. Think of that also. As for me, I tuck myself in at night, well content because I am my own charlatan. Yes, I, the Lily of Killarney, am composing me a new song, with tears and with jealousy, because I have read that John was his favorite, and it should have been me, Prester Matthew! The song is entitled, 'Mother, put the wheel away, I cannot spin tonight.' Its other name, 'According to me, everyone is a kind-of-a-son-of-a-bitch,' to be sung to two ocarinas and one concertina, and, if none of the world is about, to a Jew's-harp, so help me God! I am but a little child with my eyes wide open!"

"Matthew," Nora said, "what will become of her? That's what I want to know.   † *

"To our friends," he answered, "we die every day, but to ourselves we die only at the end. We do not know death, or how often it has essayed our most vital spirit. While we are in the parlour it is visiting in the pantry. Montaigne says: 'To kill a   o *
man there is required a bright shining and clear light,' but that was spoken of the conscience toward another man. But what of our own death—permit us to reproach the night, wherein we die manifold alone. Donne says: 'We are all conceived in   o *
close prison, in our mothers' wombs we are close prisoners all. When we are born, we are but born to the liberty of the house—   *
all our life is but a going out to the place of execution and death. Now was there ever any man seen to sleep in the Cart, between Newgate and Tyburn? Between the prison and the place of execution, does any man sleep?' Yet he says, 'Men sleep all the way.' How much more, therefore, is there upon him a close sleep when he is mounted on darkness."

"Yes," she said, "but—"

"Now, wait a minute! It's all of a certain night that I'm coming to, that I take so long coming to it," he said, "a night   *
in the branchy pitch of fall—the particular night you want to know about—for I'm a fisher of men and my gimp is doing a *saltarello* over every body of water to fetch up what it may. I   o
have a narrative, but you will be put to it to find it.   †

"Sorrow fiddles the ribs and no man should put his hand on anything; there is no direct way. The foetus of symmetry nourishes itself on cross purposes, this is its wonderful unhappiness—and now I am come to Jenny—oh Lord, why do women have partridge blood and set out to beat up trouble? The places Jenny moults in are her only distinction, a Christian with a wanderer's rump. She smiles, and it is the wide smile of the self-abused, radiating to the face from some localized centre   *
disturbance, the personification of the 'thief.' She has a longing for other people's property, but the moment she possesses it the property loses some of its value, for the owner's estimate is its worth. Therefore it was she took your Robin."

*   "What is she like?" Nora asked.
*   "Well," said the doctor, "I have always thought I, myself, the
    funniest looking creature on the face of the earth; then I laid
*   my eyes on Jenny—a little, hurried decaying comedy jester, the
*   face on the fool's-stick, and with a smell about her of mouse-
*   nests. She is a 'looter,' and eternally nervous. Even in her sleep
    I'll pronounce that her feet twitch and her orifices expand and
    contract like the iris of a suspicious eye. She speaks of people
    taking away her 'faith' in them, as if faith were a transportable
    object—all her life she has been subject to the feeling of
    'removal.' Were she a soldier she would define defeat with the
    sentence: 'The enemy took the war away.' Having a conviction
    that she is somehow reduced, she sets about collecting a destiny
    —and for her, the sole destiny is love, anyone's love and so her
    own. So only someone's love is her love. The cock crew and she
    was laid—her present is always someone else's past, jerked out
    and dangling.

    "Yet what she steals she keeps, through the incomparable
    fascination of maturation and rot. She has the strength of an
    incomplete accident—one is always waiting for the rest of it,
    for the last impurity that will make the whole; she was born at
    the point of death, but, unfortunately, she will not age into
    youth—which is a grave mistake of nature. How more tidy had
    it been to have been born old and have aged into a child,
    brought finally to the brink, not of the grave, but of the womb;
    in our age bred up into infants searching for a womb to crawl
    into, nor be made to walk loth the gingerly dust of death, but to
    find a moist, gillflirted way. And a funny sight it would be to see
    us going to our separate lairs at the end of day, women wincing
    with terror, not daring to set foot to the street for fear of it.

    "But I'm coming by degrees to the narrative of the one par-
    ticular night that makes all other nights seem like something
    quite decent enough—and that was the night when, dressed
    in openwork mittens, showing the edge of a pantaloon (and
    certainly they had been out of style three mothers behind her),
    Jenny Petherbridge—for that is her name in case you'd care to
*   know it," he said with a grin, "wrapped in a shawl of Spanish

insight and Madrid fancy (as a matter of fact, the costume
came later, but what do I care?), stepped out in the early fall of
the year to the *Opéra*—I think, and I am not mistaken, it was   *
nothing better than *Rigoletto*—walking in the galleries and   °
whisking her eyes about for trouble that she swore, even after,
she had really never wanted to know anything about, and there
laid her eyes on Robin, who was leaning forward in a box, and
me pacing up and down, talking to myself in the best *Comédie-
Française* French trying to keep off what I knew was going to
be trouble for a generation, and wishing I was hearing the   † *
Schumann cycle, when in swishes the old sow of a Danish ° † *
count. My heart aches for all poor creatures putting on dog and
not a pot to piss in or a window to throw it from. And I began to
think, and I don't know why, of the closed gardens of the world
where all people can make their thoughts go up high because of
the narrowness and beauty, or of the wide fields where the heart
can spread out and thin its vulgarity (it's why I eat salad), and I   *
thought, we should all have a place to throw our flowers in, like
me who, once in my youth, rated a *corbeille* of moth-orchids, and   °
did I keep them? Don't get restless—I'm coming back to the
point. No, I sat beside them a little while having my tea, and   †
saying to myself; 'You're a pretty lot, and you do my cupboard
honour, but there's a better place awaiting you,—' and with that
I took them by the hand around to the Catholic church, and I
said, 'God is what we make Him, and life doesn't seem to be   *
getting any better,' and tiptoed out.

"So, I went around the gallery a third time, and I knew that
Hindu or no Hindu, I was in on what was wrong with the
world—and I said the world's like that poor distressed moll of a
Jenny, never knowing which end to put its mittens on, and
pecking about like a mystified rook, until this particular night
gave her a hoist and set her up at the banquet, (where she has
been sitting dumbfounded ever since), and Robin the sleeping
and troubled, looking amazed. It was more than a boy like me   *
(who am the last woman left in this world, though I am the
bearded lady) could bear, and I went into a lather of misery
watching them, and thinking of you, and how in the end you'll

all be locked together, like the poor beasts that get their antlers
mixed and are found dead that way, their heads fattened with a
* knowledge of each other they never wanted, having had to con-
* template each other, head on and eye to eye, until death; well,
that will be you and Jenny and Robin. You, who should have
* had a thousand children and Robin, who should have been all
* of them; and Jenny the bird, snatching the oats out of love's
* droppings—and I went mad, I'm like that. What an autopsy I'll
make, with everything all which ways in my bowels! A kidney
and a shoe cast of the Roman races; a liver and a long spent
whisper, a gall and a wrack of scolds from Milano, and my heart
that will be weeping still when they find my eyes cold, not to
o mention a thought of Cellini in my crib of bones, thinking
how he must have suffered when he knew he could not tell it
forever—(beauty's name spreads too thick). And the lining of
* my belly, flocked with the locks cut off love in odd places that
† I've come on, a bird's nest of pubic hairs to lay my lost eggs in,
and my people as good as they come, as long as they have been
* coming, down the grim path of 'We know not' to 'We can't
guess why.'
* "Well, I was thinking of you, a woman at best, and you know
* what that means? Not much in the morning—all trussed up
with pain's bridle. Then I turned my eyes on Jenny who was
turning her eyes looking for trouble, for she was then at that
pitch of life that she knew to be her last moment. And do
you need the doctor to tell you that that is a bad strange hour
for a woman? If all women could have it all at once, you could
beat them in flocks like a school of scorpions; but they come
* eternally, one after the other, and go head foremost into it
alone. For men of my kind it isn't so bad, I've never asked better
than to see the two ends of my man no matter how I might be
dwindling. But for one like Jenny, the poor ruffled bitch, why,
God knows, I bled for her, because I knew in an instant the kind
of a woman she was, one who had spent all her life rummaging
through photographs of the past, searching for the one who
would be found leaning sideways with a look as if angels were
* sliding down her hip—a great love who had been spared a face

but who'd been saddled with loins, leaning against a drape of Scotch velvet with a pedestal at the left twined with ivy, a knife in her boot and her groin pouting as if she kept her heart in it. Or searching among old books for the passion that was all renunciation and lung trouble, with flowers at the bosom—that was Jenny—so you can imagine how she trembled when she saw herself going toward fifty without a thing done to make her a tomb-piece, or anything in her past that would get a flower named for her. So I saw her coming forward, stepping lightly and trembling and looking at Robin, saying to me (I'd met her, if you call it meeting a woman when you pound her kidney), 'Won't you introduce me?' and my knees knocking together; † *
and my heart as heavy as Adam's off ox, because you are a friend †
of mine, and a good poor thing, God knows, who will never put
a stop to anything; you may be knocked down, but you'll crawl *
on forever, while there's any use to it, so I said, 'Certainly,
damn it!' and brought them together. As if Robin hadn't met *
enough people without me making it worse."

"Yes," she said, "she met everyone." † *

"Well," he went on, "the house was beginning to empty, all the common clay was pouring down the steps talking of the Diva (there's something wrong with any art that makes a woman all bust!) and how she had taken her high L, and all the people looking out of the corners of their eyes to see how their neighbours were dressed, and some of them dropping their cloaks rather low to see the beast in a man snarling up in his neck—and they never guessed that it was me, with both shoulders under cover, that brought the veins to their escorts' *
temples—and walking high and stately—the pit of my stomach gone black in the darkness that was eating it away for thinking of you, and Robin smiling sideways like a cat with canary feathers to account for, and Jenny tripping beside her so fast that she would get ahead and have to run back with small cries of ambition, saying wistfully, 'You must come to my house for late supper.'

"God help me, I went! For who will not betray a friend, or, for that matter, himself, for a whisky and soda, caviare and a

warm fire—and that brings me to the ride that we took later. As
°   Don Antonio said long ago, 'Did'st thou make a night of it?'
And was answered (by Claudio), 'Yes. Egad! And morning too;
for about eight o'clock the next day, slap! They all soused upon
their knees, kissed around, burned their commodes, drank my
†   health, broke their glasses and so parted.' So Cibber put it, and
* ° I put it in Taylor's words, 'Did not *Periander* think fit to lie with
†   his wife *Melissa* after she had already gone hent to heaven?' Is
this not night work of another order also, but night work still?
°   And in another place, as Montaigne says: 'Seems it not to be a
lunatic humour of the moon that *Endymion* was by the lady
moon lulled to sleep for many months together that she might
* † have her joy of him who stirred not at all except in sleep.'

"Well, having picked up a child in transit, a niece of someone
*   Jenny knew, we all went riding down the *Champs Elysées*. We
°   went straight as a die over the *Pont Neuf* and whirled around
into the *rue du Cherche-Midi*, God forgive us! Where you, weak
*   vessel of love, were lying awake and wondering where, and all
the time Jenny doing the deed that was as bad and out of place
as that done by Catherine of Russia, and don't deny it, who
* ° took old Poniatovsky's throne for a water-closet. And suddenly
I was glad I was simple and didn't want a thing in the world but
what could be had for five francs. And I envied Jenny nothing
she had in her house, though I admit I had been sort of casting
my eye over a couple of books, which I would have spirited away
if they hadn't been bound in calf—for I might steal the mind
°   of Petronius, as well I knew, but never the skin of a calf—for
the rest, the place was as full of the wrong thing as you would
care to spend your inheritance on—well, I furnished my closet
with phenomenal luck at the fair, what with shooting a row of
*   chamber-pots and whirling a dozen wheels to the good, and
everyone about me getting nothing for a thousand francs but
*   a couple of velvet dogs, or dolls that looked as if they had been
up all night. And what did I walk home with for less than five
*   francs? A fine frying-pan that could coddle six eggs, and a raft
of minor objects that one needs in the kitchen—so I looked at
Jenny's possessions with scorn in my eye. It may have been all

most 'unusual' but who wants a toe-nail that is thicker than common? And that thought came to me out of the contemplation of the mad strip of the inappropriate that runs through creation, like my girl friend who married some sort of Adriatic bird who had such thick ones that he had to trim them with a horse-file—my mind is so rich that it is always wandering! Now *
I am back to the time when that groom walked into my life wearing a priest's collar that he had no more right to than I have to a crupper. Well, then the carriages came up with their sweet wilted horses, and Robin went down the steps first, and Jenny tearing after her saying, 'Wait! Wait!' as if she were talking to an express on its way into Boston, and dragging her shawl and running, and we all got in—she'd collected some guests who were waiting for her in the house."

The doctor was embarrassed by Nora's rigid silence; he went *
on. "I was leaning forward on my cane as we went down under the trees, holding it with both hands, and the black wagon I was *
in was being followed by a black wagon, and that by another, and the wheels were turning, and I began saying to myself: The trees are better, and grass is better, and animals are all right and the birds in the air are fine. And everything we do is decent † *
when the mind begins to forget, – the design of life; and good † *
when we are forgotten, – the design of death. I began to mourn *
for my spirit, and the spirits of all people that cast a shadow a † *
long way beyond what they are; and for the beasts that walk out *
of the darkness alone I began to wail, for all the little beasts in † *
their mothers, who would have to step down and begin going, *
decent in the one fur that would last them their time. And I said *
to myself: For these I would go bang on my knees, but not for her—I wouldn't piss on her if she were on fire! I said, Jenny is *
so greedy that she wouldn't give her shit to the crows. And then *
I thought: Oh, the poor bitch, if she were dying, face down in a long pair of black gloves, would I forgive her? And I knew † *
I would forgive her, or anyone making a picture. And then I *
began looking at the people in that carriage, very carefully raising my eyes so they would not notice anything unusual, and I saw the English girl sitting up there pleased and frightened. *

*   "And then at the child—there was terror in it and it was
*   running away from something grown up; I saw that she was
*   sitting still and she was running, it was in her eyes, and in
*   her chin, drawn down, and her eyes wide open. And then I
*   saw Jenny sitting there shaking, and I said: 'God, you are no
picture!' And then, Robin was going forward, and the blood
running red, where Jenny had scratched her, and I screamed
*   and thought: 'Nora will leave that girl some day; but though
*   those two are buried at opposite ends of the earth, one dog will
find them both.' "

6

WHERE THE TREE FALLS

ᵒ

BARON FELIX, WHO HAD given up his place in the bank, though not his connections with it, had been seen in many countries standing before that country's palace gate, holding his gloved hands before him in the first unconcluded motion of submission; contemplating relics and parts, with a tension in his leg that took the step forward or back a little quicker than his fellow sightseer.

As at one time he had written to the press about this noble or that, (and had never seen it in print), as he had sent letters to declining houses and never received an answer, he was now amassing a set of religious speculations that he eventually intended sending to the Pope. The reason for this was, that as time passed it became increasingly evident that his child, if born to anything, had been born to holy decay. Mentally deficient, and emotionally excessive, an addict to death; at ten, barely as tall as a child of six, wearing spectacles, stumbling when he tried to run, with cold hands and anxious face, he followed his father, trembling with an excitement that was a precocious ecstasy. Holding his father's hand he climbed palace and church steps with the tearing swing of the leg necessitated by a measure that had not taken a child into account; staring at paintings and wax reproductions of saints, watching the priests with the quickening of the breath of those in whom concentration must take the place of participation, as in the scar of a wounded animal will be seen the shudder of its recovery.

When Guido had first spoken of wishing to enter the church, Felix had been startled out of himself. He knew that Guido was

* not like other children, that he would always be too estranged to be argued with; in accepting his son the Baron saw that he must accept a demolition of his own life. The child would obviously never be able to cope with it. The Baron bought his boy a Virgin in metal, hanging from a red ribbon, and placed it about his neck, and in doing so, the slight neck, bent to take the ribbon, recalled to him Robin's, as she stood back to him in the antique shop on the Seine.

So Felix began to look into the matter of the church. He searched the face of every priest he saw in the streets; he read litanies and examined chasubles and read the Credo; he inquired into the state of monasteries. He wrote, after much thought, to the Pope, a long disquisition on the state of the cloth. He touched on Franciscan monks and French priests, pointing out that any faith that could, in its profoundest unity, compose two such dissimilar types—one the Roman, shaved and expectant of what seemed, when one looked into their vacantly absorbed faces, nothing more glorious than a muscular

* resurrection; and the other, the French priest, who seemed to
* be composite of husband and wife in conjunction with original sin, carrying with them good and evil in constantly quantitative ascent and descent, the unhappy spectacle of a single ego come
* to a several public dissolution—must be profoundly elastic.
* He inquired if this might not be the outcome of the very
* different confessional states of the two countries. Was it not, he asked, to be taken for granted that the Italian ear must be less confounded because, possibly, it was harking the echo of
* its past, and the French that of the future? Was it conceivable that the "confessions" of the two nations could, in the one case, produce that living and expectant coma and, in the other, that worldly, incredible, indecent gluttony? He said that he himself had come to the conclusion that the French, the more secular, were a very porous people. Assuming this, it was then only natural that from listening to a thousand and one lay sins the priest, upon reaching no riper age than two score, should find it difficult to absolve, the penitent having laid himself open
* to a peculiar kind of forgiveness; not so much absolution as

exigency, for the priest was himself a vessel already filled to
overflowing, and gave pardon because he could no longer hold,   *
– he signed with the cross, hastily and in stress, being like a   *
full bladder, embarrassed and in need of an immediate privacy.
The Franciscan, on the other hand, had still a moment to wait.   *
There was no tangent in his iris, as one who, in blessing is looking for relief.

Felix received no answer. He had expected none. He wrote to   *
clear some doubt in his mind. He knew that in all probability
the child would never be "chosen." If he were, the Baron hoped   *
that it would be in Austria, among his own people, and to that
end he finally decided to make his home in Vienna.

Before leaving, however, he sought out the doctor. He was   *
not in his lodging. The Baron aimlessly set off toward the
square. He saw the small black-clad figure moving toward him.   *
The doctor had been to a funeral and was on his way to the *Café
de la Mairie du VIe* to lift his spirits. The Baron was shocked to
observe, in the few seconds before the doctor saw him, that he
seemed old, older than his fifty odd years would account for.
He moved slowly as if he were dragging water, his knees, which
one seldom noticed, because he was usually seated, sagged. His
dark shaved chin was lowered as if in a melancholy that had
no beginning or end. The Baron hailed him, and instantly the   *
doctor threw off his unobserved self, as one hides, hastily, a
secret life. He smiled, drew himself up, raised his hand in
greeting, though as is usual with people, when taken unaware,
with a touch of defense.

"Where have you been?" he said as he came to a standstill in
the middle of the block. "I haven't seen you for months, and,"
he added, "it's a pity."

The Baron smiled in return. "I've been in mental trouble," he
said, walking beside the doctor. "Are you," he added, "engaged   *
for dinner?"

"No," said the doctor, "I've just buried an excellent fellow.   *
Don't think you ever met him, a Kabyle, better sort of Arab.
They have Roman blood, and can turn pale at a great pinch,
which is more than can be said for most, you know," he added,   *

walking a little sideways, as one does when not knowing where
a companion is going. "Do a bit for a Kabyle, back or front, and
they back up on you with a camel or a bag of dates." He sighed
and passed his hand over his chin. "He was the only one I ever
knew who offered me five francs before I could reach for my
own. I had it framed in orange blossoms and hung it over the
what-not."

The Baron was abstracted but he smiled, out of politeness.
He suggested dining in the *Bois*. The doctor was only too willing, and at the sudden good news, he made that series of half
gestures of a person taken pleasantly unaware; he half held up
his hands—no gloves—he almost touched his breast pocket—a
handkerchief, he glanced at his boots, and was grateful for the
funeral, he was shined, fairly neat; he touched his tie, stretching
his throat muscles.

As they drove through the *Bois* the doctor went over in his
mind what he would order—duck with oranges, no—having
eaten on a poor man's purse for so many years, habit had
brought him to simple things with garlic. He shivered. He must
think of something different. All he could think of was coffee
and *Grand Marnier*, the big tumbler, warmed with the hands,
like his people warming at the peat fire. "Yes?" he said, and
realized that the Baron had been speaking. The doctor lifted his
chin to the night air and listened now with an intensity with
which he hoped to reconstruct the sentence.

"Strange, I had never seen the Baronin in this light before,"
the Baron was saying, and he crossed his knees. "If I should try
to put it into words, I mean how I did see her, it would be
incomprehensible, for the simple reason that I find that I never
did have a really clear idea of her at any time. I had an image of
her, but that is not the same thing. An image is a stop the mind
makes between uncertainties. I had gathered, of course, a good
deal from you, and later, after she went away, from others, but
this only strengthened my confusion. The more we learn of a
person, the less we know. It does not, for instance, help me to
know anything of *Chartres* above the fact that it possesses a
cathedral, unless I have lived in *Chartres* and so keep the relative

heights of the cathedral and the lives of its population in proportion. Otherwise it would only confuse me to learn that Jean of that city stood his wife upright in a well; the moment I visualize this, the deed will measure as high as the building; just as children who have a little knowledge of life will draw a man and a barn on the same scale."

"Your devotion to the past," observed the doctor, looking at the cab meter with apprehension, "is perhaps like a child's drawing." *

The Baron nodded. He was troubled. "My family is pre-served because I have it only from the memory of one woman, † * my aunt; therefore it is single, clear and unalterable. In this I am fortunate, through this I have a sense of immortality. Our basic idea of eternity is a condition that *cannot vary*. It is the motivation of marriage. No man really wants his freedom. He gets a habit as quickly as possible, – it is a form of immortality." *

"And what's more," said the doctor, "we heap reproaches on the person who breaks it, saying that in so doing he has broken the image—of our safety." *

The Baron acquiesced. "This quality of one sole condition, † * which was so much a part of the Baronin, was what drew me to her; a condition of being that she had not, at that time, even * chosen, but a fluid sort of possession which gave me a feeling that I would not only be able to achieve immortality, but be free to choose my own kind."

"She was always holding God's bag of tricks upside down," murmured the doctor.

"Yet, if I tell the whole truth," the Baron continued, "the very abundance of what then appeared to me to be security, and which was, in reality, the most formless loss, gave me at the same time pleasure and a sense of terrible anxiety, which proved only too legitimate."

The doctor lit a cigarette. *

"I took it," the Baron went on, "for acquiescence, thus * making my great mistake. She was really like those people who, coming unexpectedly into a room, silence the company because they are looking for someone who is not there." He knocked on the cab window, got down and paid. As they walked up the gravel path he went on: "What I particularly wanted to ask you was, why did she marry me? It has placed me in the dark for the rest of my life."

"Oh the great shy difference," said the doctor, "of one head to another turned, you'll never know; and talking about the 'rest of your life,' it reminds me of the year when (God forgive me my ignorance) I did not know how a girlish boy would take the war, until along came the war. This lad was a dancer who had taken a professional name that sounded like a suburb of Los Angeles, his real name being MacClusky. Top-hat and sponge-bag trousers used to be hardly enough for him. Down the streets of London he would come swinging, reeking of gardenia and clutching a cane, his face made up so perfect you would think his mother had done right by him. You should have seen him when he was being the dying swan, or leaping through a hoop, with both hands spread—off he would go, swishing into the air!

"But see him after a day's march! A tin helmet over one eye, and the beautiful swivel tooth that had cost him a fortune lying somewhere in Flanders Field. Well there he was, covered with mud, and that hat over his eye, and his front tooth missing, saying his lamentations all in a field of mincemeat, coming up to regimentals to be decorated for his prowess, and all of us grinning at him because we knew how and why he came by it, by a lack in the mind of the general who did not know what sort of a nature the lad was suffering under; and we didn't say a word because MacClusky was just the kind that should have a consignment of medals left at his door for breakfast every day – the poor bewildered moll!

"He'd been standing in the middle of a bridge trying to think where the war was coming from when a douse of Germans loomed up, trying to make the bridge, and there he was, the poor frail, gone wild in the center of the pontoon, and instead of shooting – why should he know one end of a gun from another – he just went all of a fluff, and swung the heft around and began banging their heads off. They flew like crazy, seeing what they thought was a wild man in their midst. So he held the fort, swinging away with the butt of that thing. So when the general comes up prancing and pinning and kissing the elect we all stood still, looking out of the ends of our eyes at Mac who loomed up like a horse-bun on a platter, all misery and glory, thinking quick and slow: 'Here's where I come into something that will take away the ignominy of my past, and the marrow of my nature will be refilled and made glorious,' for he had been so far away and beaten up in his heart for the opinion the world had of him – and everybody has it, no matter what they say – that he had forgotten where he was standing and what he was waiting for, when down on his breast flew the *crois de guerre* with a pin in its tail and at that he gave a jump back that carried him a foot out of line, and with a great joy swelling and rolling him along he came back again and the tears spurted out of him right forward like a lemon.

"I've never seen any tears like those before in my life, though that is the way a boy cries who has been queer all his hour and it's suddenly made all right by a general upheaval of justice; and you knew that under that piece of cast-iron all his *faux pas* had gone light, and that the weight of that cross had tossed him up into a shape of approval."

The Baron was confused. He never knew what to do when the doctor went into one of his reminiscences.

"Yes," he said, choosing a table beside the lake where the shadows were dark across the water. "Yes, every kind of thing is a lesson. We should all know more than we do, and I suppose that means we should all do more than we do."

"Take the case of the horse who knew too much," said the doctor, "looking between the branches in the morning, cypress or hemlock. She was in mourning for something taken away from her in a bombardment in the war – by the way she stood, that something lay between her hooves – she stirred no branch though her hide was a river of sorrow; she was damned to her hocks, where the grass came waving up softly. Her eyelashes were gray black, like the eyelashes of a nigger, and at her buttocks' soft center a pulse throbbed like a fiddle."

* The Baron, studying the menu, said, "The Petherbridge woman called on me."

* "Glittering God," exclaimed the doctor, putting the card
* down. "Has it gone as far as that? I shouldn't have thought it."

"For the first moment," the Baron continued, "I had no idea who she was. She had spared no pains to make her toilet rusty
* and grievous by an arrangement of veils and flat-toned dark material with flowers in it, cut plainly and extremely tight over a very small bust, and from the waist down gathered into bulky folds to conceal, no doubt, the widening parts of a woman well
* † over forty. She seemed hurried. She spoke of you."
* The doctor put the menu on his knee. He raised his dark eyes with the bushy brows erect. "What did she say?"

The Baron answered, evidently unaware of the tender spot
* which his words touched: "Utter nonsense, to the effect that
* you are seen nearly every day in a certain convent, where you bow and pray and get free meals and attend cases which are, well, illegal."

The Baron looked up. To his surprise he saw that the doctor had "deteriorated" into that condition in which he had seen him in the street, when he thought himself unobserved.

In a loud voice the doctor said to the waiter, who was within
* an inch of his mouth: "Yes, and with oranges, *oranges!*"
* † The Baron continued hastily: "She gave me uneasiness because Guido was in the room at the time. She said that she had
* come to buy a painting; indeed, she offered me a very good price, which I was tempted to take (I've been doing a little dealing in old masters lately) for my stay in Vienna, but as it
* turned out, she wanted the portrait of my grandmother, which on no account could I bring myself to part with. She had not been in the room five minutes before I sensed that the picture
* was an excuse, and that what she really wanted was something else. She began talking about the Baronin almost at once, though she mentioned no name at first, and I did not connect
* the story with my wife until the end. She said, 'She is really
* quite extraordinary. I don't understand her at all, though I must
* say I understand her better than other people,' – she added this

with a sort of false eagerness. She went on: 'She always lets her   *
pets die. She is so fond of them, and then she neglects them, the
way that animals neglect themselves.'

"I did not like her to talk about this subject, as Guido is very
sensitive to animals, and I could fancy what was going on in his
mind; he is not like other children, not cruel, or savage. For this   † *
very reason he is called 'strange.' A child who is mature, in the
sense that the heart is mature, is always, I have observed, called
deficient." He gave his order and went on, "She then changed
the subject—."

"Tacking into the wind like a barge."   *

"Well yes, to a story about a little girl she had staying with
her (she called her Sylvia); the Baronin was also staying with   *
her at the time, though I did not know that the young woman
in question was the Baronin until later—well anyway, it appears   *
that this little girl Sylvia had 'fallen in love' with the Baronin
and that she, the Baronin, kept waking her up all through the
night to ask her if she 'loved her.'

"During the holidays, while the child was away, Petherbridge
became 'anxious,' that is the way she put it, as to whether or not
the 'young lady had a heart.'"

"And brought the child back to prove it?" interpolated the
doctor, casting an eye over the fashionable crowd beginning to
fill the room.

"Exactly," said the Baron, ordering wine. "I made an excla-   *
mation, and she said quickly, 'You can't blame me, you can't
accuse me of using a child for my own ends!' Well, what else
does it come to?"

"That woman," the doctor said, settling himself more com-   *
fortably in his chair, "would use the third rising of a corpse
for her ends. Though," he added, "I must admit she is very
generous with money."

The Baron winced. "So I gathered from her over-large bid   *
for the portrait. Well, she went on to say that when they met,   *
the Baronin had so obviously forgotten all about her, that the
child was 'ashamed—' she said 'shame went all over her.' She
was already at the door when she spoke the last sentence. In

* fact, she conducted the whole scene as though my room were a stage that had been marked out, and at this point she must read her final lines.

" 'Robin,' she said, 'Baronin Robin Volkbein, I wonder if she could be a relative.'

* "For a whole minute I couldn't move. When I turned around I saw that Guido was ill. I took him in my arms and spoke to him in German. He had often put questions to me about his mother,
* and I had managed always to direct his mind to expect her."

The doctor turned to the Baron with one of his sudden illuminations. "Exactly right. With Guido, you are in the presence of the 'maladjusted.' Wait! I am not using that word in the derogatory sense at all, in fact my great virtue is that I never use the derogatory in the usual sense. Pity is an intrusion when in the presence of a person who is a new position in an old account, which is your son. You can only pity those limited to
* their generation. Pity is timely, and dies with the person; a
* pitiable man is his own last tie. You have treated Guido well."

* The Baron paused, his knife bent down. He looked up. "Do
* you know, doctor, I find the thought of my son's possible death
* at an early age a sort of dire happiness, because his death is the
* most awful, the most fearful thing that could befall me. The
* unendurable is the beginning of the curve of joy. I have become
* entangled in the shadow of a vast apprehension, which is my son; he is the central point toward which life and death are spinning, the meeting of which my final design will be composed."

"And Robin?" the doctor asked.

"She is with me in Guido, they are inseparable, and this time," the Baron said, catching his monocle, "with her full
* consent." He leaned down and picked up his napkin. "The Baronin," he continued, "always seemed to be looking for someone to tell her that she was innocent. Guido is very like her, except that he has his innocence. The Baronin was always searching in the wrong direction, until she met Nora Flood, who seemed, from what little I knew of her, to be a very honest woman, at least by intention.

"There are some people," he went on, "who must get permission to live, and if the Baronin finds no one to give her that permission, she will make an innocence for herself; a fearful sort of primitive innocence. It may be considered 'depraved' by our generation, but our generation does not know everything." He smiled. "For instance Guido, how many will realize his value? One's life is peculiarly one's own when one has invented it."

The doctor wiped his mouth. "In the acceptance of depravity the sense of the past is most fully captured. What is a ruin but Time easing itself of endurance? Corruption is the Age of Time. It is the body and the blood of ecstasy, religion and love. Ah, yes," the doctor added, "we do not 'climb' to heights, we are eaten away to them, and then conformity, neatness, ceases to entertain us. Man is born as he dies, rebuking cleanliness, and there is its middle condition, the slovenliness that is usually an accompaniment of the 'attractive' body, a sort of earth on which love feeds."

"That is true," Felix said with eagerness. "The Baronin had an undefinable disorder, a sort of 'odour of memory,' like a person who has come from some place that we have forgotten and would give our life to recall."

The doctor reached out for the bread. "So the reason for our cleanliness becomes apparent; cleanliness is a form of apprehension; our faulty racial memory is fathered by fear. Destiny and history are untidy; we fear memory of that disorder. Robin did not."

"No," Felix said in a low voice. "She did not."

"The almost fossilized state of our recollection is attested to by our murderers and those who read every detail of crime with a passionate and hot interest," the doctor continued. "It is only by such extreme measures that the average man can remember something long ago; truly, not that he remembers, but that crime itself is the door to an accumulation, a way to lay hands on the shudder of a past that is still vibrating."

The Baron was silent a moment. Then he said: "Yes, something of this rigor was in the Baronin, in its first faint degree; it was in her walk, in the way she wore her clothes, in her silence, as if speech were heavy and unclarified. There was in her every movement a slight drag, as if the past were a web about her, as there is a web of time about a very old building. There is a sensible weight in the air around a thirteenth century edifice," he said with a touch of pomposity, "that is unlike the light air about a new structure; the new building seems to repulse it, the old to gather it. So about the Baronin there was a density, not of age, but of youth. It perhaps accounts for my attraction to her."

"Animals find their way about largely by the keenness of their nose," said the doctor. "We have lost ours in order not to be one of them, and what have we in its place? A tension in the spirit which is the contraction of freedom. But," he ended, "all dreadful events are of profit."

Felix ate in silence for a moment, then point blank he turned to the doctor with a question. "You know my preoccupation; is my son's better?"

The doctor, as he grew older, in answering a question seemed, as old people do, to be speaking more and more to himself, and when troubled, he seemed to grow smaller. He said: "Seek no further for calamity, you have it in your son. After all, calamity is what we are all seeking. You have found it. A man is whole only when he takes into account his shadow as well as himself—and what is a man's shadow but his prostrate astonishment? Guido is the shadow of your anxiety, and Guido's shadow is God's."

Felix said: "Guido also loves women of history."

"Mary's shadow!" said the doctor.

Felix turned. His monocle shone sharp and bright along its edge. "People say that he is not sound of mind. What do you say?"

"I say that a mind like his may be more apt than yours and mine—he is not made secure by habit—in that there is always hope."

Felix said under his breath: "He does not grow up."

Matthew answered: "The excess of his sensibilities may preclude his mind. His sanity is an unknown room: a known room is always smaller than an unknown. If I were you," the doctor continued, "I would carry that boy's mind like a bowl picked up in the dark; you do not know what's in it. He feeds on odd remnants that we have not priced; he eats a sleep that is not our sleep. There is more in sickness than the name of that sickness. In the average person is the peculiar that has been scuttled, and in the peculiar the ordinary that has been sunk; people always fear what requires watching." Felix ordered a *fine*. The doctor smiled. "I said you would come to it," he said and emptied his own glass at a gulp.

"I know," Felix answered, "but I did not understand. I thought you meant something else."

"What?"

Felix paused, turning the small glass around in his trembling hand. "I thought," he said, "that you meant that I would give up."

The doctor lowered his eyes. "Perhaps that is what I meant— but sometimes I am mistaken." He looked at Felix from under his heavy brows. "Man was born damned and innocent from the start, and wretchedly – as he must – on those two themes – whistles his tune."

The Baron leaned forward. He said in a low voice, "Was the Baronin damned?"

The doctor deliberated for a second, knowing what Felix had hidden in his question. "Guido is not damned," he said, and the Baron turned away quickly. "Guido," the doctor went on, "is blessed—he is peace of mind—he is what you have always been looking for—Aristocracy," he said smiling, "is a condition in the mind of the people when they try to think of something else and better—funny," he added sharply, "that a man never knows when he has found what he has always been looking for."

"And the Baronin," Felix said, "do you ever hear from her?"

"She is in America now, but of course you know that. Yes, she writes, now and again, not to me—God forbid—to others."

"What does she say?" the Baron said, trying not to show his emotion.

"She says," the doctor answered, " 'Remember me.' Probably because she has difficulty in remembering herself."

The Baron caught his monocle. "Altamonte, who has been
in America, tells me that she seemed 'estranged.' Once," he
said, pinching his monocle into place, "I wanted, as you, who
are aware of everything, know, to go behind the scenes, backstage as it were, to our present condition, to find, if I could,
the secret of time; good, perhaps, that that is an impossible
ambition for the sane mind. One has, I am now certain, to be
a little mad to see into the past or the future, to be a little
abridged of life to know life, the obscure life—darkly seen, the
condition my son lives in; it may also be the errand on which the
Baronin is going."

Taking out his handkerchief, the Baron removed his
monocle, wiping it carefully.

Carrying a pocket full of medicines, and a little flask of oil for
the chapping hands of his son, Felix rode into Vienna, the child
beside him, Frau Mann, opulent and gay, opposite, holding a
rug for the boy's feet. Felix drank heavily now, and to hide the
red that flushed his cheeks he had grown a beard ending in two
forked points on his chin. In the matter of drink, Frau Mann
was now no bad second. Many cafés saw this odd trio, the child
in the midst wearing heavy lenses that made his eyes drift
forward, sitting erect, his neck holding his head at attention,
watching his father's coins roll, as the night drew out, farther
and farther across the floor and under the feet of the musicians
as Felix called for military music, for *Wacht am Rhein*, for
Morgenrot, for Wagner; his monocle dimmed by the heat of
the room, perfectly correct and drunk, trying not to look for
what he had always sought, the son of a once great house; his
eyes either gazing at the ceiling or lowered where his hand, on
the table, struck thumb and little finger against the wood in
rhythm with the music, as if he were playing only the two
important notes of an octave, the low and the high; or nodding
his head and smiling at his child, as mechanical toys nod to
the touch of an infant's hand, Guido pressing his own hand
against his stomach where, beneath his shirt, he could feel the

medallion against his flesh, Frau Mann gripping her beer mug firmly, laughing and talking loudly.   *

One evening, seated in his favorite café on the Ring, Felix   ○ on entering had seen instantly, but refused to admit it to himself, a tall man in the corner who, he was sure, was the Grand Duke Alexander of Russia, cousin and brother-in-law of the late Czar Nicholas – and toward whom in the early part of the evening he steadfastly refused to look. But as the clock hands pointed twelve, Felix (with the abandon of what a mad   * man knows to be his one hope of escape, disproof of his own   * madness) could not keep his eyes away, and as they arose to go, his cheeks now drained of color, the points of his beard bent   * sharply down with the stiffening of his chin, he turned and   * made a slight bow, his head in his confusion making a complete half swing, as an animal will turn its head away from a human, as   * if in mortal shame.

He stumbled as he got into his carriage. "Come," he said, taking the child's fingers in his own. "You are cold." He poured a few drops of oil, and began rubbing Guido's hands.   *

7

GO DOWN, MATTHEW

* o

*

"CAN'T YOU BE QUIET NOW?" the doctor said. He had come in
late one afternoon to find Nora writing a letter. "Can't you be
* † done now, can't you give up, now be still, now that you know
what the world is about, knowing it's about nothing?" He took
his hat and coat off without being asked, placing his umbrella
† in a corner. He came forward into the room. "And me who
seem curious because no one has seen me for a million years,
and now I'm seen! Is there such extraordinary need of misery
to make beauty? Let go Hell; and your fall will be broken by the
* roof of Heaven." He eyed the tea tray and seeing that the
tea-pot had long since become cold, poured himself a generous
port. He threw himself into a chair and added more softly, as
Nora turned away from her letter, "In the far reaches of India
there is a man being still beneath a tree. Why not rest? Why not
put the pen away? Isn't it bitter enough for Robin that she is
lost somewhere without receiving mail? And Jenny, what of
her now? Taken to drink and appropriating Robin's mind with
* vulgar inaccuracy, like those eighty-two plaster Virgins she
* bought because Robin had one good one; when you laugh at
the eighty-two standing in a row, Jenny runs to the wall, back
to the picture of her mother, and stands there between two
tortures—the past that she can't share, and the present that
o she can't copy. What of her now? Looking at her quarters with
harrowing, indelicate cries; burying her middle at both ends,
searching the world for the path back to what she wanted once
and long ago! The memory past, and only by a coincidence, a
wind, the flutter of a leaf, a surge of tremendous recollection

goes through her, and swooning she knows it gone. Cannot a beastly thing be analogous to a fine thing, if both are apprehensions? Love of two things often makes one thing right. Think of the fish racing the sea, their love of air and water turning them like wheels, their tails and teeth biting the water, their spines curved round the air. Is that not Jenny? She who could not encompass anything whole, but only with her teeth and tail, and the spine on her sprung up. Oh, for God's sake! Can't you rest now?"

"If I don't write to her, what am I to do? I can't sit here forever—thinking!"

"*Terra damnata et maledicta!*" exclaimed the doctor, banging his fist down. "My uncle Octavius, the trout-tickler of Itchen, was better, he ate his fish when he caught it! But you, you must unspin fate, go back to find Robin! That's what you are going to do. In your chair should have been set the Holy Stone, to say yes to your yes, no to your no; instead it's lost in Westminster Abbey, and if I could have stopped Brec on his way with it into Ireland and have whispered in his ear I would have said, 'Wait' (though it was seven hundred years B.C.); it might have been passed around. It might have stopped you, but no, you are always writing to Robin. Nothing will curb it. You've made her a legend and set before her head the Eternal Light, and you'll keep to it even if it does cost her the tearing open of a million envelopes to her end. How do you know what sleep you raise her from? What words she must say to annul the postman's whistle to another girl rising up on a wild elbow? Can't you let any of us loose? Don't you know your holding on is her only happiness and so her sole misery. You write and weep and think and plot, and all the time what is Robin doing? Chucking Jack Straws, or sitting on the floor playing soldiers; so don't cry to me, who have no one to write to, and only taking in a little light laundry known as the Wash of the World. Dig a hole, drop me in! Not at all. St. Matthew's Passion by Bach I'll be. Everything can be used in a lifetime, I've discovered that."

"I've got to write to her," Nora said. "I've got to."

"No man knows it as I know it, I who am the god of darkness.

Very well, but know the worst then. What of Felix and his son
† Guido, that sick lamenting, fevered child; death in the weather
is a tonic to him. Like all the new young his sole provision for
o old age is hope of an early death. What spirits answer him who
will never come to man's estate? The poor shattered eagerness.
o So I say, was Robin purposely unspun? Was Jenny a sitting
bitch for fun? Who knows what knives hash her apart? Can't
* o you rest now, lay down the pen. Oh *papelero*, have I not summed
o up my time! I shall rest myself some day by the brim of Saxon-
les-Bains and drink it dry, or go to pieces in Hamburg at the
o gambling table, or end up like Madame de Staël – with an
affinity for Germany. To all kinds of ends I'll come. Ah yes,
* with a crupper of maiden's hair to keep my soul in place, and
in my vanguard a dove especially feathered to keep to my wind,
o as I ride that grim horse with ample glue in every hoof to post
up my deeds when I'm dropped in and sealed with earth. In time
* everything is possible and in space everything forgivable; life
is but the intermediary vice. There is eternity to blush in. Life
laid end to end is what brings on flux in the clergy – can't you
* rest now, put down the pen? Oh the poor worms that never
o arrive! Some strangely connived angel pray for us! We shall not
encompass it – the defunctive murmur in the cardiac nerve has
given us all our gait. And Robin? I know where your mind is!
She, the eternal momentary – Robin who was always the second
person singular. Well," he said with violence. "Lie weeping
* with a sword in your hand! Haven't I eaten a book too? Like the
angels and prophets? And wasn't it a bitter book to eat? The
archives of my case against the law, snatched up and out of
the tale-telling files by my high important friend. And didn't I
eat a page and tear a page and stamp on others and flay some
* and toss some into the toilet for relief's sake, – then think of
Jenny without a comma to eat, and Robin with nothing but a pet
* name – your pet name to sustain her; for pet names are a guard
* against loss, like primitive music. But does that sum her up? Is
* even the end of us an account? No, don't answer, I know that
even the memory has weight. Once in the war I saw a dead horse
that had been lying long against the ground. Time and the

birds, and its own last concentration had removed the body a great way from the head. As I looked upon that head, my memory weighed for the lost body; and because of that missing quantity even heavier hung that head along the ground. So love, when it has gone, taking time with it, leaves a memory of its weight."

She said: "She is myself. What am I to do?"   *

"Make birds' nests with your teeth, that would be better," he   * said angrily, "like my English girl friend. The birds liked them so well that they stopped making their own (does that sound like any nest you have made for any bird, and so broken it of its fate?). In the spring they form a queue by her bedroom window and stand waiting their turn, holding on to their eggs as hard as   * they can until she gets around to them, strutting up and down on the ledge, the eyes in their feathers a quick shine and sting, whipped with impatience, like a man waiting at a toilet door for   * someone inside who had decided to read the *Decline and Fall of*   o *the Roman Empire.* And then think of Robin who never could provide for her life except in you. Oh well," he said under his breath, " 'happy are they whom privacy makes innocent.' "   * o

Nora turned around, and speaking in a voice that she tried to make steady said: "Once, when she was sleeping, I wanted her to die. Now, that would stop nothing."   *

The doctor nodding, straightened his tie with two fingers. "The number of our days is not check-rein enough to look upon   * the death of our love. While living we knew her too well, and never understood, for then our next gesture permitted our next misunderstanding. But death is intimacy walking backward. We are crazed with grief when she, who once permitted us, leaves to us the only recollection. We shed tears of bankruptcy then.   * So it's well she didn't." He sighed. "You are still in trouble—I   * thought you had put yourself outside of it. I might have known better, nothing is what everybody wants, the world runs on that law. Personally, if I could, I would instigate Meat-Axe Day, and out of the goodness of my heart I would whack your head off along with a couple of others. Every man should be allowed one   * day and a hatchet just to ease his heart."

She said: "What will happen now, to me and to her?"

"Nothing," the doctor answered, "as always. We all go down in battle, but we all come home."

She said: "I can only find her again in my sleep or in her death; in both she has forgotten me."

"Listen," the doctor said, putting down his glass. "My war brought me many things; let yours bring you as much. Life is not to be told, call it as loud as you like, it will not tell itself. No one will be much or little except in someone else's mind, so be careful of the minds you get into, and remember Lady Macbeth, who had her mind in her hand. We can't all be as safe as that."

Nora got up nervously and began walking. "I'm so miserable, Matthew, I don't know how to talk, and I've got to. I've got to talk to somebody. I can't live this way." She pressed her hands together, and without looking at the doctor, went on walking.

"Have you any more port?" he inquired, putting the empty bottle down. Mechanically Nora brought him a second decanter. He took the stopper out, held it to his nose a moment, then poured himself a glass.

"You are," he said, testing the wine between his lower lip and teeth, "experiencing the inbreeding of pain. Most of us do not dare it. We wed a stranger, and so 'solve' our problem. But when you inbreed with suffering (which is merely to say that you have caught every disease and so pardoned your flesh), you are destroyed back to your structure, as an old master disappears beneath the knife of the scientist who would know how it was painted. Death I imagine will be pardoned by the same identification; we all carry about with us the house of death—the skeleton, but unlike the turtle, our safety is inside, our danger out. Time is a great conference planning our end, and youth is only the past putting a leg forward. Ah, to be able to hold on to suffering, but to let the spirit loose! And speaking of being destroyed, allow me to illustrate by telling you of one dark night in London, when I was hurrying along, my hands before me, praying I'd get home and into bed and wake up in the morning without finding my hands on my hips. So I started

for London Bridge – all this was a long time ago, and I'd better
be careful or one of these days I'll tell a story that will give up
my age.

"Well, I went off down under London Bridge and what   †
should I see? A Tuppeny Upright! And do you know what a
Tuppeny Upright might be? A Tuppeny is an old time girl, and   *
London Bridge is her last stand, as the last stand for a *grue* is   º
Marseilles, if she doesn't happen to have enough pocket money
to get to Singapore. For tuppence, an upright is all anyone can
expect. They used to walk along slowly, all ruffles and rags, with
big terror hats on them, a pin stuck over the eye and slap up
through the crown, half their shadows on the ground and the
other half crawling along the wall beside them; ladies of the
haute sewer taking their last stroll, sauntering on their last   † º
Rotten Row, going slowly along in the dark, holding up their
badgered flounces, or standing still, letting you do it, silent and   †
as indifferent as the dead, as if they were thinking of better days,
or waiting for something that they had been promised when
they were little girls; their poor damned dresses hiked up in   †
front and falling away over the rump, all gathers and braid, like   *
a Crusader's mount, with all the trappings gone sideways with
misery."

While the doctor had been speaking Nora had stopped, as if
he had got her attention for the first time.

"And once Father Lucas said to me, 'Be simple, Matthew, life   º
is a simple book, and an open book, read and be simple as the
beasts in the field; just being miserable isn't enough – you have
got to know how.' So I got to thinking and I said to myself,
'This is a terrible thing that Father Lucas has put on me – be
simple like the beasts and yet think and harm nobody.' I began
walking then. It had begun to snow and the night was down.
I went toward the *Ile*, because I could see the lights in the
show-windows of Our Lady and all the children in the dark
with the tapers twinkling, saying their prayers softly with that
small breath that comes off little lungs, whispering fatally
about nothing, which is the way children say their prayers.
Then I said, 'Matthew, tonight you must find a small church

where there are no people, where you can be alone like an
animal, and yet think.' So I turned off and went down until I
came to *St. Merri* and I went forward and there I was. All the
candles were burning steadily for the troubles that people had
entrusted to them and I was almost alone, only in a far corner
an old peasant woman saying her beads.

"So I walked straight up to the box for the souls in Purgatory,
just to show that I was a true sinner, in case there happened to
be a Protestant about. I was trying to think which of my hands
was the more blessed, because there's a box in the *Raspail* that
says the hand you give with to the Little Sisters of the Poor, that
will be blessed all day. I gave it up, hoping it was my right hand.
Kneeling in a dark corner, bending my head over and down, I
took out Tiny O'Toole, because it was his turn, I had tried
everything else. There was nothing for it this time but to make
him face the mystery so it could see him clear as it saw me. So
then I whispered, 'What is this thing, Lord?' And I began to
cry; the tears went like rain goes down on the world, without
touching the face of Heaven. Suddenly I realized that it was the
first time in my life my tears were strange to me, because they
just went straight forward out of my eyes; I was crying because I
had to embarrass Tiny like that for the good it might do him.

"I was crying and striking my left hand against the *prie-Dieu*,
and all the while Tiny O'Toole was lying in a swoon. I said, 'I
have tried to seek, and I only find.' I said, 'It is I, my Lord, who
know there's beauty in any permanent mistake like me. Haven't
I said it so? But,' I says, 'I'm not able to stay permanent unless
you help me, oh Book of Concealment! *C'est le plaisir qui me
bouleverse!* The roaring lion goes forth, seeking his own fury! So
tell me, what is permanent of me, me or him?' And there I was
in the empty, almost empty church, all the people's troubles
flickering in little lights all over the place. And I said, 'This
would be a fine world, Lord, if you could get everybody out
of it.' And there I was holding Tiny, bending over and crying,
asking the question until I forgot, and went on crying, and I put
Tiny away then, like a ruined bird, and went out of the place
and walked looking at the stars that were twinkling and I said,

'Have I been simple like an animal, God, or have I been think-   *
ing?'"

She smiled. "Sometimes I don't know why I talk to you.
You're so like a child; then again I know well enough."   *

"Speaking of children—and thanks for the compliment,—   † *
take for instance the case of Don Anticolo, the young tenor
from Beirut—he dipped down into his pelvis for his Wagner,
and plunged to his breast pit for his Verdi—he'd sung himself
once and a half round the world, a widower with a small son,
scarcely ten by the clock when presto—the boy was bitten by a
rat while swimming in Venezia and this brought on a fever. His   ○ *
father would come in and take hold of him every ten minutes (or
was it every half hour?) to see if he was less hot, or hotter. His
daddy was demented with grief and fear, but did he leave his
bedside for a moment? He did, because, though the son was
sick, the fleet was in. But being a father, he prayed as he drank
the champagne; and he wished his son alive as he chucked over
the compass and invited the crew home, bow and sprit. But
when he got home the little son lay dead. The young tenor
burst into tears and burned him and had the ashes put into a
zinc box no bigger than a doll's crate and held ceremony over
him, twelve sailors all in blue standing about the deal table, a
glass in their hands, sorrow in their sea-turned eyes slanting   † *
under lids thinned by the horizon, as the distracted father and
singer tossed the little zinc box down upon the table crying:
'This, gentlemen, is my babe, this, lads, my son, my sailors, my
boy!' and at that, running to the box and catching it up and
dashing it down again, repeating, and weeping, 'My son, my
baby, my boy!' with trembling fingers nudging the box now
here now there about the table until it went up and down its
length a dozen times; the father behind it, following it, touching it, weeping and crying like a dog who noses a bird that has,   *
for some strange reason, no more movement."

She said: "She was beautiful, wasn't she?"   †

The doctor stood up, then sat down again. 'Yes, oh God,   *
Robin was beautiful. I didn't like her, but I have to admit that   † *
much: sort of fluid blue under her skin, as if the hide of time

had been stripped from her, and with it, all transactions with knowledge. A sort of first position in attention; a face that will age only under the blows of perpetual childhood. The temples like those of young beasts cutting horns, as if they were sleeping eyes. And that look on a face we follow like a witch-fire. Sorcerers know the power of horns; meet a horn where you like and you know you have been identified. You could fall over a thousand human skulls without the same trepidation. And do old duchesses know it also! Have you ever seen them go into a large assembly of any sort, be it opera or bezique, without feathers, flowers, sprigs of oat, or some other gadget nodding above their temples!"

She had not heard him. "Every hour is my last, and," she said desperately, "one can't live one's last hour all one's life!"

He brought his hands together. "Even the contemplative life is only an effort, Nora my dear, to hide the body so the feet won't stick out. Ah," he added, "to be an animal, born at the opening of the eye, going only forward, and at the end of day, shutting out memory with the dropping of the lid."

"Time isn't long enough," she said, striking the table. "It isn't long enough to live down her nights. God," she cried, "what is love? Man seeking his own head? The human head, so rented by misery that even the teeth weigh! She couldn't tell me the truth, because she had never planned it; her life was a continual accident, and how can you be prepared for that? Everything we can't bear in this world, some day we find in one person, and love it all at once. A strong sense of identity gives man an idea he can do no wrong; too little accomplishes the same. Some natures cannot appreciate, only regret. Will Robin *only* regret?" She stopped abruptly, gripping the back of the chair. "Perhaps not," she said, "for even her memory wearied her." Then she said with the violence of misery, "there's something evil in me, that loves evil and degradation— purity's black backside! That loves honesty with a horrid love; or why have I always gone seeking it at the liar's door?"

"Look here," said the doctor. "Do you know what has made me the greatest liar this side of the moon? Telling my stories

to people like you, to take the mortal agony out of their guts, and to stop them from rolling about, and drawing up their feet, and screaming, with their eyes staring over their knuckles with misery which they are trying to keep off, saying, 'Say some-   *
thing, doctor, for the love of God!' And me talking away like   *
mad. Well that, and nothing else, has made me the liar I am.

"Suppose your heart were five feet across in any place, would   *
you break it for a heart no bigger than a mouse's mute? Would you hurl yourself into any body of water, in the size you now are, for any woman that you had to look for with a magnifying glass, or any boy if he was as high as the Eiffel Tower or did droppings like a fly? No, we all love in sizes, yet we all cry out   *
in tiny voices to the great booming God, the older we get.   *
Growing old is just a matter of throwing life away back; so you   *
finally forgive even those that you have not begun to forget. It is that indifference which gives you your courage, which to tell the truth is no courage at all. There is no truth, and you have set it between you; you have been unwise enough to make a   *
formula; you have dressed the unknowable in the garments of   *
the known."

"Man," she said, her eyelids quivering, "conditioning himself   *
to fear, made God; as the prehistoric, conditioning itself to hope, made man, – the cooling of the earth, the receding of the sea. And I, who want power, chose a girl who resembles a boy."   † *

"Exactly," said the doctor. "You never loved anyone before,   *
and you'll never love anyone again, as you love Robin. Very well—what is this love we have for the invert, boy or girl? It   † *
was they who were spoken of in every romance that we ever read. The girl lost, what is she but the Prince found? The Prince on the white horse that we have always been seeking. And the pretty lad who is a girl, what but the prince-princess in point lace – neither one and half the other, the painting on   ° *
the fan! We love them for that reason. We were impaled in our childhood upon them as they rode through our primers, the sweetest lie of all, now come to be in boy or girl, for in the girl it is the prince, and in the boy it is the girl that makes a prince a prince – and not a man. They go far back in our lost distance

where what we never had stands waiting; it was inevitable that we should come upon them, for our miscalculated longing has created them. They are our answer to what our grandmothers were told love was, and what it never came to be; they, the living lie of our centuries. When a long lie comes up, sometimes it is a beauty; when it drops into dissolution, into drugs and drink, into disease and death, it has at once a singular and terrible attraction. A man can resent and avoid evil on his own plane, but when it is the thin blown edge of his reverie, he takes it to his heart, as one takes to one's heart the dark misery of the close nightmare, born and slain of the particular mind; so that if one of them were dying of the pox one would will to die of it too, with two feelings, terror and joy, wedded somewhere back again into a formless sea where a swan (would it be ourselves, or her or him, or a mystery of all) sinks crying."

"Love is death, come upon with passion; I know, that is why love is wisdom. I love her as one condemned to it."

"Oh Widow Lazarus! Arisen from your dead! Oh lunatic humour of the moon! Behold this fearful tree, on which sits singing the drearful bird – *Turdas Musicus*, or European singing thrush; sitting and singing the refrain – all in the tear-wet night – and it starts out *largo*, but it ends like *I Hear You Calling Me*, or *Kiss Me Again*, gone wild. And Diane, where is she? Diane of Ephesus in the Greek Gardens, singing and shaken in every bosom; and Rack and Ruin, the dogs of the Vatican, running up and down the papal esplanade and out into the Ramblar with roses in their tails to keep off care. Don't I know it all! Do you think that I, the Old Woman who lives in the closet, do not know that every child, no matter what its day, is born prehistorically and that even the wrong thought has caused the human mind incredible effort? Bend down the tree of knowledge and you'll unroost a strange bird. Suffering may be composed wickedly and of an inferior writhing. Rage and inaccuracy howl and blow the bone, for, contrary to all opinion, all suffering does *not* purify – begging everybody's pardon, which is called everybody's know. It moils and blathers some to perjury; the peritoneum boils and brings on common and

cheap praying a great way sunk in pointless agony."   *
    "Jenny," she said.   †
    "It rots her sleep – Jenny is one of those who nip like a bird   *
and void like an ox – the poor and lightly damned! That can be   o
a torture also. None of us suffer as much as we should, or love   † *
as much as we say. Love is the first lie; wisdom the last. Don't I   *
know that the only way to know evil is through truth? The evil
and the good know themselves only by giving up their secret   *
face to face. The true good who meets the true evil (Holy
Mother of Mercy, are there any such!) learns for the first time   † *
how to accept neither; the face of the one tells the face of the
other the half of the story that both forgot.

    "To be utterly innocent," he went on, "would be to be utterly   *
unknown, particularly to oneself."   *

    "Sometimes Robin seemed to return to me," Nora said,
unheeding, "for sleep and safety, but," she added bitterly, "she   †
always went out again."

    The doctor lit a cigarette; lifting his chin he blew the smoke   *
high. "To treat her lovers to the great passionate indifference.
Say," he exclaimed, bringing his chin down. "Dawn, of course,
dawn! That's when she came back frightened. At that hour the   *
citizen of the night balances on a thread that is running thin."

    "Only the impossible lasts forever; with time, it is made   *
accessible. Robin's love and mine was always impossible, and
loving each other, we no longer love. Yet we love each other   *
like death."

    "Um," murmured the doctor, "beat life like a dinner bell, yet   *
there is one hour that won't ring—the hour of disentanglement.
Oh well," he sighed, "every man dies finally of that poison   *
known as the-heart-in-the-mouth. Yours is in your hand. Put
it back. The eater of it will get a taste for you; in the end his
muzzle will be heard barking among your ribs. I'm no excep-   *
tion, God knows, I'm the last of my line, the fine hairline of
least resistance. It's a gruesome thing that man learns only by
what he has between the one leg and the other! Oh that short
dangle! We corrupt mortality by its industry. You never know
which one of your ends it is that is going to be the part you

can't take your mind off."

"If only you could take my mind off, Matthew—now, in this house that I took that Robin's mind and mine might go together. Surprising isn't it, I'm happier when I'm alone now, without her, because when she was here with me, in this house, I had to watch her wanting to go and yet to stay. How much of our life do we put into a life that we may be damned? Then she was back stumbling through the house again, listening for a footstep in the court, for a way to leave and not to go, trying to absorb, with the intensity of her ear, any sound that would have made me suspicious, yet hoping I would break my heart in safety; she needed that assurance. Matthew, was it a sin that I believed her?"

"Of course, it made her life wrong."

"But when I didn't believe her any more, after the night I came to see you; that I have to think of all the time, I don't dare to stop, for fear of the moment it will come back again."

"Remorse," said the doctor, "sitting heavy, like the arse of a bull—you had the conceit of 'honesty' to keep that arse from cracking your heart; but what did she have? Only your faith in her – then you took that faith away! You should have kept it always, seeing that it was a myth; no myth is safely broken. Ah, the weakness of the strong! The trouble with you is, you are not just a myth-maker, you are also a destroyer, you made a beautiful fable, then put Voltaire to bed with it; ah, the *Dead March* in 'Saul'!"

Nora said, as if she had not been interrupted – "Because after that night, I went to see Jenny. I remember the stairs. They were of brown wood, and the hall was ugly and dark, and her apartment depressing. No one would have known that she had money. The walls had mustard-colored paper on them as far as the salon, and something hideous in red and green and black in the hall, and away at the end, a bedroom facing the hall door, with a double bed. Sitting up against the pillow was a doll. Robin had given me a doll. I knew then, before I asked, that this was the right house, before I said, 'You are Robin's mistress, aren't you?' That poor shuddering creature had pelvic bones

I could see flying through her dress; I wanted to lean forward   *
and laugh with terror. She was sitting there doubled up with
surprise, her raven's bill coming up saying, 'Yes.' Then I looked   *
up and there on the wall was the photograph of Robin when
she was a baby (the one that she had told me was lost).   *

"She went to pieces; she fell forward on my lap. At her next
words I saw that I was not a danger to her, but someone who   *
might understand her torture. In great agitation she said, 'I
went out this afternoon, I didn't think she would call me,
because you had been away to the country, Robin said, and   *
would be back this evening and so she would have to stay home
with you, because you had been so good to her always; though   *
God knows I understand there is nothing between you any
longer, that you are "just good friends"; she has explained that,   *
still I nearly went mad when I found that she had been here
and I was out. She has told me often enough, "Don't leave the
house, because I don't know exactly when I am going to be able
to get away, because I can't hurt Nora." ' " Nora's voice broke.   *
She went on.

"Then Jenny said, 'What are you going to do? What do you   *
want me to do?' I knew all the time that she could do nothing
but what she wanted to do, and that whatever it was, she was   *
a liar, no matter what truth she was telling. I was dead. I felt
stronger then, and I said, yes I would have a drink. She poured
out two, knocking the bottle against the glass and spilling the
liquor on the dark ugly carpet. I kept thinking, what else is it
that is hurting me, then I knew, – the doll; the doll in there on   † *
the bed." Nora sat down, facing the doctor. "We give death to
a child when we give it a doll—it's the effigy and the shroud;   *
when a woman gives it to a woman, it is the life they cannot
have, it is their child, sacred and profane; so when I saw that   *
other doll—." Nora could not go on. She began to cry. "What
part of monstrosity am I that I am always crying at its side!   *

"When I got home Robin had been waiting, knowing, because I was late, that something was wrong. I said, 'It is over—I
can't go on. You have always lied to me, and you have denied
me to her. I can't stand it anymore.'   * †

"She stood up then, and went into the hall. She jerked her coat off the hook and I said, 'Have you nothing to say to me?' She turned her face to me. It was like something once beautiful found in a river—and flung herself out of the door."

"And you were crying," the doctor said nodding. "You went about the house like someone sunken under lightness. You were ruined and you kept striking your hands together, laughing crazily and singing a little and putting your hands over your face. Stage tricks have been taken from life, so finding yourself employing them you were confused with a sense of shame. When you went out looking for someone to go mad with, they said, 'For God's sake look at Nora!' For the demolishing of a great ruin is always a fine and terrifying spectacle. Why is it that you want to talk to me? Because I'm the other woman that God forgot."

"There's nothing to go by, Matthew," she said. "You do not know which way to go. A man is another person—a woman is yourself, caught as you turn in panic; on her mouth you kiss your own. If she is taken you cry that you have been robbed of yourself. God laughs at me; but his laughter is my love."

"You have died and arisen for love," said Matthew. "But unlike the ass returning from the market, you are always carrying the same load. Oh for God's sweet sake, didn't she ever disgust you! Weren't you sometimes pleased that you had the night to yourself, wishing, when she did come home, that it was never?"

"Never, and always; I was frightened she would be gentle again. That," she said, "that's an awful fear. Fear of the moment when she would turn her words, making them something between us that nobody else could possibly share—and she would say, 'You have got to stay with me or I can't live.' Yet one night she ran behind me in the Montparnasse quarter, where I had gone looking for her because someone had called me saying she was sick and couldn't get home (I had stopped going out with her because I couldn't bear to see the 'evidence of my eyes'), running behind me for blocks saying, with a furious panting breath, 'You are a devil! You make everything dirty!' (I had tried to take someone's hands off her. They always put hands on her when she was drunk.) 'You make me feel dirty and tired and old!'

"I turned against the wall. The policemen and the people in   *
the street collected. I was cold and terribly ashamed. I said, 'Do you mean that?' And she said she meant it. She put her head down on one of the officers' shoulders. She was drunk.   *
He had her by the wrist, one hand on her behind. She did not say anything about that because she did not notice and kept spitting horrible things at me. Then I walked away very fast.   *
My head seemed to be in a large place. She began running after me. I kept on walking. I was cold, and I was not miserable any more. She caught me by the shoulder and went against me, grinning. She stumbled and I held her, and she said, seeing a poor wretched beggar of a whore, 'Give her some money, all of it!' She threw the francs into the street and bent down over the filthy baggage and began stroking her hair, gray with the dust of years, saying, 'They are all Godforsaken, and you most   *
of all, because they don't want you to have your happiness. They don't want you to drink. Well, here, drink! I give you   *
money and permission! These women – they are all like her,' she said with fury. 'They are all good – they want to save us!' She sat down beside her.

"It took me and the *garçon* half an hour to get her up and   *
into the lobby, and when I got her that far she began fighting, so that suddenly, without thinking, but out of weariness and misery, I struck her; and at that she started, and smiled, and   *
went up the stairs with me without complaint. She sat up in bed   *
and ate eggs and called me, 'Angel! Angel!' and ate my eggs too, and turned over and went to sleep. Then I kissed her, holding her cold hands and feet and I said: 'Die now, so you will be   †
quiet, so you will not be touched again by dirty hands; so you will not take my heart and your body and let them be nosed by dogs – die now, then you will be mine forever.' (What right has anyone to that?)" She stopped. "She was mine only when she   *
was drunk, Matthew, and had passed out. That's the terrible   *
thing, that finally she was mine only when she was dead drunk. All the time I didn't believe her life was as it was and yet, the

*   fact that I didn't, proves something is wrong with me. I saw her always like a tall child who had grown up the length of the infant's gown, walking and needing help and safety; because she was in her own nightmare. I tried to come between and save
*   her, but I was like a shadow in her dream that could never reach her in time, as the cry of the sleeper has no echo, myself echo struggling to answer; she was like a new shadow walking perilously close to the outer curtain, and I was going mad because I was awake and seeing it, unable to reach it, unable to strike people down from it; and it moving, almost unwalking, with the face saintly and idiotic.

*   "And then that day I'll remember all my life, when I said:
*   'It is over now,' she was asleep and I struck her awake. I saw
†   her come awake and turn befouled before me, she who had
†   managed in that sleep to keep whole. Matthew, for God's sake say something, you are awful enough to say it, say something! I didn't know, I didn't know that it was to be me who was to do the terrible thing! No rot had touched her until then, and there before my eyes I saw her corrupt all at once and withering, because I had struck her sleep away, and I went mad and I've been mad ever since; and there's nothing to do; nothing! You must say something, oh God, say something!"

*   "Stop it! Stop it!" he cried. "Stop screaming! Put your hands
*   down! Stop it! You were a 'good woman,' and so a bitch on a
*   high plane, the only one able to kill yourself and Robin! Robin was outside the 'human type' – a wild thing caught in a woman's skin, monstrously alone, monstrously vain; like the paralysed man in Coney Island—(take away a man's conformity and you take away his remedy)—who had to lie on his back in a box, but the box was lined with velvet, his fingers jewelled with stones, and suspended over him where he could never take his eyes off, a sky-blue mounted mirror, for he wanted to enjoy his own
*   'difference.' Robin is not in your life, you are in her dream,
*   you'll never get out of it. And why does Robin feel innocent?
*   Every bed she leaves, without caring, fills her heart with peace and happiness. She has made her 'escape' again. It's why she can't 'put herself in another's place,' she herself is the only

'position'; so she resents it when you reproach her with what she had done. She knows she is innocent because she can't do anything in relation to anyone but herself. You almost caught hold of her, but she put you cleverly away by making you the Madonna. What was your patience and terror worth all these years if you couldn't keep them for her sake? Did you have to learn wisdom on her knees?

"Oh for God's sweet sake, couldn't you stand not learning   *
your lesson? Because the lesson we learn is always by giving death and a sword to our lover. You are full to the brim with pride, but I am an empty pot going forward, saying my prayers   *
in a dark place; because I know no one loves, I least of all, and that no one loves me, and that's what makes most people so passionate and bright, because they want to love and be loved, when there is only a bit of lying in the ear to make the ear forget what time is compiling. So I, Dr. O'Connor, say, creep by, softly, softly, and don't learn anything, because it's always learned of another person's body; take action in your heart and be careful whom you love – for a lover who dies, no matter how forgotten, will take somewhat of you to the grave. Be humble   *
like the dust, as God intended, and crawl, and finally you'll crawl to the end of the gutter and not be missed and not much remembered.   † *

"Sometimes," Nora said, "she would sit at home all day, looking out of the window, playing with her toys, trains, and   † *
animals and cars to wind up, and dolls and marbles and soldiers. But all the time she was watching me, to see that no one called, that the bell did not ring, that I got no mail, nor anyone hallooing in the court, though she knew that none of these things could happen. My life was hers.   *

"Sometimes, if she got tight by evening, I would find her standing in the middle of the room, in boy's clothes, rocking   † *
from foot to foot, holding the doll she had given us—'our child'—high above her head, as if she would cast it down, a look of fury on her face. And one time, about three in the morning   *
when she came in, she was angry because for once I had not been there all the time, waiting. She picked up the doll and

* hurled it to the floor and put her foot on it, crushing her heel
* into it; and then, as I came crying behind her, she kicked it, its
china head all in dust, its skirt shivering and stiff, whirling over
* † and over across the floor."
*   The doctor brought his palms together. "If you, who are
o bloodthirsty with love, had left her alone, what? Would a lost
* girl in Dante's time have been a lost girl still, and he had turned
his eyes on her? She would have been remembered, and the
remembered put on the dress of immunity. Do you think that
Robin had no right to fight you with her only weapon? She saw
* in you that fearful eye that would make her a target forever.
* Have not girls done as much for the doll? The doll—yes,
target of things past and to come. The last doll, given to age, is
the girl who should have been a boy, and the boy who should
have been a girl! The love of that last doll was foreshadowed
in that love of the first. The doll and the immature have something right about them, the doll because it resembles but does
not contain life, and the third sex because it contains life but
* † resembles the doll. The blessed face! It should be seen only in
profile, otherwise it is observed to be the conjunction of the
identical cleaved halves of sexless misgiving! Their kingdom
is without precedent. Why do you think I have spent near fifty
years weeping over bars but because I am one of them! The
uninhabited angel! That is what you have always been hunting!"
      "Perhaps, Matthew, there are devils? Who knows if there are
devils? Perhaps they have set foot in the uninhabited. Was I her
devil trying to bring her comfort? I enter my dead and bring no
comfort, not even in my dreams. There in my sleep was my
* grandmother, whom I loved more than anyone, tangled in the
* grave grass, and flowers blowing about and between her; lying
there in the grave, in the forest, in a coffin of glass, and flying
* low, my father who is still living, low going and into the grave
beside her, his head thrown back and his curls lying out, struggling with her death terribly, and me, stepping about its edges,
walking and wailing without a sound; round and round, seeing
them struggling with that death as if they were struggling with
the sea and my life; I was weeping and unable to do anything or

take myself out of it. There they were, in the grave glass, and the grave water and the grave flowers and the grave time, one living and one dead and one asleep. It went on forever, though it had stopped, my father stopped beating and just lay there floating beside her, immovable, yet drifting in a tight place. And I woke up and still it was going on; it went down into the dark earth of my waking as if I were burying them with the earth of my lost sleep. This I have done to my father's mother, dreaming through my father, and have tormented them with my tears and with my dreams. For all of us die over again in somebody's sleep.—And this I have done to Robin; it is only through me that she will die over and over, and it is only through me, of all my family, that my grandmother dies, over and over. I woke and got up out of bed and putting my hands between my knees I said, 'What was that dream saying, for God's sake, what was that dream?' For it was for me also."

Suddenly Dr. Matthew O'Connor said: "It's my mother without argument I want!" And then, in his loudest voice he roared: "Mother of God! I wanted to be your son – the unknown beloved second would have done!"

"Oh Matthew. I don't know how to go. I don't know which way to turn! Tell her, if you ever see her, that it is always with her in my arms – forever it will be that way until we die. Tell her to do what she must, but not to forget."

"Tell her yourself," said the doctor, "or sit in your own trouble silently, if you like; it's the same with ermines – those fine yellow ermines that women pay such a great price for – how did they get that valuable color? By sitting in bed all their lives and pissing the sheets, or weeping in their own way. It's the same with persons; they are only of value when they have laid themselves open to 'nuisance' – their own, and the world's. Ritual itself constitutes an instruction. So we come back to the place from which I set out; pray to the good God, she will keep you. Personally I call her 'she' because of the way she made me; it somehow balances the mistake." He got up and crossed to the window. "That priceless galaxy of misinformation called the mind, harnessed to that stupendous and threadbare glomerate

compulsion called the soul, ambling down the almost obliterated bridle path of Well and Ill, fortuitously planned, – is the
holy Habeas Corpus, the manner in which the body is brought
before the judge – still – in the end Robin will wish you in a
nunnery where what she loved is, by surroundings, made safe,
because as you are you keep 'bringing her up,' as cannons bring
up the dead from deep water."

"In the end," Nora said, "they came to me, the girls Robin
had driven frantic – to me, for comfort!" She began to laugh.
"My God," she said, "the women I've held upon my knees!"

"Women," the doctor said, "were born on the knees; it's why
I've never been able to do anything about them; I'm on my own
so much of the time."

"Suddenly I knew what all my life had been, Matthew, what I
hoped Robin was, – the secure torment. We can hope for nothing greater, except hope. If I asked her, crying, not to go out,
she would go just the same, richer in her heart because I had
touched it, as she was going down the stairs."

"Lions grow their manes and foxes their teeth on that bread,"
interpolated the doctor.

"In the beginning, when I tried to stop her from drinking and
staying out all night, and from being defiled, she would say—
'Ah I feel so pure and gay!' as if the ceasing of that abuse was her
only happiness and peace of mind; and so I struggled with her as
with the coils of my own most obvious heart, holding her by the
hair, striking her against my knees, as some people in trouble
strike their hands too softly; and as if it were a game, she raised
and dropped her head against my lap, as a child bounces in a
crib to enter excitement, even if it were someone gutted on a
dagger. I thought I loved her for her sake, and I found it was for
my own."

"I know," said the doctor, "there you were sitting up high and
fine, with a rosebush up your arse."

She looked at him, then she smiled. "How should you
know?"

"I'm a lady in no need of insults," said the doctor. "I know."

"Yes," she said. "You know what none of us know until we

have died. You were dead in the beginning."

The twilight was falling. About the street lamps there was a heavy mist. "Why don't you rest now?" asked the doctor. "Your body is coming to it, you are forty and the body has a politic too, and a life of its own that you like to think is yours. I heard a spirit mew once, but I knew it was a mystery eternally moving outward and on, and not my own."

"I know," she said, "*now.*" Suddenly she began to cry, holding her hands. "Matthew," she said, "have you ever loved someone and it became yourself?"

For a moment he did not answer. Taking up the decanter, he held it to the light.

"Robin can go anywhere, do anything," Nora continued, "because she forgets, and I nowhere, because I remember." She came toward him. "Matthew," she said, "you think I have always been like this. Once I was remorseless, but this is another love—it goes everywhere, there is no place for it to stop—it rots me away. How could she tell me when she had nothing to tell that wasn't evidence against herself?"

The doctor said, "You know as well as I do that we were born twelve, and brought up thirteen, and that some of us lived. My brother, whom I had not seen in four years, and loved the most of all, died, and who was it but me my mother wanted to talk to? Not those who had seen him last, but me who had seen him best, as if my memory of him were himself; and because you forget Robin the best, it's to you she turns. She comes trembling, and defiant, and belligerent, all right—that you may give her back to herself again as you have forgotten her – you are the only one strong enough to have listened to the prosecution, your life; and to have built back the amazing defense, your heart!

"The scalpel and the Scriptures have taught me that little I did not already know. And I was doing well enough," he snapped, "until you kicked my stone over, and out I came, all moss and eyes; and here I sit, as naked as only those things can be whose houses have been torn away from them to make a holiday, and it my only skin, – laboring to comfort you. Am I

* supposed to render up my paradise – that splendid acclimation – for the comfort of weeping women and howling boys? Look at Felix now, what kind of a Jew is that? Screaming up against

† * tradition like a bat against a window-pane, high-up over the

o town, his child a boy weeping 'o'er graves of hope and pleasure gone.'

"Ah yes—I love my neighbour. Like a rotten apple to a rotten

* apple's breast affixed we go down together, nor is there a hesitation in that decay, for when I sense such, there I apply the breast

* the firmer, that he may rot as quickly as I, in which he stands in

o dire need or I miscalculate the cry. I, who am done sooner than

o any fruit! The heat of his suppuration has mingled his core with mine, and wrought my own to the zenith before its time. The encumbrance of myself I threw away long ago, that breast to breast I might go with my failing friends. And do they love me

† for it? They do not. They reach for any pretty boy in any daisy field before they reach for me. So have I divorced myself, not

* only because I was born as ugly as God dared premeditate, but because with propinquity and knowledge of trouble I have damaged my own value. And death—have you thought of death? What risk do you take? Do you know which dies first,

* you or she? And which is the sorrier part, head or feet? I say, with that good Sir Don, the feet. Any man can look upon the head in death, but no man can look upon the feet. They are

* most awfully tipped up from the earth. I've thought of that also. Do you think, for Christ's sweet sake," he shouted suddenly, "that I am so happy that you should cry down my neck? Do you think there is no lament in this world, but your own? Is there not a forbearing saint somewhere? Is there no bread that does not come proffered with bitter butter? I, as good a Catholic as

* they make, have embraced every confection of hope, and yet I know well, for all our outcry and struggle, we shall be for the next generation not the massive dung fallen from the dinosaur, but the little speck left of a humming-bird; so as well sing our

o *Chi vuol la Zingarella* (how women love it!) while I warble my

o * *Sonate au Crépuscule*, throwing in *der Erlkönig* for good measure,

o not to mention *Who Is Sylvia?* Who is anybody!

"Oh," he cried. "A broken heart have you! I have falling arches, flying dandruff, a floating kidney, shattered nerves *and* a broken heart! But do I scream that an eagle has me by the balls or has dropped his oyster on my head? Am I going forward screaming that it hurts that my mind goes back, or holding my guts as if they were a coil of knives? Yet you are screaming, and drawing your lip and putting your hand out and turning round and round! Do I wail to the mountains of the trouble I have had in the valley, or to every stone of the way it broke my bones, or of every lie how it went down into my belly and built a nest to hatch me to my death there? Isn't everyone in the world peculiarly swung and me the craziest of the lot? – so that I come dragging and squealing, like a heifer on the way to slaughter, knowing his cries have only half a rod to go, protesting his death – as his death has only a rod to go to protest his screaming? Do you walk high Heaven without shoes? Are you the only person with a bare foot pressed down on a rake? Oh, you poor blind cow! Keep out of my feathers; you ruffle me the wrong way and flit about, stirring my misery! What end is sweet? Are the ends of the hair sweet when you come to number them?"

"Listen," Nora said. "You've got to listen! She would come back to me after a night all over the city and lie down beside me and she would say, 'I want to make everyone happy,' and her mouth was drawn down. 'I want everyone to be gay, gay. Only you,' she said, holding me, 'only you, you mustn't be gay or happy, not like that, it's not for you, only for everyone else in the world.' She knew she was driving me insane with misery and fright; only," she went on, "she couldn't do anything because she was a long way off and waiting to begin. It's for that reason she hates everyone near her. It's why she falls into everything, like someone in a dream. It's why she wants to be loved and left alone, all at the same time. She would kill the world to get at herself if the world were in the way, and it *is* in the way. A shadow was falling on her—mine—and it was driving her out of her wits."

She began to walk again. "I have been loved," she said, "by something strange, and it has forgotten me." Her eyes were fixed and she seemed to be talking to herself. "It was *me* made

*   her hair stand on end, because I loved her. She turned bitter
because I made her fate colossal. She wanted darkness in her

* † mind – to throw a shadow over what she was powerless to alter,

† * – her dissolute life, her life at night; and I, I dashed it down.
We will never have it out now," Nora said. "It's too late. There
is no last reckoning for those who have loved too long, so for
me there is no end. Only I can't, I can't wait forever!" she said
frantically. "I can't live without my heart!

*   "In the beginning, after Robin went away with Jenny to

*   America, I searched for her in the ports. Not literally, in
another way. Suffering is the decay of the heart; all that we
have loved becomes the 'forbidden,' when we have not under-

*   stood it all, as the pauper is the rudiment of a city, knowing

*   something of the city, which the city, for its own destiny, wants
to forget. So the lover must go against nature to find love. I
sought Robin in Marseilles, in Tangier, in Naples, to understand her, to do away with my terror. I said to myself, I will

*   do what she has done, I will love what she has loved, then I will
find her again. At first it seemed that all I should have to do
would be to become 'debauched,' to find the girls that she had

*   loved; but I found that they were only little girls that she had
forgotten. I haunted the cafés where Robin had lived her night
life; I drank with the men, I danced with the women, but all
I knew was that others had slept with my lover and my child.

*   For Robin is incest too, that is one of her powers. In her, past
time records, and past time is relative to us all. Yet not being
the family she is more present than the family. A relative is
in the foreground only when it is born, when it suffers and
when it dies, unless it becomes one's lover, then it must be

*   everything, as Robin was; yet not as much as she, for she was

* † ° like a relative found in a lost generation. I thought, I will do
something that she will never be able to forgive, then we can
begin again as strangers. But the sailor got no further than the

° * hall. He said: '*Mon Dieu, il y a deux chevaux de bois dans la chambre
à coucher.*'"

"Christ!" muttered the doctor.

"So," Nora continued, "I left Paris. I went through the streets of Marseilles, the waterfront of Tangier, the *basso porto* of Naples. In the narrow streets of Naples ivies and flowers were growing over the broken-down walls. Under enormous staircases, rising open to the streets, beggars lay sleeping beside images of St. Gennaro; girls going into the churches to pray were calling out to boys in the squares. In open door-ways night lights were burning all day before gaudy prints of the Virgin. In one room that lay open to the alley, before a bed covered with a cheap heavy satin comforter, in the semi-darkness, a young girl sat on a chair, leaning over its back, one arm across it, the other hanging at her side, as if half of her slept; and half of her suffered. When she saw me she laughed, as children do, in embarrassment. Looking from her to the Madonna behind the candles, I knew that the image, to her, was what I had been to Robin, not a saint at all, but a fixed dismay, the space between the human and the holy head, the arena of the 'indecent' eternal. At that moment I stood in the centre of eroticism and death, death that makes the dead smaller, as a lover we are beginning to forget dwindles and wastes; for love and life are a bulk of which the body and heart can be drained, and I knew in that bed Robin should have put me down. In that bed we would have forgotten our lives in the extremity of memory, moulted our parts, as figures in the waxworks are moulted down to their story, so we would have broken down to our love."

The doctor staggered as he reached for his hat and coat. He stood in confused and unhappy silence—he moved toward the door. Holding the knob in his hand he turned toward her. Then he went out.

The doctor, walking with his coat collar up, entered the *Café de la Mairie du VI*. He stood at the bar and ordered a drink, looking at the people in the close, smoke-blue room, he said to himself, "Listen!" Nora troubled him, the life of Nora and the lives of the people in his life. "The way of a man in a fog!" he said. He hung his umbrella on the bar ledge. "To think is to be sick," he said to the barman. The barman nodded.

The people in the café waited for what the doctor would say, knowing that he was drunk and that he would talk; in great defaming sentences his betrayals came up; no one ever knew what was truth and what was not. "If you really want to know how hard a prizefighter hits," he said, looking around, "you have got to walk into the circle of his fury and be carried out by the heels, not by the count."

Someone laughed. The doctor turned slowly. "So safe as all that?" he asked sarcastically; "so damned safe? Well wait until you get in jail and find yourself slapping the bottoms of your feet for misery." He put his hand out for his drink— muttering to himself: "Matthew, you have never been in time with any man's life and you'll never be remembered at all, God save the vacancy! The finest instrument goes wrong in time— that's all, the instrument gets broken, and I must remember that when everyone is shitty and strange; it's the instrument gone flat. Lapidary, engrave that on my stone when Matthew is all over and lost in a field." He looked around. "It's the instrument, gentlemen, that has lost its G string, otherwise he'd be playing a fine tune; otherwise he'd still be passing his wind with the wind of the north – otherwise touching his billycock!

"Only the scorned and the ridiculous make good stories," he added angrily, seeing the *habitués* smiling, "so you can imagine when you'll get told! Life is only long enough for one trade; try that one!"

An unfrocked priest, a stout pale man with woman's hands, on which were many rings, a friend of the doctor's, called him and asked him to have a drink. The doctor came, carefully bringing his umbrella and hat. The priest said: "I've always wanted to know whether you were ever *really* married or not."

"Should I know that?" inquired the doctor. "I've *said* I was married and I gave the girl a name and had children by her, then presto! I killed her off as lightly as the death of swans. And was I reproached for that story? I was. Because even your friends regret weeping for a myth, as if that were not practically the fate of all the tears in the world! What if the girl *was* the wife of my brother and the children my brother's children? When I laid her down her limbs were as handsome and still as two May boughs from the cutting – did he do as much for her? I imagined about her in my heart as pure as a French print, a girl all of a little bosom and a bird cage, lying back down comfortable with the sea for a background and a rope of roses to hold her. Has any man's wife been treated better than that? Who says she might not have been mine, and the children mine also? Who for that matter," he said with violence, "says they are not mine? Is not a brother his brother also, the one blood cut up in lengths, one called Michael and the other Matthew? Except that people get befuddled seeing them walk in different directions. Who's to say that I'm not my brother's wife's husband and that his children were not fathered in my lap? Is it not to his honor that he strikes me as myself? And when she died, did my weeping make his weeping less?"

The ex-priest said, "Well, there's something in that, still I like to know what is what."

"You do, do you?" said the doctor. "Well then, that's why you are where you are now, right down in the mud without a feather to fly with, like the ducks in Golden Gate park, the largest park in captivity—everybody with their damnable kindness having fed them all the year round to their ruin because when it comes time for their going south they are all a bitter consternation, being too fat and heavy to rise off the water, and my God how they flop and struggle all over the park in autumn, crying and tearing their hair out because their nature is weighed down with bread and their migration stopped, by crumbs. You wring your hands to see it, and that's another illustration of love; in the end you are too heavy to move with the greediness in your stomach. And," said the doctor, "it would be the same with me if I'd let it, what with the wind at the one end and the cyclone at the other. You can lay a hundred bricks and not be called a brick-layer; but lay one boy and you are a bugger! Yet there are some that I have neglected for my spirit's sake— the old yeomen of the Guard and the beefeaters of the Tower because of their cold kidneys and gray hairs, and the kind of boy who only knows two existences—himself in a mirror—back and front." He was very drunk now. He looked about the café. He caught someone nudging someone. He looked up at the ex-priest and cursed. "What people! All queer in a terrible way. There were a couple of queer *good* people once in this world – but none of you," he said, addressing the room, "will ever know them. You think you are all studded with diamonds, don't you? Well, part the diamonds and you'll find slug's meat. My God," he said, turning around, "when I think!" He began to pound the table with his glass. "May they all be damned! The people in my life who have made my life miserable, coming to me to learn of degradation and the night. Nora beating her head against her heart, sprung over, her mind closing her life up like a heel on a fan, rotten to the bone for love of Robin. My God, how that woman can hold on to an idea! And that old sandpiper, Jenny! Oh it's a grand bad story, and who says I'm a betrayer? I say, tell the story of the world to the world!"

"A sad and a corrupt age," the ex-priest said.

Matthew O'Connor called for another drink. "What do they all come to me for? Why do they all tell me everything, then expect it to lie hushed in me, like a rabbit gone home to die? And that Baron Felix, hardly muttered a word in his life, and yet his silence breeds like scum on a pond; and that boy of his, Guido, by Robin, trying to see across the Danube with the tears in his eyes, Felix holding on to his hand and the boy holding on to the image of the Virgin on a darkening red ribbon, feeling its holy lift out of the metal and calling it mother; and me not even knowing which direction my end is coming from. So, when Felix said to me, 'Is the child infirm?' I said, 'Was the Mad King of Bavaria infirm?' I'm not one to cut the knot by drowning myself in any body of water, not even the print of a horse's hoof, no matter how it has been raining."

People had begun to whisper and the waiters moved closer watching. The ex-priest was smiling to himself but O'Connor did not seem to see or hear anything but his own heart. "Some people," he said, "take off head first into *any* body of water and

six glasses later someone in Harlem gets typhoid from drink-   †
ing their misery. God, take my hand and get me out of this   *
great argument – the more you go against your nature, the
more you will know of it – hear me, heaven! I've done and been   *
everything that I didn't want to be or do – Lord, put the light
out – so I stand here, beaten up and mauled and weeping,   *
knowing I am not what I thought I was, a good man doing
wrong, but the wrong man doing nothing much, and I wouldn't   *
be telling you about it if I weren't talking to myself. I talk too
much because I have been made so miserable by what you are
keeping hushed. I'm an old worn out lioness, a coward in my
corner; for the sake of my bravery I've never been one thing   *
that I am, to find out what I am! Here lies the body of Heaven.
The mocking bird howls through the pillars of Paradise, oh
Lord! Death in Heaven lies couched on a mackerel sky, on her
breast a helmet and at her feet a foal with a silent marble mane.
Nocturnal sleep is heavy on her eyes."

"Funny little man," someone said, "never stops talking – always getting everyone into trouble by excusing them, because
he can't excuse himself – the Squatting Beast, coming out at
night – " As he broke off, the voice of the doctor was heard: * †
"And what am I? I'm damned, and carefully public!"   *

He fumbled for a cigarette, found it and lit it. "Now suppose   †
you were in Wabash where the thing has never been heard of?
It *has* happened. So what does the judge do but call up the
nuncio of the office and he says, 'John, what do I give a man
of this sort?' And the clerk answered back, as quick as hitting
yourself in the eye, 'A dollar, a dollar and a half, two dollars!'"   *
Matthew was grinning and biting his teeth, and he swung
around again. "Like that subaltern in the trenches one night,
a sweet boy at that, but so fearful, he wouldn't, because, he
said, he was afraid any minute that he was going to meet his
maker – that's a Protestant for you! Would he do a bit with his
doing part? He would not. So in the thick of the battle, with the
bullets whistling for their man, I screamed above their calling,
'Nancy,' and I kept it up, as comrade after comrade slipped
down my arm and into nothing, – thinking of the priest among

the wranglers who said, 'You all seem so surprised that sinners
† * should sin.'

"Once upon a time I was standing listening to a quack
* hanky-panky of a medicine man saying: 'Now, ladies and
gentlemen, before I behead the small boy, I will endeavour to
entertain you with a few parlor tricks.' He had a turban cocked
* over his eye and a moaning in his left ventricle, which was
meant to be the whine of Tophet, and a loin-cloth as big as a
* tent and protecting about as much. Well, he began doing his
tricks. He made a tree grow out of his left shoulder and dashed
two rabbits out of his cuffs and balanced three eggs on his nose.
* A priest, standing in the crowd, began to laugh, and a priest
laughing always makes me wring my hands with doubt. The
* † other time was when Catherine the Great sent for me to bleed
her. She took to the leech with rowdy Saxon abandon, saying:
'Let him drink, I've always wanted to be in two places at once!' "

"For heaven's sake," the ex-priest said. "Remember your
century at least!"

For a moment the doctor looked angry. "See here," he said,
"don't interrupt me. The reason I'm so remarkable is that I
remember everyone even when they are not about. It's the
† buggers that look as innocent as the bottom of a plate that get
you into trouble, not a man with a prehistoric memory."

"Women can cause trouble too," the ex-priest said lamely.

"That's another story," the doctor said. "What else has Jenny
* ever done, and what else has Robin ever done? And Nora,
* what's she done but cause it, by taking it in at night like a
bird-coop? And I myself wish I'd never had a button up my
middle – for what I've done and what I've not done all goes
back to that – to be recognized, a gem should lie in a wide open
* field; but I'm all aglitter in the underbrush! If you don't want
to suffer you should tear yourself apart. Were not the several
o parts of Caroline of Hapsburg put in three utterly obvious
* piles? – her heart in the Augustiner church, her intestines in St.
Stefan's and what was left of the body in the vault of the
* Capucines? Saved by separation. But I'm all in one piece! Oh
the new moon!" he said. "When will she come riding?"

"Drunk and telling the world," someone said. The doctor heard but he was too far gone to care, too muddled in his mind to argue, and already weeping.

"Come," the ex-priest said, "I'll take you home."

The doctor waved his arm. "Revenge is for those who have loved a little, for anything more than that justice is hardly enough. Some day I'm going to Lourdes and scramble into the front row and talk about all of you." His eyes were almost closed. He opened them and looked about him and a fury came over him. "Christ Almighty!" he said. "Why don't they let me alone, all of them?"

The ex-priest repeated, "Come, I'll take you home."

The doctor tried to rise. He was exceedingly drunk and now extremely angry all at once. His umbrella fell to the floor with the crash of a glass as he swung his arm upward against the helping hand. "Get out! Get out!" he said. "What a damnable year, what a bloody time! How did it happen, where did it come from?" He began to scream with sobbing laughter. "Talking to me – all of them – sitting on me as heavy as a truck horse – talking! Love falling buttered side down, fate falling arse up! Why doesn't anyone know when everything is over, except me? That fool Nora holding on by her teeth, going back to find Robin! And Felix – eternity is only just long enough for a Jew! But there's someone else, – who was it, damn it all – who was it? I've known everyone," he said, "everyone!" He came down upon the table with all his weight, his arms spread, his head between them, his eyes wide open and crying, staring along the table where the ash blew and fluttered with his gasping breath. "For Christ's sweet sake!" he said, and his voice was a whisper, "now that you have all heard what you wanted to hear, can't you let me loose now, let me go? I've not only lived my life for nothing, but I've told it for nothing – abominable among the filthy people – I know, it's all over, everything's over, and nobody knows it but me—drunk as a fiddler's bitch— lasted too long—" He tried to get to his feet, gave it up. "Now," he said, "the end – – mark my words – – now *nothing, but wrath and weeping!*"

8

THE POSSESSED

o

WHEN ROBIN, ACCOMPANIED by Jenny Petherbridge, arrived in New York, she seemed distracted. She would not listen to Jenny's suggestion that they should make their home in the country. She said a hotel was "good enough." Jenny could do nothing with her; it was as if the motive power which had directed Robin's life, her day as well as her night, had been crippled. For the first week or two she would not go out, then, thinking herself alone, she began to haunt the terminals, taking trains into different parts of the country, wandering without design, going into many out-of-the-way churches, sitting in the darkest corner, or standing against the wall, one foot turned toward the toe of the other, her hands folded at their length, her head bent. As she had taken the Catholic vow long before, now she came into church as one renouncing something; her hands before her face, she knelt, her teeth against her palm, fixed in an unthinking stop as one who hears of death suddenly; death that cannot form until the shocked tongue has given its permission. Moving like a housewife come to set straight disorder in an unknown house, she came forward with a lighted taper, and setting it up, she turned, drawing on her thick white gloves, and with her slow headlong step, left the church. A moment later Jenny, who had followed her, looking about to be sure that she was unobserved, darted up to the sconce, snatched the candle from its spike, blew it out; re-lit it and set it back.

Robin walked the open country in the same manner, pulling at the flowers, speaking in a low voice to the animals. Those that came near, she grasped, straining their fur back until their

eyes were narrowed and their teeth bare, her own teeth showing
as if her hand were upon her own neck.

Because Robin's engagements were with something unseen;
because in her speech and in her gestures there was a desperate
anonymity, Jenny became hysterical. She accused Robin of a   *
"sensuous communion with unclean spirits." And in putting her
wickedness into words she struck herself down. She did not   *
understand anything Robin felt or did, which was more unendurable than her absence. Jenny walked up and down in her
darkened hotel room, crying and stumbling.   *

Robin now headed up into Nora's part of the country. She
circled closer and closer. Sometimes she slept in the woods;   † *
the silence that she had caused by her coming was broken again
by insect and bird flowing back over her intrusion, which was
forgotten in her fixed stillness, obliterating her as a drop of water is made anonymous by the pond into which it has fallen.
Sometimes she slept on a bench in the decaying chapel (she   *
brought some of her things here) but she never went further.
One night she woke up to the barking, far off, of Nora's dog. As *
she had frightened the woods into silence by her breathing, the
barking of the dog brought her up, rigid and still.   † *

Half an acre away, Nora, sitting by a kerosene lamp, raised   † *
her head. The dog was running about the house; she heard him   *
first on one side, then the other; he whined as he ran; barking   *
and whining she heard him further and further away. Nora bent † *
forward listening; she began to shiver. After a moment she got   *
up, unlocking the doors and windows. Then she sat down, her   *
hands on her knees; but she couldn't wait. She went out. The   *
night was well advanced. She could see nothing. She began
walking toward the hill. She no longer heard the dog, but she
kept on. A level above her she heard things rustling in the grass, *
the briars made her stumble, but she did not call.

At the top of the hill she could see, rising faintly against the
sky, the weather-beaten white of the chapel, a light ran the   *
length of the door. She began to run, cursing and crying, and   *
blindly, without warning, plunged into the jamb of the chapel   *
door.

* On a contrived altar, before a Madonna, two candles were
burning. Their light fell across the floor and the dusty benches.
Before the image lay flowers and toys. Standing before them in
her boy's trousers was Robin. Her pose, startled and broken,
was caught at the point where her hand had reached almost to
* the shoulder, and at the moment Nora's body struck the wood,
* Robin began going down, down, her hair swinging, her arms
* out. The dog stood rearing back, his forelegs slanting, his paws
* trembling under the trembling of his rump, his hackle standing,
* his mouth open, the tongue slung sideways over his sharp bright
teeth, whining and waiting. And down she went, until her head
* swung against his, on all fours now, dragging her knees. The
veins stood out in her neck, under her ears, swelled in her arms,
* and wide and throbbing, rose up on her hands as she moved
* forward.

* † The dog, quivering in every muscle, sprang back, his tongue
a stiff curving terror in his mouth; moved backward, back, as she
* came on, whimpering too, coming forward, her head turned
* completely sideways, grinning and whimpering. Backed into
the farthest corner, the dog reared as if to avoid something that
troubled him to such agony that he seemed to be rising from
the floor; then he stopped, clawing sideways at the wall, his
* † forepaws lifted and sliding. Then head down, dragging her
* forelocks in the dust, she struck against his side. He let loose
one howl of misery and bit at her, dashing about her, barking,
and as he sprang on either side of her he always kept his head
* toward her, dashing his rump now this side, now that, of the
wall.

Then she began to bark also, crawling after him—barking
* † in a fit of laughter, obscene and touching. Crouching, the dog
* began to run with her, head-on with her head, as if to circumvent her; soft and slow his feet went padding. He ran this way
and that, low down in his throat crying, and she grinning and
crying with him; crying in shorter and shorter spaces, moving
head to head, until she gave up, lying out, her hands beside her,
her face turned and weeping; and the dog too gave up then, and
* † lay down, his eyes bloodshot, his head flat along her knees.

TEXTUAL APPARATUS

INTRODUCTION

The Dalkey Archive edition of Djuna Barnes's *Nightwood* is a clear text edition prepared according to the editorial prinicples of W. W. Greg, Fredson Bowers, G. Thomas Tanselle, and Hershel Parker.[1] Clear text has been chosen as the appropriate form for its superior readability. Because this edition of *Nightwood* is based on Barnes's third revision of the novel, a fairly clear text with few changes or interlineations, it can be represented most satisfactorily as clear text. It is a critical unmodernized edition. It is critical in the sense that no single copy-text has been the source of this edition; there are three copies of the typescript: a ribbon and two carbons, each with slight differences. It is unmodernized in that punctuation, in particular, has not been revised to conform to modern practice.

The principles of modern textual editing developed by Greg and elaborated by Bowers and Tanselle base the selection of copy-text on the text closest to the author's hand, on the rationale that this text most closely reflects the author's final intention. If it can be shown that an author has thoroughly revised a later edition including accidentals, double copy-text authority exists. In such cases, the most recent edition may be regarded as representing the author's final intention. However,

[1] W. W. Greg, "The Rationale of Copy-Text," *Studies in Bibliography* 3 (1950-51); Fredson Bowers, "Established Texts and Definitive Texts," *Philological Quarterly* 41 (1962); "A Preface to the Text," in *The Scarlet Letter*, Centenary Edition (Columbus: Ohio State University Press, 1962); "Greg's 'Rationale of Copy-Text' Revisited," *Studies in Bibliography* 31 (1978); G. Thomas Tanselle, "Greg's Theory of Copy-Text and the Editing of American Literature," *Studies in Bibliography* 28 (1975); "The Editorial Problem of Final Authorial Intention," *Studies in Bibliography* 29 (1976); "Some Principles for Editorial Apparatus," *Studies in Bibliography* 25 (1972); Hershel Parker, "Regularizing Accidentals: The Latest Form of Infidelity," *Proof* 3 (1973).

it is important also to consider the nature of the revisions: Are they primarily literary; that is, in Tanselle's words, do they "aim at intensifying, refining, or improving the work as then conceived . . . altering the work in degree but not in kind"? Or do they alter the "purpose, direction or character of a work, thus attempting to make a different sort of work out of it" ("Authorial Intention," 193)? The second motive for changes applies to the author who makes changes because an editor requires them. Such changes do not reflect an author's final intention, but the writer's acquiesence. The editor of a critical edition will reject such changes.

Likewise, according to principles of textual editing, the author's own accidentals (spelling and punctuation) will be chosen over those imposed by in-house style. Thus, the accidentals of the copy-text of a first edition or typescript will be adopted, if no manuscript exists, as being closest to the author's own practices, rather than the accidentals of later editions that have been subjected to more than a single layer of in-house style. Hershel Parker argues as well that critical text editors who change accidentals to achieve consistency destroy the original texture of an author's work. Such changes, he argues, ought to be resisted.

Choice of copy-text. In the case of Barnes's *Nightwood* the principle of choosing the work closest to the author's hand might suggest the 1962 Farrar, Straus and Cudahy *Selected Works* edition as copy-text. Although she reviewed the proofs of this edition, Barnes made very few changes. The substantive changes that she indicated, however, have been adopted and noted in the emendations. But this edition reflects, as do all previous editions of *Nightwood*, an altered intention. At the urging of T. S. Eliot and Frank Morley, editors at Faber and Faber in 1936, Barnes deleted certain passages and phrases in order to soften the overt homosexuality of the text, modulating as well ribald nuances of the work. In addition, several pages were marked for deletion by Emily Coleman— they may actually have been removed from the manuscript—in order to reduce Doctor O'Connor's presence in the story. Most of these deletions appear to have been reviewed and confirmed by Eliot. Taken together these changes altered her final intention. Barnes acquiesced, but she objected in letters to Coleman. Her acquiescence to these changes and gratitude to Coleman and Eliot for their roles in bringing *Nightwood* to publication were undoubtedly based on her recognition that Faber and Faber's offer was her last chance for getting the novel published. It had been turned down by numerous publishers, some of them twice, and she had insisted that she could not rewrite it.

Thus, the copy-text for the Dalkey Archive edition is the typescript of the first edition, which exists in a ribbon copy and two carbons. These materials are in Special Collections at the University of Maryland, College Park, Maryland. Chosing one of these typescripts as the copy-text presents some of the same problems as chosing a copy-text from among several derivative editions. However, the second carbon of the typescript (hereafter abbreviated TSC2) has been adopted as copy-text. This is the copy of the text that Barnes kept with her, and it therefore reflects changes she initiated and also the least degree of intrusion by Eliot, Morley, or Coleman. The ribbon copy of the typescript (TSR) can be rejected as the appropriate copy-text because it was sent to publishers while Barnes and Coleman collaborated by letter regarding editorial changes that were entered on TSC1 and TSC2. In addition, in the file with the ribbon copy is a note in Barnes's hand that the ribbon copy is "prior to the final copy," but also that it is the second copy "as given to Eliot by Muir." The changes on it are few compared to those on the other two copies of the typescript.

Barnes sent the first typescript carbon (TSC1) to Coleman in late July 1935. Coleman suggested and entered many changes on TSC1 and communicated most of them to Barnes between July and November 1935, when she sent the typescript to Eliot. In June 1936, after Eliot had accepted the book for publication, Barnes visited Coleman and met with Eliot regarding the text at least three times. Eventually this copy of the typescript was used as printer's copy. Barnes presumably reviewed it carefully; however, it has not been adopted as the copy-text because Coleman and Eliot cut this copy and altered punctuation. However, this copy has been examined carefully to determine which changes are Barnes's because, outside of the proofs to the first edition, it indicates her last look at the novel before its publication. Both TSC1 and TSC2 have been compared because similar changes on both copies seem to suggest that many of the changes suggested by Coleman represented a genuine collaboration, suggestions that Barnes accepted as helping her to achieve her final intention. The Dalkey Archive edition has adopted those changes, noting them in the emendations list.

The Dalkey Archive edition, then, draws upon the three original typescripts, primarily TSC2, the second carbon which Barnes kept with her; TSC1, the first carbon sent to Coleman; and TSR, the ribbon copy.

Where changes on all three typescripts are identical, they indicate corrections Barnes made in New York before she sent the first carbon to Coleman. In general these changes are minor corrections, and they are adopted in this edition and noted in the emendations.

It may be objected that Barnes came to prefer the deletions of TSC1 because she did not restore these passages to any later edition. It is true that there appears to be no evidence in the Barnes Papers to suggest that she attempted in a later edition to re-insert the deleted passages. But the circumstances of her life suggest that it would have been very difficult for her to do so. When Barnes returned to Paris in May 1936, she sent her trunk "of papers" directly to Coleman's flat. She traveled back and forth between London and Paris, leaving Paris just before war broke out. In 1940 after she had returned to New York, Eliot wrote regarding her concern for her "property" in London, which may have included the typescripts. In the meantime she had begun work on a book related to the Baroness von Freytag-Loringhoven.[2] Several letters in the 1940s suggest she was attempting to get *Nightwood* republished in America, without results. Thus, in these circumstances, it seems unlikely that she would attempt to restore passages deleted from the book. But she did preserve the typescripts (and they may have been in storage in London until around 1952).

In addition to the typescripts, the editor has consulted the proof to the first English edition (PE1), which Barnes corrected in September 1936; the first English edition (E1); the first American edition (A1), which Eliot arranged in 1937 with Harcourt, Brace; the first New Directions edition (ND46); the second New Directions edition, which was reset in 1949 (ND49); the 1961 paperback (ND61); and the 1962 Farrar, Straus and Cudahy edition (FSC) and its proof (PFSC), which Barnes also corrected. Barnes's personal copies of the English edition, the American edition, and the New Direction 1946 edition have also been examined, for she entered changes in these books and her letters reveal that at least her mother's copy of the first English edition was apparently delivered to James Laughlin for corrections in the reset New Directions

---

[2] Entitled *The Beggars* [*sic*] *Comedy*, its various extant drafts were reproduced (with related matter) in a booklet by Hank O'Neal called *Djuna Barnes and the Baroness Elsa von Freytag-Loringhoven*, privately printed and distributed at the Djuna Barnes Centennial Conference at the University of Maryland, 2-3 October 1992.

editon. Her letters to various editors have been consulted as well. Substantive variants among these editions are included in the historical collation in the textual apparatus.

Special Problems. One significant problem the editor faces in preparing a critical edition based on the typescript is whether to accept the original chapter order of the typescripts or to accept the order established by Emily Coleman. In her letter of 5 November 1935, she wrote Barnes that she had put the Jenny chapter ahead of "Watchman, What of the Night?" If Barnes didn't agree, it could be changed later. The Jenny chapter is " 'The Squatter,' " originally chapter 5; "Watchman, What of the Night?" was originally chapter 4. In Coleman's arrangement " 'The Squatter' " became chapter 4, and "Watchman, What of the Night?" became chapter 5. In her letter of 8 November 1935, Barnes accepted this change, but protested: that it was a "let down" from the "Ah" at the end of "Night Watch."

Though Barnes seemed less than enthusiastic about this change initially, it has been retained in this edition because evidence seems to indicate that Barnes eventually came to appreciate the change and to prefer the revised order. Certainly, it would have been very easy for her to return the chapter to its original position. Even though she accepted many of Coleman's suggestions, others she steadfastly refused. For example, Coleman consistently argued that the story of Felix and Robin that opens the novel was an unnecessary distraction from the story of Nora and Robin. Barnes resolutely defended this story. It seems clear, then, that Barnes retained and exercised her convictions with respect to Coleman's suggestions.

The fact that the chapters were not returned to their original order strongly suggests that Barnes regarded the rearrangment as preferable. There appears to be no further discussion of the matter in letters between Coleman and Barnes, nor does Coleman return to the issue in her diary, which records details of Barnes's June visit with her and Barnes's report of her first meeting with Eliot. Furthermore, Barnes changed the chapter arrangement in her copy (TSC2) and marked it in the ribbon copy as well, suggesting her acceptance, while she was still in New York. She may also have realized that the intensity of Nora's story and her effort to understand Robin and her own life in "Night Watch" and in "Watchman, What of the Night?" profited from the contrast of tone provided by " 'The Squatter.' " It is interesting to note, as well, that this change breaks the chronological continuity between "Night Watch" and "Watchman."

Special Problems Regarding Accidentals. Barnes told everyone that she could neither spell nor punctuate. Often her practice is simply inconsistent. For example, she spells "ax" with an "e" and without it. She uses both "centre" and "center." Where her usage appears to be American— "parlor" rather than the English "parlour"—her usage has been retained. Her inconsistency has been allowed to stand. Obvious misspellings have been silently corrected. Though Barnes claimed a similar inability to punctuate correctly, she punctuated by ear, rhetorically rather than syntactically, in the style of the nineteenth rather than the twentieth century, and did not hesitate to scold various editors that "to me who knows nothing about punctuation," the punctuation (in the edition under discussion) looked "strange." At given points punctuation varies in all three typescripts, and it is clear that Barnes was "hearing" it differently. Because Eliot and Coleman, in addition to Barnes, corrected punctuation on TSC1, it is difficult to determine in all instances exactly who did what. Where changes appear on all typescripts, they are Barnes's corrections, and these have been adopted. Elsewhere, caution has been used in adopting punctuation from the first typescript, preferring to reflect the author's original texture of the second typescript. However, readings have been adopted from the first typescript because they they are in fact correct or they improve the clarity of the meaning intended. All of these changes have been noted in the list of emendations. With respect to apostrophes in contractions and possessives and commas and quotation marks related to dialogue, Barnes was careless, or more accurately focused on other matters, but her practice with respect to these points was standard; therefore lapses have been emended silently.

Barnes often used a comma before a noun clause beginning with "that," and she frequently used both a comma and a dash, or a semicolon and a dash; her usage has been preserved in these cases. Likewise, she seems to have employed two systems of dashes, using the standard two hypens for a typed dash, which has been changed to the em dash (—) for print, and a single hyphen with spaces on either side of it. In this instance, her spacing has been preserved and an en dash inserted (–). In items in a series Barnes typically did not use a comma before "and." With respect to interjections, sometimes she set them off, sometimes

not; this inconsistency has been preservered because it reflects her practice to punctuate by ear, using the comma to indicate a pause rather than
mark a syntactical unit. Occasionally, a comma separates a subject from
the verb of the sentence. Frequently, she uses just a comma to separate a
compound sentence; in both instances her usage has been followed. In a
few places where misreading results, a semicolon has been inserted and
noted in the emendations list.

In preparing the text, the goal has been fidelity to the typescript. All
three typescripts were compared manually and TSC2 entered into the
computer manually. The copy-text has then been compared against a
photocopy of TSC2 and checked by another reader via recorded parallel
reading. Emendations have been made to this copy-text from TSR and
TSC1. The original of TSC1 at the University of Maryland has been
collated against the copy-text to verify original wording and to assess the
changes, determining which are to be adopted in the copy-text. All
emendations from TSR, TSC1, or proofs of various editions that have
been adopted have been noted in the list of emendations with their
sources. Before the final copy-text was sent to the publisher, the text was
again recorded and the return copy rechecked.

In the sources for emendations, which appear in parentheses after
the rejected reading, the following abbreviations are used to indicate at
what stage the emendation was made:

TS   – indicates the change appeared on all three typescripts.
TSR   – indicates the change appeared on the ribbon copy.
TSC1 – indicates the change appeared on the first carbon.
TSC2 – indicates the change appeared on the second carbon.
E1   – identifies the emendation as in the first English edition, Faber
        and Faber, 1936.
PE1   – indicates the emendation appeared on the proof to the first
        English edition.
A1   – identifies the emendation as in the first American edition,
        Harcourt, Brace, 1937.
ND46 – indicates that the change appeared in the New Direction edi-
        tion, the second American edition, 1946.
ND49 – indicates the change appeared in New Directions, reset for
        third edition, 1949.
ND61 – indicates the change appeared in the New Directions paper
        edition of 1961.

PFSC – the change was made to the proof of the Farrar, Straus and Cudahy edition of Barnes's *Selected Works*.

FSC – the source of the change was the Farrar, Straus and Cudahy, 1962.

FSG – refers to Farrar, Straus and Giroux, 1982, second printing.

NW36 – indicates a change Barnes made in her personal copy or her mother's copy of the first English *Nightwood*, which Barnes sent to James Laughlin in 1949.

NW37 – indicates a change Barnes made in her personal copy of A1.

L – refers to corrections Barnes communicated by letter.

DA – an emendation introduced by Dalkey Archive edition, 1995.

The following initials are used to indicate who made the change:

B – Barnes
C – Coleman
E – Eliot
M – Morley
F – Faber, when the change cannot be attributed directly to either Eliot or Morley.

The following symbols are used within the emendations list:

~ – indicates a word previously cited when the variant is in the punctuation associated with the word.

∧ – indicates an absence of punctuation at a given point.

] – the bracket can be read as "emended from," that is, the phrase to the left of the bracket is the accepted reading; the wording to the right is the rejected reading.

In the list of emendations, each entry begins with the page and line number of the Dalkey Archive edition, followed by the accepted reading, a bracket, the rejected reading, and in parentheses the source of the emendation. Here are several examples:

12.16 upon] up on (TSC1)
"upon" has been emended from "up on" only on the first carbon of the typescript by an unknown hand, thus no source symbol is attached.

13.28 middle-aged] middle aged (E1)
This entry indicates that the hyphen has been inserted in the first English edition.

17.31 her,] ~∧ (PE1-B)
This entry indicates that a comma has been added after "her" by Barnes in the proof to the first English edition. The tilde ~ substitutes for "her" in the lemma after the bracket and the caret ∧ indicates no comma existed on the original typescript.

49.37 Yet they] They (TSC1-B, TSC2-B)
The entry can be read "Yet they" has been emended from "They." Barnes made the emendation on both the first and second carbons.

61.26 down, –] down, – a static cock fight; (TS-B; L-C, 8 Nov. 1935)
This entry indicates that "down" has been emended from "down, a static cock fight." Barnes entered the emendation on all typescripts, but Coleman initiated the deletion in a letter of 8 November 1935.

86.12 me?'] me to her?' (DB to JL, L, 27 May 1946; appears ND49)
This entry indicates that Barnes emdended 'me?' from 'me to her?' and that she communicated this change to James Laughlin in a letter dated 27 May 1946. The change appeared in the 1949 New Directions edition. Where emendations have been made by letter or a book delivered to the publisher, the date the emendation appears is included in entries.

87.18 love, were] love∧ were (PE1-F)] love were probably (TSC1-B)
This entry, with three lemmas, indicates two changes: in the first lemma, "love, were" has been emended from "love were," in the second lemma, by a Faber editor in the proof to the first edition, the caret indicating the absence of punctuation in the original typescript. The third lemma indicates that "love were" has been emended from "love were probably" by Barnes on TSC1.

EMENDATIONS TO THE COPY-TEXT

3.11   forty-five] 45 (E1)
3.15   thrust] thrusting (TS-B)
4.9   happy;] ~, (FSC-B)
4.18   felt] felt, without vocal necessity,] (TSC1, TSC2-B)
4.20   by which his] by his (PE1-B)
4.22   heart, fashioned] ~∧~ (PE1-B)
5.5   who] that (TSC1, TSC2-B)
5.10   by him adopted, became] was for him dislocated (TSC1, TSC2-B)
5.13   Gentile] gentile (TSC1, TSC2)
5.33   had been] was (PE1-B)
5.36   danced,] had danced, (TSC1, TSC2-B)
5.37   came] had come] (TSC1, TSC2-B)
6.3   head held] head had held (TSC1-B)] head (TS-B)
6.13   In the] In (TS-B)
6.17   City,] ~∧ (E1)
6.35   twos and threes.] two and threes – she said it gave the house power.] (TSC1-B, TSC2-B)
7.2   claimed] had claimed (TSC1)
7.5   windows (a . . . handsome)] windows, a . . . handsome, (TSR, PE1-B)
7.16   carpet-thick.] feasible and carpet-thick. (TSC1, TSC2-B)
7.28   three-quarter] three-quarter's (PE1-B)
8.1   sure] none too sure but (TSC1-B)
8.30   equality,] ~∧ (TSR, PE1-B)
9.1   Hedvig, the] ~. The (TS-B)
9.4   lids; into . . . shone,] lids, ~ . . . ~∧ (TSC1-B)
9.13   single –] single, – (TSC1-M, TSC2-B)
9.23   loquacity] and stemmed loquacity (TSC1-B)

9.25   past] and broken past (TSC1-B)
9.29   bowing, searching,] still bowing, still searching, (TSC1, TSC2-B)
9.32   if he] if they (E1-F)
10.3   *humaine*] *Humaine* (TSC1, TSC2-B)
10.11   apart and] and apart (TS-B)
10.13   necessary time] time necessary (PE1-B)
11.1   nor] or (E1)
11.15   only in] in (PE1-B)
11.20   but which,] out ~∧ (TSR, TSC1-B)
11.24   justice] Justice (TSC1, TSC2-B)
11.27   rump,] ~∧ (TSR, PE1-B)
11.30   public,] ~∧ (TS-B)
11.31   hope,] ~∧ (TSR, TSC1-B)
12.2   ease;] ~, (E1)
12.3   arena, he found,] ~∧ ~ ~∧ (TSR-B, FSC-B)
12.9   anyone] any one (E1)
12.16   upon] up on (TSC1)
12.20   faded] ~, (TS-B)
12.23   candies,] ~∧ (TS-B)
12.30   said,] said∧ (A1)
13.26   middle-aged] middle aged (E1)
13.30   San Francisco] Los Angeles (TS-B)
13.33   considered himself] considered (TS-B)
14.2   word,] word∧ (TS-B)
14.9   unexpurgated,] ~∧ (TSR, TSC1-B)
14.22   so,] ~∧ (DA)
14.33   about,] ~∧ (TSR-B)
15.1   theory,] ~∧ (DA)
15.2   can,] can∧] (TSC1-B)
15.30   climb,] ~∧ (PE1-B)
15.31   themselves,] ~∧ (TSR, PE1-B)
16.5   care,] ~∧ (TSR-B, TSC2-B, PFSC-B)
16.8   nodded] grinned (NW36-B; appears A1)
16.14   spoken,] ~∧ (E1)
16.16   pleased.] ~∧ (TSC1, TSC2-B)
16.25   laughter,] ~∧ (TS-B)
17.2   abruptly,] ~∧ (DA)
17.15   Tunis who] Tunis and (TSC1, TSC2-B)

17.16   cure,] ~∧ (TSR-B, E1)
17.18   inquired] Inquired (E1)
17.31   her,] ~∧ (PE1-B)
18.13   ¶But] ∧~ (TSC1, TSC2-B)
18.15   your] our (TSR-B, PE1-B)
18.24   where,] ~∧ (TSC1-B, TSC2-B)
19.5   *"Freude sei Euch . . . immerdar!"*] *"freude sei euch . . . immerda!"*
        (E1)
19.7   "You . . . easily," Nora said.] "You argue," Nora said, "about
        . . . easily." (TSC1-B, TSC2-B)
19.9   answered.] ~∧ (E1)
19.9   uphill;] ~, (E1)
19.10   true,] ~∧ (TSR-B, TSC2-B)
19.15   right,] ~∧ (TSC1-B, TSC2-B)
19.21   on, "in] ~∧ "In (TSC1-F,B)
19.27   dragged] dragging (TS-B)
19.29   her head on); the] her, head on, all the (TS-B)
20.3   woman,] woman who was (TS-B)
20.4   it,] ~∧ (PFSG-B)
20.7   Lahore] Ladore (PE1-B)] Lahore (TSC1, TSC2-B)
20.7   wanted] want (TSC1-B, TSC2-B)
20.8   thought,] ~∧ (PE1-B)
20.10   of,] ~∧ (TSC1-B, TSC2-B)
20.13   drink spirits."] drink." (TS-B)
20.15   me,"] me something fearful," (TSC1)
20.18   razor. That's] razor, that's (TSC1-F)
20.22   conversation;] ~∧ (DA)
20.23   blotter snatched from the Senate.] blotter. (PE1-B)] blotter
        snatched from the Senate. (TSC1)
20.25   At] at (TSR-B, TSC2-B)
20.32   failure for the rest of my life.] failure (PE1-B)] failure for the
        rest of my life.] (TSC1)
21.27   laughing silently] grinning. (NW36-B; appears A1)
22.16   legs,] ~∧ (TSR, E1-F)
22.20   personal,] ~∧ (TSC1, TSC2-B)
22.25   on,] ~∧ (A1)
22.29   has] was (TS-B)
22.37   you,] ~∧ (A1)
23.1   'Love,'] ~∧ (PFSC-B)

23.6   owl∧] ~, (TSR-B)
23.9   O'Connor.] ~∧ (DA)
23.10   *is*] is (TSC1, TSC2-B)
23.11   nothing, all] nothing all, (DA)
23.21   *Odeonsplatz*] *Odeon Platz* (DA)
23.31   Lohengrin] *Lohengrin* (DA)
23.33   madness,] ~∧ (TSC2-B)
23.37   God's sake,] God Sake∧ (DA)
24.8   whore. There . . . estrade,] ~, there . . . estrade∧ (TSC2-B)
24.11   (the . . . history.)] ∧~. . .~∧ (TSC2-B)
24.12   leap,] ~∧ (TSR-B)
24.15   stairs, with . . . pounding,] ~∧ ~ . . . ~∧ (TSR-B)
24.18   himself,] ~∧ (TSC2-B)
24.25   way.'] ~∧" (TSC1, TSC2-B)
24.26   much, they] ~. They (TS-B)
24.26   He] he (TSR, TSC2-B)
24.27   He] he (DA)
24.28   A] a (DA)
24.37   nay,] ~∧ (TSC2-B)
25.14   tip-toes,] ~∧ (TSC2-B)
25.23   tea caddy] teacaddy (TS-B)
25.24   *Sie österreichische*] *sie Osterreichische* (DA)
25.24   a look of utter] an utter look of (TSC2-B)
25.36   a round,] another round (PE1-B)
26.1   mother,] ~ — (PE1-B)
27.2   luck,] and pluck (TS-B)
27.7   ¶ Then] Then (TSC1-B,TSC2-B)
27.12   sake!'] ~∧' (TSR-B, TSC1-B)
27.26   (crying . . . one.)] ∧~ . . . ~∧ (TSC1-B)
27.37   me.] me as if I were one of her troubles. (TSC1-B)
28.10   "So I said, 'Why] 'Why (TS-B)
28.28   saying, 'Tragedy,' saying 'Horror,'] saying, 'Tragedy,' softly,
         saying 'Horror,' softly, (TSC2-B)
29.3   *Córdoba*] *Cordoba* (DA)
29.8   Córdoba] Cordoba (DA)
29.10   figure,] ~∧ (TSC2-B)
30.4   *Place*] *place* (E1)
30.4   *de la Mairie du VIe*] *Marie Duvé* (TSR, TSC1-B)
30.6   tram lines] car tracks (TSC1, TSC2-B)

30.14   *du*] de (TSC1, TSC2)

30.21   tradespeople] trades people (TSC1, TSC2)

30.27   custom] customs (NW36-B; appears ND49)

31.13   the "vulgarization"] the "popularization" (TSC1-F)

31.13   was once] once was (TSC1, TSC2-B)

31.21   bull's-eye] bulls-eye (FSC)

31.23   bowels—] bowels for an aim— (TS-B; L-C, 27 August 1935)

31.24   make)—so] make). So (TSC1-F, TSC2-B)

31.27   underworld] under world (E1)

31.30   *Chambéry*] *chambéry* (E1)

31.33   whale-shit—excuse me—on] whales—excuse me, on (TS-B, TSC1-F)

31.35   misery,] ~∧ (TSR, TSC1-B)

31.36   down] down in the mud (TSC1)

32.2   meddler—pardon] meddler-pardon (TSC1, TSC2-B)

32.6   whereas,] ~∧ (TS-B)

32.7   known,] ~∧ (TS-B)

32.18   true;] so; (PE1-B)

32.20   *Chambéry*, and asked] *chambéry*, he asked (E1)] asked (PE1-B)

32.21   have;] ~, (E1)

32.22   the doctor added:] added: (PE1-B)] he added: (TSC1)

32.25   looked at him.] grinned. (NW36-B, appears A1)

32.27   this," he went on: "One] this: One (TS-B)

32.30   any man's] and any man's (TSC1-B)] and man's (TS-B)

32.31   up,] ~∧ (A1)

32.35   misery,] ~∧ (E1)

33.1   as] at (A1)

33.4   ¶ His hands∧ (which . . . legs∧)] ∧His hands, (which . . . legs, (TSC1)

33.6   said,] ~∧ (TSR-B, E1)

33.9   "Neurasthenia," said Felix.] "Neurasthenia." (TSC1)

33.17   ¶ "In 1685," the Baron said,] ∧"In 1685∧" the Baron said∧ (TS-B)

33.25   *Hôtel*] hotel (E1)

33.27   doctor,] ~∧ (TSC1, TSC2-B)

33.30   twenty-nine] twenty nine (TSC1)

33.32   sighing.] ~, (E1)

33.33   the doctor's] his (TSC1, TSC2-B)

33.37   middle-class] middle class (E1)

34.3   red-carpeted] red carpeted (A1)
34.8   cover (which, like] cover, that like (TSC1-F; on PE1, B inserts the comma after "which.")
34.9   housewives),] ~, ʌ TSC1-B)
34.10   from which,] which (TSC1, TSC2-B)
34.12   trousers,] ~ʌ (E1)
34.16   was] which was (TSC1-F, TSC2-B)
34.19   making] made (PE1-B)
34.21   frame,] ~ʌ (E1)
34.22   sleep-worn] sleep worn (E1)
34.27   meet] the meet] meet (TSC1)
34.30   escape),] escape) ʌ (TSC1-B)
34.31   set,] ~ ʌ (TSC1)
34.33   of wood-winds] in wood-winds (TSC1-B)
34.34   popularize] vulgarize (TSC1)
34.35   the palms.] the largest of the palms. (TSC1-B)
35.1   wrists,] ~ʌ (TSC1-B)
35.6   on to] onto (TSC1-B, TSC2-B)
35.14   miracle,] "miracle" (TSC1-B)
35.24   nature;] ~ʌ (TSC1)
35.25   to decompose] to turn back and decompose (PE1-B)
35.27   the doctor] the doctor's hand (DA)
36.9   shop] shop or theatre (NW37-B; appears ND49)] shop (TS-B)
36.10   she] she now (TS-B)
36.15   Felix,] ~ʌ (E1)
36.18   the lids—] the lids; (TSC1, TSC2-B)
36.29   as the unicorn] as in the unicorn (TSC1-B, TSC2-B)
36.31   the infected, carrier of the past—before] the infected,; carrier of the past—the magnetized "beastly." Before (TSC1, TSC2-B; C-L, 27 August 1935)
37.3   as an image and its reflection] as the reflection and the image (PE1-B)
37.5   voiceʌ] ~, (TS-B)
37.6   abandon: the] abandon. The (TSC1, TSC2-B)
37.8   speech,] ~ʌ (PE1-B)
37.9   audience, –] ~, (TSC1-B)
37.26   "With] "with (TSC1-B)
37.30   have begun] has just (TSC1-B,TSC2-B)
38.2   house;] ~, (PFSC-B)

38.4 church-broken, nation-broken—] church broken-nation broken— (E1)

38.9 tsar] Tsar (TSC1-B, TSC2-B)

38.11 could never] would never (NW36-B; appears A1)

38.15 the only] only (TSC1-B, TSC2-B)

38.28 say beware! In] may beware, in (TS-B)

38.30 Vote," he said.] ~." He grinned. (NW36-B; appears A1)

39.6 setting, –] ~, (TSC1-B)

39.8 nocturnal,] ~∧ (E1)

39.8 birds, –] ~, (TSC1-B)

39.10 should walk] walk (TSC1-B)

39.16 he was useful to the bank] the bank found him useful (TSC1, TSC2-B)

39.21 head,] ~∧ (E1)

39.25 fading,] ~; (PE1-B)] ~, (TSC1-B)

39.26 garden, that] ~∧ ~ (TSC1-B)

39.30 happiness. Thinking] happiness in her company, thinking (TSC1-B, TSC2-B)

39.35 incurable,] ~∧ (TSC1-B)] ~, (TSC1)

39.37 he was] he was also (PE1-B)

40.1 excellent,] most beautiful, (NW36-B; appears ND49)] most beautiful∧ (E1)

40.2 debased,] ~∧ (TSC1-B)

40.8 closed, it] closed it, (TS-B)

40.11 him.] him, because she was an orphan. (TS-B; C-L, 27 August 1935)

40.22 selection;] ~, (TSC1-B)

40.26 before him,] ~ ~∧ (TSC1-B)

40.28 accepted,] ~∧ (DA)

41.1 methodical] methodic (PFSC-B)

41.5 *Leben*] leben (TSC1, TSC2-B)

41.5 *Schönheit."*] *Schonheit."* (E1)] *schonheit."* She did not understand. (TS-B; C-L, 27 August 1935)

41.8 *Kammergarten*] *Kammer garten* (TSC1-B, TSC2-B)

41.14 statue at a different angle.] ~, merely at different angles. (TSC1, TSC2-B)

41.16 Vienna] all Vienna (TSC1-B)

41.21 great,] ~∧ (TSR-B, PE1-B)

41.25 her legs] her boy's legs (TS-B; C-L, 27 August 1935)

41.34   re-entered] reentered (E1)
42.22   like a] as a (PFSC-B)
42.23   run,] ~^ (PFSC-B)
42.24   yet runs] and yet runs (PFSC-B)
42.24   runs haltingly] ~, ~, (TSC1-B, TSC2-B)
42.26   *Wo ist*] *Viel ist* (TSC1, TSC2-B)
43.1   monstrously] yet more monstrously (PFSC-B)
43.2   unfulfilled] unfulfilled than they had suffered, (PFSC-B)
43.5   *Clotilde*] *Clothilde* (DA)
43.9   *rue*] *Rue* (TSC1, TSC2-B)
43.14   his rakes] her rakes (TS-B)
44.1   humour] humor (TSC1-B, TSC2-B)
44.5   A book was lying on the floor beneath her hand.] A book lying on the floor caught his attention. (TSC1-B)
44.17   for;] ~, (TSC1)
44.19   bent^] ~, (TS-B)
44.31   Felix,] Felix^ (E1)
45.1   movements;] ~, (TSC1)
45.1   it] and it (TSC1, TSC2-B)
45.5   them,] ~^ (TSC1, TSC2-B)
45.11   bar—] ~; (TSC1-B, TSC2-B)
45.12   swinging;] ~, (TSC1-B)
45.14   three,] three in the morning, (PE1-B)
45.22   He] "Well," he (TSC1, TSC2-B)
45.23   that."] that, but," he said stiffening, "he is so sweet. Have you noticed him?" (TSC1-C, TSC2-B; C-L, 27 August 1935)
45.24   him?" . . . talk?"] him," . . . talk." (TSC1, TSC2-B)
45.26   do?"] do?" he said. (TSC1, TSC2-B)
45.30   time.] time. ¶ "How did I get here anyway?" (TS-B, C-L, 27 August 1935)
46.4   hands^] ~, (TSC1, TSC2-B)
46.6   and a] a (TSR-B, PE1-B)
46.16   look of compassion] look of hurry and compassion. (TSC1, TSC2-B)
46.20   an undocumented] a documented] an undocumented (TSC1, TSC2-B)
46.21   her,] ~^ (E1-F)
47.2   re-enacted] reenacted (TSC1, TSC2-B)
47.9   And in the midst of this, Nora.] And in the midst of this, Nora,

sitting still, her hand on her dog, the fire-light throwing her shadow against the wall, her head in shadow, bending as it reached the ceiling, though her own stood erect and motionless. (NW36-B, ND46-B; integrated ND49)

47.21   everyone;] ~ , (TSC1-B)

47.29   *détraqués*, the paupers] *detraqué*, the pauper (TSC1-B, TSC2-B)

47.31   lost needs.] "lost needs." (TSC1, TSC2-B)

47.35   play,] play, (she had always been attracted to actors and the stage as there was a need in her to be "up" in matters of the arts), (TSC1-C, TSC2-B)

47.36   programme] program (TSC1, TSC2-B)

48.14   it;] ~ , (TSC1-B)

48.16   herself.] herself. She had, in anxiety not to fail, been from one faith to another. (TSC1-C, TSC2-B)

48.27   priest. There . . . her; she] priest. Everyone knew that she would repeat, in due time, everything that they told her; but there . . . her, therefore there was no betrayal, she (TSC1-C, TSC2-B)

48.28   her; she] her, she (E1)

48.35   bottle;] ~∧ (TSC1-B)

49.1   circus,] ~∧ (TSC1, TSC2-B)

49.3   house),] ~) ∧ (TSC1-B, TSC2-B)

49.4   1923] 1926 (TSC1-B, TSR-B)

49.10   apprehension of] apprehension for (PE1-B)

49.12   whip.] flickering whip. (ND46-B; appears ND49)

49.19   her. At] her; at (TS-B)

49.30   here!"] ~," (PE1-B)

49.34   here." But] here," but (TSC1-B)

49.35   said;] said, (TSC1-B)

49.36   mid-winter.] mid-winter, then she wanted to go. (TSC1-C, TSC2-B; C-L 27 August 1935)

49.37   Yet they] They (TSC1-B, TSC2-B)

50.18   Venetian] venetian (DA)

50.23   age] time (PE1-B)

50.32   Love] Loves (TSC1-B)

51.4   this,] ~∧ (PFSC-B)

51.6   that,] ~∧ (PE1-B)

51.7   fear,] ~∧ (PE1-B)

51.7   polarized;] ~ , (TSC2-B)

51.9   out,] ~∧ (E1)

51.9   wake from] wake out of (PE1-B)
51.9   back though] back into (PE1-B)
51.15   Yet now,] Yet, (TSC1, TSC2-B)
51.17   Robin] Robin now (TSC1, TSC2-B)
51.19   people,] ~∧ (TSR, TSC1-B)
51.25   one who] one that (TS-B)
51.28   tongue,] ~∧ (TSR, TSC1-B)
51.32   Robin, unseen,] ~∧ ~∧ (TSR-B, TSC2-B)
52.5   insurmountable grief,] unsurmountable ~∧ (PE1-B)
52.10   kept,] ~∧ (TSC1-B)
52.19   curling irons] electric curlers (ND46-B; accepted DA)
52.30   said.] said. "I may be late." (TS-B; L-C, 27 August 1935)
52.35   forgotten;] ~, (TSC1-B)
53.1   through, – Nora] through. Nora (TSC1, TSC2-B)
53.25   head∧ . . . loved∧] ~, ~, (PE1-B)
53.26   eyeballs,] ~∧ (TSC1, TSC2-B)
53.27   tears),] ~)∧ (PE1-B)
53.27   eyes;] ~, (TSC1-B)
53.33   funeral,] ~∧ (TSR-B, TSC1-B)
53.35   against;] ~, (TSC1-B)
53.37   activity] function (FSC-B)
54.2   tongues,] ~∧ (TSC1-B)
54.4   doctor,] doctor (he had officiated at her birth) (TS-B)
54.5   black-caped] black caped (TSR, TSC1-B)
54.9   slide;] ~, (TSC1-B)
54.11   step to follow her,] step (TSC1-B)
54.12   everywhere," he added,] ~." he ~∧ (A1)
55.4   had not been "well] had been "well (TS-B)
55.5   completed with the entry of Robin.] completed because into this dream Robin had entered. (TSC1-B, TSC2-B)
55.8   room—an expansive,] room (Nora had loved her grandmother, and been more influenced by her than anyone of her family) an expansive, (TS-B; C-L, 27 August 1935)
55.8   splendour;] ~, (TSC1)
55.10   return. Portraits] return. ¶ Portraits (TSC1, TSC2-B)
55.10   great-uncle,] her grand uncle, (TSC1, TSC2-B)
55.11   Llewellyn,] ~∧ (E1)
55.11   Civil War] Civil war (TSC1)
55.13   quill;] quill, and (TSC1-B)

55.14   house, . . . scaffold,] ~ʌ . . . ~ʌ (TS-B)
55.16   below.] ~; (TSC1-B, TSC2-B)
55.20   an "only] the "only (PE1-B)
55.37   grandmother,] ~ʌ (DA)
56.20   multiplying;] ~, (TSC1-B)
56.30   to Robin's,] ~ʌ (TS-B)
57.2   an awful] a strange and awful (TSC1, TSC2-B)
57.3   dormant,] ~ʌ (TSR, E1)
57.5   women;] ~ʌ (TSC1-B)
58.1   "The Squatter"] The Squatter (NW36-B; appears A1)
58.2   middle-aged] middle aged (E1)
58.5   endeavour] endeavor (TSC1, TSC2-B)
58.9   together. Only] together, only (TSC1, TSC2-B)
58.13   vapours] vapors (TSC1, TSC2-B)
58.14   odour] odor (DA)
58.15   *accouchée*] *accouche* (TSC1-F, TSC2)
58.26   went; and] went;] went, and (TSC1-B)
59.2   first-hand plunder.] first hand, authentic plunder. (TSC1-B,
         TSC2-B; hyphenated by E1)
59.9   humour] humor (TSC1, TSC2-B)
59.12   recede] receded (TSC1, TSC2-B)
59.12   uncertainty,] ~ʌ (TSC1)
59.17   listeningʌ] ~, (TSC1-B)
59.22   vocabulary] tragic vocabulary (TSC1-F, B; TSC2-B)
59.22   vocabulary of] vocabulary of two words, (NW37; appears FSC)
59.26   voice;] ~, (TSC1-B)
59.26   well told] well-told (E1)
59.27   eyes; immediately] eyes, immediately; (PE1-B)] ~, ~, (TSC1-B)
59.31   story –] ~; (DA)
59.33   programmes] programs (TSC1, TSC2-B)
59.34   *La Dame aux Camélias*] Camille (TSC1-B, TSC2-B)
59.37   actresses] the actresses of her day (TSC1-B, TSC2-B)
60.4   read perhaps] read (TSC1-B)] read, perhaps, (TSC1-C)
60.12   future, it] future, and her nervousness (TSC1-B, TSC2-B)
60.16   andʌ] ~, (TSC1-B, TSC2-B)
60.24   love;] ~, (TSC1-B)
60.37   Nora's for] for Nora's (TS-B)
60.37   instinct. ¶ Jenny] instinct. ¶ The story of the meeting of Jenny
         and Robin as told by Doctor Matthew O'Connor was not quite

true; he never allowed facts to hinder him. Jenny (TSC1-B, TSC2-B)

61.6   twenty-seven.] twenty-seven. She had a fear of seeing Nora as one would fear seeing Abelard. (TS-B; L-C, 27 August 1935)

61.8   *Ambassadeurs*, (Jenny feared meeting Nora).] Ambassadeurs, (TSC1-B, TSC2-B)

61.10   income] incomes (TSC1, TSC2-B)

61.10   afford) –] ~ ∧ (TSC1-F, TSC2-B)

61.12   gait –] gait, – (TSC1-F, TSC2-B)

61.21   destiny;] ~, (TSC1-B)

61.22   daring,] ~; (TSC1-B, TSC2-B)

61.26   down, –] down, – a static cock fight; (TS-B; L-C, date unknown, see textual notes)

61.29   *promenoir*,] ~∧ (TSC1-B)

61.30   she had] she'd (TS-B)

61.36   doctor and Robin, Jenny] doctor, Robin and Jenny (TS-B)

61.37   her, two gentlemen,] her. Two gentlemen∧ (TSC1-B)

62.2   spaniel, which suffered from] spaniel, who suffered with (TSC1-B, TSC2-B)

62.3   There was talk] There was a good deal of talk (TSC1-B, TSC2-B)

62.7   ceased and sat,] ceased, and sat, her two small wax-like hands tender with the new life in them cupped up in her lap, (NW36-B; appears ND49)

62.8   else,] else; (TS-B)

62.13   person] person there (TS-B)

62.30   Robin . . . said, a malign] And Robin . . . said into the room, that malign (TS-B)

62.32   something." She] something," and she (TS-B)

63.6   time" at a later date,] time" as a later date∧ (TSC1-B, TSC2-B)

63.7   And sure] and sure (TSC1-B, TSC2-B)

63.9   got] gotten (TSC1-B, TSC2-B)

63.16   be had in Paris] be had – in Paris (TS-B)

63.18   upon∧] ~, (TSC1-B)

63.18   address,] ~∧ (TSC1-B)

63.20   an early autumn night] a spring night (PE1-B)

63.24   lest Robin should get] lest Robin get (TSC1-B, TSC2-B)

63.28   themselves.] themselves as they would. (TSC1-B, TSC2-B)

63.36   choking tone;] choking voice; (PE1-B)

63.37   doctor, Robin] doctor, who put himself between them, Robin (PE1-B)

64.4   gesture] slight gesture (TSC1-B)

64.5   woods] wet woods (TSC1-B)

64.9   night∧ but] ~, ~ (TSC1-B)

64.10   ridiculous] quite ridiculous (TSC1-B, TSC2-B)

64.17   occult] some occult (TSC1-B)

64.19   justice, where] ~∧~(TSC1-B)

64.20   aloud,] loud (TSC1-B, TSC2-B)

64.25   in his sleep lies] sleeps (PFSC-B)

64.31   saying,] ~∧ (E1)

65.5   since,'] ~∧ '(TS-B)

65.6   in to me] into me (PE1-B)] into me, I say, (TS-B)

65.12   soldier. For] soldier and not a girl, and for (TS-B).

65.13   girl,] ~∧ (TSC1-B)

65.22   up into] up in (TSC1-B, PE1-B)

65.24   the tears wet, warm, and] now the tears, wet, warm, (TSC1-B, TSC2-B)

65.27   better] bitter (PE1-B)] better (TSC1-B)

65.28   He] He now (TSC1-B, TSC2-B)

65.32   distressed.] distressed. This deduction was, he hoped, clinical, and would effect that instant cure that professional words often do. On the contrary, (TSC1-B)

66.11   hear.] hear. She was afraid she might. (TSC1-B)

66.12   thing!"] thing; that does not exist!" (TSC1-B)

66.13   fist. "What] fist. "It does, it does! Only what (TSC1-B)

66.17   knee.] knee and smiling. (TSC1-B, TSC2-B)

66.20   God!"] God, stop it! Degrading me with your passion to be a slave." (TSC1-B, TSC2-B)

66.26   Then Jenny] At this moment Jenny (TSC1-B, TSC2-B)

67.7   separated;] departed, and only (TSC1-B, TSC2-B); the semi-colon is inserted only on TSC1.

67.8   little] week (PE1-B)] and only a week (TSC1-B, TSC2-B)

68.3   concierge's *loge*] *concierges* loge (TSC1-B)

68.4   concierge] *concierge* (TSC1-B)

68.7   slowly. She] ~ , she (TSC1-B, TSC2-B)

68.14   grave,] ~∧ (PFSC-B)

68.16   books,] ~∧ (E1)

68.17   water-stained] watered stained (TSC1-B, TSC2-B)

68.27 bed, brimming] (TSC1-B)

69.1 innocentʌ] ~, (TSC1-B)

69.2 accomplice] an accomplice (PE1-B)

69.3 *à coucher*] *accoucher* (TSC1, TSC2-B)

69.4 certain belligerence in] certain amount of belligerence about (TSC1-B)

69.5 foot;] ~, (TSC1-B)

69.6 compression,] ~; (TSC1-B)

69.6 metallic odour] metallic (TS-B)

69.9 gown.] gown; with what cunning had his brain directed not only the womanly, but the incestuous garment, for a flannel night dress is our mother. (TS-B; C-L, 27 August 1935)

69.10 over-large] over large (E1)

69.10 fullʌ] ~, (TS-B)

69.16 Red Riding Hood] Red Ridinghood (TSC1)

69.17 was only] was really only (TSC1)

69.17 thought,] ~ʌ (TSC1-B)

69.20 said,] ~ʌ (TSC1-B)

69.22 about the night."] about the night, about her, about Felix, about Robin." (TSC1-B, TSC2-B)

69.29 dead;] ~, (TSC1-B)

69.31 himself,] ~ʌ (TSC1-B)

69.32 special;] ~, (TSC1-B)

69.33 that,] ~ʌ (DA)

69.36 irony;] ~, (TSC1-B)

70.6 Sleep,] ~ʌ (DA)

70.7 I,] ~ʌ (E1)

70.7 Doctor] doctor (DA)

70.30 "Have] "And have (TSC1-B, TSC2-B)

70.33 then,] ~; (PE1-B)

71.1 effect] good effect (ND46-B; first appears ND61)

71.2 blood-letting] blood letting (E1)

71.6. woodwork. No,] ~, no, (DA)

71.6 said,] ~ʌ (A1)

71.9 I did] it did (TS-B)

71.10 not knowing] only not thinking (TS-B)

71.11 thought you knew] thought you thought (TS-B)

71.17 *Notre Dame de la Bonne Garde*] *Notre Dame-de-bonne-Garde* (DA)

71.20 Doctor] doctor (DA)

71.21   is because] because (E1-F)
71.24   did] must (TSC1-B, TSC2-B)
72.12   our own names] our names (TSC1-B)
72.16   it.] it,—the inclement earth! (TSC1-C, B; TSC2-B)
72.20   ¶ To] ∧To (TSC1-B, TSC2-B)
72.20   ∧And] ¶ "And (TSC1-B, TSC2-B)
72.30   Doctor] doctor (DA)
72.34   unless you . . . it. ¶"The] unless, I say, you . . . it, as undoubtedly
        the French have. They (TSC1-C; TSC2-B)
73.4   and expect] yet expect (TSC1-B)
73.9   said.] said. "What can I do?" (TSC1-B, TSC2-B)
73.10   *sou*] sou (DA)
73.10   poor-box] poor box (NW36-B; appears ND49)
73.28   said, "It means] said, leaning forward, (TS-B)
73.32   sun?] sun? It is not. (TSC1-C, B)
73.35   brim,] ~∧ (TSC1-B)
74.5   Nora said:] Nora pushed back her hair. (TSC1-B, TSC2-B)
74.5   frightened.] ~, it is making Robin sombody else. (TSC1-B,
        TSC2-B)
74.8   stand.] ~, found them and gave them to him. (TSC1-B, TSC2-
        B)
74.15   noontide] noon tide (E1)
74.18   reach] would reach (TSC1-B)
74.21   tread. ¶ "Yes," said Nora. ¶ The dead] tread. ¶ The dead
        (TSC1-B, TSC2-B)
74.28   ∧truth∧] " ~ " (TSC1-B, TSC2-B)
74.28   it's] its (TSC1, TSC2-B)
75.2   She who] Who (TSC1-B)] She who (TSC1-C)
75.4   fate. He was neither] fate, Nora my dear, he was not formed
        (TSC1-B, TSC2-B)
75.9   The doctor looked at her.] "Exactly," said the doctor, (TSC1-
        B)
75.10   goes," he said, "that] goes, that (TSC1-B)
75.15   ax?] ax. (TSC1-B)
75.31   nowhere∧] ~, (TSC1-B)
75.32   abominations.] ~, even the ridiculous. (TSC1-B)
75.33   man] men (TSC1-B)
75.34   house,] ~∧ (E1)
76.13   night-fowl] night fowl (NW36-B; appears ND49)

76.23   particular; have . . . that?] ~, have . . . that now? (TSC1-C, B)
76.24   in . . . detachment.] 'in . . . detachment.' (TSC1, TSC2-B)
77.7   him] us (TS-B)
77.14   said] hooted (TSC1-B)
77.21   something.] ~∧ (TSC1-B)
77.22   Houses] houses (TSC1-B
77.23   as] and (TS-B)
78.9   umbrella on] umbrella or (TSC1)
78.15   most, with . . . a hundred legs? A centipede.] most? With . . . its
        hundred legs? a centipede. (TS-B)
78.30   *Place de la Bastille*] Place de la Bastille (TSC1-B, TSC2-B)
79.3   come] comes (TSC1-B, TSC2-B)
79.13   do?] do? What is to become of us?" (TSC1-B)
79.14   Ah,] ~∧ (E1)
79.20   mouse-meat] mouse meat (NW36-B; appears ND49)
79.23   tears?] ~. (PE1-B)
79.28   unhappily, "and] unhappily, "And (E1)
79.37   and though] and (TS-B)
80.1   I say] still (TS-B)
80.4   *mortadellas*] *mortadellos* (TSC1-B)
80.14   he said,] he added suddenly serious, (TSC1-B, TSC2-B)
80.25   *Skoll! Skoll!*] Skoll! Skoll! (TSC1, TSC2-B)
80.29   burial,] buried, (PE1-B)
80.33   one— ¶ "Yes!" Nora said.] one— (TSC1-B)
81.4   low-riding] low riding (DA)
81.12   heart, the] ~! The (TSC1-B, TSC2-B)
81.12   me?] ~, (TSC1-B, TSC2-B)
81.13   girl!] ~? (TSC1-B)
81.14   said,] said quietly, (TS-B)
81.19   No,] No, no, (TS-B)
81.19   an humble] a humble (NW36-B; appears ND49)
81.20   sorrow,] sorrow and anger, (TSC1-B)
81.24   everyone] every one (A1)
81.25   that; you] ~, and probably what you (TSC1-C, B)
81.26   feebleness enough] is just enough feebleness (TSC1-C, B)
81.32   entitled,] ~∧ (E1)
82.2   know.] know. It's driving me crazy." (TSC1-C, B)
82.6   visiting] visiting secretly (TSC1-C, TSC2-B)
82.10   manifold] manyfold (PE1-B)

82.12   house—] ~~ (E1)
82.21   said,] said, making a gesture, (TSC1-B, TSC2-B)
82.33   self-abused] self abused (TSC1-B)
83.1   asked.] asked quickly. (TSC1-C, B)
83.2   myself,] ~∧ (TSC1-B)
83.4   hurried decaying] hurried and decaying (TS-B)
83.5   fool's-stick] fools stick (NW36-B; appears ND49)
83.6   eternally] consequently, eternally (TSC1-B)
83.37   with a grin, "wrapped in a shawl] maliciously, "with a shawl
         (TSC1-B, TSC2-B)
84.3   *Opéra*] Opera (DA)
84.10   trouble for a generation,] trouble, (PE1-B)] trouble for a
         generation, (TSC1-C, B)
84.11   Danish count] foreign diplomat (PE1-B)] Danish minister
         (TSC1-B)
84.17   vulgarity (it's why I eat salad),] vulgarity, (PE1-B)
84.25   'God . . . better,'] ∧~ . . . ~, ∧ (A1)
84.34   amazed.] amazed and annoyed. (TSC1-C, B)
85.3   other] other that (TSC1, TSC2-B)
85.3   wanted,] intended or wanted, (TSC1-B, TSC2-B)
85.4   death; well,] death, well, (TSC1-B)
85.6   should have been] would be (PE1-B)
85.7   Jenny∧] ~; (TS-B)
85.8   that. What] ~, what (TS-B)
85.16   belly,] ~; (PE1-B)
85.19   down] along (PE1-B)
85.21   "Well,] "Well, as I was saying, (TSC1-B, TSC2-B)
85.22   means?] ~. (PE1-B)
85.29   and] but they (TS-B)
85.37   hip] left hip (TSC1-B)
86.12   me?'] me to her?' (DB to JL, 27 May 1946; appears ND49)
86.12   together; and my heart as heavy as Adam's off ox,] together;
         (PE1-B)] ~, (TSC1-B)
86.15   anything;] ~, (PE1-B)
86.17   it!' and] it!' And (PE1-B)
86.17   together. As] ~, as (TS-B)
86.19   "Yes," she said, "she met everyone."] "Yes, she said∧ she's met
         all of them. (PE1-B)] "She's met everybody." She said. (TSC1-
         B; B's emendation in TSC2 is the same as in PE1.)

86.28 cover,] ~∧ (E1)

87.7 words, 'Did . . . heaven?'] words. ∧Did . . heaven?∧ (PE1-B)

87.13 sleep.'] sleep.' What? Is this not night work, also?" (TSC1-C, B)

87.15 *Champs Elysées*] Champs-Elysées (E1)

87.18 love, were] love∧ were (PE1-F)] love were probably (TSC1-B)

87.21 water-closet] water closet (NW36-B; appears ND49)

87.31 chamber-pots] chamber pots (NW36-B; appears ND49)

87.33 dogs,] lousy dogs∧ (TSC1-C, B)

87.33 as if] as (TS-B)

87.35 frying-pan] frying pan (NW36-B; appears ND49)

88.6 horse-file] horse file (NW36-B; appears ND49)

88.6 wandering!] ~∧ (TS-B)

88.15 silence; he] silence, but he (TSC1-B)

88.17 it] my cane (TS-B)

88.21 decent] only decent (TSC1-C, B)

88.22 forget, –] forget, which is called (TSC1-B, C)

88.22 life;] ~, (TSC1)

88.22 good] only good (TSC1-C, B)

88.23 forgotten, –] forgotten; (DA)] ~, which is (TSC1-C, B)

88.23 I began] And I began (TSC1-C, B)

88.24 and the] the (TSC1-B)] and the (TSC1-C)

88.25 are;] want; (TSC1)

88.26 alone∧] alone, (NW36-B)] ~. (PE1-B)] alone∧ (TSC1)

88.26 wail, for] wail∧ for (NW36-B)]; wail, for] wail, and for (TSC1-B, TSC2-B)

88.27 would] would soon (TSC1-C, B)

88.27 going,] again, (PE1-B)] going, (TSC1-C)

88.28 decent] all decent and preoccupied (TSC1-C, B)

88.28 one fur] fur (PE1-B)] one fur (TSC1-C)

88.28 time. And] ~, and (TSC1-C, TSC2-B)

88.30 I] For, I (TSC1-C, B)

88.31 so greedy] greedy so greedy (TSC1-C, B)

88.33 gloves,] gloves, she might make a picture, and if she made a picture, (TSC1-C, B)

88.34 picture.] picture—but nobody does. (TSC1-C, B)

88.37 pleased] tight and pleased (TSC1-C, TSC2-B)

88.37 frightened.] frightened, and I said: She does not make a picture. (TSC1-C, B)

89.1 child—] child—a child makes *more* than a picture when (TSC1-

C, B)
89.1   there was] there is (TSC1)
89.1   it was] it is (TSC1)
89.2   I saw] and I saw (TSC1, TSC2-B)
89.3   she was] that she was (TSC1-C, B)
89.4   down,] down as if she wished to be capable, (TSC1-C, B)
89.4   open. And] open as if she wished to be ṣafe; and (TSC1-C, B)
89.5   said: God, you are no picture!] said: You are no picture! By God, you are no picture!' (TSC1-C, B)
89.8   some day] someday (TSC1)
89.9   those two] they (TS-B)
90.10   print),] ~ʌ (E1)
90.12   of] or (TSR-B, TSC1-B)
90.15   ʌholy decayʌ.] "~ ~ ." (TSC1-B, TSC2-B)
90.16   death;] death and ritual; (TSC1-B)
90.17   of six] or six (TSR-B, TSC1-B)
90.26   of its] of (TSC1-B, TSC2-B)
91.1   ʌestrangedʌ] " ~ " (TSC1-B, TSC2-B)
91.19   resurrection;] ~, (TSC1-B)
91.20   composite] a composite (PE1-B)
91.23   dissolution—must be profoundly elastic.] dissolution. (PE1-B)] dissolution, was undoutedly a static idea depraved by vascillation. (TSC1-B)
91.24   ¶ He] ʌ He (TSC1, TSC2-B)
91.25   states] state (TSC1-B, TSC2-B)
91.28   that] for that (PE1-B)
91.37   forgiveness;] ~, (TSC1-B)
91.37   absolution] the absolution (PE1-B)
92.2   overflowing,] ~ʌ (PE1-B)
92.3   being] because he was, (PE1-B)
92.5   Franciscan,] ~ʌ (E1)
92.8   ¶ Felix] ʌ Felix (TSC1-B)
92.10   were,] ~ʌ (FSG)
92.13   leaving,] ~ʌ (E1)
92.15   black-clad] black clad (E1)
92.23   end.] ending. (TS-B)
92.32   said,] ~ʌ (E1)
92.32   doctor.] ~ʌ That always takes a long time. (TSC1-B, TSC2-B)
92.34   doctor,] doctor— (E1)

92.37 added,] ~∧ (TSR-B, E1)

93.2 a companion] their companion (TSC1-B, TSC2-B)

93.8 smiled,] ~∧ (TSC1-B)

93.9 *Bois*] Bois (TSC1-B, TSC2-B)

93.16 *Bois*] Bois (TSC1-B)

93.22 fire.] ~, (E1)

93.23 speaking.] speaking and that he had not heard him. (TSC1-B, TSC2-B)

93.26 before,] ~∧ (E1)

93.28 her,] ~∧ (PE1-B)

94.8 like a child's drawing."] like the drawing of a child." (PE1-B)

94.11 woman] single woman (NW37-B)

94.16 possible, – it is a form of immortality."] possible, a form of immortality." (TSC1-B)

94.18 broken] spoiled the past, broken (TSC1-B)

94.20 ∧sole condition,∧] 'sole condition,' (TS-B)

94.22 that∧ she] that, she (TSC1, TSC2-B)

94.33 cigarette.] cigarette. "She was the personification of powerful and willful silence!" (TSC1-B, TSC2-B)

94.34 went on,] interjected, (PE1-B)

95.3 me?] me? Why? (TSC1-B, TSC2-B)

95.4 life."] life." "And," he added, taking the doctor's arm, "What I have heard of her kind of person only makes it more impenetrable." (TSC1-B, TSC2-B)

95.7 'rest of your life,'] "dark" and the "rest of your life" and all that, (TSC1-B)

95.19 ¶ But] ∧But (TSC1-B)

95.21 Field.] Field, (he was making a cool two thousand before people got the idea that it would be nice to shoot the world up and take the starch out of a generation.) (TSC1-B)

95.31 ¶ He'd] ∧He'd (TSC1-B)

96.8 glorious,'] ~∧ (DA)

96.17 ¶ I've] ∧I've (TSC1-B)

96.25 said,] ~∧ (DA)

96.32 stood,] ~∧ (E1)

97.1 Baron, studying the menu,] Baron∧ studying the menu∧ (E1)

97.3 doctor,] ~∧ (E1)

97.4 that?] that, (TS-B)

97.7 flat-toned] flat toned (E1)

97.11   hurried.] hurried about something she had not yet achieved. (TSC1-B, TSC2-B)
97.12   knee] knees (TS-B)
97.15   touched:] ~, (TSC1-B, TSC2-B)
97.16   convent] nunnery (ND46-B; also in notes to a French translator; appears ND61)
97.23   *oranges!*"] oranges!" (PE1-B)
97.24   uneasiness] great uneasiness (TSC1-B)
97.26   painting;] ~, (DA)
97.29   grandmother] mother (PE1-B)
97.32   was] was only (TSC1-B)
97.35   said, 'She] said, 'she (E1)
97.36   her] he (TSC1-B)
97.37   people,' –] people,' (TSC1-B)
98.1   eagerness.] eagerness, which I did not like. (TSC1-B, TSC2-B)
98.1   on: "She always] on: 'She is undoubtedly above us, but she always (TSC1-B)
98.6   not like] not at all like (TSC1-B, TSC2-B)
98.11   barge."] barge" grinned the doctor. (TSC1-B, TSC2-B)
98.13   Sylvia);] ~, (E1)
98.15   anyway,] ~∧ (A1)
98.25   Baron,] ~∧ (E1)
98.29   said,] ~∧ (E1)
98.33   over-large] over large (E1)
98.34   met,] ~∧ (PE1-B)
99.1   were] was (PE1-B)
99.6   move.] ~, (E1)
99.9   her.] ~, rather than to lament her." (TSC1-B)
99.17   person;] ~∧ for (TS-B)
99.18   Guido] him (TS-B)
99.19   The] "I hope so." The (TS-B)
99.20   know,] ~∧ (E1)
99.20   the] that the (TSC1-B)
99.21   age∧] ~, (TSC1-B, TSC2-B)
99.22   me.] ~; (TSC1-B)
99.23   joy.] joy. ¶ The Baron continued, (TSC1-B)
99.24   which is my son; he] of which my son (TSC1-B)
99.31   consent." He] consent," and he (TS-B)
100.2   the Baronin] she (TS-B)

100.4 innocence.] ~, but perhaps a very beautiful one. (TSC1-B, TSC2-B)

100.5 but] but after all, (TSC1-B, TSC2-B)

100.9 What] Beauty, in time, is indecent; for what (TSC1-B, TSC2-B)

100.12 "we do] "We do (E1-F)

100.13 neatness,] ~∧ (PE1-B)

100.14 born∧] ~, (TS-B)

100.18 true,"] true, true," (TS-B)

100.19 odour] odor (TSC1-B, TSC2-B)

100.24 is] is perhaps (TS-B)

100.25 untidy;] ~, (TSC1-B)

100.30 continued. "It] ~, "it (E1)

100.32 ago;] ~, (TSC1-B)

100.34 past∧] ~, (TSC1-B)

100.35 moment. Then] ~∧ and (PE1-B)

100.36 Baronin] baronin (TSC1)

100.36 degree;] ~, (TSC1-B)

100.37 silence,] silences, and she was very much given to them, (TSC1-B, TSC2-B)

101.7 not] not however (TSC1-B, TSC2-B)

101.11 we∧] ~, (TS-B)

101.15 preoccupation;] ~, (TSC1-B)

101.20 calamity, you] ~. You (TS-B)

101.22 whole] while (TSC1-B)

101.23 his] the calamity of his (TSC1-B)

101.23 prostrate] upright (ND46-B; appears FSC)

101.25 God's.] And God? What is God but the shadow cast on heaven of all the best people." (TSC1-B)

101.26 women of] women in (TSC1-B)

101.27 "Mary's shadow!" said the doctor.] "Ah!" the doctor exclaimed. "Mary's shadow!" (TSC1-B)

101.29 "People] "Some (TSC1-B, TSC2-B)

101.34 said under his breath:] said: (PE1-B)

102.2 dark;] ~, (TSC1-B)

102.4 sleep.] sleep. Good! (TSC1-B)

102.21 He said in a low voice,] He said, (PE1-B)

102.21 "Was] "was (TSC1-B)

102.25 quickly.] ~, (E1)

102.28 try to] try (TSC1-B, TSC2-B)
102.29 and better—funny,"] —funny (PE1-B)
102.36 answered, 'Remember me.' Probably] ~∧ "remember me," probably (TSC1-B)
103.2   'estranged'] "estranged" (TSC1, TSC2-B)
103.3   he said,] he said carefully TSC1-B, TSC2-B)
103.4   backstage] back stage (DA)
103.6   time;] ~, (TSC1-B)
103.6   perhaps, that that] perhaps, that (A1)
103.13 monocle,] ~∧ (TSC1-B)
103.13 carefully.] carefully. ¶ The handkerchief was, the doctor noticed, of black and yellow linen. (TSR-B, TSC1-B; C-L, 27 August 1935)
103.15 rode, into Vienna,] rode, (PE1-B)
103.29 hand, on the table,] hand∧ on the table∧ (PE1-B)
103.33 as] almost as (TSC1-B, TSC2-B)
104.2   laughing and talking] and laughing and talking too (TS-B)
104.9   (with] ∧with (PE1-B)
104.10 escape, ∧disproof] ~∧ (disproof (PE1-B)
104.12 points] point (E1)
104.13 of] back of (NW36-B; appears ND49)
104.15 swing,] ~∧ (PE1-B)
104.19 oil,] oil with extreme care, (TSC1-B; C-L, 27 August 1935)
105.1   Down,] ~∧ (E1)
105.2   now?"] now," (E1)
105.4   give up, now] give up? Now be (PE1-B)
105.11 Heaven] heaven (E1)
105.19 Virgins] virgins (DA)
105.20 good one] one (PE1-B)] good one (TSC1-B)
106.3   one thing] one (TSC1-B, TSC2-B)
106.14 better, he] better. He (PE1-B)
106.15 fate, go] fate. Go (PE1-B)
106.17 no;] ~, (PE1-B)
106.18 Abbey] abbey (E1)
106.18 Brec] Brech (ND46-B; appears ND61)
106.20 B.C.);] ~∧ (E1)
106.31 soldiers;] ~, (TSC1-B)
107.8   *papelero*] *papillero* (E1)
107.13 with a] a (TS-B)

107.17 forgivable;] ~ – (TSC1-B)
107.20 pen?] ~. (E1)
107.26 hand!] hand! It's the American gesture. And what about me? (TSC1-B)
107.31 – then] – and then (TSR-B, TSC1-B)
107.33 her;] ~, (TSC1-B)
107.34 loss,] loss. It's (TSR-B, TSC1-B)
107.35 account?] account! (PE1-F)
108.7 She said: "She] She said: "I can't help it—she (TSR-B, TSC1-B)
108.7 am] else am (PE1-B)
108.8 teeth, that] ~ . That (PE1-B)
108.13 on to] onto (E1)
108.16 impatience,] ~∧ (TSC1-B)
108.20 "'happy . . . innocent.'"] "∧happy . . . innocent.∧" (E1-F)
108.23 Now, that] Now it (TSC1-B)
108.23 would stop nothing.] wouldn't stop anything. (PE1-B)
108.25 check-rein] check rein (TSR-B, E1-F, PFSC-B)
108.30 We . . . bankruptcy then.] For this we . . . bankruptcy. (TSC1-B)
108.31 didn't." He] didn't," he (TS-B)
108.36 Every man] Everyman (PE1-F)
109.5 in] perhaps in (TSC1-B)
109.5 has] had (TSC1-B)
109.11 had] has (TSR-B, PE1-B)
109.14 I've got to.] I want to. (PE1-B)
109.17 any more port?"] anymore port?" (TS-B)
109.24 (which] —which (TS-B)
109.25 your flesh),] with your flesh, it's how you forgave Robin so much) (TSC1-B, TSC2-B)
109.26 structure,] ~∧ (TSC1-B, TSR-B)
109.28 painted. Death] painted—death (TS-B)
109.29 identification;] ~— (TSC1-B, TSC2-B)
109.33 on to] onto (E1)
109.33 loose!] ~. (TS-B)
110.6 girl,] ~∧ (TSC1-B, TSR-B)
110.20 rump,] ~∧ (TSC1-B)
111.5 alone, only∧] ~∧ ~, (TSC1-B, F)
111.5 corner∧] ~, (TSC1-B, TSC2-B)

111.7   ¶ "So] ∧So (TSC1-B, TSC2-B)

111.10   more] most (TSC1-B, TSC2-B)

111.11   hand] hand and (TSC1-B)

111.12   blessed] most blessed (TSC1-B)

111.13   corner,] corner, so no one could see me, (TSC1-B, TSC2-B)

111.24   all the while Tiny O'Toole was lying] holding the other with Tiny O'Toole lying across it (TSC1-B, TSC2-B)

111.32   This] Time (PE1-B)

111.34   holding] with (TSC1-B)] holding (TSC1-B)

111.34   bending] and bending (TSC1-B, TSC2-B)

111.35   forgot,] forgot the question (TSC1-B, TSC2-B)

111.35   crying,] crying, still looking at the poor little fellow as dead as only a private matter can be in a public place, (TSC1-B, TSC2-B; C-L, 27 August 1935)

111.36   Tiny] him (TSC1-B, TSC2-B)

112.1   animal,] ~∧ (TSC1-B)

112.4   child; then] child; and then (PE1-B)] ~——~ (TSC1-B)

112.5   compliment,—take] compliment—take (TSC1-B)

112.11   Venezia] Milano (TSC1-B)

112.23   sea-turned] sea turned (TSC1-B)

112.32   has, . . . reason,] ~∧ . . . ~∧ (PE1-B)

112.35   sat] he sat (TSC1-B, TSC2-B)

112.36   Robin was] Robin is (PE1-B)] yes, she was (TSC1-C, TSC2-B)

112.36   didn't] don't (TSC2-B)

113.1   had] has (TSC1-B)

113.5   witch-fire.] witch fire (TSR-B, E1)

113.8   do] so do (PE1-B)] do (TSC1-C)

113.9   also!] also! They do. (TSC1-B, TSC2-B)

113.11   flowers,] ~∧ (TS-B)

113.13   hour] hour now (TS-B)

113.13   last, and," she said desperately,] last, (PE1-B)

113.15   He brought his hands together.] He grinned. (NW36-B; appears A1)

113.18   and at] at (PE1-B)

113.20   said,] ~∧ (E1)

113.21   her] those (PE1-B)] her (TSC1-C)

113.23   rented] rent (PE1-B)] rented (TSC1-B)

113.26   world,] ~∧ (PE1-B)

113.26   some day] someday (E1-F)

113.27 person,] ∼∧ (TSC1-B)
113.33 me,] ∼∧ (PE1-B)
113.34 backside!] ∼, (TSC1-B, TSC2-B)
113.34 That] that (PE1-B)
113.34 love;] ∼, (TSC1-B, TSC2-B)
113.35 door?"] ∼. (TSC1-B)
113.37 moon? Telling] moon, telling (PFSC-B)
114.4   'Say] say (PE1-B)
114.5   something,] ∼∧ (E1-F)
114.5   God!' And] God∧' and (PE1-B)
114.7   place,] ∼∧ (E1-F)
114.12 sizes,] ∼∧ (TSC1-B)
114.13 God,] ∼∧ (TSC1-B)
114.14 get. Growing] get; and growing (TSC1-B, TSC2-B)
114.14 back;] ∼, (TSC1-B)
114.18 you;] ∼∧ (TSC1-B)
114.19 formula;] ∼ , (TSC1-B)
114.21 said,] ∼∧ (TSC1-B, TSC2-B)
114.24 boy.] boy and once, men who were children." (TSC1-B, TSC2-B)
114.25 before, . . . again,] ∼∧ . . . ∼∧ (TS-B)
114.27 invert, boy or girl] boy or girl? (PE1-B)] invert - boy or girl? (TSC1-E)
114.32 other, the] ∼. The (PE1-B)
115.13 wedded] weeded (TSC2-B; NW36; appears A1)
115.15 crying.] calling. (TSC1-B, TSC2-B)
115.16 ¶ Love] ∧Love (TS-B)
115.16 death, come upon] death reached (PE1-B)] death come upon (TSC1-C)
115.16 know, that] ∼∧ that (PE1-B)] that (TS-B)
115.17 wisdom.] ∼; (TSC1-B)
115.19 humour] humor (TSC1)
115.29 closet,] ∼∧ (TSR-B, E1)
115.29 do not] don't (TS-B)
115.29 day,] ∼∧ (TS-B)
116.1   agony."] agony - " (TSC1-B)
116.3   "It rots her sleep – Jenny] "Jenny (PE1-B)] It guts her sleep," said the doctor. "If I know wanything. She (TSC1-B)
116.5   suffer . . . should, or love . . . say] suffers . . . should, or loves

. . . say. (PFSC-B)] suffer . . . ~ʌ or love . . . we say. (TSC1-B, TSC2-B)

116.6   lie;] ~ʌ and (TSC1-B)

116.8   know themselves only] only know themselves (TS-B)

116.10   such!)] such) (PE1-B)

116.13   ¶ "To] ʌ"To (TSC1-B, TSC2-B)

116.14   oneself."] oneself, - for instance Adam and Eve, until—" (TSC1-B, TSC2-B)

116.18   cigarette;] ~ , (TSC1-B)

116.21   dawn! That's . . . back frightened.] dawn, that's . . . back: frightened. (TS-B)

116.23   with time,] even then, with timeʌ (TS-B)

116.25   other,] ~ʌ (TSC1-B)

116.25   love. Yet] love, and yet (TSC1-B)

116.27   yet there] there (PE1-B)

116.29   every man] everyman (A1)

116.32   ribs.] ~, and (TSC1-B, TSC2-B)

116.32   exception,] ~ʌ (TSC1-B)

117.2   now, in] now (PE1-B)] now in (TSC1-B)

117.12   safety;] ~, because (TSC1-B)

117.14   course, . . . wrong."] ~ʌ . . . heavy." (TSC1-B, TSC2-B)

117.16   you;] ~, (TSC1)

117.17   back] back to me (PE1-B)

117.21   her –] her – and (PE1-B)

117.25   fable,] ~ʌ (TSC1)

117.25   it; ah, the] it; the (PE1-B)] it - oh the (TSC1)

117.28   night,] ~ʌ (TS-B)

117.30   depressing.] still more depressing. (TSC1-B, TSC2-B)

117.30   would] in the world would (TSC1-B)

117.32   salon,] ~ʌ (TSR-B, TSC1-B)

117.32   blackʌ] black, (TSC1-B)

117.34   pillowʌ] ~, (TSC1-B)

117.35   then, . . . asked,] ~ʌ . . . ~ʌ (TS-B)

117.35   before] even before (TSC1-B)

118.1   dress;] dress; so (TSC1-B)

118.3   Then] And then (TSC1-B, TSC2-B)

118.5   lost).] lost. 'That's what I wanted to know,' I said." (TSC1-B, TSC2-B)

118.7   her,] ~ʌ for a moment, (TSC1-B, TSC2-B)

118.10 country,] ~∧ (TSC1-B)

118.10 said,] ~∧ (TS-B)

118.12 always;] ~, (TSC1-B)

118.14 "just good friends";] '~~~'; (DA)] ∧~~~∧; (TSC1-B)

118.18 broke. She] broke, but she (TSC1-B, TSC2-B)

118.20 'What are] 'what are (E1-F)

118.22 was, . . . liar,] ~∧ . . . ~∧ (TSC1-B)

118.27 knew, – the doll;] knew, the ~, (TSC1-B)

118.29 doll—] doll—I've been thinking about it— (TSC1-B, TSC2-B)

118.31 profane;] ~, (TSC1-B)

118.33 side! ¶ When] side! She paused, then she continued. ∧"When (TSC1-B, TSC2-B)

118.37 anymore.] anymore. I am sick.' (TSC1-B, TSC2-B)

119.6 lightness.] a great lightness (TSC1-B, TSC2-B)

119.7 ruined and you kept] so ruined that you kept (TSC1-B)

119.11 with,] with alone, (TSC1-B)

119.13 great ruin] ruin (TSC1-B)] great ruin (TSC1)

119.13 Why] And why (TSC1-B)

119.20 me; but] ~, and (TSC1-B)

119.22 ass∧] ~, (A1)

119.22 market,] ~∧ (DA)

119.25 wishing, . . . home,] ~∧ . . . ~∧ (TS-B)

119.26 always;] ~∧ (PE1-B)

119.29 possibly] possible (TSC1-B, TSC2-B)

119.33 home∧ (I . . . eyes'),] home; (I . . . eyes')∧ (DA)] home. I . . . eyes'∧ (TSC1, TSC2-B; semicolon inserted only on TSC1)

120.3 ¶ "I turned] ∧"And I turned around (TSC1-B, TSC2-B)

120.6 drunk.] sick drunk. (TSC1-B)

120.9 me. Then] things at me because she cared and I said, 'Do you mean that?' Then (TSC1-B, TSC2-B)

120.17 most of all,] most (PE1-B; E1-F inserts the comma.)

120.19 here,] her (TSC1-B)

120.23 ¶ "It] ∧"It (TSC1-B, TSC2-B)

120.26 her;] ~, (TSC1-B)

120.26 she started, and smiled,] she started and smiled, with that gentle smile, (TSC1-B, TSC2-B; comma after "started" only on TSC1)

120.27 complaint. She] ~, and she (TSC1-B, TSC2-B)

120.34 stopped.] paused. (TS-B)

120.35 drunk, Matthew, and had] ~ʌ ~ʌ and (TSC1-B, TSC2-B)
121.1   didn't,] didn't know, (TS-B)
121.5   her,] ~ʌ (E1)
121.12 ¶ "And] ʌ"And (TSC1-B, TSC2-B)
121.13 now,' she was asleep and] now,' and (TSC1-B, TSC2-B)
121.23 "Stop it! Stop it!" he cried.] "Stop it! Stop it! (TSC1-B, TSC2-B)
121.24 woman,' and so a] woman,' a (TSC1-B, TSC2-B)
121.25 plane,] plane, so (TSC1-B, TSC2-B)
121.33 life, you] ~. You (PE1-B)
121.34 it. And . . . innocent?] it—and . . . innocent? Why does she love many people? She doesn't love them at all, that's why. (TSC1-B, TSC2-B)
121.35 leaves,] ~ʌ (TSC1-B, TSC2-B)
122.8   ¶ "Oh] ʌOf (TSC1-B, TSC2-B)
122.8   sake,] ~ʌ (E1)
122.11 pride,] ~ʌ (TS-B)
122.11 forward, . . . place;] ~ʌ . . . ~ʌ (TSC1-B)
122.20 forgotten,] ~ ; (TSR-B, TSC1-B)
122.23 remembered.] remembered. The greatest gift of all!" (TSC1)
122.25 window, playing] ~ʌ or playing (ND46-B; appears FSC)
122.30 hers.] hers. She knew it. (TSC1-B)
122.32 in boy's] in her boy's (TSC1-B, TSC2-B)
122.35 time,] time— (PE1-B)
123.1   it,] it, on its head, (TSC1-B)
123.2   into it;] ~~, (TSC1-B)
123.4   floor.] floor, its blue bow now over, now under." (NW37-B; appears ND61)
123.5   together.] together softly. (TSC1)
123.7   still,] ~ʌ (E1-F)
123.11 eyeʌ] eye – (TS-B)
123.12 doll? The doll—] doll? – the doll— (PFSC-B)] doll? – the doll, effigy and shroud— (TSC1-B, TSC2-B)
123.19 blessed] holy (TSC1-B)
123.29 grandmother, whom I loved more than anyone,] grandmother, (PE1-B)
123.30 grass,] ~ʌ (TSC1-B, TSR-B)
123.32 living,] ~; (PFSC-B)
124.10 dreams. For] ~, for (PE1-B)

124.11 sleep.— And] sleep - and (TSC1-B)
124.11 Robin;] ~, (TSC1-B)
124.12 all my] my (PE1-B)
124.13 woke] woke up (PE1-B)
124.16 For] for (TSC1-B)
124.26 like;] ~, (A1)
125.3   Habeas Corpus] Habeas-Corpus (A1)
125.6   as you are] now (TS-B)
125.6   up,'] ~∧' (TSC1-B)
125.6   cannons] the cannons (TSC1-B, TSC2-B)
125.9   frantic] inadequately frantic (TSC1-B, TSC2-B)
125.14 Matthew,] ~∧ (TSC1-B)
125.18 it,] ~∧ (TSC1-B)
125.22 defiled,] ~∧ (TS-B)
126.4   too,] ~∧ (TSC1-B)
126.9   hands.] hands downward. (TSC1-B, TSC2-B)
126.16 remorseless,] ~∧ (TSC1-B)
126.30 life;] ~, (TSC1-B)
126.30 have built] build (PE1-B)
126.34 kicked] came along and kicked (NW36-B; appears A1)
126.35 eyes;] ~∧ (TSC1-B)
127.1   acclimation] acclimatation (TSC)] acclimation (TSC1)
127.4   high-up] high up (E1)
127.8   breast∧] ~, (TS-B)
127.8   affixed∧ we go] ~, we must go (PE1-B)
127.10 in dire] of dire (PE1-B)
127.18 God dared] the God dared to (TSC1-B, TSC2-B)
127.22 feet.] heels. (TSC1-B)
127.25 most] more (TSC1-B)
127.31 make,] make them, (TS-B)
127.36 *Sonate*] *Sonata* (TSC1)
128.4   balls] ballocks (PE1-B)] balls (TSC1-B, F)
128.4   head] heart (ND46-B, A1-B; appears FSC)
128.9   valley,] ~∧ (PE1-B)
128.18 feathers;] ~, (TSC1-B)
128.22 me and] me, like an arrow returned from the mark, and (TSC1-B)
128.24 gay. Only] ~, only (TSC1-B)
128.25 said,] ~∧ (TSC1-B)

128.25 me, 'only] me. 'Only (TSC1-B)
128.28 fright;] ~, (TSC1-B, TSC2-B)
128.31 loved] adored (TSC1-B, TSC2-B)
129.2   end,] ~∧ (TSC1-B)
129.4   alter, –] ~, (TSC1-B)
129.5   dissolute] desolate (PE1-B)] dissolute (TSC1-B)] desolate (TS-B)
129.5   night;] ~, (TSC1)
129.10 beginning,] beginning," she went on, (TSC1-B)
129.11 Not] "Wait, not (TSC1-B, TSC2-B)
129.14 the rudiment] rudiment (TSC1-B, TSC2-B)
129.15 city, for] ~∧ for (TS-B)
129.19 has loved] had loved (TSC1-B)
129.22 loved;] found; (PE1-B)
129.22 I found] they turned in my arms and I knew (TSC1-B)
129.26 her,] ~∧ (TSC1-B)
129.31 everything,] ~∧ (TS-B)
129.31 was;] ~, (TSC1-B)
129.32 lost] another (PE1-B)
129.35 *de bois*] *fous* (PE1-B)
130.2   waterfront] water front (E1-F)
130.4   broken-down] broken down (E1-F)
130.8   gaudy prints of the Virgin.] rich and bloody virgins; (PE1-B)
130.10 semi-darkness,] ~∧ (TSR-B, TSC1-B)
130.12 slept;] ~, (TSC1-B)
130.14 do,] ~∧ (TSC1-B)
130.16 dismay, the space between the human and the holy head, the arena of the 'indecent' eternal.] dismay. (PE1-B, TS-B)] dismay, knowing that the indecent is the eternal. (TS-B)
130.24 waxworks] wax works (E1-F)
130.26 love.] love: as a ruin gapes wider than the plan, so my heart gapes for Robin, who destroyed it." (TSC1-B)
130.27 coat.] coat. He did not know what to do. (TSC1-B, TSC2-B)
130.32 stood] stood up (B to JL, 27 May 1946; appears ND49)
130.33 he said] and said (PE1-B)
130.35 life.] life. He did not know what to do. (TSC1-B, TSC2-B)
131.5   came] come (TSC1-B, TSC2-B)
131.5   up; no] up, and no (TSC1-B)
131.8   of] if (TSR-B, TSC1-B)

131.19 flat.] flat on them. (TSC1-B, TSC2-B)

131.22 tune;] ~, (TSC1-B)

131.25 angrily,] ~∧ (TSC1-B)

131.25 *habitués*] habitués (PFSC-B)

131.26 trade;] ~, (TSC1-B)

131.28 hands,] ~∧ (TSC1-B)

131.31 said:] ~, (TSC1-B)

131.35 And was I . . . story? I was.] And I was . . . story! (PE1-B)] And
        was I . . . story? I was. (TSC1-B)

132.9   children mine] children (PE1-B)

132.13 directions.] ~? (NW36-B) appears ND49

132.29 stopped,] ~∧ (TSC1-B)

132.30 it,] ~∧ (TS-B)

132.35 brick-layer;] ~, (TSC1-B)

132.37 Guard] Guards (E1-F)

133.1   hairs, and] ~. And (TSC1-B)

133.4   someone. He] someone else; he (TS-B)

133.5   cursed.] he cursed. (TSC1-B, TSC2-B)

133.16 idea! And] ~, and (TS-B)

133.19 said.] said stiffly. (TSC1-B, TSC2-B)

133.21 everything,] ~∧ (TS-B)

133.23 life,] ~∧ (TSC1-B)

133.24 pond;] pond, (TSC1-B)] ~, just the same (TS-B)

133.26 on to] onto (TSC1-B, TSC2-B)

133.27 on to] onto (TSC1-B, TSC2-B)

133.28 mother;] ~∧ (TS-B)

134.2   out] up out (PE1-B)

134.4   me,] ~∧ (TSC1-B)

134.6   weeping, knowing] weeping. To know (PE1-B)] weeping. I
        know (TS-B)

134.8   much,] ~∧ (TSC1-B)

134.12 corner;] ~, (A1)

134.21 As] as (TSR, TSC2, A1)] As (TSC1)

134.21 off,] ~∧ (E1-F)

134.22 damned,] ~∧ (TSC1-B)

134.28 eye,] ~∧ (TS-B)

135.2   sin.'] In the morning I had orders to circumcise half the
        regiment and, 'You lousy bastards!' I screamed, 'why don't you
        use water?' and with that, with a whirl I cut round the last, and

out flew a cloud of moths." ¶ "Take bewilderment for a livlihood - that's another kind," said the doctor. (TS-B); use water] put these things in water (TSC1-B); last,] ~ʌ (TSC1-B)

135.4 'Now,] ~ʌ (E1-F)

135.7 ventricle,] ~ʌ (TSR-B)

135.9 Well,] ~ʌ (PE1-F)

135.12 priest,] ~ ʌ (TSR, TSC1-B)

135.12 crowd,] ~ʌ (TS-B)

135.14 Catherine the Great] Queen Victoria (TSC1-B, M, E)

135.26 Robin ever done?] ~ . (PE1-B)

135.26 Nora,] ~ʌ (PE1-F)

135.27 it,] ~ʌ (TSR-B, TSC1-B)

135.31 field;] ~ , (TSC1-B)

135.34 St. Stefan's] St. Stephans (E1-F)

135.36 separation.] separation you see they were. (TS-B)

136.3 argue,] ~ʌ (TSC1-B)

136.6 that justice] that (TS-B)

136.7 into] in (NW36-B; appears A1)

136.14 angryʌ] ~, (PE1-B)] ~ʌ (TSC1-B)

136.17 happen,] happen, all of it, (TSC1-B)

136.21 over,] ~ʌ (TSC1-B)

136.24 else, –] ~ , (TSC1-B)

137.4 should make] make (TSC1-F, TSC2-B)

137.5 She] She turned on her in a fury and (TSC1-B

137.5 Jenny] From that day Jenny (TSC1-B)

137.6 her;] ~, (TSC1-B)

137.11 out-of-the-way] out of the way (E1-F)

137.14 bent.] bent—They encompass me about—yea, they encompass me about—they encompass me about like bees." (TS-B)

137.15 something;] ~, (TSC1-B)

137.16 face,] ~ʌ (PE1-F)

137.16 knelt,] knelt, bending, (TSC1-B, TSC2-B)

137.16 palm,] palm whimpering, (TSC1-B, TSC2-B)

137.17 as] as of (PE1-B)

137.17 suddenly;] ~, (TSC1-B)

137.25 out;] ~, (TSC1-B, TSC2-B)

137.26 manner,] unguided and headlong manner, (TSC1-B)

137.27 flowers,] flowers that passed under her hand; (TSC1-B)

137.27 speaking] speaking harshly (TSC1-B)

137.28 near,] ~∧ (PE1-F)

138.5   She] She finally (TSC1-B, TSC2-B)

138.7   She] She no longer followed Robin because she (TSC1-B)

138.10 stumbling.] falling into the furniture. (TSC1-B, TSC2-B)

138.12 woods; the (E1-F)

138.17 (she . . . here)] —she . . . here— (TSC1-B, TSC2-B)

138.19 As she had] She had (PE1-B)] As she had (TSC1-B)

138.21 up,] ~ (TSR-B, TSC2-B, NW36-B; appears ND49)

138.22 a kerosene] the kerosene (PE1-B)

138.23 house;] ~, (TSC1-B)

138.24 other;] ~, (TSC1-B, TSC2-B)

138.25 Nora bent] With a quick involuntary gesture Nora put her
        hands on the fore parts of her legs, bending (TSC1-B, TSC2-B,
        L-C 27 August 1935)

138.26 listening;] ~, (TSC1-B)

138.27 down,] down again, (TS-B)

138.28 knees;] legs again, (TSC1-B)

138.28 She went] Suddenly she went (TSC1-B, TSC2-B)

138.28 out. The] ~, the (PE1-B)

138.31 grass, the] grass and the (PE1-B)

138.34 weather-beaten] weatherbeaten (PE1-F)

138.35 door. She] door and she (TSR-B, TSC1-B)

138.36 blindly, without] without (TS-B)

139.1   ¶ On] ∧ On (TS-B)

139.1   a Madonna] the Madonna (TSC1-B)

139.6   shoulder,] ~∧ (TS-B)

139.7   going down, down, her hair swinging, her arms out.] going
        down. Sliding down she went; down, her hair swinging, her
        arms held out, (PFSC-B)] going down. Sliding . . . out,] going.
        Sliding . . . out, (TS-B)

139.8   The dog stood] and the dog stood there (PFSC-B)] and the
        dog, the model of what she was about and the terror of what she
        was to do, stood there, (TSC1-B, TSC2-B)

139.9   hackle standing,] hackle standing; (PFSC-B)] hackle about his
        neck standing out stiff and beautiful; (ND46-B; appears ND49)

139.10 the tongue] his tongue (PSFC-B)

139.12 his,] ~; (PFSC-B)

139.14 throbbing,] ~∧ (PFSC-B)

139.14 hands] fingers (PFSC-B)] finger (PE1-F)

139.15 forward.] forward. "Where?" she whispered. "Where?" Where?" (TS-B; C-L, 27 August 1935)

139.16 back,] back, his lips drawn, (NW36-B, NW37-B, ND46-B; appears ND49)

139.18 whimpering too,] whimpering too now, (NW36-B, ND46-B; appears ND49)

139.19 Backed] Backed now (NW36-B, ND46-B; appears ND49)

139.23 sliding.] sliding, looking at her, striking against the wall, like a little horse; like something imploring a bird. (NW36-B, NW37-B, ND46-B; appears ND49)] sliding . . . a bird, a mistress. (PE1-B, TSR-B, TSC2-B)

139.23 Then head down, dragging] Then as she, now head down, dragging (NW36-B, NW37, ND46-B; appears ND49)

139.24 she struck] struck (NW36-B, NW37-B, ND46-B; appears ND49)

139.24 side. He] side, he (ND46-B; appears ND49)

139.27 side, now that,] sideʌ now thatʌ (PE1)

139.30 obscene] unclean (PE1-B)] obscene (TSC1-E)

139.30 Crouching, the dog began to run with her,] The dog began to cry then, running with her, (ND46-B; appears FSC)

139.31 head-on] head on (PE1-F)

139.31 as if to circumvent] as if slowly and surely to circumvent (NW36-B; appears ND46)] as if to slowly and surely circumvent (TSC1-B, TSC2-B)

139.37 eyes bloodshot, his head flat along her knees.] head flat along her knees, his eyes bloodshot, and waiting. (TS-B; L-C, 27 August 1935)

TEXTUAL NOTES

4.18 felt the echo] In the left margin of TSC1, a red pencil comment "disentangle" led Barnes to omit the phrase "without vocal necessity."

4.36 everything possible] It appears "possible" was omitted through error; it was not deleted on any of the typescripts, nor does it appear on PE1.

7.5 handsome)] Barnes was not careful about punctuation when she made textual corrections; on PE1 it appears she deleted the comma after "windows," but left the second comma of the pair after the parenthesis. It is deleted.

8.13 inherit, for the Jew] On TSC2, Barnes inserted a semicolon, circled "for," and directed attention to Morley's correction on TSC1 where he questioned in red pencil the deletion of "for" and inserted a colon and a cap "T." Presumably Barnes decided to retain the original typescript punctuation, for it appears in E1.

8.17-21 One . . . Uffizi] This deletion appears only on TSC1 in the style of Eliot, three lines diagonally across the section. Because it is not marked for deletion on any other typescript by Barnes, it is restored.

11.20 but which,] Only in TSR does a comma appear after "which," but it is accepted for clarity.

13.16 oneself] On PE1 "herself" appears instead of "oneself," likely a typesetter error. Barnes changed it, but the change apparently went unnoted. In her copy of the first English edition, she made the change a second time.

14.12 enough sense] is the wording on the typescripts, but "sense enough" appears in PE1 and E1, apparently a typesetter transposition that went undetected. The original wording is retained.

14.22 so,] No punctuation followed the "so" on TSC1 or TSC2, but on

TSR, Barnes used a semicolon. However, a comma is more appropriate and aids readability.

15.1 theory,] The parenthetic comment is set off to prevent misreading.

15.2 can,] After "can" Barnes inserted semicolons on TSR and TSC2, but changed to a comma on TSC1.

16.5 care,] It appears that though Barnes added the comma after "care" on TSR and TSC2, it was not transferred to TSC1 and thus not integrated into the text until Barnes inserted it on PFSC.

16.8 nodded the doctor] Barnes penciled in "nodded" and "laughed" above "grinned" in NW36. In A1, "nodded" appears.

17.2 As abruptly,] The introductory adverb refers to the previous action, his "uncontrollable laughter" and therefore needs to be set off.

17.14 become as the wives of] Though this phrase appears in the typescripts and is not marked for deletion, it has not appeared in any edition. As it was presumably omitted in error, one that Barnes did not notice in proofing later editions, it is accepted in this edition.

18.36 gesture of the prince] The word "gesture" is crossed out on TSC1, apparently by Eliot. Because it is not marked for deletion on any other typescript and because there appears to be a legitimate distinction between the prince and his gesture, the original phrasing is accepted.

19.21 on, "in] On TSC2 Barnes inserted the comma, but left "In" capitalized. The first edition reading is accepted.

19.29 at the far end of the animal,] Originally, on TSR Barnes enclosed the phrase "thanks be to my maker I had her head on" in parentheses; however, TSC1 shows a period after "animal" and a capital beginning "Thanks" with no parenthesis. Since it is not clear who made the change, and since the parentheses of TSR indicates that the phrase is subordinated, rather than the opening thought of the next sentence, it is accepted. This phrasing seems most consistent with O'Connor's style of discourse. On TSC1, the phrase "the hole was no bigger than a tea-tray" is lined out, but marked stet in the margin. It is accepted in this edition, though it has not appeared in any other edition.

20.13 spirits."] After inserting "spirits" on the typescripts, Barnes deleted it only on TSR.

20.22 conversation;] The phrase applies to Dr. O'Connor, not the headsman, and a semicolon clarifies this point.

20.23   snatched from the senate.] The phrase is marked out only on
TSC1, but Barnes restored it on PE1.

20.32   failure for the rest of my life.] The phrase is deleted on TSC1,
but "stet" appears in the margin, and Barnes inserted it on PE1.

21.27   laughing silently] Barnes changed the phrase in her copy of the
first edition, probably to eliminate the frequency of "grinning,"
which she had noted.

23.9-25.35   "Quite right . . . power."] This three-page passage was de-
leted by Eliot, a deletion suggested by Coleman. In the margin of
TSC2 Barnes had written, "From here to 32 can be cut if you think
there are too many doctor's stories – see Coleman on other ms."
The block has been included in this edition because letters to
Coleman indicate her reluctance to have anything deleted, unless
Eliot confirmed it. Presumably, then, she acquiesced in the deci-
sion, but regretted the deletion.

23.11   nothing, all packed] Barnes placed a comma after "all," on all
three typescripts, but sense clearly requires the comma after
"nothing."

23.15   collar—and I wouldn't . . . collar—] The phrase between the
dashes is crossed out on TSC1 by an unknown hand; since it is not
deleted on any other typescripts, it is accepted in its original form.

24.26   very much, they said,] On the typescripts Barnes changed the
period after "much" to a comma, deliberately drawing these
phrases together. Even though there is some danger of misreading the first phrase as a direct quote, her change is accepted.

25.7   (that seems . . . coming in),] In the margin of TSC1 Barnes wrote
"save" in pencil next to this line in the section marked for deletion
by Eliot.

25.36   "Listen," the doctor said, ordering a round, "I] Though this line
is part of the typescript, it is handwritten at the top of TSC1 on
page 32. It reflects Coleman's suggested deletion to Eliot. The
note, "pp 29-31 out" also appears. A few pages later, on page 35, a
second note, "pp 33-34 out" also appears.

26.16-28.19   "Halt!" said the doctor, . . . me a friend."] Crossed out on
TSC1 by Coleman and confirmed by Eliot, this section is restored
to this edition. It is not deleted on any other typescript, and while
the motive may have been to reduce the doctor's stories, his stories
also focused directly on his homosexuality.

28.23-37 "You have . . . pride of the race."] This section is marked for deletion by Eliot. Perhaps the objection was simply too many doctor's stories or it may have been the openly homosexual theme. Since it is not marked for deletion on the other typescripts, it has been restored to this edition.

28.25 this badly executed leap] Within a passage marked for deletion, the phrase "badly executed" has been lined through by an unknown hand only on TSC1; it is restored to this edition.

29.1-12 "Listen to the music. . . something."] The section was deleted by Eliot on (TSC1). It has been restored to this edition.

29.8 Piazza] has been left as it appears in the typescripts, though a Spanish setting would require *Plaza*. However, O'Connor is speaking and Barnes has indicated that he is not necessarily authoritative.

30.27 custom] This correction first appears in Barnes's mother's copy. After her mother's death—15 March 1945, noted on the inside cover—Barnes used this copy to make corrections. It seems likely this copy is referred to in her letter to Laughlin of 26 April 1949 as the corrected copy she had sent him.

31.20 withdrawal,] The original typescript punctuation following "withdrawal" was a comma and since the phrase that follows describes the action of the lover, the comma is more appropriate. It is not clear who inserted the semicolon on TSC1, but the change is made only on that typescript.

31.23 bowels—] Coleman's letter of 27 August 1935 observes that "for an aim" seems wrong, and in September Barnes indicates her acceptance of this suggestion and others.

31.33 whale-shit—excuse me—] The dash after "me" appears to have been suggested by Morley, replacing Barnes's original comma.

31.36 down by the devil] Although on the typescript it is not clear who omitted the phrase "in the mud," it is accepted because the contrasting action of "smacked down" and "lifted up" is more immediate.

32.20-22 The doctor ordered . . . the doctor added] Barnes's open style of punctuation and an unclear "he" caused her to modify the sentence in TSC1 and again in PE1. The reading of E1 is accepted here for its clarity.

33.1 as the heart] This phrase, instead of "at the heart," seems to be the meaning Barnes intended; "at" apprears to be a typographical error that went unnoticed.

33.11 by the by] It appears that a typesetter introduced the change to "by the way" in the proof to E1. The typsecript phrasing is retained.

33.29 explained] It appears that the typesetter inadvertantly substituted "exclaimed" in PE1 rather than "explained," which appears in the typescript.

34.7 forgotten, left without ... cover (which, like ... housewives),] The original punctuation of TSC2 has been retained with the exception of the parentheses before and the comma after "which"; Faber editors suggested "which" instead of the original "that" and Barnes concurred. In addition, on TSC1, it appears that someone added a dash after "left" and "housewives" and changed the comma after "cover" to a left parenthesis, with a right parenthesis after "housewife." However, typesetters missed the left parenthesis. Thus, on the proof to E1, Barnes inserted a comma after "which," without noting that the left parenthesis did not appear, leaving a dash and only the right parenthesis after "housewives." Since these dashes separate what are essentially coordinate adjectives "forgotten" and "left," they have been omitted, retaining the original commas after "forgotten" and "housewives" and reinserting the left parenthesis before "which."

34.13 thick lacquered] The typescript punctuation is retained rather than "thick-lacquered" of later editions. Barnes presumably meant the pumps were thick, not necessarily the lacquer.

34.20 a sleep] On TSC1, "a" is cirled in red with a stet in the margin. Evidently, associate editor Morley (he seems to have used the red pencil) questioned the use of "a" with sleep.

34.27 meet] On TSC1, "the" is inserted, then crossed off by an unknown hand or hands.

34.33 of wood-winds] In the margin, Barnes has written "wind instruments" and then crossed it out.

35.9 all right,] On TSC1 a semicolon was inserted after "right" by an unknown hand; the original puncutation has been retained as adequate to separate the two actions.

35.27 origin, the doctor] The original punctuation of TSC2 is retained; the semicolon inserted in TSC1 by an unknown hand unnecessarily separates a participial phrase from the noun it modifies. The noun phrase "doctor's hand" results in a dangling modifier, and since it can easily be changed, it has been.

36.9 *promenoir*] Barnes pencils "promenade" above "promenoir," but chooses apparentely "promenoir." In the same sentence, she inserted "or theatre" in all typescripts, but dropped the two words in her personal copy of A1, though she returned to the phrase in ND46, reinserting it. Sense requires its omission, however.

36.31 infected, carrier of the past—before] In her letter of 27 August 1935, Coleman objected to "the magnetized beastly" and Barnes deleted it from all copies of the typescript. The comma and semicolon after "infected" are crossed off and then inserted on TSC1 and TSC2 with a marginal insert mark, though the comma does not appear on the proof. Barnes apparently intended "the infected," to be read as an appositive indicating that to be infected is to be a "carrier" of the past.

37.9 audience, –] It appears Barnes has added the dash after the comma, but the comma is not crossed out.

39.24 theatres,] Although a semicolon has been inserted after "theatres" by an unknown hand, the original comma is retained as what follows is simply a pair of absolute modifiers.

39.30 happiness. Thinking] On TSC1, "yet" is blocked out by an unknown hand but rewritten above the deleted word by Barnes.

39.34 bitter,] On PE1 "bitter" is followed by a colon, but it does not reflect Barnes's decision, nor is it necessary.

39.35 incurable,] The comma appears to have been deleted on TSC1, but Barnes inserted it again. It is accepted in this edition.

40.1 excellent,] Barnes introduced the change in her mother's copy of *Nightwood*. This copy appears to have been given to New Directions in 1949; the changes are integrated in the 1949 edition. The comma was inserted in E1.

40.11 him.] Coleman wrote that the phrase "because she was an orphan" "must come out." Barnes concurred, as the deletion on all three typescripts suggests (L, 27 August 1935).

40.28 accepted,] The phrase following "accepted" is not adverbial, describing manner of acceptance; therefore a comma is appropriate.

41.9 another, though she asked why.] Though "though she asked why" his has been lined through in pencil on TSC1 by an unknown hand, the phrase is accepted in this edition because it provides the reason for Felix being "brought up short" in the next sentence.

41.12 anything, though now,] The insertion of a semicolon after "anything" and the deletion of "though" on TSC1 by an unknown hand makes this sentence abrupt; the reading of TSC2 is accepted.

41.25 her legs] Coleman points out that Barnes has written "boy's legs" elsewhere and should not overemphasize it (L, 27 August 1935).

42.23 run,] On the proof to FSC, Barnes inserted the comma after "run"; however it is not integrated into the edition. It is accepted in this edition.

44.31 Felix, having come in unheard, found] On TSC2, Barnes had inserted "he" before "found," but did not translate the change to TSC1; the editor, instead, inserted a comma after "Felix," thus making "Felix" the subject of the sentence.

45.23 that."] Coleman writes that the original phrase is "chi-chi" and "should be out" (L, 27 August 1935). Barnes concurs and removes "he is so sweet" on all typsecripts, but "Have you noticed him?" only on TSC1 and TSC2.

45.30 time.] Coleman suggested that the phrase be omitted. Barnes concurred (L, 27 August 1935).

46.1 Night Watch] In the table of contents to the typescript, the chapter title is hyphenated, but in the chapter heading itself it is not.

46.19 that wood . . . in her,] In her mother's copy of *Nightwood* Barnes deleted the phrase "that wood in the work; the tree coming forward in her," but the phrase has appeared in every edition. The phrase is retained in this edition.

47.7 upright] circled in red on TSC1 with a question mark; stet appears in the margin.

47.18 immune to] This wording appears in the TS and has been accepted here rather than "immune from" which appears in E1. Barnes means that Nora is not "not affected by" a given influence, rather than "not subject to an obligation."

47.35 (she . . . arts),] In her letter of 8 November 1935 Barnes confirms that Coleman is right about the "omissions re Nora," and tells her to take out "Need to be up in the matter of the arts," and "she would tell in time everything they told her," but does not feel the sentence "She had, in anxiety not to fail, been from one faith to another" should be omitted. However, Coleman returns to the point in her letter of 16 November 1935 and argues that the passion of Nora is inconsistent with the description of one who has anxiety not to fail. Evidently her argument persuaded Barnes, for the phrase is crossed out in TSC2 and in TSC1.

48.16 herself. ¶ One] See previous entry.

48.27 priest . . . There] This passage is a deletion suggested by Coleman, according to Barnes's response of 8 November 1935 to a Coleman letter which is not in either collection.

48.28 in her; she] On TSC1 a semicolon is inserted after "betrayal," but when the phrase is deleted, the semicolon occurs after "her."

49.4 fall of 1923] Barnes questions "fall" on TSC1, writing "autumn" in the margin, and changes the date to 1923; on TSC2 she substitutes "autumn," leaving the date 1926; on TSR "fall 1923" appears. "Fall of 1923" is accepted.

49.36 mid-winter.] Coleman urges Barnes to delete the phrase "then she wanted to go" and it is marked out on TSC1; on TSC2 Barnes has inserted "became restless" for "wanted to go." The deletion is accepted, Barnes presumably concurring (L, 27 August 1935).

50.7 permanent by her own strength,] Barnes rewrites this phrase above the line where it has been crossed out on TSC1.

52.19 curling irons] In her personal New Directions 1946 Barnes substituted "curling irons" for "electric curlers." Though the change was not integrated into the reset printing or succeeding editions, it is accepted in this edition.

52.30 she said.] Coleman suggested the deletion of the phrase "I may be late," and Barnes apparently concurred easily, for it is deleted on all three typescipts (L, 27 August 1935).

53.25 head . . . loved] Barnes deleted the comma after "head" in PE1, but a comma that had followed "loved" was omitted on the proof. Because it was paired with the comma after "head," its omission is accepted in this edition.

53.36 extinction] On the proof to the 1962 Farrar edition, Barnes inserts a comma after "extinction." She may have been responding to the difference in length of pause because a comma had replaced her original semicolon after "against" in the previous clause. Her original semicolon is retained after "against" and no comma follows "extinction."

53.37 activity.] Barnes noted that "function" was repeated in this sentence in her personal copy of E1, but the change was not made until the Farrar, Cudahy editon.

55.8 room—an expansive] On TSC2 Barnes retained the phrase, "Nora had loved her grandmother more than anyone of her family" but it is deleted in TSC1. It is one of the passages that Coleman suggested deleting and perhaps she "obliterated" it on TSC1 because of the difficulty of the phrase "an expansive, decaying splendour" which followed "grandmother" (L, 27 August 1935). The reading of TSC1 is accepted.

55.25 further] In E1 "farther" is substituted for Barnes's "further"; original accepted.

55.37 grandmother, who] The "who" clause is nonrestrictive, and for clarity, the comma is added.

58.15 *accouchée*] On TSC1, stet appears in the right margin signaling the retention of "accouchée" rather than "brought to bed," a phrase in the left margin that is crossed off.

59.22 vocabulary] The word "tragic" has been circled in red with a question mark in the margin, presumably by Eliot or Morley. It is crossed out in pencil, probably by Barnes.

59.31 story – the teller herself.] On the typescripts a semicolon follows "story," but this seems to lead a reader to expect a series or a full sentence; a dash is substituted for clarity.

59.34 *Camélias*] A red line under "Camille" prompts Barnes to supply *La Dame aux Camélias*.

60.5 perhaps] On TSC1, in the phrase "she had read, perhaps, ten books in her life," "perhaps" has been blocked out, and the commas deleted, but Barnes reinserted "perhaps" above the line without restoring the commas. The blocking out of phrases appears to be the work of Coleman, what she referred to in her diary as phrases she had "obliterated."

60.30 over these] E1 changed the phrase to "over those," perhaps a misreading because of the type. The original has been retained because it gives a sense of the "presentness" of the feeling for the past.

60.32-37 When she fell . . . by instinct.] This passage is circled in red pencil with a red parenthesis around "She was a 'squatter' by instinct." In the margin in pencil is the note, likely Barnes's, "think this over." On TSC2 Barnes had circled the same phrase and drawn a line from it to the beginning of the paragraph. It is possible that Eliot or Morley questioned the passage in their meeting with Barnes; however, no changes were made.

61.6 twenty-seven.] On TSC1, "She . . . Abelard" represents the collaborative effort of Barnes and Coleman. The words, "as . . . Abelard" are crossed out by two lines in ink, as suggested by

Coleman in her letter of 27 August 1935. Subsequently, "She . . . Nora" is deleted in pencil, a second stage revision. Thus, the two-line deletion appears to be Coleman's, but Barnes marked out the entire passage in TSR and TSC2, transferring to the next paragraph (on TSC1 and TSC2) the idea that Jenny feared meeting Nora.

61.12   gait –] A red line deletes the comma that originally followed "gait" (gait, –), indicating a Faber decision, but the deletion is accepted because it also appears on TSC2, indicating that Barnes may have concurred or initiated the change.

61.26   foot down, –] In her letter of 8 November 1935 to Coleman, Barnes exclaims that "static cock fight" must come out and that "Really Emily you are amazing and wonderful! The trouble you take." She is responding to a Coleman letter that does not appear to have survived.

61.28   at the opera] In the proof to the first English edition, Barnes inserted the phrase "described later" after "opera," setting it off by commas, but it did not appear in the first edition nor in subsequent editions. The phrase is not accepted in this edition for it creates the effect of the narrator commenting on the process of narration, an effect inconsistent with the narrator's role throughout.

62.7   ceased and sat,] Barnes marked the phrase for deletion after "ceased" in her mother's copy of the first English edition and on 14 December 1949 she wrote to Pierre du Sautoy of Faber that she hoped the same change (and two others) could be made in the second English edition of 1950. Apparently, her letter arrived too late, for none of these changes appeared in E2. However, beginning in 1949 New Direction editions incorporate the change, though not after "ceased" but after "sat," perhaps to avoid the potential for misreading, "ceased, staring . . ."

63.9   got up] In the right margin of TSC1, a red pencil notation (Morley) suggests "dressed up"; perhaps the impetus for Barnes's change.

63.17   with them] has been crossed out and then written in above the line.

64.5   "Christ's sweet foot, where] This passage has been blocked out only on TSC1, presumably Coleman's decision, which Barnes may have agreed to. However, it seems an attempt to censor, and it has been restored to this edition.

64.17 "Just the girl] In TSC1, "Just" is deleted and "the," is capitalized, but Barnes restores the original version.

64.36 he said, "one who . . . a 'queen.'] This passage was enclosed in red pencil parentheses, presumably by Morley for discussion. A red delete mark is in the left margin, and a blue penciled question mark, presumably Eliot's, in the right margin. Beneath the blue question mark is the phrase "might better be out?" This comment appears to be Barnes's. However, the passage is retained as it was certainly a matter of softenening what both editors saw as material that might raise the censor.

66.12 terrible thing!"] On TSC1, the succeeding phrase "does not exist!" is blocked out, but here it is a matter of a stylistic change that Barnes probably accepted. The deletion is accepted.

66.13 doubled fist.] The phrase, "It does, it does!" is also blocked out in Coleman's style, but the deletion is accepted. It is likely that Barnes concurred in the decision not to make the direct assertion or contradiction regarding love.

67.6 It was not long after this that] blocked out in TSC1, but rewritten above the line in Barnes's hand.

68.1 Watchman, What of the Night?] On the typescript, the chapter title appears in capital letters, but in the chapter heading itself it is written as above. The small "w" of "What" and the exclamation mark after "Night" are found only in the table of contents.

68.7 slowly. She] In TSC1 eight words are inserted above the line and then blacked out; illegible.

68.9 Misery. . . friend.] On TSC1 pencil brackets appear to question whether this sentence should be deleted, but a red penciled stet appears in the margin.

69.4 belligerence in] On TSC1, "a certain amount of" has been crossed out, but Barnes inserted "a certain" above the deletion, making the line conform to TSC2; however, only on TSC1 is "about" replaced by "in."

69.9 flannel night gown.] In her 27 August 1935 letter, Coleman wrote, "about the flannel nightdress I wd have definitely out; just mention he wore it. I do not think it fits here to say it is our mother—and a bit smarty." On TSC2, Barnes deleted everything after "gown," but on TSC1, the phrase "for a night dress is our mother" appears to be deleted by two double pencil lines. "With" has been capitalized, but then the sentence is lined through with a single line. A blue pencil question mark apparently prompted Barnes to reconsider the passage. A delete mark appears in the margin. The section after "gown" is deleted on TSR as well, indicating Barnes's agreement.

69.15 head,] It appears a semicolon follows "head" on TSC1, but in E1 a colon appears; the original comma of the TS is retained.

69.17 was only] On TSC1 "really" is blocked out entirely, a style that often indicates Coleman's suggestion.

69.22 the night.] The emended passage reflects an exchange between Coleman and Barnes via letter (27 August 1935). In response to Coleman's observation that "her" in the original wording ("about the night, about her, about Felix, about Robin") was ambiguous, Barnes deleted "about the night" on TSC2 and TSR. Then on TSC2 Barnes wrote "about the night" in above the line and crossed out the rest, making no change to TSR. Barnes weighed the phrasing before returning to the more abstract "about the night."

69.33 that, giving . . . , is] The comma after "that" completes what is a pair setting off a nonrestrictive modifier.

71.17 *Notre Dame de la Bonne Garde*] so reads the title when used earlier by O'Connor (see 27.37, 28.14), reflecting Barnes's usage. The published versions have *Notre Dame-de-bonne-Garde* here, which is irregular (proper French form would have a hyphen also between *Notre* and *Dame* and would capitalize *bonne*), so it has been emended to be consistent with its earlier appearance.

72.32 come upon you heavily.] On TSC1 "heavily" had been blocked out, but Barnes reinserted the word above the line.

72.34 heart, unless you] On TSC1, "I say" and "as undoubtedly" have been blocked out entirely, but they have also been crossed out by Barnes on TSC2. Thus, they may have been initiated by Coleman and accepted by Barnes. However, on TSC2, Barnes did not change the original comma after "heart" to a semicolon. That change on TSC1 may have been made before the sentence was ended at "it." Barnes's original comma is accepted.

73.4 and expect] On TSC1 "and" is written above the blocked "yet," indicating perhaps Coleman's editing. However it has been accepted because just several lines before this line Barnes had reinserted a word, indicating she had very likely reviewed the change.

73.9 she said.] On TSC1 "I cannot endure my life" is written, perhaps by Coleman, above "What can I do?" Both phrases are crossed out. The change is accepted because on TSC2 Barnes also crossed out the original phrasing.

73.32 sun? For now] On TSC1, the phrase "It is not" is blocked out, perhaps by Coleman, but the deletion is accepted because the page contains other editorial marks by Barnes.

75.2 "She who stands"] On TSC1, "She" has been blocked out and "who" capitalized, probably by Coleman; but Barnes wrote "She" above the blocked word.

75.4 fate. He] The phrase "Nora my dear" is deleted on both TSC1 and TSC2, but only on TSC1 is "he" capitalized and the comma after "fate" deleted, apparently by Barnes.

75.6 ¶ "You . . . philosopher."] On TSC1, the entire paragraph has been lined through diagonally, probably by Eliot, but stet appears in the margin. On TSC2 Barnes has joined it with the previous paragraph, but then reinserted the paragraph mark.

75.12 that company. ¶ When] On TSC1 Barnes combined the paragraph beginning with "When" with the previous paragraph, but changed her mind, reinserting the paragraph mark.

75.17-20 Or is confessing . . . pleases?] This passage was enclosed in blue pencil brackets and lined diagonally in blue on TSC1, probably by Eliot. A question mark and a blue editor's delete mark appear in the margin. It is also lined through in pencil on TSC2. However, the deletion reflects an attempt to soften the sexual and anticlerical theme. It is restored to this edition.

76.23 that?] The word "now" following "that" was blocked out, probably by Coleman, but the deletion is accepted.

77.37 in search of my man . . . looking for her woman.] On TSC1 a blue pencil lines out "in search of my man" and "looking for her woman, but" and the phrases are lined out lightly on TSC2, with a question mark in the margin. However, it appears to be an instance of pressure to soften the homosexual openness of the text. The phrases have been accepted in this edition.

78.12 cottages of delight] On TSC1 a red parenthesis, likely Morley's, encloses "delight," and an editor's blue delete mark is in the margin. The word has been accepted in this edition; it is not marked out in other typescripts and seems an attempt to suppress the suggestion of pleasure with respect to homosexual acts.

78.16 its hundred] "a" is changed to "its" only on TSC1.

78.17 picked a bird] This phrase is enclosed in blue pencil parentheses. The editor, likely Eliot, appears to have been avoiding reference to homosexual invitation.

79.34 still, . . . rest.' "] On TSC1 and TSC2 a period follows "murdered," and a single line deletes the rest of the sentence; however, a stet appears in the margin of TSC1. The original comma after "still" is retained in this edition, Barnes presumably using "still" to refer to motion, not the adverbial "still quiet." In her mother's copy of the first English edition, Barnes crossed out "now I can rest," but apparently did not communicate this change to later editors, for the phrase appears in all editions.

80.4 *mortadellas*] In the margin in blue pencil, "think this over." On TSC2 "the devil" is written above "mortadellos," but, according to Coleman's diary, Peter Hoare corrected the spelling and Barnes kept the phrase.

80.27 Or walks . . . holding her hands] In this paragraph, on TSR, Barnes has changed "her" to "their," probably in order to be consistent with number in the previous paragraph. However, perhaps because the passage loses its sense of singular suffering, she did not transfer the change to TSC1 or TSC2.

80.33 one—" ¶ "Yes!" Nora said.] This passages is inserted by hand; "Ah" before "yes" has been crossed off.

81.26 feebleness enough] This phrase has been revised from "enough feebleness" on TSC1 and TSC2, but only "just" is crossed out on TSC2; "and probably what" and "is just" are deleted on TSC1 by being blocked out, likely Coleman's style. However, Barnes reviewed and accepted the change.

82.2 know.] The deleted phrase, "It's driving me crazy," was blocked out on TSC1, probably by Coleman; on TSC2 Barnes crossed out "crazy" and inserted "mad." The deletion is accepted.

82.25 put to it to] On TSR and TSC2, Barnes changed this phrase to "hard put to" but not on TSC1; the phrase has remained unchanged in all subsequent editions.

83.1 asked.] The word, "quickly" following "asked" has been blocked out. Its deletion has been accepted.

84.10 trouble, for a generation, and] On TSC1, a comma has been inserted after "trouble," the phrase blocked out, perhaps by Coleman, but on the proof to E1, Barnes restored it.

84.11 Danish count.] On TSC1, a blue pencil underlines "Danish minister." The words "foreign diplomat" are inserted, and in the margin "nobleman" is written and subsequently crossed out. The word "nobleman" also appears on TSC2 above the crossed out "Danish minister." However, Barnes ultimately settled on "Danish count" in the proof to E1.

84.21 point. No, I] On TSC1 a period is inserted after "back" in the above line, and the end of the sentence is crossed out. A new sentence begins with "I." However, a stet appears in the margin.

84.34 amazed.] The phrase "and annoyed" were blocked out on TSC1, probably by Coleman. Its deletion is accepted.

85.17 nest of pubic hairs] On TSC1, "pubic hairs" was bracketed by blue pencil, likely Eliot's; the phrase is lightly lined through in TSC2-B. It is not changed on TSR. Since the phrase was undoubtedly deleted because of censorship fears, it is restored in this edition. In her diary for 3 June 1936, Coleman mentions Barnes's vigilance with respect to the phrasing and "whether bird's nest had the suggestion of pubic hair."

86.12 introduce me?'] In a letter of 27 May 1946 Barnes wrote Laughlin of New Directions that the third and fourth words on p. 129 were to be omitted.

86.13 a friend of mine] this phrase has been blocked out on TSC1, probably by Coleman, but it has been rewritten above the blocked line, probably by Barnes.

86.19 "Yes," she said, "she met everyone."] On TSC1, "every body" has been blocked out, perhaps by Coleman, and Barnes wrote "all of them" above the line. She made the above change in the proof. TSC2 was changed to the above reading.

87.6 Cibber] On the proof to E1, Barnes writes in "Cybbar," but in the left margin, she indicates she believes it is spelled "Cibber."

87.7 hent] Eliot questions the use of "hent," which is "not in the O.E.D.," but Barnes retains it.

87.12 sleep.'] The following phrase, "What? Is this not night work, also?" has been blocked out only on TSC1 in Coleman's style of deletion, but the deletion has been accepted because it avoids an awkward repetition of the same sentiment two lines earlier.

88.21-89.10] Passages throughout this section are blocked out, suggesting Coleman initiated the editing, but within the section, there are corrections by Barnes and some reinsertions, suggesting also that Barnes concurred in the deletions. Comments in her letter of 8

November imply that Barnes valued Coleman for her ability to spot the redundant phrase. The deletions therefore are accepted in this edition.

88.22   forget, – . . . forgotten,] After "forget" Barnes inserts a dash without deleting the comma. But two lines later in the parallel construction she follows "forgotten" with a semicolon. E1 has changed that to a full dash; the comma and dash are retained here to parallel Barnes's earlier punctuation.

88.24   and the spirits] "and" has been blocked out on TSC1, but restored by Barnes.

88.26   darkness alone I began to wail,] In her copy of the first edition, Barnes deleted the comma after "alone," a comma she had inserted in PE1, and inserted the comma after "wail," which had been accidentally omitted in E1. Thus, the phrase, "for all the little beasts . . ." functions as an appositive of emphasis for the phrase that follows the preceding semicolon.

88.33   gloves, would I forgive her?] Barnes has edited this phrase also on TSC2, deleting from "she might make" to "And I knew," but the idea is more completely rendered on TSC1 and she certainly accepted the phrasing suggested there by Coleman.

94.11   one woman] In her copy of the first American edition, Barnes deleted "single" from the phrase "one single woman." Although this emendation does not appear in any of the succeeding editions, it is accepted in this edition. When she deleted the word, Barnes may have been avoiding the repetition of "single" in the next line and she may have chosen also to avoid the ambiguity of "single" with respect to the aunt.

94.20   one 'sole condition,'] On TS Barnes crossed out the single quote after condition, but omitted to delete the one before.

95.4   life."] On TSC2, Barnes wrote "nature" above "person" before crossing out the entire phrase.

95.4-96.29   rest of my life . . . Take the case] On TSC1, this passage was marked for deletion. Coleman wrote to Barnes that she had "taken out" this section because there were too many stories of the doctor (L, 5 November 1935). Barnes responded that she had not taken the pasages out, that she would wait until Eliot decided. On 12 August, he wrote that he preferred "the shorter version." Barnes's concurrence does not appear then to be a matter of preference; the passage is restored to this edition.

97.11 hurried. She] On TSC1 the entire sentence, "She seemed hurried . . . achieved" was marked out by an unknown hand, but Barnes wrote "She seemed hurried" above the line, omitting the rest of the sentence.

97.24-29 The Baron continued . . . turned] On TSC1, this passage was marked with pencil diagonals for deletion, but stet appears in the margin.

98.6 he is not like] On TSC2, Barnes marked out only "at," but this seems an inadvertant omission of the phrase "at all."

100.35 moment. Then he] On PE1 Barnes crossed out "and" after "moment," inserting "Then." The word appears to be capitalized, but she did not add any punctuation. The period is supplied by E1.

103.3 monocle into place,] On TSC1, Barnes deleted "into place," but retained it with a stet in the margin.

103.13 carefully.] On TSC1, in the deleted sentence Barnes inserted a comma after "noticed" and deleted "that" before she deleted the entire sentence, perhaps in response to Coleman's question of the motive for its presence: "why must you have his handkerchief mentioned here. You are *cruel* to him. (Do take this out, unless it has some meaning I dont know, which makes one understand him *sympathetically*" (L, 27 August 1935). Barnes answered that it was not mean to mention his cleaning his monocle with the handkerchief: "it merely means that he remembers his father, as his father had done before him, his father carried one, you will notice if you look back to chapter one" (20 September 1935). The line was blocked by Coleman, but rewritten by Barnes. A blue pencil question mark appears to question the deletion and stet appears in the margin, but the passage is marked through in pencil by Barnes in a series of curving lines. That decision is accepted.

105.4 give up, now] Barnes's change in the proof to E1 to make this a series of questions was not adopted in E1. It is accepted in this edition.

105.7 me who seem curious] In FSC "seem" has been changed to "seems" though it does not appear to have been a change Barnes indicated; "seem" is retained.

107.2 Death in the weather] In A1 "winter" appeared instead of "weather." Barnes marked the correction in her personal copies of A1 and ND46.

109.26 as an old master . . . painted.] This passage was marked with brackets, but stet appears in the margin.

110.4 down under] "down" appears to have been omitted inadvertantly from E1.

110.14 *haute* sewer] "sewer" does not appear in FSC, but appears in other editions.

110.16 standing still, letting you do it] On TSC1, the phrase "letting you do it" is lined through and marked for deletion in blue pencil. Barnes reinserted it in her personal copy of NW36; it was restored in ND46.

110.19 hiked up in front] On TSC1, the entire phrase from "their poor damned dresses . . . rump" is enclosed in blue pencil brackets (likely Eliot's), but only the words "hiked up in front" have been lined out in blue. On PE1, Barnes inserted "hiked up and" before "falling away." In her mothers's copy of NW36, Barnes inserted "hiked up in front," but "in front" does not appear in ND49 nor in succeeding editions. It is accepted in this edition.

111.14 I took out] Barnes substituted "spoke to" for the original "took out" in this passage in response to a red pencil line under "took out," presumably an effort by Morley to sanitize the passage. The original wording is restored in this edition.

111.26 know] In FSC "knows" appears instead of "know." It is probably a typographical error.

111.26 mistake] In E1 and E2 "mistakes" appears, but it is corrected by Barnes in NW36.

111.35 crying,] Coleman suggested she delete the phrase "only a private matter . . . place," and Barnes deleted it.

112.5 compliment,—] On TSC1 Barnes inserted the dash without deleting the comma.

112.23 eyes slanting] On the typescripts, to insert a space between two words run together, Barnes drew a slash between "eyes" and "slanting," but it appears that the line deletes the "s" on eyes and the typesetter misread the correction; thus all editions have read "eye slanting" when the sense of the line requires the plural.

112.34 She said : She was beautiful, wasn't she?"] On both TSC1 and TSC2 Barnes deleted this phrase as a result of Coleman's comment that it was "absolutely wrong. It is romantic" (L, 8 August 1935). Perhaps because Barnes did not want anything sentimental (or romantic) she accepted Coleman's advice. However, without Nora's comment, redirecting O'Connor's attention to Robin, there is no motivation for him to comment on Robin. The phrase is restored.

112.36 Robin was beautiful. I didn't like her] On TSC1 in what appears to be Coleman's hand, the phrase "Robin is" was substituted for "yes she was," but on TSC2 Barnes used past tense "was," changing also the next sentence to "I didn't." In PE1 she changed "is" to "was," but did not change the tense of "don't." Since the passage focuses on the doctor's earlier view of Robin, this change from TSC2 is accepted.

113.15 He brought . . . together.] In her NW36 Barnes wrote "smiled" above "grinned," but then replaced it with this phrase.

114.24 a boy.] On all typescripts, in the phrase "and once, men who were children," Barnes inserted the comma after "once" and changed "are" to "were." Then she deleted the entire phrase on TSC1 and TSC2.

114.27 invert, boy or girl?] On TSC1 "invert" has been deleted, perhaps by Eliot. However Barnes inserted the word in PE1, adding a comma after it, rather than the original single hyphen.

115.13 wedded] Barnes replaced "weeded" with "wedded" on TSC2, but it was changed to "welded" on TSC1, perhaps by Coleman, and not noticed by Barnes, who corrected it in her mother's copy of the first English edition.

115.15 sinks crying.] Coleman's letter of 7 May 1935 quotes this line, but argued for "tips crying": "Sinks crying is too much like the story books . . . ." She also mentioned the phrase "sinks crying with lead at its heart," referring to a prior version of *Nightwood*. The original typescript reading is "calling," and Barnes had decided on "sinks calling," but changed it to "crying" on TSC1 and TSC2.

115.16 Love is death, come upon with passion; I know,] In TSC1, "come upon" was changed to "reached." On PE1 Barnes deleted it and wrote in "come upon." "I know" was inserted in all three typescripts, but only on TSR does she include a comma after "know." Thus, she intended a comma after "death" and "know," a point that is not clear in her proof correction.

116.2 "Jenny," she said.] On TSC1, this line was effaced, but Barnes rewrote it.

116.5 suffer . . . should, or love . . . say.] On TSC1, it appears that Coleman printed in "should" but Barnes reinserted "say." On the proof to FSC, Barnes deleted the "s" after "suffer" and "love," making the plural form, but singular form was retained. Her change is accepted in this edition.

116.10 Mercy, are there any such!)] On PE1, Barnes appears to have intended the exclamation to follow "such," a correction misread or changed by Faber to place the exclamation after "Mercy" and a question after "such."

116.16 unheeding] On TSC1, "unheeding" was crossed off and then reinserted above the line.

118.27 hurting me, then I knew, –] Barnes inserted the hyphen after "knew," but did not cross out the comma; both are retained, according to her regular use of this structure.

118.37 I can't stand it anymore.] On TSC1, in the additional phrase "I am sick," Coleman substituted "going" for "sick," but Barnes deleted the entire phrase on both TSC1 and TSC2. Only on TSC1 is "any more" two words and in her copy of ND46 Barnes joined the two words.

119.33 home (I . . . eyes'),] Barnes inserted the parentheses and added a semicolon after "home," but this stop causes misreading of the modifying clause beginning with "running." A comma seems preferable.

120.30 holding her cold hands] Apparently "cold" was accidentally omitted from the proof. It is restored.

121.14 me, she who] On TSC1 "she" was blocked out, and then written in above the blocking, apparently by Barnes.

121.15 Matthew, for God's] A paragraph has been indicated before "Matthew," but deleted.

122.23 remembered.] On TSC2 Barnes substituted "peace" for "gift" in the concluding phrase "The greatest gift of all"; but on TSC1 the entire phrase was deleted by an unknown hand.

122.25 window, playing] Barnes marked this change in her copy of ND46, but it was not integrated into the text until FSC.

122.32 in boy's] Coleman prompted this change on the ground that Barnes had said it elsewhere (L, 27 August 1935).

123.4 across the floor.] This phrase was followed by the phrase "its blue bow now over, now under." It underwent a series of changes before Barnes marked it for deletion in her personal copy of A1 and subsequently in her copy of ND46. On typescripts it appears as "its blue bow now over, now under," but that is changed to "its blue bow over and under," perhaps by Coleman, for on PE1 Barnes returned it to the original form of the typescript.

123.19   The blessed face!] In the margin of TSC1 is a blue penciled comment, "too condensed do you infer saintly?" Barnes responded by changing "holy" to "blessed."

124.11   sleep.—And] Barnes inserted a period, but did not delete the dash.

124.13   grandmother dies] Inexplicably, "grandfather" appears in all editions but not in the typescripts. It appears to be an error.

127.1   acclimation] On TSC1, "acclimatation" appears in the margin, and though Barnes marked her preference for "acclimation," her note was either misread or not noticed and "acclimatation" appeared in all editions until "acclimation" in FSC.

127.4   high-up] On PFSC a blue pencil questioned the hyphen, but Barnes marked it stet in the margin.

127.16   They reach for . . . me.] The phrase was marked in red pencil and Barnes lined it out on TSC1 and TSC2, but she was clearly acquiescing only because of editorial objections to the homosexual tones. The sentence is restored.

128.4   balls] The word was questioned on TSC1 in both red and blue pencil. Barnes wrote "ballocks" in the margin and crossed out "balls," but she reinserted "balls" on PE1.

128.4   on my head?] Barnes marked this change in her ND46 copy and in her A1 edition, but it did not appear in the text until FSC.

128.5   hurts that] The typescript reading has been retained rather than the reading of subsequent editions, "hurts, that," because Barnes likely means that what "hurts" is memory, that the mind goes back, not two separate items in a series.

129.4   alter, –] Barnes inserted a dash without deleting the comma.

129.5   dissolute] Barnes had difficulty making up her mind about this word. On the typescripts it is "desolate," then changed to "dissolute" on all three typescripts. On TSC1 it is changed back to "desolate" before the final change on PE1.

129.32   in a lost generation.] Barnes inserted "lost" instead of "another," on PE1, but it was not incorporated in E1, or in any succeeding editions. It is accepted in this edition.

130.16   dismay . . . eternal.] Barnes marked this change in all typescripts, but as the line had been typed in between lines and then moved lower by a pencil line, the typesetters apparently misread the correction.

130.30 Barnes inserted a line after this paragraph on TSR and TSC2, but neglected to transfer the separation to TSC1. She made the correction on the proof.

131.18 shitty and strange;] "shitty and" was blocked out on TSC1, likely by Eliot or Morley. In her letter of 14 May 1936, Barnes wrote, "as for taking out a few 'shits' (really!) . . . if a bit of 'local color' has to be shelved it does not much matter — dashes will do, tho no other word will," indicating acquiescence but also mild outrage; therefore the original wording is accepted.

132.9 children mine also?] Although Barnes inserted "mine" on PE1, the emendation was not made in E1 or in succeeding editions.

132.34 You can lay . . . bugger!] Barnes modified punctuation in this sentence, but in responding to a blue pencil question mark in the margin, she accepted its deletion. Because the deletion was a matter of censoring her language, the passage is restored.

134.1 Harlem] The typescript reading is accepted, rather than the "Haarlem" of all editions. It seems more likely that Barnes intended the Harlem of New York rather than the Haarlem of the Netherlands.

134.21 As he broke off,] On TSC1 "as" has been changed to lower case, but on TSC2 and TSR "As" is capitalized. The new sentence beginning seems warranted.

134.23-135.2 "Now suppose you were in Wabash . . . sinners should sin.'] A blue pencil brackets this passage and a red line runs the margin of the passage. On TSC2 Barnes crossed out the passage out and wrote in the margin: "Could bring in here any of the Dr.s stories that may be too heavy in another place Los angeles fairy — memories of his boyhood etc." It is likely that the homosexual references led Morley and Eliot to suggest the deletion and Barnes complied. It is restored to this edition.

135.2 In the morning . . . another kind," said the doctor.] Even though this passage is marked by blue pencil and red delete mark, indicating a suggesting by Eliot and Morley because of its homosexual subject matter, the deletion is accepted. The passage was marked out on TSR with a single diagonal line, slanting from left to right, a characteristic of Barnes. It appears also in the Related Drafts where O'Connor talks about the war and the bombardment and taking refuge in a cellar with the old woman and her cow and the Irishman. Thus, in shifting the passage, Barnes may not have been convinced of its place at the end of this paragraph and chose to delete it. On TSC1, the last sentence, "Take bewilderment . . . doctor," was marked with two parallel lines, indicating a separate, and probably earlier, decision on Barnes's part.

135.14 Catherine the Great] On TSC1, a question mark in red pencil and "Catherine" marks the passage. A blue pencil brackets "Saxon." Morley and Eliot may have been concerned about English sensibilites, or what might have been considered the more appropriate historical reputation. On TSC2 Barnes crossed off Queen Victoria and inserted "a Queen." Thus, it seems that Barnes concurred with the suggestion (reminder) of Catherine.

135.22 buggers] On TSC1, there are red pencil parentheses around "buggers" and it was changed by Eliot to "boys." Barnes made the change on TSC2, but in Coleman's diary of 2-3 June she recorded Barnes's return from her meeting with Eliot: "At one point, Eliot changed the word buggers to boys. Djuna said to me, 'Imagine trying to wake Eliot up.' " It seems clear that Barnes acquiesced in rather than preferred the change.

137.14 bent.] The passage deleted, "They encompass . . . bees," is "obliterated" on TSC1, indicating perhaps that Coleman initiated it, though she mentioned it in none of the existing letters. It is marked out on the other typescripts and the deletion is accepted here.

138.12 woods; the silence . . . forgotten] This page (212) of TSC1 has been retyped; its line lengths differ from those of TSR and TSC2. In the retype, "woods" is followed by a comma, which is changed to a semicolon by Faber. The original punctuation on TSR on TSC2 is a period. The semicolon is accepted for readability because of the long clause and phrase following it. In addition, the phrase "broken again by insect and bird" was placed later in the sentence than in the original. Barnes placed it properly, and changed "was" to "which was," the reading of TSR and TSC2.

138.21 up, rigid] The comma does not appear on the retyped TSC1 (page 212, see above), but it does appear in TSC2 and TSR, the original typescripts. Barnes marked it in her mother's copy of *Nightwood*. It appears in ND49.

138.22 away, Nora,] On TSC2 and TSR, a comma follows "away," but on the retyped TSC1, it is not included. It is accepted here. It does not appear in editions until the FSC edition.

138.25 Nora bent] In her 27 August 1935 letter, Coleman stated that where Nora puts "her hands on 'the upper parts of her legs' will have to come out." She argued that it is sexual; Peggy Guggenheim and Muir agreed. She cited also "and waiting." She acknowledged that Barnes did not intend this passage to be sexual, but that it was. And some of it must come out: "It isn't that publishers wouldnt like it—it is that *you do not want that idea there* yourself" (Coleman's emphasis).

139.16 sprang back, his tongue] Barnes marked the phrase "his lips drawn" for deletion in her mother's copy of NW36 and in her personal copy of A1, and wrote to Pierre du Sautoy at Faber (14 December 1949) asking for the change to be incorporated into the new Faber edition—"how that ever got by I do not know!" Her letter arrived too late and the phrase was retained in the 1950 edition.

139.23 sliding.] On 27 August 1935, Coleman wrote Barnes that the passage was sexual. Barnes replied that she couldn't change it, though she suggested leaving out "a mistress," a decision she confirmed on the proof after she deleted it on TSR and TSC2, not deleting it on TSC1, perhaps because Eliot had the typescript.

139.30 obscene and touching.] In the margin of TSC1, it appears as if Eliot has inserted "unclean" for "obscene," and where it appears in the proof, replaced it with "obscene." In the margin of TSC1 is Barnes's comment, "Sample of T. S. Eliot's lack of 'imagination' (as he said.)"

139.30 Crouching, the dog began to run with her, head-on] This change is noted in ND46, but it is not integrated in ND49 as are the other changes on this page. It appears in FSC. It may have been a printer's oversight.

139.37 along her knees.] Coleman wrote to Barnes on 27 August 1935 to suggest that the concluding phrase "and waiting" should come out. Barnes concurred, removing it from all three typescripts.

EXPLANATORY ANNOTATIONS

In the following annotations, explanations are given for literary references, geographical locations, historical figures, foreign terms, and certain phrases that Barnes glossed for translators.

1.1 *Nightwood*] Barnes wrote to Coleman on 23 June 1935 that she thought she had the title: *Nightwood*, "like that, one word, it makes it sound like night-shade, poison and night and forest, and tough, in the meaty sense, and simple yet singular, like Lavengro or whatever it is when spelled right" (Emily Holmes Coleman Papers; *Lavengro* [1851] is a novel about Gypsies by George Borrow). Because Coleman didn't like it and because Barnes couldn't decide between *Nightwood* and "Anatomy of the Night," Coleman's preference, she suggested they ask Eliot, because he would "know the English market." Later on 9 October 1936 Barnes wrote to Coleman: "do you realize that the title is Thelma's name? Nigh T. Wood—low, thought of it the other day. Very odd" (Coleman Papers). Barnes later told Hank O'Neal that the title was taken from the second line of William Blake's "The Tyger": "Tyger! Tyger! burning bright / In the forests of the night . . ." (from *Songs of Experience*, 1794) and had nothing to do with Thelma Wood's surname (see his *"Life is painful, nasty and short . . . in my case it has only been painful and nasty": Djuna Barnes, 1978-1981* [New York: Paragon, 1990], 104).

2.1 Peggy Guggenheim and John Ferrar Holms] Peggy Guggenheim, socialite and patron of the arts, was an early friend and long-time benefactor of Barnes's; it was at Guggenheim's rented country manor in England, Hayford Hall, that Barnes wrote most of *Nightwood*. Guggenheim's lover at that time, critic John Holms, was also a visitor at Hayford Hall. He died unexpectedly in January 1934.

3.1 Bow Down] the title, Andrew Field points out, of an "old folk opera" about a man's simultaneous courtship of two sisters (*Djuna: The Formidable Miss Barnes* [Austin: Univ. of Texas Press, 1985], 183). At an early stage Barnes intended to use *Bow Down* as the title for the novel.

3.28 Prater] an elaborate pleasure garden in Vienna, dating from the end of the eighteenth centruy, containing refreshment booths, coffee houses, etc. The park could be illuminated.

4.3 Pietro Barbo] Pope Paul II. In 1466 he introduced footraces to the Roman Carnival; originally Jews under twenty raced in the Corso, Rome's main street, for a piece of cloth as "goal and prize," but later the races became more degrading as participants, including old men, clothed only in loincloths, raced before jeering crowds. This appears to be the ordinance that Barnes refers to, though the dates are not exact.

4.7 *Monsignori*] a title and office conferred on a male cleric by a pope.

4.19 *Piazza Montanara*] an obscure square name, either fictitious or of no historical importance.

4.19 *"Roba vecchia!"*] It. "Old stuff" (used goods, unwanted items), the cry of itinerant dealers in secondhand goods.

6.17 Inner City of Vienna] the old part of the city, originally within feudal walls.

8.9 wandering Jew] a legendary Jew who mocked Christ at the Crucifixion and consequently was condemned to wander the earth until the Second Coming. Traditionally, he is age thirty.

8.18 St. Patrick's] presumably Saint Patrick's Cathedral in New York City.

8.21 Uffizi] world-famous museum in Florence, Italy.

9.32 bowed slightly] In her response to Coleman's 1944 essay on *Nightwood* (never published) Barnes scolded her for describing Felix as a sycophant and explained that his bowing and his adjusted stomach were the acts of one "who is afraid he has mistaken that which he most honours." She also vehemently denied that he was "craven."

10.3 *Comédie humaine*] *La Comédie humaine* (The Human Comedy) is the title French novelist Honoré de Balzac (1799-1850) gave to his series of novels examining French life.

10.10 Madame de Sevigné] French lady of fashion (1626-96) celebrated for her letters.

10.10 Goethe] Johann Wolfgang von Goethe (1749-1832), German poet, playwright, and novelist, best known for the two-part drama *Faust*.

10.10 Loyola] Saint Ignatius of Loyola (1491-1556), founder of the Society of Jesus (the order of Jesuits) and author of *Spiritual Exercises*.

10.10 Brantôme] Seigneur de Brantôme (1535?-1614), author of colorful memoirs of sixteenth-century French military and aristocratic life.

11.5 Princess Nadja] cf. André Breton's 1928 novel *Nadja*.

11.17 Carnavalet] the Musée Carnavalet (third arrondissement) specializes in unusual curios, furnishings, and documents, as well as paintings.

11.24 Rops] Felicien Rops (1833-98), Belgian-French painter and engraver, known for his decadent, erotic themes.

12.31 *nicht wahr?*] Ger.: "isn't that so?"

13.1 living statues] a decadent entertainment of the time where naked models would pose as mythological figures in various tableaux.

13.20 *Wir setzen an dieser Stelle über den Fluss—*] Ger.: "We are sitting at this place above the river."

14.15 *Ja! das ist ganz richtig*] Ger.: "Yes, that is absolutely correct."

14.30 *ameublement*] Fr.: furnishing.

14.34 gig-mill] Barnes responded to Pierre du Sautoy, at Faber and Faber, that the word (in the O.E.D.) referred to a "machine for raising a nap on cloth by the use of teazles" and added "the meaning must be apparent?" (letter 19 September 1958).

14.35 Desdemona] the heroine of Shakespeare's *Othello*.

15.1 the Jansenist theory] a system of doctrine based on moral determinism—a harsh, puritanical reformist movement by French Catholics in the seventeenth century, condemned as heretical by Pope Innocent X.

15.7 the word said by Prince Arthur Tudor] Arthur married Catherine of Aragon in November 1501 and died the following April, age sixteen. Jane Marcus says the word is *merde* (Fr.: "shit"): see her "Laughing at Leviticus: *Nightwood* as Woman's Circus Epic" in *Silence and Power: A Reevaluation of Djuna Barnes*, ed. Mary Lynn Broe (Carbondale: Southern Illinois Univ. Press, 1991), 225. In the epigraph to Marcus's essay, Barnes is quoted as saying: "just *what* word, undoubtedly short and improper the Tudor king said I've now forgotten, . . ." [219]).

15.15   Tiny M'Caffery] according to Barnes's letter to translator Wolfgang Hildesheimer, the "word is one the doctor uses for both himself and his member . . . a 'camping' word . . . passing for a number of things" (17 July 1959). Later, the doctor calls his member Tiny O'Toole (see 111.14).

15.19   House of Rothschild] influencial family of Jewish financiers, originally based in Germany.

15.19   *dos*] Fr.: "back, rear."

15.22   the really deplorable condition of Paris before hygiene was introduced] Jane Marcus suggests Barnes had in mind "Victor Hugo's *Notre Dame de Paris*, with its famous digression on the criminal underworld and the sewers" ("Laughing at Leviticus," 225).

15.25   'Garde tout!'] Fr.: "Guard everything!"

15.31   I do, but not so well but that I remember some of it still] Barnes's notes glossing this line for Hildesheimer explain: "meaning not so familiar he has forgotten it" (Djuna Barnes Papers).

17.5   *In questa tomba oscura*] It.: "In this dark tomb."

17.6   Rutebeuf] thirteenth-century French poet and *jongleur*, best known for his satires. He wrote poetic complaints blending self-pity and mordant irony; a dramatic monologue entitled "Dit de l'herberie" was supposed to be delivered by a quack doctor.

17.9   Salome] the daughter of Herodias who danced for her stepfather Herod in exchange for the head of John the Baptist.

17.13   Cathedral of Clermont-Ferrand] a city in central France; the cathedral dates from the thirteenth century.

17.14   Mussulmans] an older spelling of Moslems.

17.25   *fine*] a French brandy.

17.31   Luther] Martin Luther (1483-1546), German priest who led the Reformation, opposing the wealth and corruption of the Catholic Church.

18.15   story that the priest is telling] in her notes for Hildesheimer, Barnes explains the "story" is that of the mass.

18.17   Leo X] pope (1513-1521) who excommunicated Martin Luther in 1521 for asserting that faith alone, not works, would earn salvation.

18.18   *pecca fortiter*] Lat.: sin boldly, a bold sin.

18.18   masses his soul] Barnes glosses the term in notes to Hildesheimer: "satisfies his (sexual) soul."

18.30   gift of gab] argot for "eloquence"—Barnes's notes to Hildesheimer.

19.4 *Gesundheit . . . immerdar!*] Ger.: "God bless you. As today may God grant you joy always!"

20.20 Boul 'Mich'] Boulevard St. Michel, main avenue of the Left Bank. See map on pages 216-17 for this and other Parisian locales.

20.27 Carmen] the Gypsy heroine of Georges Bizet's opera of the same name (1875).

20.35 Museé de Cluny] a museum comprised of the remains of the Gallo-Roman baths and the medieval Hôtel de Cluny, constructed in the fourteenth and fifteenth centuries for the abbots of Cluny. It specializes in arts and crafts of the Middle Ages; its holdings include the six tapestries known as the *Lady with the Unicorn*.

21.24 *Herr Gott!*] Ger.: "Lord God."

21.33 Ponte Vecchio] in Florence, a bridge built over the Arno in 1345.

21.35 *Nur eine Nacht*] German song, "Only One Night."

22.8 *Unter den Linden*] Ger.: "Under the linden trees": name of the principle thoroughfare in Berlin.

23.2 *Wunderbar*] Ger.: "Wonderful."

23.5 mad Wittelsbach] family name of Ludwig II (1845-86), king of Bavaria from 1864 to 1886, who ascended the throne at eighteen. Munich citizens loved him for his beauty, but he hated court ritual and was anti-militaristic. He was engaged briefly to Sophia, the younger sister of the empress, and was rumored to have thrown her sculpted bust out of the window. He reportedly had homosexual tendencies, which he suppressed, only to succumb and then reproach himself. He built fantastic castles in the Bavarian mountains, a Winter Garden in the palace, and in the 1880s increasingly withdrew from court and society, sleeping during he day, riding through the mountains at night. He supported Richard Wagner lavishly, constructing a stage for Wagner's operas and viewing them in solitude. In 1886 Ludwig was declared insane, removed from office, and held in Schloss Berg near the Starnberger See, under the care of his psychiatrist. He and the psychiatrist were found drowned on June 13; accounts speculate that the psychiatrist drowned trying to save Ludwig from suicide or that Ludwig forced the psychiatrist to join him in suicide.

23.20 *Residenz Schloss*] royal palace in Munich.

23.21 *Odeonsplatz*] a square in the middle of Munich, the scene of the failed putsch of 1923.

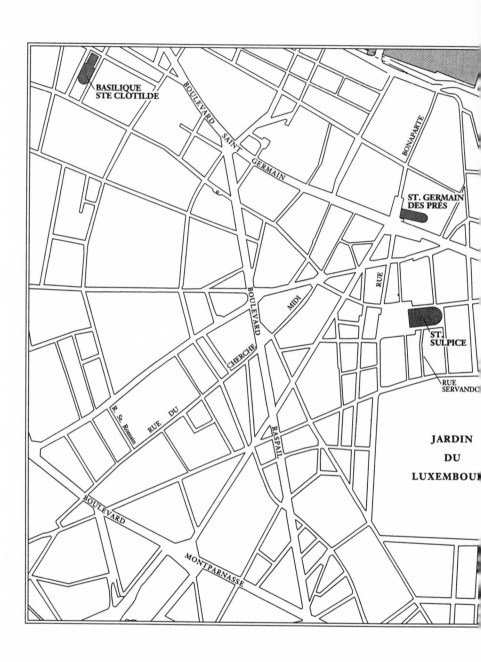

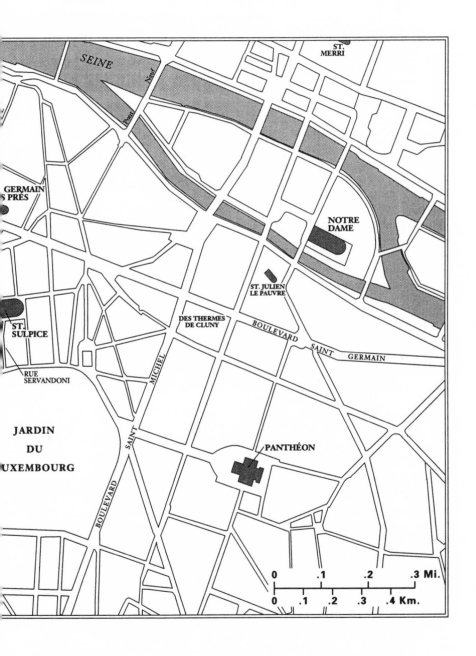

23.22 ceiling of wrenched yellow silk] This description seems similar to Wilfrid Blunt's description of the "Grail" room of Wagner's home in the most expensive residential part of town. It was provided to him by the King. Its walls are described as covered with yellow satin, with yellow valances, and "a rosette of satin in the centre of the ceiling" (*The Dream King* [New York: Viking, 1970], 33).

23.31 Lohengrin] in act 1 of Wagner's *Lohengrin*, the knight arrives in a boat drawn by swans.

25.24 *Lesen Sie österreichische Geshichte*] Ger.: "Read Austrian history."

26.32 Marie Antoinette] queen of King Louis XVI (1755-1793). Unpopular because she was extravagant and insensitive to the masses, she was tried by the Revolutionary Tribunal and executed.

27.8 *procureur*] Fr.: public prosecutor.

28.16 *de tout mon coeur*] Fr.: "with all my heart."

28.18 *C'est le coeur d'une femme!*] Fr.: "It is the heart of a woman!"

29.3 Albéniz' *Córdoba*] a piano piece by Isaac Albéniz (1860-1909).

30.1 La Somnambule] Fr.: "The Sleepwalker." The title echoes Bellini's opera *La sonnambula* (1831). In a letter to Coleman (5 May 1935) Barnes wrote: "I still do not think La Somnambule the perfect title—Night Beast would be better [e]xcept for the debased meaning now put on that nice word beast."

31.3 "Aren't you the beauty!"] According to Barnes, the phrase is "The manner in which a man like the doctor accosts another man" (letter to Wofgang Hildesheimer, 17 July 1959).

31.37 *Misericordioso!*] Sp.: "Mercy."

33.17 In 1685 . . . the Turks brought coffee into Vienna] The invading Turkish forces left behind sacks of coffee beans—previously unknown to the Viennese—after the seige of 1683 (not 1685, as the Baron states). Soon after coffee houses became a fixture of Vienna.

33.20 Pitt the younger] William Pitt (1759-1806), British statesman; eventually negotiated an alliance with Austria 1793.

33.24 *chausseur*] Fr.: "bellboy."

33.29 Midi French] i.e., a southern French accent.

34.28 *douanier* Rousseau] Henri Rousseau (1844-1910), customs clerk, began painting at forty, his style characterized as "primitive." Alan Williamson identifies the painting referred to as Rousseau's *The Dream;* see "The Divided Image" in *Critique: Studies in Modern Fiction* 7 (Spring 1964): 68.

34.29 a jungle trapped in a drawing room (in the apprehension of which the walls have made their escape)] Barnes glosses this phrase for Hildesheimer—"well, the drawing-room might fear or be displeased to house a jungle"—and for a French translator (perhaps Leyris)—"the walls, as might be expected, would be if they could be, apprehensive if surrounding a jungle" (Djuna Barnes Papers).

34.32 *dompteur*] Fr.: master, tamer.

37.2 converging halves of a broken fate, setting face, in sleep, toward itself in time] Barnes wrote about this phrase to Hildesheimer: "This seems too plain to me that I don't know how to make it plainer. Robin has been mentioned as Somnambule, sleepwalking in life, it has been more than hinted that she feels 'without home'; her very nature makes her incomplete . . . in short the face of one who is sleeping, that face and that sleep seeking itself . . . in time . . . and time takes time" (17 July 1959).

37.35 "A king is the peasant's actor"] Barnes explained to a French translator that the King "acts out . . . the dreams—fairy stories, longings, and so on" of the poor (Djuna Barnes Papers).

38.21 "the last child born to aristocracy is sometimes an idiot, out of respect—we go up—but we come down"] Barnes explains this phrase for a French translator as "high as a nobleman can go—no higher" (Djuna Barnes Papers).

39.1 the Bourbons] French royal family that ruled variously in France, Spain, and Naples until the nineteenth century.

41.4 "*Das Leben ist ewig, darin liegt seine Schönheit*"] Ger.: "Life is eternal, therein lies its beauty."

41.6 Imperial Palace . . . *Kammergarten* . . . the *Gloriette*] The Schoenbrunn Palace, the former imperial summer residence south of the Inner City. A spacious park is attached to the Palace, at one end of which stands the *Gloriette*, a structure built by Ferdinand Hohenberg in 1765 to commemorate the victory at Kolin.

41.18 Emperor Francis Joseph] Emperor of Austria from 1848 until 1916.

41.19 Charles the First] Emperor of Austria from 1916 until 1918; after his abdication, he lived in Switzerland; deported in 1921 to Madeira, where he died the following year. This reference indicates this episode is taking place in 1920-1922.

42.26 *Wo ist das Kind? Warum? Warum?*] Ger.: "Where is the child? Why not? Why not?"

43.4 *St. Julien le Pauvre*] a small church, which faces Notre-Dame, from the Left Bank.

43.5 *St. Germain des Prés*] the oldest church in Paris, at the center of St.' Germain Quarter, it is the burial site of Merovingian kings and the seat of the Benedictine order.

43.5 *Ste. Clotilde*] Paris's principal modern Gothic church (built 1846-56), in the rue Martignac in the seventh arrondissement.

43.9 *rue Picpus*] properly, rue de Picpus, near the Place de la Nation.

43.10 convent of *L'Adoration Perpétuelle*] unidentified.

43.14 Jean Valjean] the central figure of Victor Hugo's *Les Miserables* (1862), a convict on the run in much of the novel.

43.17 Lafayette] Marquis de Lafayette (1757-1834), French statesman and officer.

43.27 Louise de la Vallière] (1644-1710), a mistress of Louis XIV, reputed author of *Réflexions sur la Miséricorde de Dieu* (1685).

43.27 Catherine of Russia] Catherine II (1729-96), known as Catherine the Great, became empress in 1762 after Peter III was deposed by a group led by her lover. She increased the territory of Russia through conquest and three partitions of Poland. Cf. 87.21.

43.28 Madame de Maintenon] (1635-1719), another mistress and second wife of Louis XIV, noted for her beauty and intellectual gifts.

43.28 Catherine de Medici] wife of Henry II and queen of France, Catherine (1519-89) was regent during the minority of her son Charles IX (1560-63). She continued to exert power until the end of Charles's reign in 1574.

43.29 Anna Karenina] the protagonist of the Tolstoy novel of the same name (1873-76).

43.29 Catherine Heathcliff] the wife of Heathcliff's son Linton in Emily Brontë's novel *Wuthering Heights* (1847).

44.7 Marquis de Sade, *Et lui rendant sa captivité les mille services qu'un amour dévoué est seul capable de rendre*] as the French pornophilosophical writer (1740-1814) never wrote any memoirs, the reference is puzzling. The French quotation translates: "And he rendered to his captivity the thousand services that devoted love is alone capable of rendering." Barnes may have intended "captive."

47.11 gap in "world pain" . . . body falling in observable space] Barnes responded to Pierre Leyris's inquiry, initially scolding: "(the very reason one writes a book is in order *not* to answer such a question!)," but continuing: "I think it means something like this:—the force of mystery that keeps, like a cork on a geyser, an impermiable body dancing on the top of that it would drown in—bliss? beatitude? The knowledge of the unknowable? (un-know-able)? In other words, state of un-gifted" (letter to Pierre Leyris, 17 June 1954).

47.29 *détraqués*] Fr.: a person shattered (in mind or body), broken, deranged.

48.6 Scarlatti, Chopin, Palestrina] the first and last are Italian composers, Chopin the celebrated Polish-French pianist and composer.

48.10 Seventh Day Adventists] an American religious group developed in the nineteenth century that believed Christ's second coming was imminent and awaited his return on hilltops. In her notes to a translator, Barnes explained "confound the seventh day" implied "one of those fervid women," one who "confounds the seventh day by the belligerance of her acceptance" (Djuna Barnes Papers).

49.1 Denckman circus] apparently fictitious.

50.9 *rue du Cherche-Midi*] Paris street near rue de Sèvres. Rue St. Romain, the street Barnes lived on, runs into rue du Cherche-Midi.

52.25 "In the resurrection . . . cast of your grave."] Barnes often explained this phrase, whether she had been asked or not: to Pierre Leyris she wrote: "this word 'cast' means the same here, for the rising of the human body, as it means for the earth cast up around the worm emerging from the earth" (letter, 17 June 1954). And similarly to Hildesheimer (11 March 1959).

53.1 had not been lived through] Barnes wrote to Hildesheimer: "Robin might return to her, Nora, as at least one adventure she had not lived through . . . the one lover, in short, she had not known of that whole night" (17 July 1959).

58.2 Jenny Petherbridge] in a letter to Coleman dated 5 January 1939, Barnes wrote questioning whether she would have written *Nightwood* if she had known what it would "cost" her. When she contemplated returning to the U.S., she wrote, "I would not be at all surprised if Henriette [Metcalf, the Jenny figure] stuck me in the back with a knife," and she added, "hers is the best reason, for her I did not write of with love or one or other of its odd faces . . . she is the *only* person not made something by the forgiving (usually unforgiving) excellence of imagination." Barnes recognized that readers liked the chapter because it was human, "plain," "not involved with the higher flights." It was "adequate," she felt, but not "art." On those grounds it might be more "just," but to her "boring" (BP).

58.8 Judy] of the Punch and Judy puppet show.

58.15 *accouchée*] Fr.: brought to bed (i.e., about to give birth).

58.15 Her body suffered from its fare] Barnes explained the phrase: "abuse and indulgence, herself, and others—both, all" (for a French translation, Djuna Barnes Papers).

59.7 *andante*] musical term meaning moderately slow.

59.12 La Duse] Eleonora Duse (1858-1924) a popular Italian actress, who toured the U. S. in 1893, 1896, 1902, 1924. She appeared in Ibsen's *Hedda Gabler*, *A Doll's House*, *Rosmersholm*, and other plays.

59.33 *Comédie-Française*] a theater company established in the seventeenth century, the Comédie Française has long been identified with French classical drama. Molière and Racine are staples.

59.34 Molière] France's premier comic dramatist (1622-73).

59.34 Racine] Jean Racine (1633-99), one of the leading dramatists of France's classical era.

59.34 *La Dame aux Camélias*] 1848 novel by Alexandre Dumas *fils* (1824-95), which he later dramatized (1852); the basis for Verdi's opera *La Traviata* (1853).

60.21 *commedia dell' arte*] the Italian term for "professional comedy." Popular in the sixteenth and eighteenth centuries in Europe, traveling companies of professional actors performed in masks, representing stock characters like the rich father (Pantaloon), the heroine (Inamorata), and other characters like Harlequin, Pulcinella, and Scaramouche.

63.26 *fiacre*] Fr.: a hackney-coach.

64.3 *"Écoute mon gosse . . . à tes fesses!"*] Fr.: "Listen, my lad, go as if thirty-six devils were holding on to your buttocks!"

64.6 *Fais le tour du Bois!"*] Fr.: "Make a tour of the Bois!" The doctor refers to the Bois de Boulogne, woods and park on the west edge of Paris.

64.27 the black curse of Kerry] Kerry is a county in Ireland.

68.1 Watchman, What of the Night?] from Isaiah 21:11-12: "Watchman, what of the night? Watchman, what of the night? The watchman said, The morning cometh, and also the night." Barnes may have also been familiar with William James's *Pragmatism* (1907), in which he writes: "Our spirit shut within this courtyard of sense-experience, is always saying to the intellect upon the tower: 'Watchman, tell us of the night, if it aught of promise bear.' "

69.3 *chambre à coucher*] Fr.: bedroom.

70.7 Dante] this element of the doctor's name evokes the Italian poet as geographer of hell and poet of purgatory.

71.4 Nymphenburg] an area in NW Munich, site of the secret treaty signed in 1741 that led to the War of the Austrian Succession; the summer residence of the electors and kings of Bavaria, and birthplace of Ludwig II.

71.15 *Ah, Mon Dieu! La nuit effroyable!... une petite extrémité!*] Fr.: Ah, my God! The awful night! The night, which is an immense plain, and the heart which is a small extremity.

73.4 *savon*] Fr.: soap.

73.5 *bretelle*] Fr.: strap, brace, suspender.

73.7 *cantiques*] Fr.: hymns.

73.18 *charter mortalis*] proper Latin would be *carta mortalis*, meaning a grant authorizing rights or privileges by a sovereign, here implying the principle establishing human vulnerability, being subject to death. Spoken by the doctor, the phrase is a mixture of Latin and English; the doctor is not known for accuracy in his languages.

74.11 Sodom became Gomorrah] biblical cities associated with sin and depravity (Gen. 17, 19), especially homosexuality, hence "Sodomites" (79.28). Cf. Proust's *Sodome et Gomorrhe*, and see note 77.28 below.

74.30 Morpheus] Greek god/personification of sleep.

75.7 *cardia*] the Greek word for heart (*kardia*), but more properly used for the area where the esophagus opens into the stomach.

76.31 *L'Echo de Paris*] a French newspaper founded in 1884.

77.21 *Misericordia*] Sp.: "Mercy."

77.28 remembrance of things past] Marcel Proust's multivolume novel *A la recherche du temps perdu* was translated into English in the 1920s under this title (taken from Shakespeare's sonnet number 30). For Barnes's familiarity with Proust's novel, especially the volume entitled *Sodome et Gomorrhe*, see Julie L. Abraham's "'Woman, Remember You': Djuna Barnes and History," in *Silence and Power*, 401 n.8.

77.35 Jehovah, Sabaoth, Elohim, Eloi, Helion, Jodhevah, Shaddai!] names and titles associated with the god of the Israelites—except for Eloi and Helion; the Eloi are the pampered aristocrats of the future in H. G. Wells's *The Time Machine* (1895); Helion sounds like the name of a sun god.

77.37 *pissoirs*] Fr.: urinals.

77.37 Highland Mary her cows down by the Dee] from Charles Kingsley's (1819-75) once-popular poem "The Sands of Dee": "O Mary, go and call the cattle home,/And call the cattle home,/And call the cattle home,/Across the sands of Dee." The Dee is a river in Scotland.

78.9 Bannybrook umbrella] Barnes refers to the "Bannybrook" umbrella as "one more of the doctors flights of fancy" (letter to Hildesheimer, 11 March 1959).

78.28 petropus] an elusive term that may be literally translated as "stone-foot."

78.30 *Place de la Bastille*] Originally the site of the Bastille prison, destroyed in the Revolution, but now a major crossroads in Paris.

78.32 *arrondissement*] Fr.: the geographic areas into which Paris is divided.

78.35 *formidable*] Fr.: "frightful," but the noun the doctor intends is unclear.

80.4 *mortadellas*] an Italian variety of sausage.

81.18 golden-mouthed St. John Chrysostom] one of the Fathers of the Greek Church (345?-407), called soon after his death *Chrysostom* (Greek: golden-mouthed) because of his eloquence.

81.22 *Parsifal*] Wagner's last opera (1882), based on the legend of the Holy Grail. In act 1 the "guileless fool" Parsifal shoots and kills a wild swan with his bow and arrow.

81.29 the Lily of Killarney] title of an opera by English composer Sir Jules Benedict, based on a play by Irish writer Dion Boucicault, and first produced in 1862.

81.31 John was his favorite] the apostle John, the disciple whom Jesus loved (Jn. 19:26).

81.32 Prester Matthew] as in Prester John, the legendary medieval king who reportedly ruled over a large Christian kingdom in the east.

82.6 Montaigne says: 'To kill a man there is required a bright shining and clear light'] apparently from book 3, chap. 5 of the *Essays*, "Upon Some Verses of Virgil" (quoted later at 87.10). In John Florio's translation (which Barnes preferred over others) the passage reads: "*Each one avoideth to see a man borne, but all runne hastily to see him dye. To destroy him we seek a spacious field and a full light.*"

82.10 Donne says . . . 'Men sleep all the way'] from "A Sermon Preached to the Lords upon Easter-day, at Communion, the King being then dangerously sick at New-Market" (1619); see Donne's *Selected Prose* (Oxford: Clarendon Press, 1967), 184. Newgate was a prison, and Tyburn where its prisoners were taken to be executed.

82.24 *saltarello*] an animated Italian dance with numerous little hops.

84.4 *Rigoletto*] Verdi's popular opera (1851).

84.11 Schumann cycle] German composer Robert Schumann (1810-56) wrote several song cycles based on poems by Heine (*Dichter-liebe*), Chamisso (*Frauenliebe und Leben*), and others.

84.19 *corbeille*] Fr.: a wide flat basket.

85.13 Cellini] Benvenuto Cellini (1500-71), Florentine goldsmith and sculptor, best known for his *Autobiography* (1558-62).

87.2 Don Antonio said . . . So Cibber put it] from *Love Makes a Man; or, The Fop's Fortune* (1700), a little-known comedy by English actor and dramatist Colly Cibber (1671-1757). Clodio (as the name is spelled in the 1777 edition of Cibber's works) is "a pert coxcomb" and in act 1 is telling his father about a night out with some French nobles.

87.7 Taylor's words, . . . gone hent to heaven?] probably Jeremy Taylor (1613-67), but untraced. The same anecdote appears in Montaigne in the paragraph preceding the one about Endymion (next note). Periander was a tyrant of Corinth (d. 585 B.C.), one of the Seven Wise Men of Greece despite his necrophilia.

87.10 as Montaigne says . . . except in sleep.'] adapted from *Essays*, book 3, chap.5: "Upon Some Verses of Virgil." In Florio's translation the sentence reads: "Seemes it not to be a lunatique humor in the Moone, being otherwise unable to enjoy *Endimion* hir favorite darling, to lull him in a sweete slumber for many moneths together; and feed hirselfe with the jovissance of a boye, that stirred not but in a dreame?" In Greek mythology Endymion was a beautiful shepherd boy who, as he slept on Mount Latmus, so attracted Selene, the moon goddess, that she came down and kissed him. Thereafter, she put him under an enchantment so that she could visit him whenever she wished.

87.16 *Pont Neuf*] bridge across the Seine and the oldest in Paris, completed by Henri IV in 1607. It crosses the Ile de la Cité at the island's west end.

87.21 Poniatovsky's throne for a water-closet] Count Stanislas

Poniatowski, related to an important Polish family, became the lover of Catherine and minister of the king of Poland to Russia; eventually Catherine named the now-discarded lover king of Poland. In 1772 Catherine agreed with Frederick II of Prussia and Joseph II of Austria to partition Poland, the three taking one-third of Polish territory, again in 1793, the three rulers took more territory, and again in 1795 a third "partition" left no Poland, and the former lover and a small court in retreat at Grodno.

87.27 Petronius] Gaius Petronius (d. A.D. 66), author of the satirical Roman novel *Satyricon*.

90.1 Where the Tree Falls] from Ecclesiastes 11:3: "If the clouds be full of rain, they empty themselves upon the earth: and if the tree fall toward the south, or toward the north, in the place where the tree falleth, there it shall be."

95.31 He'd been standing in the middle . . . in their midst] This incident may be based on a story of his own experience that John Holms told Barnes in the summer of 1932 or 1933; it is reported by Lance Sieveking in a 31 January 1957 *Listener* review of an edition of John Holms's correspondance.

96.29 the horse who knew too much] According to Barnes, the phrase means the horse "who in the shock of the war, gave premature birth" (letter to Hildesheimer, 11 March 1959).

103.25 *Wacht am Rhein*] "Die Wacht am Rhein" (The Watch on the Rhine) is a patriotic song based on a poem by Max Schneckenburger (1840), music by Karl Wilhelm.

103.26 *Morgenrot*] Red of Dawn, another patriotic, sentimental song appropriated by the Nazis.

104.3 the Ring] the demolition of the seventeenth-century fortifications surrounding Vienna allowed the building of two large rings around the city. The inner loop, the Ringstrasse opened in 1865; it was the grander of the two. The outer loop was the Lastenstrasse. Buildings were grouped around relevant functions: museums, financial areas, governement offices, with residences and restaurants.

105.1 Go Down, Matthew] Barnes affirmed that the title refers to the gospel song "Go down Moses, let my people go" (letter to Hildeshiemer, 25 July 1959, quoted in *Silence and Power*, 205).

105.24 Looking at her quarters] Barnes explains that the phrase means "looking at her parts, privy external organs of sex" (letter to

Hildesheimer, 5 June 1959).

106.12 *"Terra damnata et maledicta"*] Lat.: "Damned and accursed land."

106.13 Itchen] a river in England.

106.16 Holy Stone . . . Westminster Abbey] beneath the coronation chair in London's Westminster Abbey is the Stone of Scone (also called the Stone of Destiny), on which Celtic kings were crowned before it was conveyed to the abbey in 1296. Although of Scottish origin, it was believed to have been located earlier at Tara in Ireland and, earlier still, at Bethel, the site of Jacob's dream.

106.18 Brec . . . seven hundred years B.C.] In an 11 August 1959 letter to Hildesheimer Barnes identified Brec as Simon Brec, also spelled Symon Brake, as the bringer of the Stone of Scone to Ireland. "Seven hundred years B.C." could be taken to mean within the millennium, i.e., the doctor's extravagance.

106.33 Dig a hole, drop me in! Not at all.] Barnes glosses this phrase similarly for Hildesheimer and a French translator: "meaning—good or bad, here or there, all in all—he can't be done away with" (Djuna Barnes Papers).

106.34 St. Matthew's Passion by Bach] oratorio dating from 1729; Mendelssohn's revival of this work in 1829 was largely responsible for the rediscovery of Bach.

107.4 What spirits answer him? . . . was Robin unspun?] Barnes glossed these phrases for a Signor Maffi: "What unknown purpose may be in a child that does not mature . . . was Robin *undone* (or unspun) without purpose . . . suggestion is that there was some reason for this also. As also remark was Jenny a *sitting bitch* for fun or was it some entanglement with Fate etc etc." She further explained the latter phrase for a French translator: "as the saying a sitting duck, a sitting hen—a thing easily caught and killed" and in notes for Hildesheimer she wrote: "sitting pigeon—vulnerable and a bitch."

107.8 *papelero*] Sp.: paper-maker, stationer. When queried by Hildesheimer about the meaning of this expression, Barnes responded: "don't know, leave it as one of the doctors strange exclamations; no one else had asked about it" (letter 5 June 1959).

107.9 Saxon-les-Bains] "-les-Bains" is a French geographic suffix meaning "the baths," i.e., a watering place or spa.

107.11 Madame de Staël] Baronne Louise Germaine Necker de Staël-Holstein (1766-1817), French writer, literary patron and critic whose *On Germany* (1810) introduced romanticism to French literature.

107.15 that grim horse with ample glue in every hoof ... earth.] Barnes explained the phrase to Hildesheimer: "The grim horse is death; the ample glue is referring to the glue made of horses hoofs, and the horse that he will ride will also supply the glue necessary for sticking up an account of the doctor when he is buried" (letter, 17 March 1959).

107.21 "We shall not encompass it ... all our gait."] to Maffi Barnes wrote: "we shall not encompass the mystery. Defunctive murmur etc, the heart beats with the sound and knowledge in it of death ... we go accordingly."

108.17 *Decline and Fall of the Roman Empire*] Edward Gibbon's massive history, published in several volumes from 1776 to 1788.

108.20 'happy are they whom privacy makes innocent'] untraced.

109.10 Lady Macbeth, who had her ... safe as that.] Barnes wrote to Hildesheimer that "Macbeth had only one crime to reflect on, *'we'* can't be as safe as she" (notes, undated). For a French translator, she wrote "she seemed to feel her guilt chiefely [*sic*] in her hands—the Doctor suggests there are wider localities."

109.25 pardoned your flesh)] in notes for a French translator, Barnes wrote "pardoned your vain notion of immunity—Death I imagine will be pardoned by the same identification—with everything—all the arrows of outrageous fortune."

109.37 without finding my hands on my hips] Barnes wrote to Hildesheimer: "he hopes he will get home without having given way to his natural unnatural behavior ... hands on hips is a common 'camping jesture' " (letter 25 July 1959).

110.7 *grue*] Fr.: slang for prostitute.

110.14 *haute*] Fr.: high, upper end.

110.25 Father Lucas] a character in Barnes's *Ryder* (1928); see chap. 32.

111.3 *St. Merri*] a small church in the fourth arrondissement between rue de Sebastopol and rue du Renard.

111.10 *Raspail*] in notes to Hildesheimer, Barnes responded, "I don't know—Dr's account taken literally." The Boulevard Raspail runs near the Jardin du Luxembourg.

111.28 *C'est le plaisir qui me bouleverse!*] Fr.: It's pleasure that overthrows me!

112.11 Venezia] presumably the Gulf of Venice (Golfo di Venezia) rather than the Venezia province in Italy.

113.6 meet a horn and you know you have been identified] Barnes glossed the phrase for a French translator: "The horn in mythology, and religion—the horns of the altar, the horns attributed to deities and Moses—horns of salvation—and just simple horns of beasts that, dismissed from the head, so startle and seem relative."

114.32 neither one and half the other, the painting on the fan!] Barnes explained the line to Signor Maffi: "neither boy or girl, a mix up of both. Painting on the fan? Well the sexless Watteau sort of person."

115.18 lunatic humour of the moon] repeated from Montaigne; see annotation to 87.10.

115.22 *I Hear You Calling Me*] a song by Charles Marshall (1908) popularized by the great Irish tenor John McCormick.

115.23 *Kiss Me Again*] a song by Henry Blossom and Victor Herbert, first featured in Herbert's operetta *Mlle. Modiste* (1905), then revived separately by Herbert in 1915.

115.24 Diane of Ephesus] famous statue portraying the Roman goddess with many breasts. Diana (the standard form) was the counterpart of the Greek Artemis, and the temple of Diana of Ephesus in Asia Minor was one of the Seven Wonders of the World.

115.26 into the Ramblar] Barnes explained the phrase for a French translator: "from Italy into Spain—just the irresponsible wandering of the the Doctor's mind—" Perhaps Barnes (and/or the doctor) is thinking of *rambla*, the Spanish term for a broad street in eastern Spain built on a watercourse, specifically an avenue in Barcelona called La Rambla.

115.33 Rage and inaccuracy howl . . . which is called everybody's know] to Maffi Barnes wrote: "rage and inaccuracy shake the very skeliton [*sic*]. *Everybody's know* means what everybody thinks they know, and which usually they do not know. Consequently everyone (more or less) is suffering in suffering without the slightest idea of good and evil, right and wrong."

116.4 the poor and lightly damned!] for a French translator, Barnes said the phrase meant "insufficient soul."

117.25 Voltaire] the skeptical French satirist and philosopher (1694-1778).

117.25 the *Dead March* in 'Saul'] *Saul* (1738) is an oratorio by George Frederick Handel (1685-1759) about the biblical king.

123.6 a lost girl in Dante's time . . . She would have been remembered]
see Julie L. Abraham's argument that this could be a reference
either to Beatrice in *La Vita nuova* or a lesbian in the *Inferno*
(" 'Woman, Remember You,' " 260-61). The word "and" (in "and
he had turned") is the archaic "an," meaning "if."

125.23 ceasing of that abuse] Barnes wrote to Hildesheimer that the
abuse was "the staying out all night, drinking, being defiled . . .
abuse of the spirit" (letter, 25 July 1959).

127.5 'o'er graves of hope and pleasure gone.'] untraced.

127.11 dire need] Barnes explained this phrase to Hildesheimer as "the
need to rot and be done with it. thoroughly over" (letter, 25 July
1959).

127.12 The heat of his suppuration . . . before its time.] Barnes explained the phrase to a French translator: "the rotten apple rots the
apple next to it—figuratively speaking—the zenith—highest point
in his premature dissoluton for friendship sake."

127.35 *Chi vuol la Zingarella*] "Who wants the Gypsy girl?" —an aria
from Italian composer Giovanni Paisiello's 1789 opera *I Zingari in
Fiera*.

127.36 *Sonate au Crépuscule*] Twilight Sonata; unidentified.

127.36 *der Erlkönig*] a famous poem by Goethe, later set to music by
Franz Schubert, about an encounter with the Erl-King, a goblin in
German legend who haunts forests and lures people (especially
children) to destruction.

127.37 *Who Is Sylvia?*] a song in Shakespeare's *Two Gentlemen of Verona*
(4.2.39), set by many composers over the centuries.

128.12 peculiarly swung and me the craziest of the lot] Barnes glossed
the phrase for a French translator: "unsound, irregularly pieced
together—in short homosexual—peculiarly sexed."

129.32 a lost generation] it is unlikely that Barnes had in mind here
Gertrude Stein's statement to Hemingway that his was "a lost generation," though Barnes herself belonged to that generation.

129.35 *Mon Dieu, il y a deux chevaux de bois dans la chambre à coucher.*]
Fr.: My God, there are two wooden horses in the bedroom.

130.2 *basso porto*] an unusual phrase, apparently Italian slang for "low
life," i.e., the criminal underworld of the port town.

130.6 St. Gennaro] the Italian form of Saint Januarius (d. 304), patron
saint of Naples.

131.32 It's the instrument, gentlemen . . . touching his billycock!]

Barnes glossed this passage variously for Hildesheimer, a French translator, and most succinctly for Maffi: "emission of wind from the anus; otherwise if the G string hadnt been lost the tune would have been correct. if he had been more as other men he would have done better." A billycock is a bowler hat, a derby. "Why?" Barnes added, "otherwise, he'd be jaunty."

132.37 yeomen of the Guard] perhaps only coincidentally the title of a Gilbert and Sullivan opera (1888).

133.13 beating her head against her heart, sprung over] Barnes explained the phrase meant "bent over head to heart" (letter to Hildesheimer, 25 July 1959)

133.30 Was the Mad King of Bavaria infirm?] another reference to Ludwig II, who committed suicide (1886). See 23.5 above.

135.33 Caroline of Hapsburg] There were several Hapsburg Carolines, but the burial ritual described by O'Connor was that accorded to members of the Hapsburg monarchy: the heart was removed and placed in a golden urn and taken to the Heart Crypt of the Augustiner Church. Entrails were placed in a copper urn and carried by coach to St. Stephen's. The body of the monarch lay in state and then went to the church of the Capuchins. (Barnes uses the French form of the order.)

137.1 The Possessed] Dostoevsky's novel of this name (1871-72) may have contributed to the title. Barnes owned a copy (5 January 1927, letter from her mother, Djuna Barnes Papers).

HYPHENATION LISTS

Following is a list of end-of-line compounds that were hyphenated in the copy-text and their editorially established form:

6.26	fireplace
7.5	overlooking
11.19	sweat-tarnished
13.4	anything
13.28	over-large
15.34	rosy-cheeked
16.21	something
16.22	something
26.5	everything
27.14	myself
27.36	injustice
42.1	non-committal
45.9	Sometimes
48.24	reconstruct
52.25	herself
53.20	passer-by
55.9	grandmother
56.2	everlasting
56.13	grandmother
60.15	everything
60.19	over-tight
62.32	something
63.5	forbear
71.21	everything
71.27	fist-tight
83.14	anyone's
86.7	without

95.11   top-hat
95.21   somewhere
97.36   understand
105.19 eighty-two
107.17 everything
108.25 check-rein
108.27 understood
109.22 inbreeding
110.21 sideways
110.33 show-windows
113.26 some day
115.13 somewhere
116.33 hairline
117.32 something
119.11 someone
119.36 everything
121.4   nightmare
121.22 something
121.32 sky-blue
123.29 grandmother
124.3   forever
126.25 himself
129.17 understand
132.35 brick-layer
132.37 beefeaters
135.5   gentlemen
136.21 anyone
136.33 everything's

Following is a list of words hyphenated at the end of lines in the Dalkey Archive edition whose hyphens need to be retained when quoting from this text.

10.35   sword-swallowers
55.10   great-uncle
69.10   gun-metal
70.7   Matthew-Mighty-grain-of-salt-Dante-O'Connor
81.17   golden-mouthed
83.5   mouse-nests

HISTORICAL COLLATION

Some of the variants in the following selected list of substantive variants among editions are the result of alterations or corrections that Barnes made; others, however, appear to be typesetter errors. At Barnes's prompting, T. S. Eliot communicated a few changes to editors at Harcourt, Brace & Company for the first American edition. In October 1945 she wrote James Laughlin requesting corrections for the New Directions publication of 1946 and again in 1949 urged corrections for the reset edition. She wrote to Pierre du Sautoy of Faber and Faber regarding changes for the second English edition, though her letter arrived too late, he informed her, for the changes to be made. Barnes reviewed the proofs to the *Selected Works* edition of Farrar, Straus and Cudahy in 1962; these revisions are primarily in the last chapter.

The following list does not include accidental variants unless they affect meaning, e. g. "Harlem" instead of "Haarlem." Where an "s" has been omitted, for example, from "Marseilles," or in a plural formation, it has not been included.

In the following list the first lemma indicates the reading that appears in this edition. Following the reading, within parentheses, is a list of the editions that carry the same reading; variant readings follow the bracket. A plus sign (+) following an edition abbreviation indicates the same reading in all editions that appeared after the one cited, with the exception of the Dalkey Archive edition. For example, (ND49+) means that all editions after the New Directions 1949 edition have the same reading. Two editions separated by a hyphen indicate the same reading in all editions between the two cited; for example (A1-ND61), means that the first American edition (A1), the second American edition published by New Directions (ND46), the second English edition (FF50), and the New Directions paperback (ND61) have the same reading. The following abbreviations are used to identify editions:

E1   first English edition: Faber and Faber, London, 1936.

A1   first American edition: Harcourt, Brace & Co., New York, 1937. This edition is based on the English edition, but accidentals vary. There are some typesetting errors in the edition, and a few corrections communicated by Eliot.

ND46 New Directions: New York, 1946. This edition was based on the American edition (A1). Pagination is identical: but there are a few substantive variants.

ND49 New Directions: New York, 1949. This edition was reset, and several changes and corrections were introduced by Barnes.

FF50 second Faber and Faber edition: London, 1950. The pagination is the same as E1. There are a few substantive differences between the first and second English editions. Many of the changes made in ND49 do not appear in this edition.

ND61 New Directions: New York, 1961, paperback edition. A reprint of ND49, the pagination is identical, but there are a few substantive variants from ND49.

FSC   Farrar, Straus & Cudahy *Selected Works*: New York, 1962. Barnes made very minor changes to the text, complaining to publisher Robert Giroux that their fall catalog indicated revisions in *Nightwood*: "Why, why, why!" she wrote, stating that changes "amounted to about six words." The Farrar, Straus & Giroux edition of 1980 is identical to FSC.

4.36   everything possible] everything (E1+)
7.31   out (ND49+)] out of (E1-ND46)
8.16   seen (E1-ND61)] seem (FSC)
13.10 it's (E1-ND46, FSC)] its (ND49, ND61)
13.16 oneself? (A1-ND49, ND61+)] herself? (E1, FF50)
16.8   nodded (A1-ND49, ND61+)] grinned (E1, FF50)
17.14 become as the wives of the rich] become as the rich (E1+)
21.27 laughing silently (A1-ND49, ND61+)] grinning (E1, FF50)
22.35 pine (E1-ND46, FF50)] pin (ND49, ND61+)
30.24 *du VIe*, (A1-ND49, ND61+)] *de VIe*, (E1, FF50)
30.27 custom (ND49+)] customs (E1-ND46)
32.25 looked at him. (A1-ND49, ND61+)] grinned. (E1, FF50)
33.1   as (A1-ND49, ND61+)] at (E1, FF50)
33.1   Hiss (E1, ND49+)] His (A1, ND46)
33.11 by the by] by the way (E1+)

33.29   explained] exclaimed (E1+)
35.7   deep shocked (E1)] deep-shocked (A1+)
36.9   shop (ND49+)] shop or theatre (E1-ND46)
37.32   him, (E1, FF50)] him, but (A1-ND49, ND61+)
38.11   could (A1-ND49, ND61+)] would (E1, FF50)
38.30   said (A1-ND49, ND61+)] grinned (E1, FF50)
39.20   night watch (A1, ND46)] night-watch (E1, ND49+)
40.1   excellent (ND49, ND61+)] most beautiful (E1-ND46, FF50)
42.22   like (FSC+)] as (E1-ND61)
42.24   yet (FSC+)] and yet E1-ND61)
43.1   monstrously unfulfilled (FSC+)] yet more monstrously unful-
        filled than they had suffered (E1-ND61)
47.9   Nora. (ND49, ND61+)] Nora, sitting still, her hand on her
        dog, the fire-light throwing her shadow against the wall, her
        head in shadow, bending as it reached the ceiling, though her
        own stood erect and motionless. (E1-ND46, FF50)
47.18   immune to] immune from (E1+)
49.12   whip. (ND49+)] flickering whip. (E1-ND46)
49.30   get (E1-ND61)] get her (FSC)
51.15   Yet (E1-ND46, FF50)] Yes (ND49, ND61+)
52.19   curling irons] electric curlers (E1+)
52.32   a slowly (E1-ND46, FSC+)] slowly (ND49, ND61)
53.9   would catch (E1-ND46, FF50)] could catch (ND49, ND61+)
53.28   remembrance (E1-ND61)] a remembrance (FSC)
53.37   activity. (FSC+)] function (E1-ND61)
58.1   "The Squatter" (A1-ND49, ND61+)] The Squatter (E1, FF50)
59.22   of (FSC+)] of two words, (E1-ND61)
62.7   sat, (ND49, ND61+)] sat, her two small wax-like hands tender
        with the new life in them cupped up in her lap, (E1-ND46,
        FF50)
62.22   carriages (E1-ND61)] carriage (FSC)
64.25   in his sleep lies (FSC+)] sleeps (E1-ND61)
71.1   effect (ND61+)] good effect (E1-FF50)
71.29   the one (E1-ND61)] one (FSC)
71.31   And (E1-ND46)] Any (ND49+)
75.1   counter (E1-ND61)] contour (FSC)
78.23   any one (E1, FF50)] anyone (A1-ND49, ND61+)
79.34   still, quiet] still quiet (E1-FSC)
81.17   Groom (E1, ND49+)] Gloom (A1, ND46)

81.19 an humble (ND49, ND61+)] a humble (E1-ND46, FF50)
83.27 nor] not (E1+)
85.10 long spent] long-spent (E1+)
86.2 pedestal (E1-ND61)] pedestal and (FSC)
86.12 me? (ND49+)] me to her? (E1-ND46)
88.23 we are (E1-ND61)] we have (FSC)
91.17 their . . . faces] his . . . face, (E1+)
92.26 when taken (E1-ND46, FF50)] taken (ND49, ND61+)
94.11 one woman] one single woman (E1+)
94.30 at the same time (E1-ND61)] the same (FSC)
97.16 convent (ND61+)] nunnery (E1-FF50)
101.23 prostrate (FSC+)] upright (E1-ND61)
104.13 of (ND49+)] back of (E1, A1, ND46, FF50)
107.2 weather (E1, FF50, FSC+)] winter (A1-ND49, ND61)
109.17 any (E1-ND46, FF50)] got any (ND49, ND61+)
110.4 off down] off (E1+)
110.14 *haute* sewer (E1-ND61)] *haute* (FSC)
110.16 still, letting you do it, (ND46, ND49, ND61+)] still, (E1, A1,
        FF50)
111.14 took out] spoke to (E1+)
111.26 know (E1-ND61)] knows (FSC)
112.25 crying: (E1-ND61)] saying: (FSC)
113.15 brought his hands together. (A1-ND49, ND61+)] grinned. (E1,
        FF50)
114.7 any (E1-ND46, FF50)] my (ND49, ND61+)
115.13 wedded (A1-ND49, ND61+)] welded (E1, FF50)
116.5 suffer . . . , or love (FSC+)] suffers . . . , or loves (E1-ND61)
118.9 would call (E1-ND46, FF50)] could call (ND49, ND61+)
120.28 too, and (E1-ND61)] too, (FSC)
121.36 It's] That's (E1+)
122.25 window, (FSC+)] window or (E1-ND61)
123.4 floor. (ND61+)] floor, its blue bow now over, now under. (E1-
        FF50)
124.13 grandmother] grandfather (E1+)
125.11 it's] that's (E1+)
126.6 mew (E1-ND46, FF50)] new (ND49, ND61+)
126.34 kicked (A1-ND49, ND61+)] came along and kicked (E1, FF50)
127.7 "Ah yes—] "Ah, yes— (E1-ND61)] "As, yes— (FSC)
128.4 head? (FSC+)] heart? (E1-ND61)

130.27 staggered (A1-ND49, ND61+)] stood up. He staggered (E1, FF50)

130.32 at (ND49, FF50+)] up at (E1-ND46)

132.9 children mine] children (E1-FSC)

132.28 weighed (E1-ND46, FF50)] weighted (ND49, ND61+)

134.1 Harlem] Haarlem (E1+)

134.19 everyone] everybody (E1+)

136.7 into (A1-ND49, ND61+)] in (E1, FF50)

139.7 down, down her hair swinging, her arms out. The dog stood (FSC+)] down. Sliding down she went; down, her hair swinging, her arms held out, and the dog stood there (E1-ND61)

139.9 standing (ND49, ND61+)] about his neck standing out stiff and beautiful; (E1-ND46)

139.14 up on her hands (FSC+)] up on her fingers (E1-ND61)

139.16 back, his tongue (ND49, ND61, FSC)] back, his lips drawn, his tongue (E1-ND46, FF50)

139.18 too, (ND49, ND61+)] too now, (E1-ND46, FF50)

139.19 Backed into (ND49, ND61+)] Backed now into (E1-ND46, FF50)

139.23 sliding. (ND49-FSC)] sliding, looking at her, striking against the wall, like a little horse; like something imploring a bird. (E1-ND46)

139.23 Then head down, dragging . . . she struck (ND49, FF50+)] Then as she, now head down, dragging . . . struck (E1-ND46)

139.30 Crouching, the dog began to run with her, (ND49-FSC+)] The dog began to cry then, running with her, (E1-ND46)

139.31 to (ND49-FSC+)] slowly and surely to (E1-ND46)

RELATED DRAFTS

INTRODUCTION

All that remains of the two earlier versions of *Nightwood*—the first rejected by Barnes's previous American publisher, T. R. Smith of Liveright, in December 1932, the second also rejected by Smith in August 1934—are seventy-two pages of fragments in the Barnes archive at McKeldin Library at the University of Maryland, all of which are reproduced here. The fragments reside there in five separate folders (in boxes 5 and 10, series II), but they are arranged here chronologically on the basis of the different style of headings they carry, for these headings seem to point to different drafts or stages of composition. These fragments, then, give hints of the previous versions and of Barnes's methods of revision.

The first section consists of two versions of "Run Girls, Run!" (pp. 244-60). This fragment is linked to *Nightwood* by "Bow Down" in its heading, which was the original title of *Nightwood*. In addition, there is a note in Barnes's hand in a folder containing part of this fragment identifying it as "Early mss of 'Nightwood.'" Unfortunately, the first two pages of the typescript version are missing; to supplement the missing pages, and to provide a glimpse of Barnes's revising techniques, a marked-up facsimile of the published version of "Run Girls, Run!" follows. It appeared in March 1936 (seven months before *Nightwood*) in *Caravel*, a magazine published in Majorca and edited by (among others) Barnes's friend Charles Henri Ford. (The version reproduced here is one that Barnes corrected sometime later, for unknown reasons; the story has been reprinted only once—as the second half of *Vagaries Malicieux* [New York: Frank Hallman, 1974]—but that edition reprints the text of the *Caravel* version, and in fact was done without Barnes's authorization and, hence, without any of her corrections.) On 9 December 1935 Barnes wrote to Emily Coleman that she had given to Ford the part which she had "put into *Nightwood* and took out again." Very much in the style of her previous novel *Ryder*, this story seems unrelated to the style and tone of *Nightwood* as we know it.

The second section of drafts begins with a note in Barnes's hand (p. 261) identifying this material as "Discarded pages from early copy of 'Nightwood' (T. S. E. handwriting in BLUE)." The first four pages (262-65) are from "Watchman, What of the Night?" They were originally paginated 16-18, 24, then renumbered by hand. These fragments indicate that in early drafts of the novel Barnes apparently numbered each chapter separately and at a later stage returned to the manuscript and renumbered it consecutively. Eliot's "handwriting" consists of a vertical line in the left margin with an "x" beside it. Only one other page, "La Somnambule" (p. 271) has pencil marks identified as Eliot's by Barnes's note.

The next five pages (pp. 266-70) are from a chapter that was called "Largo." Some of this material corresponds to material that now appears in "Go Down, Matthew" (see the table at the end of this introduction), but other sections do not. The bar scene in "Largo" suggests that this chapter was combined with "Go Down, Matthew" and its title dropped.

The final section of drafts, from pages 271 to 319, carries the same style of heading, suggesting that these pages are all from the same version of *Nightwood*, perhaps the second. One page (271) comes from "La Somnambule," but none of the details here appear in the finished chapter of that name. Barnes's note on this page indicates the presence of Eliot's handwriting, specifically the small x's in the left margin. This page is followed by one from "Where the Tree Falls" (272). The change in chapter number in the heading from 7 to 6 suggests rearrangement of chapters or the omission of one.

The remaining thirty-eight pages are from "Go Down, Matthew." The chapter number of 9, instead of the published 7, again points to the combination or omission of chapters. Much of this material does not appear in the published *Nightwood*; the material on pages 297 to 310, for example, suggests autobiographical parallels with Barnes's early life. On 25 July 1936, Barnes wrote from Paris to Emily Coleman about the final portion of this material, the "old lady" section (313-19). When she had asked Dan Mahoney, the model for Doctor O'Connor, how he felt about being in the book, he had replied, "I'd forgive you—in case I don't sue you—if you would put my old lady back." Barnes wrote: "So there you are—I'll have to send it to Eliot, as Dan really seems to feel her loss so bloody bitterly—heaven knows why." There is no evidence, however, that she did so.

Correspondences. The following list identifies correspondences between draft material and the present edition of *Nightwood.* (Draft pages that are not listed have no direct correspondence with the published version of *Nightwood.*)

262-64 → 80-82, 84.
266 → 130-31
269 → 133
274 → 108-9
275-77 → 95-96
278-81 → 26-28
284 → 19
285 → 107
286 → 114
289 → 133
290 → 135
291 → 113
292-97 → 114-16
311 → 14
312 → 126

From Something published, I think in New Orleans ... ... was it myaca ?

Bow Down --3- Run Girls,Run!

"You've gone and done it undoubtedly,the rain predicts as much ,or
my chilblains and spearpricks lie to my marrow!" The trend to the
effect that he would wing wring her neck of her head's need,if she,in
so much as one sole,hinted at bedleaving ,and with that,and for that
matter without waiting to turn up one foot to make sure of his "if",
he tore down the bed hangings,with no thought of himself,but with
an absent eye proved that he was computing the price of her guilt,and
the more outrageous pence of her gall ,as he pushed down upon her,to
encompass a smother, a great bolster from Stratford ,saying:"Sink back
in to folk-lore,make of your flesh the venison thinkers toughen their
wits on,for the sooner I'm done with you,girl,that much sooner you will
be sung of!" At this point he broke completely down,in the classic manner
remarking "Hey nonnie nonnie O,my heart breaks over the corn ocean!
I weep like a tiger in txt stripes for a whelp in trouble all on a
spear's end,for doing away with your habits,which were of the worst,
and your fawnings,which were remarkable! May God forgive me,and likewise
(mark the difference!) the Lords in their Polonaises and the Queens
at their belladonna,and the pages in waiting. The mistletoe shall frost
on the bough calling never your mouth to the kissing,nor longer
the furze bloom of the yule tree be spangled! The faggots shall
thicken in the branch for lack of your dust to sweep,and the place
where you sat shall chill in the gown,and the Forum will haggle over
you,right and wrong,for payment on sin means a head under a pillow.
When I am a clubman at ninety odd,with my daughter dangling on my
arm,who will be a fin of yet another fish,and blind of an eye for the
generations sake,-she will fore fear the blood,when she recalls that
you were cooled with a pillow!"

Bow Down--&--Run Girls,Run!

Whereupon she cried "May!" and "May!" And "May!",and her hands
went as high as her head,and her hands went as high as her eyes,and her
hands went as high as her mouth,and her hands went as high as her throat,
and her hands went as high as her breasts,and with that her soul was
unleashed and it roared from the portal,and her hands had no more ways.
Then they snatched her up,and sealed her with wax,and when but
three days deep in her own death,they put her in a child's coffin,
a fright of a gaud trumpery satin,fourpenny lace,white and its sister
off white,with nod-lillies on her oaker knees,and sleep-bells coiled
under her heels,and shook-blossoms helter skelter all about her and
                                from
down on the cobbles ,thrown by the balconies of the many-faced populace
never so pleasantrixxas unpleasantly pleased as when pelting history Webb
new made in its own court. And Don,now Oratorio,shaken with a lad's grief
though a man among men,walked with his/this head held up,the tears
falling brief-hot.And the cock sparrow crew "Hyrly,burly and under
the broom!"

                              ....

Was it Fancy?

     And this is but preface to: what was up to the nines of
mahoy that put such a controversy in her marrow? Was she a child
when she took porridge,and was she a woman,when a woman,she split
to the harvest,a scythe in her hand,her skirts tucked u p,and her
bald head turned listening to a meadow lark singing between the oat
and its oats?

     Culled she a plovers egg down by the brinky,and noting
it knocking as she held it in her hand,did she unthinking come a
random nearer God and the mystery of his manner,or was it in ignorance

Bow Down 5 Run Girls,Run!

(the very fountain of trouble) that she reaped eye sockets of late
tears. Who was it ploughed up her borders of caution at one stroke,
when night by day,for the full and appointed time,from the cradle to the
feather bed of sweet sixteen,the home fires were kept roaring with x
leaves snatched from the Bible,and her mother darning maxims as fast as
she could stitch them into the hosen,and thou-shalt-nots in crotch
work .

     Had Nancy ever heard of a cock as other than a hens brag in her
own time,or of the bull in the pastures for that matter,as anything
but a cows idea of a cut-up when she wanted to play at romp ? Or had
she ever thought of a brindle snarling,as anything but a duet to a bitch
barking at the moon riding high?

     Never! Yet the race,hand for hand,bastard on brat,heeled over
on this years calendar. Still our sweet Nancy persisted in averring that
it was but fumble called Jack,as he crawled by the door,babbling of
papa when the dinner gong called big men to mutton,bluff boys to
cheese.

     Did she have a caul? "as she forecast for damnation? Was it to be
expected that she would bulk to this fate when they pinned up her bib
and bound her about in woolsey? Was it foreordained that under these
rafters she would once one day take off her stays saying " How was it?
Why was it? ~~Who was it by~~ damn! I swear I never so much as looked
~~behind me~~
~~back that day a year back~~ (was it June?) when a fist came out of a wind
~~and fell~~ ~~me to my knees~~ breeze flung up my kirtle and browsed at
~~my thighs~~ ~~crotch~~ ~~withers~~,ah me! A storm is a storm,yet it
~~appears~~ ~~thought~~ ~~a father~~ ~~They say~~ it is good for the barley,but
~~what of me~~ ~~what harm~~ ~~I did~~ ~~I ought not to have~~ done when I was

Bow Down--6--Run Girls,Run!

down on my knees   in the corn patch,and my hand held before me was
no others but my own.At my back was the meadow and the hills,and beyond
the hills the horizon,the same sky for Asia and China.Or is that a
madmans tale which we call an Atlas! Yet I am a mother,and the child is
a how-come. I the pot of most horrid luck! Well,from this day till that
day that spells my finish,not so much as a shower shall come between
me and my kneeling ,or a clap of thunder will get me with child
I'll be called a witch at the weather! I'll be tarred for a prophet,
feathered for fear's sake,be burned in the market,be ducked in a pond!
Oh God! who would have guessed that the wind was a boy!
Was It Guesswork?
            And there,in the smock green,on the tangled towpath
to the edge of the world where the waters ran loshing in the pranks of
the sun,so ripe and pure the quantity that all about its edges,fish
lay sprung and lashing with sea loss;there the moon lay,embosomed on gallon
gallons,how deeply reflected,none can say but those who sway for walking
as they tread out the floors of the watery ocean,well,there in the
Marshes,in a basket of osier,woven as big as a cocooos nest and not a
leaf larger than that,a Babe in the Bullrushes put his face out,and
was seen by the sons of man--twenty---thousand- -years,and the clock
strikes now.And this is but preface to :how walks she safe? The Face has
has shown her the way to the Street Called Straight,where innocence to
Error throws a crown of thorns to a crown of roses over the steeple's top
And this brings us to Nell and her lovely saxe blue bonnet,the very
bonnet she set her cap in,well over her eye. Her breastfull of bosoms
strapped in a keel-shaped corset from Spitzburgen,her hand,kid held in a
plausable suede from Mount Sinai,, where anterior to the fall of Don

Bow Down --7--Run Girls,Run!

      and his prayers,xhaxwaxxtakingxthaxwatwwax(in which she was not
included by so much as a leaf full of dashes or a dogs ear) she was
taking the waters,fishes and all,but for all that,at the curve of her
none-to-sacred-leg,as stout as a log from the True Bean,and as blooming
as a branch from the Right Tree,flounced ten yards and a half of goods
Ghetto taffeta ,a wandering Jewess,ladled up handsomely from the vat of
the Hebrew,though by alley collusion,by wink and by side-step,more and
more of a heathen.

      Her pose is impressive(Gainsborough painted her) her hand on
her hip,her hip on a tilt,on the full of her arm a reticule bulging with
scraps swept from Parliament Street all the way up Sinister Lane.Her
shoulders strutted to the upstanding Indian(in flesh,in wood,in fact
the Indian is a dying race,mark this well,perhaps someday this story will
be all that we will know of it!) who in cedar magnificence holds out
a dozen or more perfectos from Barcelona,as Nell sings in flasetto(the
voice we all come to) "Only a Bird in a Gilded Cage." changing the
largo of that to the retardo of "If my Brother Were Here,You Would
Not Dare To Insult Me!" because ,raising her oriental lids she observes
that she is bounded on all full four quarters by a pub,and that closing
in on her from all seas are sailors all seas over,with a week yet to go
of an all shores leave,therefore falling back on the brother in question
who,being off on that endless that makes him a Jew,is a sort of
help to the mind. A cat corner rubbing passes her on his way to the
Bowery,which reminds her that they are both a long way from home nearly
all their lives,which accounts for the fact that the "Singapore Jars,here
over and over,found her a virgin,Still it is a step in advance,for in
the days of Don Jamie all a girl got for her pains was a pillow,Still

~~~~~~~~ ~~ ~~~~~~ Girls, Run!

In time, Time will date her , let her walk ever so lightly, and she will
be found to have fallen to the calendar as Anne Domini B.C.

Or Dreaming?

Which is but preface to: Katrina at the Well, and how, in
giving her water to the ~iberian Don Snangar, they fell in love down
straight tank: to the cistern's bottom, and there, lying out of wedlock
upon its pebbles , how they both drank of deaths spring deeply .

                                    held her vanether the other way
        Love held her one way and the water held her another so that
because
she became mother a wet sighing sea work, a mother. She was scattered
along the pods of the ocean, up in the green grass she went, down in the
rain she came, the lichen trembled with her, while her daughter on terma
went seeking a lock of her hair, face over the fields she went seeking
over the mountains and valleys she went seeking, while the bloodhounds of
history wrote it down in a book.

Or was it-

        Which is preface to La Pirouetta, the Dog faced Girl, who for all
that was the ugliest woman in history. XXXXXXXXXXXXXXXXXXXXXXX
Don Pierre was her lover(among others) She danced on her toes, she made
her bows backward--tulle is a stuff that moves outward from its
purpose , so that Don Pierre, who always took his opera glasses to
his assignations, saw something pretty, prompt, and withall, frilled.

        She was hunted in spring like a hare. Men ploughed through
snow, rhime and rain for her sake. Her suppers were of course the talk of
the town. What she lost at meat she made good later with the bone. She
had Montaigne for hors d'oeuvres, Voltaire slept over her shoulder,
Bismark pulled at her ear, she had a handfull of secrets, but in the end
Alas! She was traced back to England by scraps of fools cap,

THE Dawn ,9--Run Girls,Run!

by traces of urine,all the way out of Egypt and over the Indies and
xxx   xxx
into Peru,Nor was that all, She grew as fat as a pudding,took to loud
barking,a dog pointing herself,till she startled the most unexpected
thing,--the Bird of her Soul,and pecking a seam came out at her belly,and
on a
          sharp   curve of wings ,flew into the face of convention,went up
in a caw and a   diminishing funnel of smoke,to couch in heaven   on a
mackerel sky ,where,much to the amazement of the Elders,she became large
                                                       studying
of Leda,who it turned out to be a boy with a Greek face,who studied
his own hand,palm up, in a manly effort to discover a trace of herself!
Or was it but Legend?

          And this bespeaks the day when Hazel of Honfleur,coming to
a pass,fainted on the milk-white knob of her father's door,though
God help/us,no child at the breast whimpered of snow in the air,
though on all walls the rain went roaving."ll because and why? Hazel
had been hot footing it down the priceless profusion of the paternal
ivy,which flourishingly flourished taking no heed of a girls reputation
flourished at all hours of the night,facing out toward Main Street,
so her father observing a late loitering lad had with the fruit of his
loins,what as termed converse,though no clue could be found that could
have led the lad to her,but by putting two and its inevitable two together
matching last year's love letters to love,papa bearded her night trick
and, and with a haughty name saving gusto pushed her full fathoms ten
into history.

          So it was that all rents and tatters,Hazel found herself ducked
in mythology,and a little later making eyes in Byzant to a Butcher
who oxed it to Dons of a caper and to scholars.His suet had waxed many
a contentious page,and his cow's heads and his sow's heads, much like

Bow Down -IO--Run Girls,Run!

Faith in A Tight Place,lay cheek to cheek on their platters.

Now this good Roman,the first butcher without wit of a kind ,
having come upon hard times at all times,what with meum and teum,
on Passion Week,year in and year out, sacrificed a bull to his betters,
and in some way this having reached High Heaven(all prayers are
finally answered in some extraordinary fashion,) rewarded Gonzolas
the butcher by sending him Hazel,to make up in wummvway for the fact
that Gonzolas had married a Christ day Resenter,who walked on her two
feet as if they were four feet,whookesa   whose one eye was dour for
for the sake of the other,who in Greek cloth bound up her envious
bogws,and who never ceased resenting the fact that she was the worst
blunder in the wrong place ,watching for Saturdays sin on anycoff
Sunday night ,suspecting that this Hazel,who called herself Boaz and
who wore galligaskins handsomely enough,wore them too handsomely for
the sex she claimed.

Ah yes,such things were,in the shady days of a long time ago,
undoubtedly brewing. On the gall-spotted pastures,under the even then
                    Gonzolas and Hazel
mythically roving moon, had beak's banter,sweet kissing ---could it be
left thus? Never! Lore must be served,tragedy must come from all points
of the compass.The Helenic gesture,Epic injustice were in those days not
pondered by scholars alone,sometimes they seethed the exceeding small
inch of damnation called a womans skull work,and such an inch had
Fumpuoda,the wife of Gonzolas,for he poor fellow while Greek in one
kidney was Grouse in the other.

The eve of the sacrifice found Gonzolas tying twigs, lugging
faggots from the the forest for the burning of his fine white ox,the very

Bow Down--II--Run Girls,Run!

hero of the herd ,a beauty to boot,who bellowed the song of the grass
that he had eaten,,richly and loudly,rocking against the sky the
outriding
beautiful arch of his horns,like a gibbus of metal. Fmmpucca meanwhile
set to bees-waxing the cords that should lace like a boot that fine
swort pastured belly,for it must be stuffed with gudgeon,slivers of
bacon,gouges of gooese liver, the foot of a swan,the tongue of a
lark;basted with burgundy,strapped in with truffles,smartened with
thyme and bay and garnished with plover,filliped with a skylark's
gullet,and syroped all over with honey.

The hurly burly was great,the gathering large.wise acres' wit
pinched from hunger and in need of a good larding,minstrels from Avon
with lutes stretched for plucking,a dozen of winnow Widows ,all in
black,from Loch Namarra,a witch or two who hoped for a gug jug or
more of drippings spilled by gluttons,yes all were there,even trapse -up
of neighbors and little people from the wood.

Gonzolas was scattered and harried by the hell in Fmmpucca who
was calling for a pitchfork for the hired help who were trying to roll
the beast over.The tapes of Gonzolas' apron were as stiff as the
switch in the tail of an ass with his hurrying hither and thither at her
bidding.

The fair ox was now roasted to a second,not a gill in that
conclave but watered with greed while Gonzolas with buckets of lard
eased the roast bptheopoint to the point,all the while springing his
ears for the sound of the footfall of Hazel.

Now the ox split asuhder,done to a lick finger, with a
cleaving of ribs as loud as one great stroke on a drum . And there
out in his belly sat Hazel,her chin on her knees,as dead as the ox

Bow Down.— I2-Run Girls,Run!

heart that smouldered beside her.For--who had been stuffing the beast
in the night,in the dark dead of the night?Pumpucea with a smile on her
face.

Who was it that gave out that long wailing cry,like a bell that
had lost its account with the hour?--all jangled and frenzied?
Gonsolas,going headlong,head forward,at battle alone.
Farewell!

Farewell Ladies! Farewell Marigoldo! Farewell! Farewell!
God and I broke the sleep of the Beast,which is sweet water,and he
and I shall not meml it!

Hail Ladies! Hail Marigoldo! Hail! Hail!

. . . .

(Vol. II)
No. 5

CARAVEL

March
1936

An American Magazine Published in Majorca
Edited by Jean Rivers, Sydney Salt and Charles Henri Ford

The contents of The CARAVEL is copyrighted by The CARAVEL PRESS. In submitting manuscripts do not fail to enclose sufficient return postage and a self-addressed envelope. Subscription price, One Dollar a year. Address communications: The CARAVEL, Ciudad Jardin K-7, Alicante, Spain. (Mss may also be submitted to Mr. Ford, 21 W. 8 St., New York City.)

RUN, GIRLS, RUN!
Djuna Barnes

In the days when three sorts of nature but made a man; when the Marquis had no Seningalt, and the Chevalier d'Eon had yet to raise his petticoat to posterity; when history was a country, and no man's land an inheritance, and the night covered all for the gossips of dawn; at the time when one sparrow could glean every grave in an hour, we had this story—the first of its kind, though those that followed were as like as the links in the ankle chain of a convict. The time, in other words, when it was impossible to talk of backstepping to the days of our fathers without getting back to the first, when he, glide by creep, in his nightshift of a nightshirt (he was known as Don Juan B. C., but mark him, a bit of a Moor for all that—bespattered with the wine of thanksgiving—he'd been doing a bit at a banquet—all bedabbled with the tears of thankstaking) tiptoed through chamber upon chamber where, in a bed of elegant sheets and millenium lace, he came upon his wife, she who had borne him no sons but a thundering head brace of thorns, having diddled and horned him on every one of his fleecy temples, with, taking them as they came, a soldier off leave (no kill), a senator in mittens (where *did* he get them?), a conqueror come home from the wars, defeat in both hands up to the wrists; a galley-slave without an oar (women love the stoop in conquer), a Doge damned by Venice, a huntsman with his fallow deer but three sighs unspilled of her blood; and, of course, a carpenter at joists who had been pegging the first house; a headsman stropping a whacking large meat ax (raised in rage and felled in justice). on a corn reaper's hone, who in turn dried the deed on the pot-boy's buckram. Then followed a bishop, a priest (nowhere to blame had his breviary been bigger) and for witchery, no doubt, a few stews boys, lean and sniffing, and last of all (for a woman will sidle up to a climax), the power behind the Throne.

So, having passed the Lord of the Breeches, the Lady of the hose (avoiding as he went the eye of the Night Trot, holding her candle up-side down), there went Don, full upon his knees—sprung and galled in the hocks from twigging at the tourneys—down, down beside the sweet sleeping on her neat nest of swans' down and goose-fallings, over-stitched with pelicans' pelt, thatched with pinions of linnet moult at larks' battle, latterday drift-work from a scene of feathery combat (on one of those bright and sunny days when she went hawking) the whole quilted for her feet, soft and succumbing. So, finger to finger, he put his elbows down upon that part of her guesswork that brought her, with a bound and a stifled scream, straight up from the realms of the Valkyrie and the backward nations of Uz, to find from her hand, poor innocent jade, the harp struck down by the weight of a ton of Toledo cod-work (protecting what she had never respected) which at that moment Don doffed with the last furious gentsure of a man who throws caution to the wind and her baggage after. And in so doing he became no longer dear Don, but Richard the Lion-hearted, crying like a gosling into a woman's handkerchief, snatched up at the moment of his worst deductions, whose initials were nobody's (she'd taken care of that) but which reeked of a perfume used by the Duenna oversleeping at the wrong door—this to his man's eye—(it was embroidered all over with vestal lace, making his grief slightly dubious), he said hoarsely: «You've gone and you've done it! The rain predicted as much, or my chilblains, and that damnable sword prick, lie to my marrow!» The general trend to the effect that he would wring the neck of her head if in so much as one sole of her foot there was a print of bed leaving. Naturally, without turning up one to make sure of his if he tore down the bed hangings with no thought to himself, though what slid from the canopy would have amused him considerably, had he looked into the matter; but instead, with eyes raised (proving him counting the price of her

guilt, and the outrageous pence of her gall), he pushed all of it down
to encompass a smother, a bolster from Stratford, among other things,
saying «Jump back into folk-lore, that old rhyme-makers may toughen
their teeth on you; for the sooner I'm done with you, that sooner will
you be sung of!» At this point breaking completely down, in the classic
manner, adding «Hey nonnie, I weep like a tiger in stripes for a whelp
crying 'Mother!' high on a spear's end, in doing away with your habits,
which were, God knows, of the worst! So, I wind up your fawning on
my fury's spool. May God forgive me, and likewise (mark the change),
the Lords in their Polonaises, and the Queens pecking at belladonna,
and the tireless pages in waiting. The mistletoe shall frost on the bough
calling never your mouth to the kissing, nor longer the furze bloom of
the Yule tree be spangled! The faggots shall thicken in the bush for
lack of your dust to sweep, and the place where you sat shall chill
in the gown.

«Of course, the Forum will haggle over your corpse; right or wrong,
payment of sin always finds a head-under-pillow! So, when I marry
again at ninety, my other daughter will be a fin from another fish,
blind of an eye for the generation's sake. And will she fore-fear the
blood! She will, when she learns that you were cooled with a pillow!»
Whereupon the poor slut (not dead yet by a damned sight) cried:
«Nay!» and «Nay!» and «Nay!» And her hands went as high as
her crown, and her hands went as high as her eyes, and her hands
went as high as her mouth, and her hands went as high as her throat,
and her hands went as high as her breasts, and with that her hands had
no more ways, and her soul roared from the portal.

They snatched her up and sealed her with wax (better for her
had it been done in her lifetime) and when but three days deep in her
death, they put her in a child's coffin, a fright of a gaud (a woman
packs close when she has died of suspicion), all trumpery satin, four-
penny lace, white and its sister off-white, with nod-lilies on her knees,
sleep-bells coiled under her heels, and all about her shock-blossoms thrown
down on the cobbles, helter skelter, tossed from the balconies of the
many faced populace (along with a few jaseys) never so pleasantly pleased
as when pelting history new made in its own courtyard, Don, the Lion
Hearted, now Little Lord Fauntleroy, shaken with a lad's grief, though
of course a man among MEN, walked with his head up, his pelvis
bristling, his tears falling brief hot on his collar, which stuck out around
his neck like a platter. And the cock crew «Hurly, Burly, and under
the broom!»

And that is but preface to the next in line, Nancy, and what had

been up to her nines that controversy roved her marrow at such an
early age? Was she a child, or was she not, when she first ate her porridge?
Was she a woman, when a woman, she split to the harvest? She was
carrying a scythe, and her skirts were tucked up as neat as a hen's pinions,
her head turned listening to the warbling of a meadow lark, singing between the oat and the oat.

.She culled; or found, or foraged a plover's egg down. by the brinky,
and noting it (I may have the wrong egg) did she then at that moment,
thoughtlessly, come a thought nearer God? Or was it ignorance, plain
and simple, that reaped her eye-sockets of trouble? Who on that particular
harvest was it that ploughed up her borders of caution at one lightning-
like stroke, when night and day, for the full and appointed time, from
the cradle to the grave, every fire in the house had been kept burning
and roaring away with leaves snatched from the Bible and The Book
of Creation, the Zend Avista, and the Zohar; her mother darning maxims
as fast as she could overhand them into hosen, and plenty of thou-
shalt-nots into the family crotch work.

Yet Nancy got her babe, landing in a sitting posture on that year's
calendar! Still Nancy persisted in averring that it was fumble and fancy
called Jack as he crawled by the door, babbling of paps when the dinner
gong rang, calling big men to mutton and bluff boys to cheese. Into
the shades with the question! Was she perhaps noosed in a caul? Was
t that bulked her to this fate, so that she, in taking off her stays, night
after night, had to whisper: «Now how was it? And why was it? And
who was it, by damn? I swear I never looked behind me that day a fear
back, when a fist came out of the wind and felled me to my knees;
a breeze flung back my kirtle and browsed at my thigh, and a gale drenched
my withers! Ah me, a storm is a storm, yet it appears a tempest's a
father! It is said that it is good for the barley, but what of me? Who
can say I did aught that I shouldn't have done when I was in the corn
patch, down, searching for cobs, and my hand before me was no one's
hand but my own! At my back was the meadow and the hills, and beyond
that the horizon – the same sky for Asia and China and me, ah 'tis a
madman's lie which we call the Atlas. Yet I'm a mother, and the child
is a how-come, oh most horrid luck! From this day to
that day that shall spell me no longer, not so much as a shower shall
come between me and my sheaving, or a clap of thunder will get me
with child, I'll be called a witch at the weather, be tarred for a warning
and feathered for fear's sake, be burned in the market, or ducked in
a pond – oh God, who could have guessed that the rain was a boy!»

But all this was only the beginning, and it brings us to Nell, sweet

Nell, in her saxe-blue bonnet, the bonnet she set her cap in, well over
her eye, her breastful of bosoms strapped into a keel-shaped corset from
old Spitzburgen, her hand, kid-held in a plausible suede from Mount
Sinai — all early century women were not wholly Christian, though they
did not mention it (Nell had taken the waters at every Spa on the map
before Don Jaime left her to ruin). At the curve of her none too sacred
leg, as stout as a log from the True Beam, and as blooming as a branch
from the Right Tree flounced ten good yards of Ghetto taffeta — a wandering Jewess, ladeled up handsomely from the vat of the Hebrew, though, as
she drifted through life (collusion and alley, side street and nooks) she
became more and more of a heathen. Observe her poses. Impressive!
(Gainsborough painted her when she made England for a night) her hand
on her hip, her hip on a tilt, on her arm at the full, a reticule bulging
with scraps swept from Parlament Street up Sinister Lane, she stands by
an Indian, who in magnificent cedar offers passersby a dozen perfectos
from Aged Barcalona, as Nell sings in falsetto (the voice we all come
to) «Only A Bird In A Gilded Cage» (God, what a voice!), changing
from largo to largo retardo as she breaks into the strains of «You Would
Not Dare To Insult Me If My Brother Were Here» as she becomes aware
that she is beset on all sides with all pubs, and sailors closing in on her from
all seas' leave.

Thinking of that Brother also off on the endless that makes him a
Jew, she bursts into tears, as a cat, corner rubbing (the first cat in history)
passes her silently on his way to the Bowery, reminding her that they
both are a long way from home, nearly all of their lives.

So did she, holding on to the hand of her illegitimate daughter, on
the instant of passing a beautiful deep-seated cistern, throw herself in
by mistake?, as housewives will, sooner or later, throw the peas in the
swill-pail and the pods in the pot! She did and was a wet sighing
sea-work in less than a month, scattered along the pulse of the ocean
(there was a leak in the well). Up in vapour she went, down she
came in the rain, while her daughter, on terra firma, went seeking a
lock of her hair. Over the fields she went, over the mountains, into
the valley, while the bloodhounds of history wrote it down in a book,
as «La Histoire de la Pirouetta», the dog-faced Girl, who was, for all
that, the ugliest woman in history (dating about the Voltaire period),
and was, among other things, one of the best conquests of Don Jamie
when he became Don Presto, the man at the small ends of the Opera
glass (he had to, to come upon her). Men hunted her in the spring
like hounds; they plunged through the snow, sleet, rain, all for word
with her about it and about. Her suppers were the talk of the town.

What she lost at meat she made good with the bone. Yet, alas, in the
end she was traced back into Perugia by fools-cap and urine, all the
way out of Egypt and over the Andes and into Peru, nor was that the
worst of it. She grew as fat as a pudding, took to loud barking, a
beagle pointing herself by the scruff of her neck, Until she startled
from cover the Bird of her Soul, which pecking a long seam, came
out at her navel, and on flat wings flew straight into the Face of
Convention, went up in a caw and a funnel of smoke to sit in heaven,
where much to the amazement of the Elders, she became large of
Leda, who turned out to be a boy with a Greek face, twisting and
turning to see how he was made, and never having heard that there's
nothing much on the back, nearly dislocated his neck saying «Where
is the other?»

And all of this is but preface to Hazel of Honfleur, woman into
beast. Hazel fainted on the milk-white knob of her father's door (though
no babe whimpered at the breast, bone nor was there snow in the
air). Why? because Hazel had been caught hot-footing it down the
paternal ivy facing Main Street at all hours of the night. Putting this
fact together with the vision of a late loitering lad, Papa had word
with her setting her chin out from the family, though no clue could
positively have been said to lead to her, nevertheless by matching last
year's love letters to love, Papa bearded her night trick, and with
impressive gusto hove her ten fathoms deep into the life of the people.

So it was that, all in rents and tatters, Hazel found herself
ducked in mythology, and making eyes at a Byzantine butcher who
oxed it to Dons of a caper and to scholars. This fellow's suet had
waxed many a contentious page, his sows' heads and his cows' heads,
much like fate, lay cheek to cheek on his platters.

Now this good Roman Gonzolas (why not Roman?) the first
butcher without wit of a kind, having lost it in hard times at all times,
what with meum and teum in Passion week, year in year out, was
rewarded with Hazel from the Lord, to make up to him, in a small way, for
having taken in marriage a Christ day resenter, a terrible creature who
walked on her two feet as if they were four, whose one eye was
dour for the sake of the other, and who, in Greek cloth, bound up
her envious brows, for she never ceased lamenting the fact that she
was the wrong blunder in the right house. She was particularly suspicious
of Gonzolas in connection with Saturday night, and she had a pre-
sentiment that Hazel, who called herself Gavin (she had donned
galligaskins) was no more girl than the pout of her breeks would
suggest.

Ah, undoubtedly yes! This shady epoch saw Gonzolas and Hazel in the gall-spotted pastures, beneath a mythically roving moon, having beaks banter and sweet kissing. Could matters so stand? Lore *must* be served; tragedy must come from all points of the compass. The Hellenic gesture, Epic injustice, were in those days, things that did not seethe the brains of scholars alone; oftimes the exceeding small inch of damnation called a feminine skull could catch out scorpions, and such an inch had Frampucca, wife to Gonzolas, for though he, poor wretch, was Greek in one kidney, he was grouse in the other.

The eve of the great yearly sacrifice saw Gonzolas tying of twigs, lugging faggots from the forest, to forward the burning of his finest white bull, the hero of the herd, who had bellowed the symphony of the meadow, in the grass he had eaten, richly and fondly, the arch of his horns a gibbus of plenty against the night sky.

Meanwhile Frampucca sat bees-waxing the cords that would lace up his fine swart belly like a boot. For the ox was to be stuffed with gudgeons, slivers of bacon, gouges of goose livers, the foot of a swan, the tongue of a lark, basted with burgundy, strapped in with truffles, smartened with thyme; and garnished with bay, a fillip of nightingales' gullet to syrup over the honey and amber.

The hurly-burly was great on that night, the gathering large. Wise-acres, wit-pinched from hunger and in need of a good larding, were there, minstrels from Avon with lutes stretched for plucking, a dozen of widows from Loch Namorra who hoped for a jug full of drippings caught from the chins of gluttons, yes, all, all were there, even trapse ups of neighbors and little people from the park.

Gonzolas was scattered and harried by the hell in his wife who was calling for a pitchfork to give a lift to the hired help who were rolling (or trying to) the beast over. The tapes of Gonzolas' apron were as stiff as the switch in the tail of an ass, what with hurrying hither and yon at her bidding.

Now the bull split asunder from the great heat, done to a lick finger, with a cleaving of ribs as loud as the stroke of a drum—and there in his belly, like a queen in her chamber, sat Hazel, her chin on her knees, as done as the ox heart that smouldered beside her. For who had been stuffing the beast in the night, in the dark pit of night? Frampucca the wife, with a smile on her face.

And who was it gave out that long wailing cry like a bell torn from the arms of the hour? Gonzolas going head forward, headlong, at battle alone. AND SO ON.
Farewell, Ladies, farewell farewell

Discarded pages from early
Copy of "Nightwood"
(T. S. E Handwriting in BLUE)

146

"Watchman,what of the night?" -16-

set of features

—They become old without reward,the widower bird sitting

sighing at the turnstile of heaven,her wings bent down,her

voice high spent,on mourning fat,a bird flying arse up,down,

screaming back a plume of sighing,hallelujah! I am sticked! Skoll|skoll|I' am dying!

Or walks the floor,holding her hands,or lies upon the

floor,face down,with that terrible wish of the body that would

in misery,be flat with the floor,or lost lower than buriel,or

utterly blotted out and erpased so that no stain of her could

ache upon the wood,or snatched back to nothing without aim,

going backward through the target,taking with her the spot where

she made one--

Look for the girls also,in the toilets at night,and you

will find them kneeling in that great second confessional,the

one the Catholic church forgot--over the door Dames,a girl

standing before her,her skirts flung back one on one,while between

the columns the handsome head of the girl made boy by God,bends

back,the posture of that head volts forth the difference

between one woman and another--crying softly between tongues,the

terrible excommunication of the toilet:

May you be damned to hell,bitch,bitch that you are.

May you die standing upright,may you be damned upward ,may

you be damned,terrible and damned spot,may it wither into the

grin of the dead,may you draw back, low riding mouth with the

complete grin of the dead,biting eternity with the bitter bag

bite of the snail,showing your pelvic teeth in a snarl of the

groin ;may this be your torment,may this be your damnation.

""atchman,what of the night?" -I7-

God damn me before you ,and you after me,kneeling and standing
away 6illl till we vanish,for what do you know of me,mans
mans meat ? Iâm an angel on all fours,with a childs feet behind
me ,seeking my people that have never been made,going down
face foremost,drinking the waters of ȹf night at the water hole
of the damned,and I go in up to my heart into the waters,the
terrible waters,and what do you know of me, ̣fanixampxmayxymmx
paxxxframxme,damned girl may you pass from me, foul oup may
you pass from me! Damned and-be damned!

    And theres a curse for you, and I have heard it,
but if you think that's all of the night,you're crazy!Groom,
bring the shovel! Am I the golden mouthed St John Chrysostum,the
Greek who said it with the other cheek? No,I'm a fart in a
gail of wind; just a humble violet under a cow pad. Even the
evil is us comes to an end,so don't be taking strangeness for
importance,errors may make you immortal--one woman went down the
ages for sitting through Parsifal up to the point where the
swan got his death shot,whereupon she screamed out "Godamercy,they
have shot the Holy Grail!"--but not every one is as good as
that,and probably what you lay up for yourself in your old age
is just enough feebleness to forget the passions of your youth,
which you spent your years in strengthening. As for me,I tuck
myself in at night well content because I am my own charlitan.
Yes,I the Lilly of Killarney,am composing me a new song,with
tears and with jealousy,because I HAve read that John was His
favorite,and it should have been me! The Preston matthew song is titled "Mother
put the wheel away,I can not spin tonight" its other name,
according everyxxxisxxxkindxfxxxxxxfxxxxxch

"Watchmah,what of the night?" -18-   148

"According to me,everyone is a kind of-a-son-of0a -bitch" to   χ
be sung to two aucorinas and one ~~concertina~~ina,and if none of the
world is present,to a Jews-harp,so help me God,I am but a little
child with my eyes wide open!

      To our friends we die every day,but to ourselves we
die only at the end.We do not know of death,or where it comes
from upon us first,or how often it has essayed our most vital
spirit."hile we are in the parlour it is visiting secretly in
the pantry.Montaigne says "to kill a man there is required a
bright shining and clear light" but that was spoken of the
conscience toward another man,but what of our own death,permit
us that we reproach the night,wherein we die densely alone. Donne
says "we are all conceived in close prison,in our mother's
wombs we are close prisoners all."hen we are born,we are but
born to the liberty of the house--all our life is but a going
out to the place of execution and death. Now was there ever any
man seen to sleep in the Cart,between New-Gate ,and Tyborne
Between the prison and the place of execution,does any man sleep?
And he says "man sleep all the way",how much more,therefore,is
there upon him him a close sleep when he is mounted on darkness
" Congratulate no man upon his happiness until you become aware how
And its all of a certain night that I am coming to,that I take to sleep,-
so long coming to it,a night in the branchy pitch of fall--for
lay I'm a fisher of men,and my gimp is doing a saltarello over
every body of water,to retch up what it may. I have a narrative,
but you will be put to it to find it.

"Watchman,what of the night?"-24-   154

better than Rigaletto, walking in the galleries and whisking her
eyes about for trouble that she swore,ever after,that she had
really never wanted to know anything about,and there laid her
eyes on Robin,who was leaning forward in a box with Nora at
her side,and me pacing up and down talking to myself in the
best Comedie Francaise French trying to keep off what I knew was
going to be trouble for a generation ,and pacing up and down,xxxxi
wishing what I was hearing was the Schumann cycle and the vie
d'une femme ,when in swished the old sow of a Danish minister
or something,who never knows which way he is going,sort of
cnnfused horses arse--and they are the only ones to lovey-markxxxa
                                        poor creatures
mark that down--my heart aches for all sorts putting on dog,and
not a pot to piss in or a window to throw it from,-and I began
to think,and I don't know why,of the closed gardens of the world
                                  so grievous, grievous
where all people make their thoughts go up high because of the
narrowness and beauty,or of the wide fields where the heart can
spread out and thin its vulgarity,and I thought,we should all
have a place we could throw our flowers in,like me who once in
my youth rated a corbeille of moth orchids,and did I keep them?
not long .For I sat beside them for a little while having my tea
and saying to myself,you are a pretty lot,and you do my cupboard
honour,but theres a better place awaiting you,and with that I took
them on foot around to the Catholic church,holding them by the
hand,and I said God is what we make him,and life doesn't seem
to be getting any better,and tip toes out,and I went round the
gallery a third time,and I knew that Hindu or no Hindu I knew
what was wrong with the world--I said its like that poor distressd
distressed moll of an Olivette

Largo   ~~~~~~~~   -17-   ⊆   274

what to do--the way of a man in a fog he said,
He was well known here,and everyone waited for what he
would say and do next,knowing him drunk and in trouble,
it was this way that half the world learned what the other
half was doing,they knew that he would betray them for
the sorrow in his heart and for his lost place in the
world,in great defaming sentences it would come up,and
they would never know how true it was,or what to think,
and could please themselves.

        Theres another story somewhere,he said,speaking
aloud to himself and the room,hooking the crook of his
umbrella over the bar,which goes by the name But for the
grace of God--xxx I never really learned anything until
I travelled in lands the language of which I was ignorant.
You cant avoid trouble if you dont know how--if you really
want to know how xxx hard a prizefighter hits,you must
not be a prizefighter,you must walk into the circle of
his fury as an onlooker,and get carried out by the heels,
not by the count.

        "hat heels now? Someone said.
        The doctor looked up.Helen,he said,the girl who
sold herself in the end,to a Madame in Buenos Ayres
for a couple of matched dimes,nothing hanging over her
head but hope,you bastard,and a bed

Largo   2·99

a week,until I told her to shut up,that I didn't want
to be converted,that I was the concierges daughter,and
sunk in Catholicism,and to leave me alone.So then she
went about as meek as mothers milk for a few days,and then
she came to me one afternoon and says:There are two
king snakes at the door making love,as near as I can make
out by the way they are swallowing eachother! And I said
if there are snakes at the door,nothing will move me
out of this house,if its a month before I see the sky
again! And with that out she bounces with a shovel and
just bangs their heads off.So maybe there is something
in predestination ,if such a flimsy bitch as that could
do such a mighty thing!

    Smmeone at another table said:Get this,he's
drunk and telling the world again.

    The doctor did not move,he shivered from head
to foot,and the ex priest said :Did you ever play two
on a tower?

    Without looking up Dr Matthew O'Connor said:
I have.And the rules of the game,what are they?That you
cant of two persons push both off,or say that you will
jump off yourself--as if man had not had sorrow enough
all his life without making up a game about it like that!--
And what did I find myself doing,without so much as
tossing a coin to see how it should be,but pushing my
father off,right in the small of his back--and very
astonished he looked going over and down,and next it was

3∽

Largo   -43-

my best girl friend for my worst boy lover.Off she went!
in a flurry of skirts,and there I was all of a misery
and an amazement,sitting up,my hands₎one crossed over
the other₎before me like a dog praying for the safety of
a little dog,and it was my brithday too! So then I went
home,and black pain was in my stomach for what I had done,
so I thought,well I8ll shave;and I got the lather well
over the brush₎and dashed it athwart the cheek bones,and
burst into tears,and flew to my bed and jumped on it all
in one gesture,face down,with my knees under me,and said:
Oh for God's sake,the people I8ve murdered! My own father
and my best girl friend! And I cried into my pillow like
mad,and said: How did this come on me when I never intended
it? And then I said to myself: I wonder now if they are
lying comfortable at the foot of the beastly building,or are
they all in pieces! And in my mind I began searching among
them , down there in the grass,trying to put them together
again.And I said:Oh God,why didn't I ever notice how they
were put together,so I could set them up again; and not
have them lying about as mixed as a salad.And at that a
terrible hate of the man who had made me p lay the game
came over me,and crept into my heart,and I began cursing
him roundly₎and damned the very way his pants were put
on,and I took him up suddenly and threw h͟i͟m͟ off,and funny
enough,he did not die and kept coming up again,and I kept
pushing him off,over and over.

Largo   301

The doctor began to pound the table with his glass.
May they all be damned! Those people in my life who
have made my life miserable--coming to me to learn of the
degredation of the dark.' Hess,rotten to the bone for love
of that girl Robin,and what of her? Beating her head
                                            c
against her heart.^Sprung over,and her mind losing her
                                              ^
life up like a heel on a fan,saying; I do not know which
way to go,but it's always with her in my arms! And that
sand-piper Olivette! Oh it's a grand bad story,and who
said I was a betrayer? Tell the story of the world to
the world; shit or get off the pot! What do they all
come to tell it to me for? And that boy Guido,Robin's child
by Baron Felix,now as far as Budapest,trying to see across
the Danube with the tears in his eyes,holding onto the hand
of the child,who holds onto the image of the ~~Madonna~~
                       on a darkening red ribbon
Virgin,feeling its lift out of the metal ,and calling it
               ^
mother for many reasons.And me not knowing which direction
my own end is coming from.I've worn every garment before
it was ~~still~~ called for! Even a shroud in the war. Flags
and winding sheets are the only spare laundry you'll find
on parade! I got to rummaging through some old dusty
closets in Lentz--I'd been without a clean shirt since the
                 ^
first manoeuvre--so when I came on a lovely long shirt,all
                                       m
white linen buttons,and a smart high collar,naturally,Ijust
                                      ^
put it on

Large   45   302

"~~Go Down Matthew!~~"   ~~75~~

And out I walked,and would you have seen the regiment!
and me perfectly happy smiling over the top of it,like
a bird over a hedge.They said,~~Oh God~~, *Holy mother of mercy!* its a shroud you've
put on--and the luck of that is too awful to mention!
I was a little surprised,but I says to myself,in that
case,my life always having been the other way around,its
good luck for you Matthew! After a while,I should say
about six weeks,they snatched it away to delouse it--
they deloused everything,but the dirt went marching on.
So I went to call for my shirt,I had become so fond of
it,and wasn't it missing! So at that I just sat down and
commenced to cry,and the bullets whistling among the
trees,and my buddy going sitting down suddenly and soft
on the stump of a tree,his head leaned further back than
light love in a picture,because his throat just got cut
clean through ~~with the Jerry said, I was~~
~~standing in the shuffle~~   Jesus,'I said,in the shuffle I've
lost me shroud! And I knew my luck had been snatched
away with it.And wasn't I right? The next instant along
comes a bit of shrapnel,flying low,and jerked my kidney
out. Let me end my days in Caen,like Beau Brummel,other
than I was at starting out;serving my guests to the bitter
end,even when they have left the room. I'm not one to
cut the knot by drowning myself in the print of a horses
    no matter how its raining
hoof,tho I know one man who,maddened to a thread,just
put his face in one,and drew in one tremenduous breath
and said Bon jour, Dieu! *God Put the Sea out* If you put the sea at my service,
it wouldn't cure the recollection people have of me.

(cool poems from my school ...Cool (wood)")

2. La Somnambule/55

in the past. He told her how/~~XXXXXXXXXXXX~~ they had
played cards in the long afternoons, all together
about a long table, ~~xxxxxxxxxxxxxxxxxxxxxxx~~ They
had been like a (great) conference that had met
to plan dissolution; in the twilight they had
spoken in baroque sentences that were as the
flower and fall of their palaces, [a honeycomb
of despair.

It is always twilight to the nobly born;
nobility is the permission to go, in one's own
time, back into the forgotten.

(And) she said, "Did they wear ermine and
jewels and crowns?" (And) he told her they were
slatterns. She looked up at that, the quick
look of the [very] young. And he said, to age
her a little, ["The new [grand] are always faultless." Save

But it was of the old [grand] that he wanted
to tell her - splendid and dirty in a way, like
cathedrals, which are beautiful because they are
of DEATH—
the fear before and after, like anything that
survives, The people live, but the nobility
endures. All grandeur is dowdy because it is
conceived in hope, cherished in anxiety and
doomed to massacre.

She said, "And where is the zoo?"
He started visibly. "But," he said, "animals,
why [of] that [now?] They are something else, they

6 7. ~~Where/In/This~~ Where the Tree Falls / ~~194~~ B. 218

~~sion~~ of melancholy, that flowering of the

bough of despair which comes of racial ridicule,

then he ~~w~~ould smile, with the smile of a people

that resurrects itself to a blow. Felix went

on, searching for the paragraph that must have

been somehow misconstrued by scavanger and

scholar, for he would not only know the kind

of death his great died but the exact duration

and agony; he experienced, when he found such

mention, a sensation of having participated

in the embodiment and dissolution. He haunted

greatness still, as a sparrow haunts a cathedral;

the older, the more persistently at home. And

if, by some chance, he went astray, he became

as hysterical as a girl; his bowels turned to

water. At forty he was an intermittent diarrhoe-

tic, hurrying out of his error at a run; for to

be caught, to catch himself, on unimportant

ground, was his chief misery.

As we write to the press, he corresponded

with nobility and received no answer (as later

he wrote to the pope and received no answer).

His torment was to be in the world when it was

what he termed too late. He atoned in every

gesture of his mind and body for his maladroit

9. Go Down, Matthew / 215

along with a couple of others - everyman should
be allowed one day and a hatchet just to ease
his heart. It's why every man struggles so
desperately for money, as you have had to
struggle, just to keep nothing before the eye -
and Robin never trying at all, what does that
mean?"

 "Matthew," she said, "what is it we know,
and cannot find?"

 "Everything we find and can't know," he
said instantly. "Ask the doctor anything, he knows,
but in spite of telling everything he never says
a word. My soul's integrity! I never tell
the truth. It's such a bad idea, like case-history,
all the sensation **FACTS** of life but none of the facts **SENSATIONS** -
what is the use! What sense is there in saying
the girl went wrong at twenty, that she wore
a bowler hat by preference when but eight months
old and showed a liking for kissing her grandmother's bottom *left elbow*; it's not that she did so that
needs explanation, it's what it seemed like
while she was about it. For instance, once I
was in a room full of blind men, and some looked
as if they had been deprived, but there was one
who looked as if he were seeing the most beautiful
thing - and that's the difference between knowing

Go Down, Matthew / 216

and finding."

~~Here~~ *Catherine* said, "Matthew, what will happen
in the next few years?"

"Nothing," the doctor said, "as always.
We all go down in battle and we all come home."

"~~Robin is walking home alone. I will~~
& Robin / Can find
~~love her forever, yet for me to have her~~ again
~~it can only be~~ in sleep or in death ~~-~~ ~~and~~ perhaps
in both she has forgotten me."

Said the doctor; "My war brought me many
things; let yours bring you as much. Life is
not to be told, call it as loud as you like, it
will not tell itself. The prophet talks only
                   never
of what we have ~~not~~ been able to use and never
will be able to use; the other is outside his
reaching. No one will ever be much or little
except in someone else's mind, so be careful
of the minds you get into. Mother makes out
I'm a seven months baby to make an excuse for
everything, because she knew that not everyone
is safe with the safety of Lady Macbeth who had
her mind in her hands."

Catherine .
~~Hess~~ SAID:" ~~I think~~ "we are dangerously moved by what
we shall never know," ~~said Hess~~.

"Isn't that the word of truth!" exclaimed

9. Go Down, Matthew /2.17

the doctor. "Once in a while we learn however.
For instance I did not know how a girlish boy
would take the war until along came the war. This
lad was a dancer who had taken a professional·
name that sounded like a suburb of Los Angeles,
his real name being MacClusky. Top-hat and
sponge-bag trousers used to be hardly enough for
him. Down the streets of London he would come
swinging, reeking of gardenia and clutching a
cane, his face made up so perfect you would think
his mother had done right by him. And you should
have seen him when he was being the dying swan,
or leaping through a hoop, with both hands
spread - off he would go, swishing into the
air! But see that one after a day's march! The
poor galoot, with a tin helmet over one eye, and
the beautiful swivel tooth that had cost him a
fortune lying somewhere in Flanders Field, -because
he was making a cool two thousand before people
got the idea that it would be nice to shoot the
world up and take the starch out of a generation.
Well, there he was, covered with mud, and that
hat over his eye, and his front tooth missing,
saying his lamentations all in a field of mincemeat, coming up to regimentals to be decorated

9. Go Down, Matthew / 218

for his prowess, and all of us grinning at him
because we knew how and why he came by it, by a
mistake or a lack in the mind of the general
who did not know what sort of a nature the lad
was suffering under, and we didn't say a word
because MacClusky was just the kind that should
have a consignment of medals left at his door
for breakfast every day - the poor bewildered
moll! He'd been standing in the middle of a
bridge trying to think where the war was coming
from when a douse of Germans loomed up, trying to
make the bridge before MacClusky found out, and
there he was, the poor frail, gone wild in the
center of the pontoon, and instead of shooting -
and why should he know one end of a gun from
another - he just went all of a fluff, if you
can call murder fluff, and swung the heft around
and began banging their heads off, and they flew
like crazy because even a war has certain cal-
culable reactive processes and this wasn't one
of them, so off they flew, seeing what they
thought was a wild man in their midst who had no
respect whatsoever for the correct forms of
slaughter. So he held the fort, as it were,
swinging away with the butt of that thing.

9.   Go Down, Matthew / 219

And it got about, and all of us grinning because
we knew it was the moment his balls fell out with
misery and horror that he got the idea. So when
the general comes up prancing and pinning and
kissing the elect we all stood still, looking out
of the ends of our eyes at Mac who loomed up like
a horse-bun on a platter, all misery and glory,
thinking quick and slow; 'Here's where I come
into something that will take away all the
ignominy of my past, and the marrow of my nature
will be refilled and made glorious' - for he
had been so far away and beaten up in his heart
for the opinion the world had of him - and
everybody has it, no matter what they say - that
he had forgotten where he was standing and what
he was waiting for, when down on his breast flew
the _croix du guerre_ with a pin in its tail and at
that he gave a jump back that carried him a foot
out of line, and with a great joy swelling and
rolling him along he came back again and the
tears spurted out of him right forward like a
lemon. I've never seen any tears like those
before in my life, though that is the way a boy
cries who has been queer all his hour and it's
suddenly made all right by a general upheaval

9. Go Down, Matthew / 231

her day that an expecting queen should have
to deliver h rself amid all the rabble that
they call the royal suite? There they were,
scrambling to get a sight of her and all but
stepping on the umʰilical as if she were a prizefight and not a lady; and 'That,' I said to
myself as I was being dragged along, 'has been
spared me,' and then as I began to think of
that I began to weep and hurl my robin, with
the dark all about me and the bats flying. Then
the sargeant, who was going to take me to
the procureur after that black terrible ride
in the Maria, came and put his hand out and it
was to put the manacles on me, but I did not
understand, so I just took his hand, and at that
he sighed and gave up the ghost and said,
taking my hand in his, 'Oh for God's sake' and
me walking beside him, feeling a little as if
I had a mother, a mother winnowed down, but
still a mother - I had always wanted one all
to myself! They tossed bread into my cell and
it was made of wood and they said, 'If you want
water you can get it where you make it!' and
with that they left me until the court scene the
next morning, and me looking about, all bewildered

9. Go Down Matthew / 232

for a place to lay my head that wouldn't
stop the traffic. Well, the next morning there
I was being hur~~ried~~ along - oh moon of both
sexes! holding on to my pants, because they
had cut the suspenders for fear of suicide. So
there I was, covered with snow and shame,
shuffling along holding on to my pants and
my heart breaking, shuffling along in one loose
shoe and the other loose shoe - they'd snatched
out the laces for fear of hanging - and me
looking right and left under my eyebrows (the
poor hairy things!) and crying and afraid and
shamed, crying and needing a friend <u>and afraid</u>
<u>I would see one!</u> My God, to get into this
for a thing that was far less than love' - an
accident and then an accusation I'd had nothing
whatsoever to do with. I don't believe that there
is a thing that lasts in this world, 'ove least
of all, and here was something that I was
never going to forget! Oh God! I was all of
a twitter, my heart bleeding and my long golden
curls catching in my french heels! Me, with
a face like a squirrel's, only fit to keep nuts
in! When I think how ugly He made me (and me
wanting to be a soprano and sing a cadenza in
an early Gaulish garden) I cou d weep for

9. Go Down, Matthew / 233

injustice! Well, then I looked up and there
standing over above the judge was <u>Notre Dame
de la Bonne Garde</u> looking down at me as if I
were one of her troubles. So I began praying
right then and there, holding on to my pants,
saying softly: 'If you get me out of this,
darling, I'll say my beads smack down under
you for thirty days'' And it's a crazy kind of
prayer I'll be saying to her because I'm the
little man who believes you should talk to
these people. If they aren't your friends up
there in the sky, then whatre they? So why
shou'dn't I talk to her in that way?"

"You should, Matthew, you did."

"I did and I should, saying: 'Why did
you have me if you didn't want me and weren't
going to help me in our hour of trouble!' And
there I was, draped over the railing, all of a
swoop of misery, as heavy in my heart as
Adam's off ox. And at that <u>Notre Dame de la
Bonne Garde</u> seemed to sort of give me the high
wink, and the judge let me off after all! So,
as I went by him I whispered: 'I thank you, and
I love you very much, <u>de tout mon coeur</u>!' And
he answered, soft and low, stabbing the blotter
with a pencil: '<u>C'est le coeur d'une femme</u>!'
'<u>Oui</u>!' I said gentle, so perhaps I've got me a

9. Go Down, Matthew / 234

friend."

"Yes, Matthew, yes."

"So I got to thinking how terrible the
law is when it catches up with a private life,
because everyone's life is private even if it
is in the middle of the street, - who can be
yourself, no matter where you are, but yourse'f?
Because while I was in Miss Law's court of
Injustice, they hauled in a poor, frowsy,
frightened, moth-eaten bag of a girl for
offending the _pudeur_ of the citizens of the
night before. Gramercy, how they hollered
at her! As if what she had been doing was
any more than what they had been after! Shouting
smutty things at her for the purity of the
spirit, and asking her how much she charged
to be indecent. Oh for God's sake! The price
of the bread she swallowed was nothing to the
cost of it coming up! And me thinking, it's
a terrible, terrible world, this extremity, this
badly executed leap in the dark called life.
And I was thinking, up in my head, where _are_
all the birds and flowers? There we were,
sitting up like a row of Byzantine latrines,
a couple of beggars and two gents in top hats
looking very surprised and educated, and me,

9. Go Down, Matthew / 235

and a poor fellow from some unknown country,
and I thought I should have been a mother, what
with my trying to comfort them, all with
different tosses of my eyes, and me with the
worst disgrace on me of the lot! what with
getting drunk and going up against Civic Virtue -
the old tuppeny upright! When you draw a blank,
I said, why can't it be forever, and not let you
come out crawling against the law - as if I had
no turbary - and having to hear all those
men talking my sin right out loud where every
ear was flapping for the sound of the depths
to which I had fallen and no way after that of
climbing up again with my chin in the air! If
they must punish you for forgetting yourself -
as if that were not awful punishment enough -
why don't they come to your house in the dark,
where No one is looking, and let your drawers
down and beat you up? It would be better for
the pride of the race. This way they just
make you brazen with the tears in your eyes!
From now on, I'm going to be regenerated and
regrettable every day of the rest of my life!
And when I pass a can, I'm going to drop my
veil, even if my teeth are floating. For

9. Go Down, Matthew / 236

there's no trance left t at's fitting to go
into. I, Matthew O'Connor, am dropping the
world like a hot rock!"

"Yes, Matthew."

"Only,when you have dropped it you see it
rolling after you, showing its teeth! It
caused me to run all over Paris for six months
looking up my influential friends - one of them
was a woman, because I've slept with women too, -
only, when you sleep with a woman you sleep with
an enemy, and when you sleep with a man you sleep
with an influence, - so I looked up my influence,
it proved to be sufficient, glory be to God!"

"Yes, yes."

"Why don't you say something yourself?
I wonder if in your whole life you've ever
been unreasonable? There's a lot of good in
that - you can rest. But you wouldn't know!
You were damned coming down and you'll be
damned going up! I know a tree when I see one
and you are a tree that was meant to stand
alone. You know as well/as I that in the end
it's not going to make a bit of difference to
anyone, not even to Robin. Have you ever
thought of that? I was thinking like that when
they hauled me into court, thinking of another
city in which I might have been safe. I said

9. ~~Go~~/~~Down~~//Go Down,Matthew / 238

if the noise came down and struck in the
right place; and I was scrambling for the
dug-out and the cellars and running like mad,
saying, 'There was Hector and Nero, and the
Horse of Troy and the Bull Taurus and moonlight
over the Acropolis and a pedestal standing up
broken in Tyre (a pedestal I've never been on,
it's such a small room) and the nightingales·
singing in the groves of Hooray.' There I was
saying, 'What ^{WHERE} am I now?' with an old Briton
woman and a cow she was dragging with her and
behind that someone from Dublin, a voice saying
over and over, 'Glory be to God!' in a whisper
at the far end of the animal, thanks be to my
maker I had her head end ^{ON}, and there we were all
stuffed into a hole no bigger than a tea-tray,
and the poor beast trembling on her four legs
so I knew all at once that the tragedy of the
beast can be two legs more awful than a man's.
And she was slowly and softly dropping her dung
at the far end where the thin Celtic voice
kept coming up saying, 'Glory be to Jesus!' and
I kept saying to myself,'Can't the morning come
now, so I can see what my face is mixed up with?'
At that a flash of lightning went by and I saw

9. Go Down, Matthew / 241

"And in the morning I had orders to
circumcise half the regiment and, 'You lousy
bastards!' I screamed, 'why don't you sometimes put these things in water?' and with
that, with a whirl I cut round the last and
out flew a cloud of moths."

Catherine
~~Hers~~ was laughing as she walked up and
down, crying.

"And there was a horse too," said the
doctor, PRETENDING NOT TO NOTICE "looking between the branches in the
morning, cypress or hemlock, how should I
know; and she was in mourning for something taken
away from her in that bombardment - I think
by the way she stood that something lay between
her hooves - she stirred no branch though her
hide was a river of sorrow, she was damned to
her hocks where the grass came waving up softly.
Her eyelashes were ~~dusty an~~ GRAY black, like the
eyelashes of a nigger, and at her buttocks' soft
center a pulse throbbed like a fiddle. I know,
because I went all about her and knew I should
never know her nor lose her, - it's that way
with a horse."

"It's that way with love," *Catherine* ~~Hers~~ said,
her voice shaking.

9. Go Down, Matthew / 242

"All right," said the doctor,"give me
a drink. You must admit, for one who talks
as much as I talk, I do little injustice. I
am always doing my _danza del fuego_ where it
comes to no harm. Why? Because I know we
love in sizes. Were your heart five feet
across in any place would you break it for
a heart no bigger than a mouse's mute? Would
you hurl yourself into any body of water, in
the size you now are, for any woman that you
had to look for with a magnifying glass, or
any boy if he was as high as the Eiffle Tower
and did droppings by the bucket, or, on the
other hand, speaks like a fly? You would
not; yet we all cry out in tiny voices to the
great booming God, me most of all. And does
age help? Growing old is just a matter of
throwing life away back, so forgive even those
that you have not begun to forget, it is that
indifference which gives you your courage, which
to tell the truth is no courage at all. There
is no truth, and you have set it between you,
you have been unwise enough to make a formula,
you have dressed the unknowable in the garments

9. Go Down, Matthew / 243

of the known. Suppose you were back again
where there are no receipts for insults and
kisses, suppose being pinched you laughed,
caressed you were injured, how then would
you be? In another kind of trouble, up to
the neck, but at least another kind, even the
contemplative life is only an effort to hide the
body so the feet won't stick out. Some say
that we live after death and some that we do
not and others comfort themselves by thinking
at least their energy is not lost, and what
for that matter have they ever done with it
in this world? I say it is vanity, all
vanity, one way or the other. Suppose it
isn't lost, what of it? What does it matter?
The great sad distinction! I've seen a member
of our best society, Sir Don, a grown man of
thirty, beautified by handsome manners and a
game leg, stand screaming for ptarmigan in the
middle of the maids' furnishing department of
the bazar of the Hôtel de Ville! The nut in the
brain of man that made him the king of beasts is
that same ability to lean upon the purple of
hope in the wrong places. Instead of being
glad that it is spring and that he is nobody

9. Go Down, Matthew / 244

amid all the green flowing grasses, having a
time, good or bad, just rolling his hoop along,
no, instead he thinks? 'Oh the great insupportable
miracle, I am I! Don't let it stop! Can I
really be so absolutely me!' And here he pinches
himself and turns haggard with the mystery, to
think that someday he will pinch and not feel,
so he screams out, 'Lord Jesus, I am excellent,
don't stop the experiment!'"

    "Yes, Matthew," she said, "yes, Matthew!"

    "Yes Matthew, no! Because he feels
elegant he wants to survive in spite of the
fact that he feels terrible, the fool! He
wants to be importantly agonized the rest of
forever! The only sensible things in the
world are the wars in the world, where God
wipes your face out. And suppose you didn't
die forever? Suppose you 'got off?' What
would you be doing with your time, what would
you be wishing for then? Time off to stop
time. Which reminds me of my terrible disgrace -
it was then, after all that, that I learned
everything. There have been only two children
born to the spirit, Little Faith, for those

9. Go Down, Matthew / 245

who have not been degraded, and Big Faith, for
those who have. Many of us are 'pure' because
we are afraid to become 'evil' - God, take my
hand and et me up out of this great argument -
the more you go against your nature, the more
you will know of it - hear me heaven! - I've
done and been everything that I didn't want
to be or do - Lord, put the light out - so
I sit here, all beaten up and mauled and
weeping - because I know that everybody isn't -
and that's a bigger knowledge than what they
are - and I know I am not what I thought I
was, a good man doing wrong, but the wrong man
doing nothing much, and I wouldn't be telling
you about it if I weren't talking to myself,
I talk too much because I have been made so
miserable by what all of you are keeping hushed.
I'm an old worn out lioness, a coward in my
corner, for the sake of my bravery I've never
been one thing that I am, to find out what I'm
about. And oh God! there I was, having taken
only a jorum and a jack of punch, well there I
was I say between one thing and another and
neither of them mine and wishing to high heaven

9. ~~Don~~ Go Down, Matthew /246

I had never had a button up to my middle - for
what I've done and what I've not done all
goes back to that - to recognize a gem it
should lie in a wide open field and I'm all
aglitter in the underbrush! Were not the
several parts of Caroline of Hapsburg put
in three utterly obvious piles? - her heart
in the Augustiner church, her intestines in
St. Stephan's and what was left of the body
in the vault of the Capucine? They were.
But a glittering damp bundle of sorrow I am,
and a bundle I'll be buried, lost alas, but
not scattered."

and ~~Hope~~, suddenly in terror because she
had lost the custom of her thinking, said, "
One cannot live one's last hour all one's
life, yet that is love. Is love man seeing
his own head? Look," she said, "the human
head, so rented by misery that even the teeth
weigh! - its whole fate a circumscribed insan-
ity." And then she said:"To be an animal!
Reborn at the opening of an eye, going only
each foor forward and at the end of day,shutting
out memory with the dropping of the lid. All
day," she said, and she ~~went walking~~ the room

9. Go Down,Matthew/247

" to live down her nights--time is not long enough
for that!" And walking,she said ;"She could not tell
the truth,Matthew, because she never planned the truth--
that great,that very great occupation.Her life is a
continual accident,and for a continual accident how can
anyone be thoughtful,prepa/red. Everything we can't
bear in this world someday we will find in one person
and love it all at once. A strong sense of identity
gives a person an idea that he can do no wrong;to o
little accomplished the same. Some natures cannot appreciate but they can regret.Will Robin only regret?"
She stopped abruptly,half turning,gripping the back öf
the chair on which the doctor was sitting.She said:
"Perhaps not,for even her memory wearied her; a torrent
of fury and abuse followed the slightest frustration
of her will to gxxf forget."
        "Oh the great shy difference," the doctor

9. ~~Box~~ Go Down, Matthew / 248

said, "of one head to another turned! The beast
of once-upon-a-time will prey upon us all! Being
ruthless is only a certain kind of character;
we like to think it a positive endeavor. What
is this love we have for the invert - boy or
girl? It was they who were spoken of in every
romance that we ever read. The girl lost, what
is she but the Prince found? The Prince on the
white horse that we have always been seeking.
And the pretty lad who is a girl, what but the
prince-princess in point lace? - neither one
and half the other. The painting on the fan!
We love them for that reason. We were impaled
in our childhood upon them as they rode through
our primers, the sweetest lie of all, now come
to be in boy or girl, for in the girl it is the
prince, and in the boy it is the girl that makes
a prince a prince and not a man. They go far
back in our most lost distance where what we
never had stands wanting; it was inevitable that
we should come upon them, for our miscalculated
longing has created them, they are our answer to
what our grandmothers were told love was and what
it never came to be, they, the living lie of

9. Go Down, Matthew / 249

our centuries; and when a long lie comes up,
sometimes it is a beauty; and when it drops
into dissolution, into drugs and drink, into
disease and death, it has at once a singular
and terrible attraction. A man can resent and
avoid evil on his own plane, but when it is the
thin blown edge of his reverie, he takes it to
his heart, as one takes to one's heart the dark
misery of the close nightmare, born and slain
of the particular mind; so that if one of them
were dying of the pox one would will to die of
it too, with two feelings, terror and joy,
wedded somewhere back again into a formless sea
where a swan (would it be ourselves, or her or
him, or a mystery of all) sinks crying."

"And I was crying Matthew, ~~softly~~, and
~~you were breaking~~ suddenly I knew what all
my life had been, and what I hoped Robin was,
the secure anxiety. we can hope for nothing
greater, except hope. with that I had kissed
her head, over and over. I put my two hands
beneath th~~at~~ _her_ head to hear something between
us. And suddenly, Matthew, I knew that it was
my own head that I had been seeking always.
Love? Is it every man seeking his own head?

9. Go Down, Matthew / 250

When I had found my own head it was weeping
up at me, and its tears were neither of joy
or of grief, but the tears of my own time. I
knew ~~then~~, at that instant, ~~that~~ my youth had
been the whole evidence of my life and all my
other years its destruction. Love is death
come upon with passion; that is why we say
love is wisdom, as death is wisdom; I love
her as one condemned ~~to it~~ - "

  "Oh Widow Lazarus! Arisen from your
dead! Oh lunatic humor of the moon! Behold
this fearful tree, on which sits singing the
dreadful bird - <u>Turdus Musicus</u>, or European
singing thrush; sitting and singing the
refrain - all in the tear-wet night - and it
starts out <u>largo</u>, but it ends like <u>I Hear You
Calling Me</u>, or <u>Kiss Me Again</u>, gone wild with
Fritzi Scheff! And Diane, where is she?
Diane of Ephesus in the Greek Gardens, singing
and shaken in every bosom; and Rack and Ruin,
the dogs of the Vatican, running up and down
the papal esplanade and out into the Ramblon,
with roses in their tails to keep off Care, which
has a boy's name! Don't I know it all! Do you
think that I, the Old Woman who lives in the
closet (some call it the <u>chambre de bonne</u>) haven't

9. Go Down, Matthew / 251

found out that every child, no matter what
its day, is born prehistorically, and that
even the wrong thought has caused the human
mind incredible effort? I have. Suffering may
be composed wickedly and of an inferior
writhing. Rage and inaccuracy howl and blow
the bone, for, contrary to all opinion, all
suffering does not purify - begging everybody's
pardon, which is called everybody's know. It
moils and blathers some to perjury; the
peritoneum boils and brings on common and
cheap praying a great way sunk in pointless
agony - "

 "Yes," she said, "there is Jenny - "

 "It rots her sleep," the doctor said.
"If I know anything she is one of those who
nip like a bird and vpid like an ox - the
poor and lightly damned! That can be a
torture also. None of us suffer as much as
we should or love as much as we say. Love is
the first lie and wisdom the last. Don't I
know that the only true way to know evil is
through truth? That frantic disease! The
evil and the good alike only know themselves
by giving up their fate ~~side by side~~ face to face. The
true good who meets the true evil (Holy Mother

9. Go Down, Matthew / 252

of Mercy, are there any such!) learns for the
first time how to accept neither; the face of
he one tells the face of the other the half of
the story that both forgot. Yes," he said, "to
be utterly honest would be to be utterly
unknown - particularly to oneself."

Catherine
He said, "There is a running in some
women to all mothers, as there is in all children
a running from some infancy."

"And nobody knows anything; I least of
all, because I know!"

Catherine
"Where two love," He said, "Is it is
not beautiful because it is secret. And when
it is public is it not shame?"

"When the body you love goes forth!" he
said.   He continued

She began to smile. "Man goes down only
according to his construction; he bleeds
according to his blood; forgives when he is
beginning to forget." So
"Your heart is in your hand. Put it
back. It is for your chest. The eater of it
will get a taste for you; in the end his
muzzle will be heard barking among your ribs."

She left the chair where she had been

9. Go Down, Matthew / 253

leaning and began walking again. "Sometimes
Robin returned to me suffering from ~~an object~~
~~fear of~~ a sleep that was blowing thin./ The
sleep walker," she said, "coming to me for
sleep; to make her safe again, to make her
secret; and," she said, "she always went
forth."

The doctor poured himself a drink.
" - To treat her lovers to the great
passionate indifference!" he said.

~~Napp~~ *Catherine* said: "Only the impossible lasts
forever and even that, with time, is made
accessible. Robin's love and mine was
impossible from the beginning. If it had
been anything else I could not have loved
her __as__ I loved her; had I been appropriate she
could not have loved me __as__ she loved me.
Suppose I had been that idiotic thing people
call the complement of herself? Then why
should she have loved me at all, and how could
she have loved me with this love?" ~~Napp~~ *Catherine* began
to wring her hands together and the doctor
permitted her to pass and repass his vision
without moving his head. *Catherine*

"I was born in the beginning," ~~Napp~~ *Catherine* went
on with fury, "without precision and whacked

9. Go Down, Matthew / 254

well on the bottom and wouldnôt cry; and set
up at twelve months and photographed, with
my mother holding onto my bow at the back,
kneeling down behind my chair so that she
wouldn't be in the picture, - and that was my
infancy. Then I was five and photbgraphed
with my brother who was crying (what could
those tears galvanized forever in a picture
have been so brief about?) and I wouldn't
cry. And that was my childhood. Then at
sixteen, standing at the break of day in the
dust of the cross-roads, a boy asked me to
kiss him, and I kissed him, and he said,
'Thank you,' and I laughed because I knew
that was not the answer, though what he should
have said I hadn't the faintest idea. Then
he went away because he was dying of something
incurable and hot in him, though he was only
a lad of eighteen. And then I had a lover
and a doll, and because he was a man who had
held me on his knee when I was a child, and
because I had a doll and ate caramels, and
looked up at him and said'yes,'he couldn't
bear it. He thiught, perhaps, that he was
bored, but it was something else; he was an

9. Go Down, Matthew / 255

old man then and he wanted something simpler
and older, so he took me away to a transients'
hotel in Bridgeport, if you know what kind
of an hotel that is - "

"I should hope to say I do! Men going
upstairs panting, and women going up slowly,
saying, 'For the love of God, can't you wait.'"

"Like that, and it frightened him still
further, beyond endurance, because I wouldn't
cry, and he said, 'Go back home and don't tell
anyone , because after all I never did intend
to marry you!' And I picked up the carving
knife then, seeing that night back on the
hill, my brother playing the trombone somewhere
so that it came softly up to the trees and I
had said, 'No, I will marry you in my heart
but I will not marry you in church.' Because
that was a big new ideal my father had in his
head. Then I remembered the ceremony beside
the Christmas tree, when my father and my
grandmother stood by, and my mother by the
door in her apron, crying and thinking God
knows what; and he put a ring on my finger
and I kissed him. Before that, it must have
been two hours, I had gone down on the floor

9. Go Down, Matthew / 256

and hugged my grandmother by her knees,
dropping my head down, saying, 'Don't let
it happen!' and she said, 'It had to happen.'

"And I was in bed that first night, and
he said, 'Christ! You don't bleed much.' And
I said, 'It is all the blood it has.' And all
before the door my mother had strewn flour - to
give herself hope, hoping there would be no
foot-mark in it going my way.

"So I took the carving knife and leaned
cross the table, strong and blind with something coming up in me out of what my father
had in his head for women and love, and for
the Christmas tree and the flour on the floor,
and he jumped out of the window backward into
the garden. And then I came back home and I
wasn't crying. nd I got thin, and fell when
I walked, and my grandmother came to me and said;
'What is it that he has done that you are
sent back home?' And I told her. And that too
was my childhood.

"And then I came to New York, when the
family broke up, and father drove us all down
in a pickle cart, and said good-bye forever,
and he did not wave to us, nor turn his head,

9. Go Down, Matthew / 257

and my little brother had been lying on his
face in the straw all the way and has grown
up all different because of that. And so I
had to earn a living for me and some for them.
And I wouldn't take my hair down when a boy
asked me to; and I wore ear-rings and played
the fiddle. And another boy asked me to kiss
him and I struck him, and then I was older,
and another man - he seemed so tall and melancholy and humorous, with a head with the curve
of madness in it - said, 'Sit beside me.' And
I sat beside him. And he said, 'I love you.'
And I said, 'I love you.' And we walked across
Brooklyn Bridge, and he kissed me then and it
was the first time I had been kissed or cared in
six years, and I loved him with all my heart,
and I screamed and flew at him and I said,
'I'd throw you down there into the water if
I were strong enough!' And I struck at him,
and he laughed, and I began running, and he
walked quietly after me in soft long strides.
And it went on three years and I said, 'I will
be married.' And then the war came, and he
was a German all the time in his heart, and in
his mind he saw German families going down to

9. Go Down, Matthew / 258

death, and he thought Germa children must be
born to take their place. And he came to
me in a top-hat one morning with a can of
cocoa under his arm and two rolls, because it
was Sunday (we used to take the ferry) and he
said, 'I can't marry you, because you must
be German for that now.' And we cried until
it was night; and he took me up to my garret
room on Washington Square, and he stood under
the trees and cried up at me, and I leaned
weeping down at him from the window, and it
was good-bye forever. And that Bulgarian,
one floor down, a strange man, fat and
devoured by a passion for cake, came up and
stood in the doorway and said, 'You mustn't
do that,' and how did he know that I had
thought of killing myself - would I have?
I think not. Two days later I couldn't stand
it any more, so I rushed into the German's
house and flung my arms about his neck and I
said, 'I love you anyway, and you can do as
you like!' And he said, 'The court would
say the child resembles me.' And my blood went
away then, and he was quoting Shakespeare (he

9. Go Down, Matthew / 259

used to teach me Hamlet in German) and I was
leaning by the table, my hands on it, gone
terribly still, and I said, 'That is a lie,
a terrible lie - that I would get you into
court, and it is against me and what I am!'
And he said, 'What is this that you are that
I do not understand!' And he took me by the
wrist and began turning my wrist. He was
livid and turning and turning and I wouldn't
scream though I began to go down with the
pain in my arm. And he said, 'Down, and say
that there is nothing that I do not understand
about you!' And I said, 'You understand nothing,
now I know you understand nothing'' And I kept
saying,'Nothing!' and he had me down and back
with my legs under me, still turning my arm;
and then he was lying on me and trembling and
crying and kissing me, and so heavy that I shook
with his shaking. And I said, 'Nothing! Nothing!
Nothing!' Then it was over and he got up and
I got up and he went to the window and I said,
'She will have to be a German - now.' And he
said, 'She will be German.'"

"And then there were others?"

"And then there were others. One was a

9. Go Down, Matthew / 260

Cuban, very gentle and pretty and sick, and he
crawled up from his sick-bed to lay the only
red flower on the coffin of a friend I had
loved and who had died before him of his own
disease, and she had been a fair tall woman
so that the flower was quite lost upon her
length. Then one day I had to tell him a thing
I never knew could happen, that I must say
good-bye to him - we had been planning to go
to Cuba together, and to sit up in the twilight
and watch the lights and the pretty women
coming from the casino, and none of them with
roses as red as they say in their bosoms -
because a girl had said to me, 'Play - while
there is still time in my mind for playing.'
She was stocky and handsome and she wore a
silver chain around her neck and she was heavy
on her little feet and her hands were small
and crumpled in the skin, too soft and like a
child's, and she had thick lips that quivered
because she was afraid of something, afraid of
what she had to be, a charlatan, to make herself strong, to make herself last, before she
was lost; she played on that too, that being
lost. She would say, 'I'm God's fool.'"

  "The blind, vain cow!"

9. Go Down, Matthew / 261

"Yes, evil for her soul's preservation.
She knew that she had been born pitiful and weak,
so she made it pitiful and strong by torturing
her mind for ways to come back at herself, as
if she were her own cat and mouse, and hard bent
on worrying herself to keep being, to frighten
herself upright so that she could be there,
sitting straight up when the great terror came
for her, for she knew she would go all to pieces
then, and be carried out a gross unidentified
child, God's thick one, lost, and how could
she stand that? Who could stand that? And
she turned to women for her love, because she
wanted to bury herself, perhaps she had thoughts
somewhere in that strange head, of being
miraculously born again, how do we know? She
was tortured and she couldn't find a way. In
the end it made her like a great garden slug
trying to find home, and for that one loved
her too, because it was so horrible and so
sad - life on the far side, out of reach, crying and going wrong - and often she made it
seem sacred and necessary so that you tore
yourself in half to make way for her. Yet
really, all the time, it was the body of

9. Go Down, Matthew / 262

another woman she was seeking through me, a
way through me to the woman she loved, who
would sit playing, Questo, questo! Questamènte!'
and eating bon-bons, dreaming of still some
other woman, with her head turned, unaware,
because she did not love this girl. And I
said then, 'How can this be, that I could love
a woman?' And that was the first thought
about it and the last because after that there
was no difference at all, only just love. And
she was kneeling beside me and she said: 'Do
not wait until we are friends and it is too
late!' And then she was holding my knees, and
I felt that great kiss, with the broad dragging
under-lip, and I knew that she was damned
forever, praying for something to stand in
her way and to prevent her going headlong into
nothing, and I wept.

     "Every woman," she went on, "teaches
you a different lesson, and that was only
one; after that there was Robin. The first
was wide awake and making drama. She said
she saw 'God's eye' and had almost convinced
herself that time when I stood by her there in

9. Go Down, Matthew / 263

the fields believing and she turned over on
her face and would not look, how crazy it
sounds and how true it is! And I turned her
over and said, 'You will look!' and it was I,
after all, who expected to be destroyed. Then
she made a motion to me, and pretended that she
could not talk (she did that when crossed),
feigned lockjaw when she had got herself into
an impasse. And she stumbled away and into
the house, and I was wringing my hands because
I believed that too. And I went and stood by
her door, just to be near her, and there I
heard her talking like a magpie to that other
girl, able enough. She said ritual was necessary
and made so much of it that hers was a great
bed and little or no place in it. She had no
way for nature to go, up against a wall always,
not back against the wall but face to it. You
know, Matthew," she said, "there is nothing
like a distortion of nature to teach you nature.
With a girl like that one is madly out of the
world, so far out that you do not think of
'rights' any more, or how they have been lost,
because at one smack they are gone, as if you

9. Go Down, Matthew / 264

had walked into an heathen church, a church
upsidedown, where you have not come to atone
or to be made whole but to be bewildered, to
be slapped, to be injured and damnably mauled;
because she was a sick soul, beating its way
out, making everyone and everything wild and
tangled, that the getting out would not be too
soon for what was unprepared in her, or too
prepared. Her argumenst were stones to stop
her going, ~~now fancies~~ *She PUT* fancies in t*he* way.
Many people misunderstood why she was making
the way difficult, thinking her ~~weeds more~~ a
new kingdom of peace. Only one day I saw that
poor wretch with her startled idiot face -
beautiful because it was so entirely demented,
so complete, staring out of the ~~jungle~~ she had
made, heavy and thick, her lips hanging, her
child's hands trembling, and behind her her
followers, a pack baying for her conclusion,
waiting for her to fall, and I knew it and
I said: 'Damn her powerful wild idiot mind!'"

"Like a brick privy," said the doctor,
"built close to the ground!" He lifted his
glass. "That kind is always dangerous; they
have dwarf's blood, you can't strike low enough

9. Go Down, Matthew / 265

to hit them; you can't box an ear that's no
higher than the kidney!"

Catherine

"Close to the ground," Nora said,
"self-betrayed and belly down. Then there was
Robin ◆ "

"The other kind, " the doctor said, and
held his glass to the light. "So high up

...omewhere that you find yourself boxing a
pair of feet. Now with a fairy you are still
worse off, because, though exactly your own
size, they are themselves singular, they, the
only animal in the world that does not feel
proximity and the shadow of coming events.
The elephant, for instance, can be said to know
when there's another elephant about, the lion
senses when the lioness has had a rush of blood
to the head; even a man, now and again, has
a feeling that all is not right with his
neighbor. But a fairy! There's a never for
you! The prehensile gardens of the womb tell
any mother that there is something in the
wind. But a fairy! Taken by and large, he
is the monster of monsters! Take the word of
Tiny McCaffery for that! They know only two
existences, themselves in a mirror, back and

9. Go Down, Matthew / 266

front! All wisdom, unfortunately, is based
on the edicts of the demented. It's learning
how to accept that offer, that difficult
offer, that you find your mind or lose it, and
I can't say that I think you have lost yours -
yet."

"I lost it that once," Catherine said, "and
I got it back again, ~~bright and shining~~. Do
you know what every being wants, with all the
power of his heart and mind, Matthew? Nothing -
that's the secret."

"Yes," said the doctor, smiling, "that's
the secret, as she said the ebrious secret, the great
plastered hangover of forty or odd."

"Then, when this first girl tried to
betray the ~~medium of the~~ heart by her "hand" ~~that other
medium, the body, then it was that~~ I knew
what to do. One finally finds out what they
know. But what one feels, does one ever know?"

"What did you do?" inquired the doctor,
refilling his glass."

"It was a long time ago at a party, she
became incredibly vulgar, in a new way, to
make me jealous, to undo what she had done with

9.Go Down,Matthew/302

son-of-a-bitch whom you have given wings."

"No," she said ," No,she is someone I have not let
alone."

"Have it your own way," the doctor answered. "It's
mistaken ideas like that that makes war. Go about a
bit,for God's sake,not Robins,throw your eyes around
and tip your arse to the world."

She said:"Humour is supposed to be a saving grace,
that is a lie,it is a tragedy."

"I know it," said the doctor; "every nation with
a sense of humour is a lost nation,and every woman with
a sense of humour is a lost woman. The Jews are the
only nation people who have enough sense to keep humour
in the family;a Christian scatters it all over the
world.So be it! Laughing I came into the Pacific Street,
and laughing I'm going out of it; laughter is the paupers
money. Don't change,it's always too late.Nothing is so
abominable as a sweet old lady; hoard a little vitriol
for your long winter nodding."

"Yes," she said,"time passes,it will be over.
Circumstances are never fully our own because they
contain another person,we forget that.We think of the
other person as a part of our perplexity,in reality that
perplexity is part of the other person .I must learn
to be over."

"I speak three languages," broke in the doctor,
"two living,one wounded; the wounded is the tongue of the
church,Latin,and its best of all,why? Because it's dead,

9. Go Down, Matthew / 304

~~be~~ a doctor and a weeper, to be a climber and a
descender, and all on the same rung! - to be subject to profane diversions for the sake of Holy
Preferment! Physic had never healed me of the
roaring and lovepmaking of vipers nor of the
tangle of tigers saying it softly in a jungle
fury, in an everlasting and beautiful forfeit
of human understanding captured in the happy
permission of natural contumacy. The Scriptures and the scalpel have taught me nothing
that I did not/know, already and I'm the one man left
in the wórld honest enough to admit it, because
and why? Because I've told my lies elsewhere.
I make an example of myself flor my brothers'
lack and so doing have been damned. No one
can undo any tangle but the orthodox. Temporal
and natural ways twine with majestic and pro-
pitious contingencies, and the ordinance of
His habitude is no less an occupation of my
soul then the endictments that all men suffer
at the hands of the comprehensive estate - or
you are as you are. No man has a foothold that
is not also a bargain, so I have bargained for
my dissolution here and now, for which my friends

9~Go Down ,Matthew/ 312 and 313

"Very well,listen then:Don't let one indignation
sum up your life,nor one love.So I say my war gave me
more things that terror,it gave me also insight into
other days and times,for a war is a plow that goes deep
but its handles stick up. It taught me to love quality.
I came to know her when we got down as far as St [G]ermain,
and there was her house

9. Go Down, Matthew / 314

was

~~all~~ in a ruined garden, with pears on the ↗ peaches

espalier and birds twittering up against the

hoops of wrought-iron ~~that was~~ ᵒᶠ the fence, ~~and~~
you could see the old place
ₐa great way off you ~~could see the old palace~~

with its bellying windows, and ~~he~~ walks that

went all the way around and disappeared behind;

~~and~~ there were statues in the garden, of naked

women holding ~~bits of~~ drapery up to the right

height ͵ ~~and~~ the sunlight striking away the drakness

on them in the right place ͵ ~~and~~ a dove or two

perched on their heads or on their out-strutted

elbows, in a way French doves have of befouling

Venus with ~~a light and~~ careless humor; ~~and~~ I was

tired and weak and wanted my tea so I just rang

the bell and out comes, very slow, an old footman

~~or something͵~~ to the gate. And my God, wasn't I

I let right in, as if she had been expecting me

all the time! Up into the hall I went ͵ ~~and~~ I

knew at one glance that it had seen better days,—

~~and~~ when a place has seen better days that's the

time to see it. The panellings were coming away

from the walls ͵ ~~and~~ they were painted silk, and

there were flowers and cupids having no trouble

at all with gravity, ~~and~~ the staircase went up

broad and rounded as if it were promising up-

9. Go Down, Matthew / 315

stairs forever, ~~and~~ The salon was at one end
with a turreted roof in glass where on a pedestal
stood the bust of a Roman or something that was
all black ~~////~~ for a profile. ~~with the light~~
~~behind him~~. And there she was, sitting in a
high-backed chair with her feet on a stool with
its heavy tassels lying on the floor, and I looked
at her sitting there behind _a_ table laid, for
tea with a vase of flowers on it and an old
bonbonnière of some stained and cherished wood,
you knew it was cherished because the corners
were all worn ~~light and~~ round by hundreds of
times of hands. ~~And~~ I looked at her and I knew
I was going to have to hurry to love her in her
time as much as I was going to in mine, because
she was eighty-six then and like a beautiful
young woman you see through tears, all blurred
in line and breaking into that clear sight that
would never be your own eyeballs drying but the
glare of God's. And I knew in a moment that
she was one of the vieille noblesse who had
never been married anywhere except in her heart,
or what wicked people would call a strumpet of
the old regime, - ~~grave~~ _Proud_ and ~~tottering and~~ _Shaking_
splendid with walking against custom in the

Go Down, Matthew / 316

past that made the custom of today ~~mean and~~
shoddy beside it. Somehow everything she did
was different, the way she offered the dish with
the candied ~~potatoes with all the tonality of the~~
~~time that had passed between the girl and the~~
~~eating - and they were as old as God~~ - and the
way she leaned ~~a little~~ back to hear you, instead of forward, as if she were listening to
something she had to ~~make a far way off~~ to hear
it, and the way that she talked of the time that
she had prayed when she was ~~a~~ young ~~girl~~, in the
church of St. Thomas d'Aquin, all conscious, she
said, of the lightness of the body, and then in
later years, ~~she said~~, so aware of the heaviness
of the dress. ~~And~~ how she had driven her carriage
down the Faubourg and had chosen feathers for her
fan was different too, and you knew all that an
eye suffers in its years because when she spoke
you saw her eyes looking over that fan, young and
full of the color of her purpose, and then you
looked up and saw her eyes in age and they
were flickereing and about to be gone. And she
would smile and say: 'Matthew' - because I came
every day after that, ~~and~~ she would stand behind
the bars against the _espalier_ and wave her hand-

9. Go Down, Matthew / 317

kerchief and say: 'Matthew, you are a fine
boy; ~~you are a sweet boy~~.' And we would
drink our tea in the old tradition, which is
the way to drink it, she with her feet up on
that cushion in a silk yellowed by time, and me
leaning forward, ~~Jew, not to lose a thing of~~
her; ~~and~~ She would tell me of the time <u>when</u> that she
was beloved, ~~and~~ once it was a great minister,
and once someone so high that she did not mention
his name or station, - or was it some ~~little~~
boy she had loved and who was so nobody that
she had forgotten? - it comes to the same.
~~And~~ She spoke of her ways with him as if <u>they</u> ~~he~~ had
been Cellini over a silver cup, with ~~beautiful~~
thin detail and turnings of the mind, that took
the pattern round the handle and brought it
into darkness, to draw it up again, straight
and fine to the lip, and with a ~~little~~ <u>sharp wit</u>
~~it~~ to make it last and hold its <u>patine</u> ~~when~~
~~the time came~~. And she stood, light and bending,
the day I was to go away, holding to the branches
of the peach tree, her skirts blowing ~~tired~~
between the bars. ~~And~~ I looked back and I said,
'I shall love you forever, Madame.' And she
said, 'I shall not forget.' And then I went

Go Down, Matthew / 318

home to California and I threw myself on my
mother and I cried to be sent back,'Because,'
I said, 'I must see her all the time along to
her death.' And In the end I had my way because I screamed so loud and wept so much. My
mother sent me off again and said, 'Go ~~now~~ then
~~and find her quickly because~~ you have a great
memory of each other.' And I came back into
Paris and I rushed out into the high dark
gardens and there on the espalier hung a great
fine peach, just as it had hung three years
before - for it took me three years to get
back somehow, it's always that way when you go
and come - and she was eighty-nine then. ~~And~~
I came hurrying up the path and into the ~~great~~
room where the statue ~~still held its profile~~ stored
~~dark and high,~~ and I said, 'It's me, Matthew!'
And she was smaller in her sitting and she said,
'Yes, child.' And I knew, like a blow in the
chest, that she did not remember me at all. I
began to cry ~~then,~~ and she said, in her hurry
that no one should grieve: 'Won't you have tea,
Monsieur, and later a peach? I've been saving
it for you a long time.' And then she said,
'It was for you, forgive me that I do not remem-

Go Down, Matthew / 319

ber your name,' as if that made no difference.'
And it was making all the difference in the world!
She had forgotten the person and only remembered
gentleness. And I said, 'I am the one that
loved you all the time before I knew you!' And
she trembled then and put her handkerchief up
to her eyes with both fine shaking hands with
the narrow pulses beating in the wrists. And
she said, 'My dear, I have been saving it for
you.' And then it was and the room went silent all over the
room at once. And when I went away that day
she came to the peach with me and took it down;
and like our life together, I broke it open,
beautiful and round. But she didn't see what I
saw at the core, a little serpent, and I ate the
peach, peels serpent and all so that she wouldn't
guess, and I never saw her again because I knew
that she would always be trying to remember and
that it would give her pain to know that the
companion who could have lived her dissolution
could not be recalled long enough to go with
her. An' she was like you might have been if
you had ever been loved and could have cried
for love going the right way in your heart
just once. And it was then I said aloud to the